THE
GOLDEN
COUPLE

Greer Hendricks spent over two decades as an editor. Prior to her tenure in book publishing, she worked at *Allure* magazine and earned her Masters in Journalism from Columbia University. Her writing has been published in the *New York Times* and *Publishers Weekly*. Greer lives in Manhattan with her husband, two children and very needy dog, Rocky. *The Golden Couple* is her fourth novel.

Sarah Pekkanen is the internationally and *USA Today* bestselling author of several novels including *Skipping a Beat*. A former investigative journalist and feature writer, her work has been published in the *Washington Post*, *USA Today* and many others. She is the mother of three sons and lives just outside Washington, D.C.

The two women began working together in 2010 when Greer became Sarah's editor. They formed an instant connection, which grew into a close friendship, and they now write *New York Times* bestselling psychological thrillers together.

By Greer Hendricks and Sarah Pekkanen

The Wife Between Us
An Anonymous Girl
You Are Not Alone
The Golden Couple

THE
GOLDEN
COUPLE

GREER HENDRICKS

AND

SARAH PEKKANEN

MACMILLAN

First published in the United States 2022 by St. Martin's Press, New York

First published in the UK 2022 by Macmillan
an imprint of Pan Macmillan
The Smithson, 6 Briset Street, London EC1M 5NR
EU representative: Macmillan Publishers Ireland Limited, 1st Floor,
The Liffey Trust Centre, 117–126 Sheriff Street Upper, Dublin 1, D01 YC43
Associated companies throughout the world
www.panmacmillan.com

ISBN 978-1-5290-5609-9

1 3 5 7 9 8 6 4 2

A CIP catalogue record for this book is available from the British Library.

Printed and bound by CPI Group (UK) Ltd, Croydon, CR0 4YY

Visit **www.panmacmillan.com** to read more about all our books
and to buy them. You will also find features, author interviews and
news of any author events, and you can sign up for e-newsletters
so that you're always first to hear about our new releases.

For Jen Enderlin

PART
ONE

Ten sessions might not seem like nearly enough time to solve complex therapeutic issues, but according to Avery Chambers, her unique brand of intensive short-term counseling changes lives. Her highly controversial process, which some decry as dangerous, is predicated on amplifying core universal emotions such as fear, anger, sadness, and happiness. By pinpointing her client's root issue, and using it as a lightning rod to draw in these emotions at high levels, she can slay the demons that plague people, Chambers claims. Among the success stories she lists are clients who have overcome phobias, left emotionally abusive relationships, and changed up their jobs and cities. Each of her ten sessions has a specific title, and they always follow the same order, but when pressed to reveal more details, Chambers demurs. "If my clients know what to expect, my process won't be as effective. I'll only tell you this: it always starts with The Confession."

—Excerpt from "D.C.'s Maverick Therapist" profile, copyright *The Washington Post Magazine*

CHAPTER ONE

AVERY

I NEVER KNOW what to expect when I open my door to new clients.

The preliminary phone call only reveals so much. In this case, it came from a woman who introduced herself as Marissa Bishop.

My marriage is in trouble, she began. *I need to talk to my husband about something, but it's a bit complicated. I thought if we came in together—*

I'd cut her off there.

I don't want any bias to color my perception before we meet. Plus, the initial communication is for scheduling and security screening only. The actual work doesn't start until the first of our ten sessions. Still, I gleaned a fair amount of information about Marissa Bishop during our brief conversation: She has money, since she didn't balk at my fee. She's polished and well-spoken, using complete sentences rather than the fragments and fillers people often rely upon in spoken communication. And she's nervous; her voice wavered.

The doorbell chimes, indicating the Bishops' arrival, a few minutes late for our 7:00 P.M. appointment at my home office.

Are evenings okay? My husband works long hours; he has a demanding schedule.

If I decide to work with them, this lack of punctuality won't happen again. I send a quick text to the man I'm seeing later tonight: **8:30 works. Do you have any limes?** I set my phone to silent mode, then tuck the bottle of expensive tequila a client brought me earlier today into my tote bag. Therapists aren't supposed to accept gifts from clients. But I'm not one to follow the rules.

I'm also no longer a therapist; I lost my license five months ago.

I rise and walk to my front door, peering through the peephole before I pull it open. Marissa and Matthew glide across the threshold as if they're accustomed to making an entrance.

They're tall and sleek; their blond hair and classic features a perfect match. He's in a business suit and an overcoat that looks like cashmere. She wears a camel-colored cape that falls to the top of her high-heeled boots.

"Welcome. I'm Avery Chambers." I reach out a hand.

His grasp is strong and dry. "Matthew Bishop," he replies. I take in his square chin, light blue eyes, and broad shoulders.

Then I turn to his wife. I inhale a light floral perfume as I lean forward to shake Marissa's delicate hand. Her fingers are ice-cold.

"Sorry we're a little late. There was traffic," she says as her eyes skitter away from mine.

I lead them to my first-floor office, closing the door behind us. Matthew helps his wife off with her cape before he removes his overcoat, hanging them on the wood-and-brass standing coatrack, then takes a seat on the couch. A confident man, assured of his place in the world.

They're not touching, but they sit close enough together that it would be easy for them to do so. They don't look like a couple in trouble. But appearances are often misleading.

I pick up a fresh yellow legal pad and pen and claim my usual chair, directly across from them. My home office is uncluttered and comfortable, with a few ficus trees, a deep bay window, and colorful abstract prints on the walls. Back when I worked in a building with other therapists, many of them displayed family photos on their desks, turned inward so as not to distract their patients. My desk was then, and is now, bare.

I start the session the way I always do: "What brings you here tonight?"

Marissa wrings her hands, the large diamond on her ring catching the overhead light. Her flawless skin is pale.

"I thought—" She coughs, as if her throat is tight. This isn't easy for her.

"Would you like some water?"

She manages a smile. "Do you have anything stronger?"

She's joking, but I make a quick decision and stand up and retrieve my tote bag. "Tequila?" I hold up the blue-and-white-patterned bottle.

Matthew looks surprised, but recovers quickly. "I would've gotten here earlier if I'd known you were serving Clase Azul Reposado." His pronunciation is flawless.

I take three of the little plastic cups from my watercooler and fill each with a generous shot.

"Cheers." I tilt up my cup. A familiar, welcome heat fills the back of my throat as I reclaim my seat.

Marissa sips hers; she looks more like a white-wine kind of woman. But Matthew tosses his back easily.

"We're here to talk about Bennett, our son," Matthew says. He looks at his wife.

I don't betray my surprise, even though Marissa didn't mention a child in her initial phone call.

She reaches for her husband's hand. "Actually, sweetheart, that isn't exactly why we're here. I need to tell you something." Her voice quavers again.

The shift in the room is palpable; it's as if the temperature plummets.

Here it comes: The Confession.

I wait for it as Matthew stiffens, his features hardening. He doesn't blink as he stares at Marissa. "What's going on?"

His wife blindsided him. She lured him to me on false pretenses. Not the best way to begin our work, but maybe it was the only way to get him here.

"I've wanted to tell you this for a while. I just didn't know how." A tear rolls down her cheek. "I broke your trust, and I'm so sorry."

He pulls his hand away roughly. "Cut to the chase, Marissa."

She swallows hard. "I slept with someone," she blurts. "Just once. But—"

"*Who?*" Matthew's question cuts like a knife through the air.

She covers her flat stomach with her hands, as if she feels its blade.

This won't be the first time I've helped a couple through an infidelity. Back when I was a licensed therapist—instead of a consultant, which is my title now—I saw iterations of it nearly every week: the wife who had an affair with a coworker, the husband who cheated with a neighbor, the fiancé who had a fling with an old girlfriend. But something about Marissa's revelation feels different.

Or maybe it's Matthew's reaction.

Typically, spouses experience shock when confronted with news such as this. Anger doesn't descend until later.

Matthew's rage is immediately palpable, though. His hands clench into fists, the plastic cup crumpling in his grasp.

"It wasn't anyone you know," Marissa whispers. "Just a man I met at Pinnacle Studio."

"What?" Color floods his cheeks. "You fucked a guy from the gym?"

She bows her head, as if she feels she deserves his coarse language.

I lean forward. It's time for me to reenter this scene. "Matthew, I know how hard it must be for you to hear this."

He whirls to look at me with blazing eyes. I lean closer to him, meeting his gaze unflinchingly.

"Really? You *know*?" He spits out the words. "Were you in on this, helping her set me up to get me here?"

I lift up my hands. I'm not going to give him an answer, but I can absorb his rage. I've dealt with angrier men than him.

Marissa raises her head. "Matthew, she didn't know why we were coming. And I was scared that if I told you at home—"

She doesn't finish her sentence. My eyes drift to the mangled cup in his hand and wonder if Matthew's emotional outbursts are ever accompanied by physical ones.

Matthew stands, towering over his wife. She stares up at him beseechingly.

Their body language speaks volumes: she's frightened.

What I need to find out is if she's scared of losing her husband or scared of *him*.

I rise unhurriedly to my feet. I don't shout, but my tone carries force. "Do you love your wife?"

Matthew turns to look at me. His face is twisted; too many emotions are tangled up in his expression for me to determine which one is now dominant.

He doesn't answer my question. I maintain eye contact. With men such as Matthew, it's important to demonstrate assertiveness.

"If you love your wife"—I enunciate every word—"then please sit back down. I can get you through this."

He hovers, on the brink of a decision. I could say more to sway him. I could let him know I've worked with many couples who've endured far worse issues than infidelity. I could tell him about my success rate, which is even higher now that I've shed the constraints of traditional therapy and created a new method, one that's all my own.

But I don't. I wait him out.

"I don't see how talking about bullshit like my issues with my father and my dreams can help us get through this," he says.

If I had to lay down odds on whether he'll storm back out through the door, I'd put them at fifty-fifty.

"Matthew," Marissa begs. "Avery's not like that. Please, give this a chance."

He exhales, his rigid shoulders softening. Then he plants himself on the couch, as far from his wife as possible.

I reclaim my seat as well.

What Matthew doesn't know is that I've just made a decision, too. The Bishops intrigue me; I'm going to take them on.

"Here's how this will go. You have ten sessions." Knowing the time frame for our work together is essential for a client. What they can't know is my agenda.

In my process, each session has a title, beginning with The Confession, then cycling through Disruption, Escalation, Revelation, Devastation, Confrontation, Exposure, The Test, Reconciliation, and concluding with Promises.

"You cannot skip our sessions or be late. No traffic excuses or last-minute deadlines. In between our appointments, you can talk about your son, your careers, the weather—really anything. But it's best if this space remains pure, so I recommend avoiding discussing what will come up here. I also suggest you don't reveal information about our time together to anyone else while our sessions are ongoing."

Marissa nods eagerly. I take Matthew's stony silence for acquiescence.

There's a hitch in my energy, which I'm careful to mask. All couples have secrets. The Bishops are no exception. There's more than just infidelity here. Marissa's cheating is a symptom, not the source of their fundamental breakdown.

Twelve minutes ago, they breezed into my office—glamorous, affluent, enviable. The golden couple. Now the underlying tarnishes they've never allowed the public to see are already beginning to show.

It's going to get a lot uglier soon.

"When do we start?" Marissa asks.

"We already have."

CHAPTER TWO

MARISSA

Marissa feels as if she and Matthew have hurtled off a cliff. They're in free fall. She just spoke the terrible words out loud: *I slept with someone.*

On the drive to Avery Chambers's office in Cleveland Park, D.C., Marissa almost suggested canceling the session. She knew Matthew wouldn't have minded. It had been her idea to schedule the meeting, which she insinuated was to talk about their eight-year-old son, Bennett, who had been bullied by a classmate last year.

Marissa reached out to Avery after reading an article in *The Washington Post Magazine* that described Avery's unconventional "anti-therapy." The profile contained biographical details about the forty-one-year-old: she grew up in Chicago, attended Northwestern, is an avid runner, and loves to travel to off-the-beaten-path destinations. Several of her former clients were interviewed—"She literally saved my life," one proclaimed—and so were a few detractors, including the head of the American Psychological Association, who was quoted as saying, "Avery Chambers does not represent or uphold the sacred tenets of our profession." An accompanying photo revealed the silhouette of a woman with a tumble of long hair looking out a window.

In person, Avery is more attractive and stylish than Marissa expected, with her radiant olive skin and full lips. She wears a belted green suede dress and three-inch heels that make her almost as tall as Marissa, and a stack of gold bangles adorns her right wrist. Avery doesn't wear a wedding band. Marissa wonders if this matters. Would it be better if Avery had a husband? Would that enable her to more effectively understand the nuances of a complicated marriage?

And certainly Marissa and Matthew's union is complicated. A decade into their marriage, Matthew, a partner in a D.C. law firm, spends more evenings at business events than by her side. Marissa feels lost in a constant swirl of activities: running her boutique, Coco; cooking delicious but nutritious meals for her family; staying trim and fit enough to slide into the pair of faded Levi's cutoffs she's had since high school; and serving on the auction committee at Bennett's private school.

Avery's voice pulls Marissa into the present. "You need to answer four questions, Marissa. Keep it short. One: Have you ever cheated on Matthew before?"

"No! Never!"

Her whole body is shaking; she's freezing. Normally Matthew would notice and wrap an arm around her or offer her his suit jacket. She desperately wants to stand up and walk past her husband to get her cape, but it feels perilous to enter his space now. He's blazing with fury; he's the heat to her ice.

"Two." Avery must sit in that chair day after day, absorbing sordid and sad stories. She's in the epicenter of the rage and pain and disgust ricocheting around the room; it seems impossible that she's immune to it. Yet she looks utterly calm, and invincible. "Will it ever happen again?"

"No, I promise."

Avery nods. "Three: Is it truly over with the other man?"

"Yes," Marissa whispers. The moment carries a solemnity; it has the feel of a vow. Matthew finally turns to look at her. There's a sheen in his eyes, just as there was on their wedding day when she walked down the aisle, in a cream silk dress with a long train, past two hundred guests.

Avery is studying both of them intently, Marissa realizes. What is she thinking?

The silence stretches out.

"What's the fourth question?" Marissa finally asks.

"That's for Matthew to decide. But not right now. Matthew, when you leave here, I'd like you to think about the essential information you need to know in order to move on."

He nods, just once. But it already feels like progress.

Coming here was a good decision. Avery's no-nonsense approach suits Matthew's personality. He likes charts and precise plans; he's a cut-to-the-chase kind of guy. Back when Bennett was being bullied, Marissa tried talking to the other child's parents. Matthew hired a boxing coach to teach their then second-grader how to throw an uppercut.

"Let's go back to happier times." Avery jots something on her notepad. "Tell me about one of your favorite moments together, Marissa."

There are so many for Marissa to choose from, whole albums of memories. She selects one of the glossy snapshots: "Just last year, Matthew and I were invited to a black-tie dinner at the Kennedy Center. It was magical. We hired a car and driver and danced all night. He looked so handsome. It was because of his work on behalf of the World Wildlife Fund that we went—"

Avery cuts her off. "That's an Instagram post. Give me something real."

Marissa flinches. In those few words, Avery has cut to the core of what their marriage has become: curated moments served up in public, while in private the emptiness between them slowly expands.

Matthew hasn't seemed bothered that their conversations have become more about to-do lists than ideas or feelings, or that their hands no longer find each other during long drives, entwining atop the gearshift. She can't even remember how long ago Matthew began getting out of their bed as soon as the alarm sounded in the morning, instead of reaching for her.

"Something real," Marissa repeats. She feels as if she were about to fail a final exam. Then she closes her eyes and it comes to her.

A snowstorm blanketing the city; her and Matthew at home. Baby Bennett napping. Matthew building a fire, while she makes mugs of hot chocolate spiked with rum. The two of them sitting on a chenille blanket playing Scrabble, then abandoning the game to make love.

"It wasn't rum. It was Grand Marnier," Matthew says when she finishes. His voice is still hard, but have its edges softened just a little?

Avery leans closer to Matthew. "Now I want a memory from you. I want you to recall some incredible sex you had. Something really steamy."

Marissa lowers her eyes, her cheeks flushing, wondering which moment Matthew will pick. He might not play along. But if he does, will he share the same recollection that bloomed in her mind? That trip to St. Barts when they snuck into the outdoor cabana in the middle of the afternoon, their bodies slick with suntan lotion and sweat. The taste of salt and coconut on his skin. They hadn't had raw, passionate sex like that in a while. Years, truthfully.

Matthew squeezes the crumpled plastic cup in his hand again, making a loud crackling sound. "I can't think about any good times with Marissa right now."

Avery stands up and retrieves a trash basket from behind her desk. "Let's get rid of those cups." As she returns to her chair, Avery continues, "And I'm not talking about Marissa."

Marissa's head snaps up in time to catch a smile playing on the edge of Avery's lips. "I want you to tell me about the greatest sex you had with another woman."

"Are you serious?" Matthew asks.

"Yes. Your mind is being flooded with ugly images right now. You're imagining your wife with another man. So let's have her think about you with another woman."

Matthew is doing it; Marissa can tell by the way his gaze grows unfocused. She bets she knows exactly whom Matthew is thinking about: Natalie, the woman he dated for a year during college and still maintains a friendship with. Natalie's young daughter attends the same private school as Bennett, and Natalie is the cochair of the auction committee; she is impossible for Marissa to avoid.

However, when Matthew speaks, he shares a different memory. "Okay, fine. I was a first-year law student and this hot TA approached me in the library. I was in the stacks and she snuck up behind me and slid her arms around my waist, under my sweatshirt. We ended up in her apartment. . . . We did it three times that night. It's still my record." Matthew pauses. "Do you really want me to go on?"

Naturally Matthew would boil it down to numbers, to a record. He is highly competitive.

And for a moment, so is she. She feels like the runner-up.

She's never heard this story before. So she and Matthew both kept secrets, she thinks.

Avery taps her pen on her pad and seems to make a decision. "Marissa, would you step out for a few minutes? There's a chair just outside the door where you can sit."

Marissa hesitates, then rises. This appointment is nothing like what she expected. Leaving the two of them alone feels dangerous.

As Marissa exits Avery's office, she glances back at her husband, but he isn't looking her way.

The wide, wood-planked hallway contains a single upholstered chair, next to a table holding a Mission-style lamp and vase of red tulips. Marissa is too agitated to sit. She moves closer to the door. She can hear the low rumble of Matthew's voice, but she can't make out a single word.

Avery could be asking him anything. Nothing seems out of bounds for her. *Losing my license was the best thing to ever happen to me—and to my clients,* Avery was quoted as saying in the *Post* article. Marissa stares at the door. If she pressed her ear against it, just for a minute . . .

Then a thought strikes her: there could be a video camera somewhere. It would be humiliating to be caught.

Finally, she pulls out her phone and taps a message to Bennett's babysitter: **All okay? If Bennett wants a brownie, he can have one. I snuck black beans into them so they're secretly healthy. :-)**

Just as she finishes, the door to Avery's office opens. Marissa quickly tucks her phone into her bag.

"The sitter." Marissa's unsure why she feels the need to explain her actions.

"Come back in."

Marissa studies Matthew's face as she reenters the room. It reveals nothing.

"A lot of times people confess an infidelity because they can't stand the guilt." Avery's tone isn't judgmental or forgiving; she's matter-of-fact. "They do it to ease their own conscience. Is that why you brought your husband here?"

Marissa thinks carefully about her answer, making sure it is truthful: "I wanted to tell Matthew because it was the right thing to do."

Avery raises an eyebrow. "You two are going to have to put in a lot of work."

Marissa nods eagerly. "I'll do anything." Beside her on the couch, Matthew is as still as a stone. Marissa wonders if Avery thinks they need more fixing than the average couple with an infidelity issue.

Avery asks a few more questions about major stresses they've experienced. Marissa describes the two miscarriages she suffered before having Bennett, and the failed fertility treatments they endured afterward. Matthew talks about the death of his mother to leukemia five years earlier. Marissa debates mentioning the deep rift between Matthew and his father—a successful D.C. lobbyist—but she decides not to risk bringing up another upsetting topic.

Avery rises. "Thursday, same time?"

Matthew pulls out his iPhone and frowns at the screen. "I've got a client dinner. Getting here will be a pain in—"

"No problem," Avery says smoothly. "Where do you live?"

"Chevy Chase," Marissa replies. "Just over the D.C. line."

"I'll come to you. Nine P.M.?"

Matthew blinks in surprise. "Fine."

Marissa isn't getting a vote in this, she realizes, even though she'll be the one cleaning up after dinner, and making sure Bennett is asleep early, and figuring out logistics such as where they'll sit and whether it's appropriate to serve drinks or food.

"Keep Monday and Thursday evenings at seven P.M. free for the next few weeks," Avery instructs them.

Avery already seems to know how to handle Matthew; he's nodding, responding to her succinct instructions.

Which means Avery probably also has a strategy for managing her, Marissa thinks.

CHAPTER THREE

AVERY

THE SKY IS PITCH-BLACK as I veer left onto Connecticut Avenue and head toward home, reaching for the bottle of water in my cup holder to rinse the sour taste of tequila from my mouth. The D.C. roads are quieter at this time of night—or technically, early morning—with just a few people straggling in and out of the bars and restaurants that line either side of the street. Most residents are asleep—including Derrick, the man I just left.

His scent lingers on my skin. Derrick's cologne is too woodsy for my taste. If I were planning to have a long-term relationship with him, I might give him a bottle of my favorite brand. But neither of us is looking for a commitment. Still, the hours I just spent with him are among the most pleasurable I've passed all week.

At twenty-six, Derrick has retained the powerful physique and athleticism that earned him a full scholarship to the University of Maryland, where he served as a tight end on an undefeated team. Unlike a lot of good but not great college ballplayers, Derrick never labored under the illusion that he'd turn pro. After graduation, he found a job with a company that sells state-of-the-art security systems, ones that are much more expensive and comprehensive than those typically purchased by homeowners.

I met him fairly recently, when he came to my house to install mine.

My phone buzzes with an incoming text just as I reach my Cleveland Park neighborhood. I don't dig into my purse to read it. It could be Derrick checking to see if I've made it home safely, or my stepdaughter, Lana, who has a fickle relationship with time. It could also be my mother, letting me know she's extending her stay at the south-Indian ashram where she's been ensconced for the past two months. I finish off the water in my bottle and turn onto my street.

My gut clenches as I realize something is off: my house is too dark.

The lamp on the table just inside my front door should be shining brightly. It's set on a timer precisely so I don't have to enter a shadowy home.

Just a few months ago, I would've blithely gone into the darkness.

Now I slowly pull into the driveway, my headlights illuminating my front porch. The wooden swing is swaying ever so slightly in the wind, but there's no other sign of movement.

I've got Mace on my key chain, my bushes are cut too low to provide cover for anyone, and my alarm system is almost impossible to override. Still, I leave on the car engine and keep my headlights blazing while I step out of my old BMW and approach my front door, reaching into my purse for my phone.

My neighbors are close-by on either side, but their places are also dark, and on a cold night in mid-March, no one is likely to have a window open.

The bottom porch step creaks as I step onto it.

I reach my doorknob and test it. The lock is still engaged. I twist a key into it, then unlock the dead bolt. When I give the door a little push, it soundlessly glides open. I wait a moment, listening hard. I can't sense a presence inside.

A table in my foyer holds a vase of red tulips, a shallow glass bowl, and the lamp. Down the hall to the left is my office; the living room is to the right.

I click the switch on the lamp, the sharp, sudden noise seeming to echo through the house. When it doesn't come to life, I twist it again. Nothing. I touch my index finger to the bulb. It's warm. I unscrew it and gently shake it, hearing the telltale rattle that indicates it burned out.

Sometimes the simplest explanation is the correct one, but I can no longer risk making those kinds of assumptions.

I flick on the overhead hall light, then walk back to my car to turn off the engine. My phone buzzes again as I reenter my house, and I instinctively glance down.

A text lands on my screen: **Please. It's an emergency.**

Directly above it is the message that came in while I was driving: **Sorry to bother you, but could you call me?**

They're both from Cameron, one of my first ten-session clients. Cameron is a sweet, shy thirty-two-year-old who completed his work with me last fall.

Cameron came to see me because he was having panic attacks. His first-session confession was clear, even though he didn't explicitly state it: he was miserable in his marriage. His wife, Skylar, was a controlling, narcissistic woman who wanted to completely dominate Cameron.

Cameron's life changed radically as a result of our work together. So did mine.

The last time I heard from him, he'd moved out and was enjoying life on his own in an apartment.

After I slip off my boots and hang up my coat, I call him. He picks up before the first ring ends.

"Avery?" His voice is frantic. "Skylar found out I was dating someone and tried to kill herself! She took a bunch of pills and called me to say goodbye!"

I'm not all that surprised, but I don't mention this to Cameron. "Where are you now?" I ask as I climb the stairs and enter my bedroom.

"Sibley Hospital."

I peer into the mirror over my bureau and frown, wiping smeared mascara from beneath my eyes. I'm exhausted and it's after midnight, but I pull a sweater and jeans out of a drawer. "I'll be right there."

Other people's issues are so much easier to fix than my own.

Cameron sits on a bench just outside the hospital entrance, his shock of red hair and familiar army-green puffer jacket—the one that's a size too big—making him immediately recognizable. Keeping my pace steady and unhurried, I walk toward him, my exhalations forming little white puffs in the frigid night air. As I draw closer, I notice one of his shoelaces is untied. I resist the urge to lace it up for him. With tears streaking his open, innocent face and a smattering of freckles across his nose and cheeks, he looks young enough to still be in high school.

"It's going to be fine." I put my hand on his shoulder. "C'mon, let's go inside."

He rises and follows me as I step onto a mat that triggers the automatic doors, and we enter the ER. Only one other person—a middle-aged man sitting in a plastic bucket seat, staring at his phone—is in the waiting area.

As I lead Cameron toward a sofa, I think about how I'm going to manage this temporary setback. A meek man with an oppressive, manipulative ex is a toxic mix.

"Maybe I shouldn't have told her I started dating someone." Cameron collapses onto the couch.

"Let's take a step back. You're still helping Skylar out financially, right?"

"Yes, I'm paying half the mortgage until the house sells. And sometimes I go by if she needs help with stuff."

"Stuff?"

"Yeah, like if something goes wrong around the house. I told her to call me instead of dealing with it herself because once she got up on a chair to open this window that was stuck and she fell. She only got a few bruises, but it could have been worse."

Convenient, I refrain from saying.

"Maybe it was all too abrupt." Cameron's lower lip trembles.

"That's exactly what Skylar wants you to believe. She didn't intend to kill herself."

Cameron flinches. "How do you know that?"

"Look, if Skylar really wanted to die, she wouldn't have phoned you." While a suicide attempt is usually a cry for help, in Skylar's case I can say with near certainty it's an attempt to regain some control over Cameron.

Right now, my former client is more of a danger to himself than Skylar is to herself, and I need to shock him straight. "So, what do you think the solution is, Cameron? Give up your new life and move back in with Skylar?"

Exhilaration courses through my veins; casting aside the filters that constrained me when I was a therapist is so deliciously freeing.

I lean in closer to him. I'm fond of Cameron; he has as tender and pure a heart as anyone I've ever met. "There will always be something with her. And if you give in now, in another few months, you'll be right back where you were before."

I'm reaching him; I can see it in his slower breathing and in his increased eye contact. "What should I do?"

A traditional therapist would gently help Cameron find his own solution, even if it took years. Even if it was the wrong one.

"You need to tell Skylar you're sorry she's hurting, but it isn't going to change anything."

"I-I want to, but . . ."

"The longer you wait, the harder it's going to be." Cameron's ex-wife is a powerful force in his life; I need to be stronger. I stand up and stretch out my hand. "Let's go. You're not doing this alone."

He hesitates, then rises and follows me to the security guard manning the desk. I tell the guard we're here to see Skylar Sullivan, and we present our driver's licenses and sign in. A nurse appears a few moments later and leads us to Skylar, who lies on a gurney with curtain walls separating her from the patients on either side. Her dark hair is spread out over the white pillowcase, and I notice she's wearing an awful lot of makeup.

"Skylar," Cameron says softly.

Her eyelids flutter open. "Cameron," she whispers. "I knew you'd come."

She stretches out a hand, leaving her manicured fingers dangling midair, until he moves closer and takes them. She doesn't notice me; her sole focus is on Cameron.

I pick up the chart at the foot of Skylar's bed and scan the notes. She swallowed twenty milligrams of Lunesta, a sedative. Not enough to kill her. She didn't even need to have her stomach pumped. Just enough to give her ex a bad scare.

"You know I hate hospitals." Skylar's voice trembles. "Will they let you take me home?"

"I don't think you'll be able to leave tonight."

Her face falls. "But when I do, you'll be there, right? You'll stay with me."

This is it, the moment when my ten sessions will collide with his ex-wife's force of will.

"No." Cameron swallows hard and releases her hand. "I have my own apartment now."

She inhales sharply. "But I'm not well! I need you!"

As I put down the chart, Skylar's head swivels toward me. I see recognition come into her eyes.

"What is *she* doing here?" Skylar's eyes narrow. "Get out or I'm calling the cops again!"

A machine beeps shrilly, and by the time the same nurse who led Cameron and me to Skylar opens the curtain, I'm already backing out of the makeshift room.

"You feeling okay, Skylar?" The nurse checks the machine's screen. "Your blood pressure and pulse just shot up."

I hope Skylar will be kept here for another day or two. In the meantime, I'll email Cameron another snippet of the video clip I've created, the one that features a zoom-in on Skylar's furious, pinched face as she berates him with vicious words.

I showed Cameron that video during our fourth session together, the one I've titled Revelation. Seeing and hearing his wife disparage him, as he cowered on the couch, unshackled something in Cameron. It saved him.

Sometimes, we need to look at our lives from a different angle to recognize the dysfunction and damage certain relationships are causing. When Cameron saw—truly saw, for the first time—how abusive Skylar was to him, he began to gather the courage to move out.

That video also cost me my license. I'd snuck into Cameron and Skylar's house in D.C. to record it; neither of them knew I was hiding in a closet, filming the argument I'd instructed Cameron to stoke. When Skylar found out by hacking into Cameron's emails, she reported me. Luckily, Cameron told the police he'd given me permission to enter his home and film him, which means the criminal charges didn't stick. Only the professional repercussions did.

So in a way, that video freed me, too.

Back in the hospital's waiting room, I pause at the watercooler by the guard's desk. A night of tequila and sex has left me parched, and the dry hospital air isn't helping. I pull a plastic cup out of the dispenser sleeve and fill it, gulping it down without pause. Then I fill it again.

When I toss the cup into the trash bin, it lands atop a pile of others—including one that someone crushed. I stare at it for a moment, remembering Matthew's hand closing tightly around the cup I gave him, then I head back outside.

My BMW is right where I left it in the parking lot, beneath a tall, bright lamp, but I still glance into my back seat before unlocking my door. It's one of my newer habits, along with requesting a picture ID from prospective clients and making sure they match the photos before I let them into my house.

Skylar isn't my only enemy.

It takes a minute for the heat to come on, and I'm already driving toward Matthew and Marissa's house by the time the blowing air has chased the chill from my body.

Clients reveal only so much when they come to see me. I want to get a fuller picture of the Bishops, and I'm wide-awake, so I might as well start now.

They live in Chevy Chase, just over the D.C. line in Maryland, an area where even a small plot of undeveloped land can go for seven figures. Their home is exactly as I expected: grand and sprawling with a beautifully maintained lawn, enclosed by a tall wrought-iron fence and gate. It's easy to imagine Marissa clipping flowers from the garden in a wide-brimmed hat while Matthew tosses a baseball to his son, and to picture them on their graceful front porch, sipping cocktails as the sun dips lower into the sky.

Only one thing is off, and it's the inverse of what occurred just an hour or so ago, when I arrived home to discover my house was unexpectedly dark.

At nearly 2:00 A.M., the Bishops' place should be cloaked in shadows and completely still. But a glow illuminates one of the second-story rooms. I squint and glimpse the form of a person moving around inside.

Which one of them can't sleep?

Insomnia can grip us for many reasons: stress, guilt, fear, and rage are among them.

An uneasy mind is difficult to quiet.

CHAPTER FOUR

MARISSA

MARISSA WINCES AS THE empty glass shatters against the terra-cotta tiles of the kitchen floor.

"Damn," she mutters, grabbing a paper towel and bending down to pick up the shards. Too much coffee and too little sleep have made her jittery.

"*Mom*," Bennett says. "That's a dollar for the curse jar."

Technically, she feels the word is only a borderline swear, but she isn't going to debate this with her eight-year-old. She scans the floor, knowing she has probably missed a few sharp slivers, as she hears the rush of water abruptly cease one floor up. On typical mornings, Matthew showers while she applies moisturizer and makeup, the two of them discussing the day's logistics: whether he'd be home for dinner that night, or if they should repaint the dining room. Ever since their session with Avery, though, her husband has been sleeping in the guest room and avoiding the master bathroom until she is downstairs.

Marissa reaches for another glass and fills it with freshly squeezed grapefruit juice, then glances at the spelling list on the counter.

"*Song,*" Marissa prompts Bennett, who sits atop a kitchen stool, eating Kashi cereal topped with fresh blueberries, which he seems to be pushing aside with his spoon.

"S-O-N-G."

"Perfect." Marissa turns the turkey bacon sizzling on the stove. "How about *strong*?"

She keeps quizzing Bennett on the *ong* words as she sprinkles a quarter cup of grated Gruyère in the omelet she is preparing. Usually breakfasts such as these are reserved for Matthew's birthday, Father's Day, and the occasional lazy Sunday. But this is the third day of her efforts to make amends.

It has been easy to follow Avery's instructions and avoid talking about their session because Matthew has barely been home.

She hopes his silent fury is beginning to burn out.

"Wrong," Marissa prompts Bennett as Matthew's footsteps approach the kitchen. Marissa slides the omelet onto a plate alongside three slices of bacon and sets it down on the counter, then turns to greet her husband: "Good morning."

"Hey, guys!" Matthew's voice is jovial, but he turns his back to her as he ruffles Bennett's hair. "I'm driving you in today, kiddo. Run and grab your backpack."

"You are?" Marissa asks as Matthew grabs a single slice of bacon. She always takes their son to school; Matthew doesn't even know the car-pool rules. "You need to drop him off at the south—"

"We'll figure it out. I'll wait for him in the car."

Bennett reappears in his coat with the backpack that always looks so big on his narrow shoulders. She hugs him, holding on a moment longer than usual and breathing in the scent of the tangerine-vanilla shampoo she just started carrying in her boutique.

"Bye!" she calls out, watching as he climbs into the back seat of Matthew's Land Rover.

During the ten seconds her husband spent in her presence, the welcoming ambience she'd carefully cultivated—the brewing coffee, the bouquet of violet hydrangeas on the counter—was irrevocably altered.

"I love you," she says, even though she knows neither of them can hear her.

Marissa remains perfectly still at the window in the suddenly silent kitchen, watching, until the car disappears from view.

Twenty minutes later, Marissa slides her key into the lock of her boutique and the door glides open. She steps inside Coco and inhales a slow, grounding breath.

The landscape of her personal life is jagged and frayed, but all the pieces in this intimate, elegant space are in place. Located just a few miles from their home, across the D.C. line, the boutique carries a medley of luxury goods: everything from antimicrobial, cushioned yoga mats to baby-soft cashmere hoodies—items her customers didn't even know they needed until they became cherished possessions.

She can hear her lone employee, Polly, in the back room, unpacking the boxes, which arrive several times a week from far-flung locations, containing hand-painted trays from Santa Fe, or wildflower honey from Vermont, or fragrant bath salts from Paris. Usually, Marissa doesn't get into the boutique until after 9:00 A.M. But Matthew's surprise declaration left her with an extra forty-five minutes that would have been spent taking Bennett to school. She'd felt too unmoored to stay in their home alone.

Marissa hired Polly just a month or so ago, after her former assistant accepted a managerial job at Saks. Polly opens and closes the shop almost every day, which allows Marissa to be on-site only during the time that Bennett is in school. Marissa knows being able to craft her own schedule is a luxury, but it isn't as idyllic as it sounds. She still has to respond to emails at all hours— especially because many of her suppliers are in different time zones—and she often attends to ancillary tasks, such as following up on delayed shipments or uploading new photos to the store's website or Instagram, from the bleachers of Bennett's baseball games or in the early morning when she's the only one awake in the house. In a sense, she's always on call.

Marissa moves an antique perfume bottle an inch to the right as she passes a display table, calling out, "Good morning, Polly."

"Marissa!" Polly steps out of the back room, holding a mug of tea with a red-and-white-striped paper straw. "You're here early. We finally got in those gorgeous hurricane globes, but two are broken."

"Wonderful." Marissa rolls her eyes. "How difficult is it to wrap things properly?"

"I'm sorry—should I send them back?" Polly looks stricken, as if it were her fault.

"No, no, I'll handle it. Sorry, rough morning. Ignore me, I'm grumpy."

"Everything okay?"

"I just didn't sleep well."

"Well, you look awesome. As always. Love your shirt."

Marissa gazes down at her navy blue blouse; she's forgotten what she's wearing. "Thanks. Matthew gave it to me for Christmas."

Polly is young and eager, and usually Marissa welcomes Polly's many questions, knowing she wants to learn the ropes. Marissa doesn't mind explaining the ins and outs of owning a small business. But today, she craves quiet. The second session with Avery is tonight, and Marissa can think of little else. Just before she left the house, she sent Matthew a text reminding him, but he hasn't replied. What if he doesn't come home in time?

"Should I change up the window display?" Polly abruptly tips her head and untucks her hair from behind her ears in a strange, jerky motion.

"Sure. Let's do something cute with the bathrobes and slippers." Marissa already has a vision in her mind; she'll let Polly give it a shot, then she'll tweak it.

But for once, Polly isn't peppering Marissa with questions. She's still fiddling with her long brown hair.

"I'll get started." Polly starts to spin around, and that's when Marissa notices the distinctive chunky gold-and-onyx earrings Polly is wearing—earrings that adorned Marissa's own earlobes just yesterday. She'd taken them off and left them on her desk when her AirPods died and she'd had to press her cell phone to her ear.

"Polly? Are those my—"

"You left them here," Polly blurts, a cherry-colored flush spreading across her fair skin. "I'm sorry, I was worried they'd get lost—I was just—I thought I'd hold them for you. . . ."

"I see." The earrings are pierced; it feels a little gross that Polly slid them into her lobes. It would've been easy for her to simply put them aside in a safe place.

Polly removes the earrings and holds them out in her palm, casting her big brown eyes toward the floor.

Marissa takes the jewelry, making a mental note to sanitize the pieces before wearing them again.

"Okay, let's see what you come up with for the window," Marissa says briskly. "I've got to make a few calls. I'll come look when I'm done."

As Polly heads toward the front of the store, Marissa walks into the tiny kitchen and makes herself a cup of ginger chai, pulling a paper straw from the supply drawer. She'd taught Polly the trick of using one to not only preserve lipstick, but avoid staining your teeth.

Marissa settles in at her desk, attending to emails and calls. She has just hung up with the candlestick vendor when her phone buzzes with an incoming text. The name on the screen electrifies her.

You doing ok?

He isn't supposed to be texting her. She'd told him they both had to forget their illicit night ever occurred. *It was a mistake. It can't ever happen again,* she'd said the next morning when he'd phoned.

She should be annoyed that he is continuing to reach out. But she's strangely touched.

The truth is, she hasn't been able to erase the memory of their time together.

The first time she noticed him—*really* noticed him—she was drawn to his physicality, his strong shoulders and biceps flexing as he lifted and pulled. He'd turned and smiled at her with a boyish grin that let her know he'd caught her watching.

She stares down at her phone, willing herself to ignore his message.

Three dots appear, almost as if he knows she is looking, waiting to see what he'll write next.

I know I shouldn't say this, but I can't stop thinking about our night.

She hasn't stopped thinking about it either. Still, if she could undo it, she would. She'd give quite a lot for it never to have happened.

Yet, something unexpected is woven into Marissa's shame and regret—a deep thread of warmth that comes from the sensation of feeling cherished. Of being truly seen.

It wasn't just raw sex between them; his kisses were slow and tender and he held her afterward, seemingly reluctant to let her go. *Marissa,* he'd whispered, his voice husky.

"Marissa?"

She flinches and looks behind her. Polly stands there, holding a fresh cup of tea, just inches away. Close enough, perhaps, to have read the screen of Marissa's phone.

Marissa flips it over in her hand, feeling her heart pound.

"You startled me." Marissa stands up and takes a step away from her desk.

"I'm sorry." Polly's usually easy to read. But Marissa can't tell from Polly's expression whether she glimpsed those incriminating lines on the phone. "I just wanted to let you know the window display is done. I think you'll like it."

Marissa wants to push back; her needy young assistant is grating on her. Polly takes a sip of the ginger chai that Marissa favors and Polly has recently proclaimed to be her own favorite. The shirt she's wearing is tucked in the front and left loose in the back—the same way Marissa always wears her shirts.

It never annoyed Marissa until now. "I'll be there in a minute," Marissa says firmly.

"Okay." Polly skitters away and Marissa quickly deletes the messages.

It's 10:00 A.M., time for Coco to open. Marissa selects one of her Spotify playlists, and Chris Martin's voice croons through the speakers.

She walks to the front of the store and looks at Polly's display. It's exactly what Marissa asked for: two cozy his-and-her robes draped over a tufted chair, with matching slippers set out. Polly has added a life-size, decorative silver pug dog atop a rug, and a pair of chunky painted mugs on a little glass table. Anyone would want to sink into that scene.

Marissa stares at it. She feels Polly's eager eyes on her; she swears she can hear Polly's excited breaths. Polly is standing too close to her again; her presence makes Marissa feel itchy.

"Good effort, but it isn't quite right." As soon as the words come out, Marissa regrets them. But not enough to try to smooth them over.

CHAPTER FIVE

AVERY

I COLLAPSE ONTO THE GRASS, gasping. Romeo flops down beside me, his tongue lolling out, his stubby tail thumping the air. "You're not even winded, are you? Show-off."

He rolls over, exposing his pink stomach for a scratch. I comply. "Such a good boy." I can't help it; I'm a sucker for dogs, especially ones such as Romeo, who no longer have any reason to trust humans, but continue to do so.

It's a crisp forty-degree day, but clumps of tourists mill around the grassy National Mall stretching between the Washington Monument and the US Capitol. It's my favorite loop to run. For the past few months, ever since I completed the requisite volunteer training, I've been stopping by the animal shelter on my drive here to pick up a jogging buddy. The shelter's director always finds me a dog who needs the activity; at first I ran with a Labrador mix, then a handsome gray dog who was part whippet. Those two were quickly adopted.

For six weeks straight, my dates have been with Romeo, a pit bull. "He's a lover, not a fighter, which is why he was dumped here," the shelter director told me. "But we can't find him a home. People take one look at him and move on to the next crate."

Romeo does look fierce, with his powerful jaws, muscular body, docked ears, and scarred face. But inside, he's a marshmallow. My breathing slows as he leans against me, and I soak in his welcome warmth. Then

I glance down at my watch and see it's almost noon. I'm going to be late if I don't hurry.

I reluctantly stand up and stretch my tight calves, then give Romeo's leash—the bright yellow one with the hopeful words ADOPT ME! printed on it in black letters—a tug. He dutifully pads to my parked car, slurps up the water I pour into a collapsible bowl, then hops into the passenger's seat for the ride back to the shelter.

I've grown to hate having to return Romeo to his kennel, even though the shelter is a clean, pleasant space staffed by bighearted volunteers. One of them tosses a rawhide bone into Romeo's cage when we arrive.

Romeo walks obediently inside. He curls up on his worn bed in the corner and stares at me through the metal bars with limpid brown eyes, ignoring the bone.

"Come on, that looks delicious!" I say as I head toward the exit.

I hear a little whimper.

I turn around: "I'll be back in a week."

He drops his head onto his paws, his gaze never wavering.

I swear I can feel the sadness of the dog who wouldn't fight back, even to protect himself, for the entertainment of despicable people.

"This is a terrible idea."

I go find the shelter's director, to tell her I want to adopt Romeo.

On my drive home, I blast the Indigo Girls and make a mental list of the supplies I will need for Romeo when I pick him up tomorrow—bowls, a new leash, toys, kibble. I find myself smiling as I imagine Romeo's nails clicking on my hardwood floors as he follows me around my house, and him snoozing by my side as I write up client notes. Then I picture him chewing on my favorite leather pumps.

As I pull into my driveway, I see my stepdaughter, Lana, sitting in the driver's seat of her Honda, parked behind the old Mercedes that her dad used to drive.

I turn off my engine and step out as she mirrors my movements.

"Sorry I'm late." I stretch out my arms.

"It's okay. I just got here."

As we hug, I notice a streak of pink paint in her hair. Lana runs kids' birthday parties at a decorate-your-own-pottery store. "Princess theme?" I touch a chocolate-brown curl. She inherited her thick locks from her dad, along with his love of roller coasters and Monty Python and aversion to mayonnaise. Lana and her cerebral, intense father had little else in common, though.

I unlock my front door and gesture for Lana to come in. She still has a key, since Paul shared custody with his ex-wife after their divorce and Lana lived with us part-time as a teenager, but she stopped using it when she graduated from college and moved into a nearby apartment. It could have been a disastrous mix: a thirteen-year-old girl and her father's new wife cohabitating under one roof. But Lana and I formed a bond that's all our own.

"Want some coffee?" At her nod, I drop a pod into the Keurig and reach into the cupboard for the box of almond biscotti.

I crunch into one as I lead Lana into the living room. Two packing boxes are stacked by the fireplace, containing memorabilia Paul stored in the basement.

When my husband died, he left his generous life insurance policy to Lana, and he willed our home to me. I got rid of a few things immediately, such as his containers of medicines and the hospital-style bed that we'd set up in Lana's old bedroom, so he could have the brightest room in the house. We'd tried to offset the grimness of all the medical supplies by erecting a trio of bird feeders just outside the windows so Paul could watch the fluttering of blue jays, finches, and soft-brown sparrows. We'd also covered the walls with family photographs of Paul, Lana, and me in happier times and brought in his vintage Crosley turntable so he could hear his beloved jazz music.

It took me a little while to box up Paul's clothes and donate them to a homeless shelter. Now, just a few of Paul's belongings still occupy our rooms, including his vast DVD collection of black-and-white movies, hundreds of records to go with his turntable, and books ranging from the classics to spy thrillers. Sometimes when I walk by his office, I almost expect him to swivel around in his black leather chair, calling out, "Luv?"—in the British accent that won me over the first time we met, when I went to Politics and Prose to attend his book signing.

These boxes represent another layer of clearing away; they're filled with Paul's academic awards, old letters, photographs, and Lana's childhood artwork.

"Take anything you want," I tell Lana.

She sinks onto the carpet and crosses her legs. But she doesn't reach into the top box.

I study her face. "You okay, sweetie?"

She sighs. "I just miss him so much."

If Lana were one of my clients, I'd open the box myself and hand her the first item. But instead I hug her. "If you're not up for this, we can do it another time."

"No, no. I'm fine." She sucks in a deep breath, then lifts up a flap and pulls out a big padded envelope filled with loose photographs. She begins flipping through them: Lana sitting on a spotted pony; blowing out six blazing candles atop a pink-frosted cake; standing in between her parents; beaming through a mouthful of braces at what must have been her junior high school graduation.

My eyes linger on that photo. It was taken shortly before I met Paul; neither he nor his ex-wife is wearing a wedding ring in the picture. Paul's hair was still a riot of dark curls back then, with just a few strands of silver glinting in the temples. He was tan and fit; strong enough to scoop me up in his arms and carry me to bed on our wedding night.

So different from the frail man who I held in my arms as he took his final breath, eight months ago.

Maryanne, Lana's mother, stands on the other side of her daughter, looking as if she smells something sour—an expression I've come to associate with her.

"How's your mom?" I ask.

"Oh, you know, the same." Lana's eyes flit away from mine. Maryanne and Paul separated long before he and I met, but Maryanne never liked the idea of him with someone else—let alone someone who was nearly two decades younger. Years after he and I wed, Lana confessed to me that her mother still referred to me as *her*.

Deeper in the box are first-edition copies of Paul's three books—all bestsellers. I've saved copies for myself, too. Lana flips open his debut, titled *You, Me, and the Couch,* and stares at the dedication: *For Lana, my precious daughter.*

She runs her fingertip over the words, and we both blink back tears. The sight of the book is transporting me back to the first time I ever glimpsed Paul. He was standing behind a podium, microphone in hand, enthralling the crowd that filled every seat in the Politics and Prose bookstore. I was twenty-four, attending grad school at George Washington University to get my master's degree in social work, and I walked in late for Paul's reading. I wasn't good at setting boundaries back then and I'd allowed one of the clients at my internship to overstay his session. Paul's gaze met mine as the door closed behind me. *Sorry,* I'd mouthed.

I'd read a few of his articles, and I admired his insights into the complexities of the human mind as well as his dexterity with language. But I was unprepared for his physical magnetism.

His eyes, still holding mine, crinkled as he spoke his next words: "That's when the police came rushing in to arrest my patient, who tried to hide behind me. As if a rumpled psychiatrist was any defense against a SWAT team. Bloody hell, did he think I'd whack at them with my reading glasses?"

That accent. His fierce intelligence. His graceful movements and the elegant yet strong-looking hands that gripped the pen when he signed my book: *To Avery, I can already tell you'll make a brilliant therapist.*

I emailed him a week later—it was easy to find his contact information through his office, and I had a legitimate question about one of the cases he'd described in his book. At least that's what I told myself. We fell into a correspondence that felt natural and exhilarating. I instinctively knew I had to be the one to ask him out because of our age difference. So, one night after a couple glasses of wine, I carefully crafted a note suggesting we meet for coffee or a drink. I closed my eyes as I pressed the key to send it.

Our first date was twenty-four hours later. Within six months, I'd moved into his home, located in a comfortable, eclectic neighborhood not far from the National Zoo.

Lana sets down her dad's book, breaking my reverie. I take a sip of coffee while she looks through old letters she wrote to Paul from sleep-away camp, reading aloud a few funny bits.

I'm about to suggest that we make lunch together when her phone rings. Her face lights up: "Sorry, it's this guy I've been seeing—"

"Take it!" I get up to go into the kitchen to give her privacy. I check the contents of my refrigerator to see what I can cobble together, but the items aren't inspiring: a half dozen eggs, baby carrots, a bottle of Dom Pérignon, slightly wilted lettuce, and leftover quesadillas from my favorite Tex-Mex place.

"Avery?" Lana pokes her head in as I'm suspiciously sniffing a container of hummus. Her voice is different—higher and airy. "Sorry, but I've got to run. Greg got off work early and I need to pick him up."

"Ooh." I give her a playful poke in the ribs. "Who's Greg? Come on, tell me while I help you pack up your car."

As we load the boxes into the trunk of her Honda, I learn Greg works at the hardware store a few doors down from the pottery shop, and they met on a lunch break last week. "We both ordered the same veggie sandwich!" she exclaims as she hops into her car.

Her eyes are now sheened with excitement instead of tears. At the moment, picking up a guy she's just met has eclipsed everything else of importance to her.

Lana doesn't always have the best instincts when it comes to men; before I can share her happiness over her new relationship, I need to meet Greg. I extract a promise from her to bring him by soon, then lean in through the open window and give her a kiss.

She roars away, over the speed limit, as I reenter my house.

With the boxes gone, I have only one more area to clean out. I should be getting some work done—I want to check in on Cameron and research Bishop, Simms & Chapman, the corporate law practice founded by Matthew Bishop and two partners—but I've postponed this particular task for far too long already.

I climb the steps to Paul's study and sink into his big chair. His long wooden desk used to be cluttered with papers and journals and a decorative jar filled with pens and our framed wedding photo; Paul tended to get messy when he lost himself in work. Now it's bare, as mine is, just one floor below.

I pull out Paul's deep middle desk drawer. It's filled with letters and cards. Most handwritten, a few printed out, some in somber cream envelopes and others in pastels. There must be a hundred of them.

Every one of them is addressed to me.

I pick up a handful. They feel heavy with the weight of the written sentiments inside. I let the envelopes slide through my fingers into the trash basket. I glimpse a few familiar names on the return addresses— one of Paul's favorite colleagues, another from my grad school roommate—as they fall. I grab another handful, then another, sending them tumbling through the air into the trash, until no more remain.

Following Paul's funeral, I'd intended to write back to every sympathy note that arrived. But I never even opened them.

How could I respond to people who wrote about my terrible loss, my unimaginable pain, and exhorted me to remember that even though it might seem impossible, time would heal all of my wounds?

The complicated truth, which I've never revealed to anyone, is that I stopped loving my husband long before he passed away.

Paul was passionate and dynamic—at first. I attributed his occasional withdrawals as being a necessary component of his work. His patients were demanding and he had to remain keenly alert and focused all day. He operated at a high level; he required solitude and quiet to concentrate on his research and writing at night. As the years passed, his need to be alone grew more intense. His absences, both emotional and physical, became harder to excuse.

Naturally we tried therapy. Every week for a solid year we sat side-by-side on a couch in Dr. Friedman's office, fighting to bridge the chasm between us. I attempted to be more understanding. Paul vowed to make more of an effort to engage emotionally with me. Neither of us succeeded.

We ended therapy, and I turned my focus toward ending my marriage: I'd rent a little place in Georgetown, something near the vibrant intersection of Wisconsin Avenue and M Street. I'd keep the office space I shared with three other therapists; my commute would be a little bit longer, but I'd make it work. Paul and I would remain cordial. Lana and I would remain close. I'd begin dating, a prospect that filled me with excitement.

I'd just begun to look for an apartment when I was jarred awake late one night by the incessant shriek of the teakettle. Turn it off, Paul, I thought irritably. When he didn't, I groggily made my way downstairs, to the brightly lit kitchen, where Paul lay on the tiled floor, a carton of half-and-half spilled beside him.

A seizure, an impossibly young-looking doctor with blue-framed glasses told me. But that was a symptom; the root cause was an aggressive brain tumor.

Paul lived for another nine months. Visiting nurses handled most of his medical care. At night, Paul and I reclaimed our companionship by watching his beloved old movies as well as comedies such as *Schitt's Creek* and *The Office.*

His life was ending. Mine was on hold.

I didn't mourn my husband when he died. I'd already come to terms with losing him.

I finally felt free.

CHAPTER SIX

MARISSA

MARISSA LIES NEXT TO BENNETT in his twin race-car bed, her body as jittery as her mind, willing her son to sleep.

He's been resisting her efforts tonight, first insisting he needed to give fresh water to Sam, his pet gecko, then begging her to read a third *Harry Potter* chapter—almost as if he intuits how much she needs him tucked away in preparation for Avery's house call and is lodging a protest.

Finally, Bennett's breathing evens out, and Marissa hoists herself up, maneuvering over a big plastic wheel. She takes a step toward his door, not daring to exhale. Her hand touches the knob.

"Mama?"

She turns around. "Sweetie, please, you have to go to sleep."

But she crawls back in next to him, even though this violates one of her primary parenting rules, because she knows it's the fastest way to ensure he'll drift off.

Avery will be here in less than thirty minutes. Matthew still isn't home. Marissa desperately wants the half glass of crisp white wine she left on the kitchen counter, which she intended to sip while she finished tidying up. She also needs to change out of the pants and top she wore all day and set out a pitcher of water and three glasses on the side table in the library, the spot she's chosen for their session. Most important, she craves a few minutes to mentally prepare, to center herself for whatever this evening's session will bring.

What will Avery think of their house? They moved in when Bennett was only a few months old, purchasing it after a builder razed two old, smaller homes to expand the property. He'd clear-cut towering oak and old maple trees and brought in a landscape architect to create a backyard oasis that featured multitiered decks, a pool and a hot tub surrounded by intricate stonework, and—Matthew's favorite touch—a built-in grill and gorgeous gas fireplace with groupings of furniture beneath a pergola. They'd celebrated Bennett's eighth birthday outside with a *Star Wars*–themed party. Matthew, wearing a Chewbacca mask, flipped burgers and hot dogs for the kids while Marissa served shrimp and veggie kebabs and negronis to the adults.

It's an idyllic location, though that opinion isn't shared by the neighbors, who tried to halt construction, even calling the police when bulldozers arrived to remove the trees. But the builder had secured the proper permits, and work proceeded.

The local paper published a small item after several neighbors filed a petition with the homeowners' association. It would be easy to find, should Avery decide to look. Although Marissa and Matthew were identified as the purchasers of the new home, what the article neglected to mention was that they signed a contract *after* the demolition of the two old homes and mature trees. The destruction wasn't done at their behest. Still, every time Marissa drives past one of the people whose names appeared on the petition, her stomach muscles tighten and she keeps her gaze fixed straight ahead.

Bennett rolls onto his side, releasing a little sigh, as Marissa's hand begins to rub gentle circles on his back. Bennett is thinning out; he's going through a growth spurt, and his shoulder blades feel pronounced yet delicate beneath her palm. Sometimes when she looks at him, she sees glimpses of his father; other times she recognizes touches of herself in his long lashes and high cheekbones.

He's close to sleep; she can sense it.

A noise comes from downstairs. Her hand stills as she strains to listen, but there's no alert chiming on her cell phone, or sound of the heavy front door shutting, or Matthew's footsteps thudding up the stairs.

Only the wind, she thinks.

She steals a glance at her watch: 8:48. Twelve minutes until Avery arrives.

Where is Matthew?

Agitation roils within her body. She can't face Avery alone. Plus, Avery made it abundantly clear that she won't tolerate a lack of punctuality.

Maybe she shouldn't have told Matthew about her disloyalty. Then this could have been an ordinary night, with her working on her laptop in bed while Matthew lingered at his business dinner. She could have greeted her husband with a quick kiss when he arrived home and continued selecting colors for handwoven silk scarves for Coco while he took off his suit and changed into boxers and a T-shirt in the walk-in closet. Some women wouldn't have confessed; they'd talk to a therapist alone or confide in a friend. But when Marissa thought about the women in her life, there wasn't anyone to whom she felt close enough to go to for advice.

Ever since the night of her betrayal, guilt had gnawed at Marissa; it was difficult to eat, concentrate, and sleep. She'd begun to busy herself with little tasks whenever she was around Matthew so she didn't have to look him in the eye.

It was a partial confession, though. She hasn't told Matthew everything. She can't.

Is it truly over with the other man? Avery had asked.

I know I shouldn't say this, but I can't stop thinking about our night, he'd texted.

Marissa will never touch him again. That part of her vow she can keep.

But she won't—she *can't*—exist without ever seeing him again.

Marissa slowly counts to sixty, then gets out of Bennett's bed again. She finally catches a break; he's asleep.

Marissa is slipping on jeans and a cashmere sweater when her cell phone pings, alerting her to a presence at the front door. Matthew is home, with one minute to spare. He couldn't have cut it any closer.

As she hurries down the stairs, she hears a voice, but it isn't Matthew's. It's Avery's. Marissa can't make out her words, but picks up the rumble of Matthew's laughter. It's a sound she hasn't heard recently.

By the time she reaches them in the kitchen, Matthew is standing by the sink filling a glass with water from the tap while Avery leans against the granite island, seeming to take in everything: Marissa's half-finished glass of Chablis, the spaghetti pot soaking in the sink, Bennett's splayed-open lunch box with the crusts of his turkey sandwich and Fruit Roll-Ups wrapper inside.

The tap has a built-in purifier, but Avery wouldn't know that and it feels overly casual for Matthew to hand her the glass with a drip rolling down the side. Another thing feels awkward: Matthew is still in his dark suit and crisp white shirt. Avery wears a wide-legged black jumpsuit cinched with a silver-studded leather belt and heels, as if she's come here from a cocktail party.

Marissa feels acutely underdressed.

"Sorry! It took a little while to get Bennett to bed. I trust you found our place okay. Can I get you anything else?"

She realizes she's babbling as she reaches for the half-full wineglass and tips the contents into the sink.

"Hope you're not doing that on my account," Avery says.

Marissa laughs; it sounds forced.

Matthew fills a water glass for himself but doesn't offer one to Marissa. His face is ruddy, an indication he's had a few drinks. There would have been wine with the meal, and perhaps an after-dinner Scotch.

"Shall we go sit?" Marissa suggests.

She turns toward the library, but Matthew is already heading in the other direction, into the family room. Not there! she thinks. But she silently follows; she doesn't want to start the night by contradicting even a small choice of her husband's.

The room is set up for relaxed evenings, with a big TV affixed to one wall and a large sectional couch and two oversize chairs grouped around a coffee table. Matthew claims one of the chairs, and Avery selects the other one, setting her water on the little side table. This leaves the couch for Marissa.

She hesitates, then sinks into it. Avery remains standing, her tote bag still slung over her arm. She surveys the room, then walks over to the built-in shelves, which are filled with books, knickknacks, and photographs.

Avery stares at the photos for what feels like an uncomfortably long time, her back to Marissa and Matthew.

What captured her attention? Marissa wonders. The photo of the three generations of Bishop men in front of a Christmas tree—Matthew; his father, Chris; and Bennett? The black-and-white formal portrait of Matthew's maternal grandparents, who could trace their lineage to the *Mayflower*? Or maybe Avery's gaze is caught on the silver-framed wedding photo of Marissa and Matthew surrounded by their loved ones— both sets of parents; Matthew's younger sister, Kiki; Marissa's younger brother, Luke; plus their bridesmaids and groomsmen.

But the picture Avery reaches for is one of Marissa and Matthew as teenagers, sitting side-by-side on a dock, their feet dangling in the water of the lake where they first met.

Avery turns around and glances at them, then looks back down at the picture. "Is this the two of you?"

"Yeah, back when I had a six-pack," Matthew jokes.

One of the qualities Marissa loves most in her husband is that he is so confident he can be self-deprecating. She tries to catch his eye to give him an appreciative smile, but he's avoiding her gaze—just as she did to him when she had something to hide.

The photograph is a bit blurry and faded, but Marissa cherishes it. It was taken shortly after her fifteenth birthday, in a small town on the Eastern Shore of Maryland, where Matthew's family owned a summer house and Marissa's parents ran a gourmet-food market that was open year-round but did the bulk of its business from June through August. Marissa spent most of those warm days behind the glass counter, scooping lobster salad onto brioche rolls and slicing peaches for her mother's cobbler, but whenever she had time off, she untied her red apron and headed to the shore to meet up with the gang of teenagers who gathered at a particular narrow, sandy stretch by the long wooden pier.

There were two groups: the summer kids, who owned shiny eighteen-speed bikes and Sunfish sailboats and wore polo shirts with upturned collars, and the locals, who knew the best spots to pick blackberries and which clerk at the convenience store would sell them Coors and Seagram's wine coolers. The class divide didn't seem as sharp during the warm nights—everyone had on bathing suits and ate hot dogs around a bonfire and mingled and developed crushes—but they all knew it existed. How could they imagine otherwise when the boy scooping up a girl and playfully pretending to toss her off a dock had a mother who worked as a housecleaner for the girl's family and had likely made her bed that morning?

Or when the summer guy with streaky blond hair—and, yes, a gorgeous six-pack—licked the icing off a cupcake Marissa had frosted just that afternoon before turning to her and saying, "Want to try out my Jet Ski?"

The photograph in Avery's hands was taken a few days after Marissa and Matthew shared their first kiss, toward the end of a summer that had been unlike any other.

Marissa can still remember every detail: the chirp of a nearby cricket, the distant sound of Guns N' Roses over someone's boom box, and the feel of his hands cupping her face. And the way he put his arm around her after they broke apart and walked toward the group on the sandy shore, as if he was claiming her.

She hadn't realized how much she'd needed that strong, solid arm around her. It steadied her at a time when the world seemed filled with dangerous, steeply pitched terrain. Earlier that summer, Marissa's beloved best friend from childhood, Tina, had died. It was as if Matthew stepped into the gaping void Tina had left, counteracting the deep sorrow and grief that gripped Marissa.

"Have you two been together since you were teens?" Avery asks now.

"No," Marissa replies, just as Matthew replies, "Yes."

"Well, this should be interesting," Avery says as she puts back the photo and finally claims her seat.

CHAPTER SEVEN

AVERY

"The answer is actually yes and no," Marissa rushes to explain as I pull my yellow legal pad out of my tote bag. "We dated as teenagers, but we didn't really grow serious until after college."

"Maybe we have different definitions of together." Matthew stares hard at his wife.

She flinches. "Matthew, come on! We both saw other people before we got engaged. Just a few nights ago you mentioned sleeping with some random TA from law school. Plus, you were with Natalie for almost a year. It's obvious she still has a crush on you—"

"But I never cheated." Matthew needs an outlet for his anger, but these types of potshots are not constructive.

"Who's Natalie?" I ask mildly.

Matthew exhales. "An ex-girlfriend. I went out with her for a while when I was in college and we've stayed in touch. It wasn't a big deal. I even set her up with one of our good friends when he moved to D.C. last year, but they didn't hit it off."

A shadow crosses Marissa's face and she leans back on the sofa.

I write *Natalie* on my notepad, drawing a circle around the name, wondering how hard she'll be to find. Not very, if she lives as public of a life as the Bishops. The location of Marissa's boutique, the name of Matthew's company, their son's private school—Marissa served up all that information in the questionnaire I required them to fill out.

Other details have been equally easy to ascertain: their favorite neighborhood restaurant (La Ferme), their most recent vacation destination (Palm Beach), the last book Marissa adored (Ann Patchett's *The Dutch House*), and how Bennett looked after he caught his first pop fly in baseball (more shocked than elated).

My crack about Marissa serving up glossy Instagram posts was spot-on. I confirmed it by checking out her social media accounts after the Bishops' first session.

I redirect our conversation: "Matthew, at our last meeting I asked you to think of a question."

"Yeah, I've got one." He leans forward. "Did you know you were going to lose your license?"

He's twisting the rules; the query was supposed to be for his wife, not me. But men such as Matthew are accustomed to controlling a room; he was blindsided during our first meeting, so now he's trying to keep me off-balance as a way of evening the score.

It's obvious Matthew has done some investigating of his own, I think as I take an unhurried sip of my water.

"I read the *Washington Post* profile," Matthew adds when I don't immediately reply.

I look at Marissa. "Did you?"

Marissa clears her throat. "Yes. . . . A friend forwarded it to me a little while back. Actually, it's the reason I sought you out."

She's providing these details, even though I didn't ask for them, because she's essentially truthful. Or because she wants to appear that way.

Matthew is even more difficult to decipher. His trust and pride have been badly wounded, and that is coloring our experience together.

"No, I didn't know I was going to lose my license." I put down my glass. "But as I told *The Post,* I've never regretted it."

The *Washington Post* reporter sought me out when he learned by reading the police blotter about the criminal charges Skylar filed. I agreed to the interview because I knew I could control the narrative better than anyone else. The reporter and I sat in my living room on two consecutive afternoons, and I shared the evolution of my ten-sessions system. He asked questions and jotted my answers in his notebook, like a kind of reverse therapy.

I recounted some of my story, but not everything. When the reporter asked how I came up with my protocal, I told him I'd had a burst of inspiration during a long run, and that even though my unorthodox methods meant I could no longer be a licensed therapist, my results spoke for themselves.

In his provocative, mostly flattering profile the reporter dubbed me "D.C.'s Maverick Therapist."

I answered all of his questions without lying; I just omitted pieces of the truth. I need to do the same thing now to earn Matthew's confidence.

"I'm glad you brought up the article, Matthew. It's important for us to be direct with each other. You can ask me anything. I'm not promising I will answer, but you can ask."

He nods. "Okay. How is talking for ten sessions—actually, eight and a half more sessions—going to fix me and Marissa?"

I smile. The second session is Disruption, and I've been waiting for this opening to introduce it. "You're right. Talking alone won't help. We could sit here for dozens of hours and not solve anything. So, I'm going to have free rein in your lives—to a reasonable degree. I'm not going to read your diaries or plant a camera in your house or spy on Bennett. But in order to help you, I need to really know you. Not just what you tell me."

"Free rein?" Marissa echoes. "What does that mean, exactly?"

"I just came from the outdoor patio at La Ferme."

Marissa's brow creases. She doesn't get it yet. "We go there all the time!"

"I've never been there before, but I thought I should check it out. The truffle popcorn really is delicious."

There's a moment of silence. I watch their confused expressions morph as they get my underlying meaning. Matthew half rises from his seat, immediately on the defensive. "What the—!"

"Matthew's addicted to that popcorn!" Marissa says. "But how—"

"Most therapists only know what you tell them," I say. "Even if you try to be one hundred percent honest, you create an illusion based on your perceptions and unconscious biases. I need to access who you are when I'm not around in order to learn the truth, and for our work together to be effective."

Clients understand they're in for something different when they come to see me. But they don't realize the full scope until they learn I'll be scrutinizing their lives on my own time and on my own terms. Some of them terminate our contract on the spot. But most stay; sometimes even the ones I least expect.

Matthew's a private man. Unlike his wife, he leaves almost no footprint on social media. His body language is resistant; his arms are now folded across his chest.

This might be too much for him.

What's more interesting to me, though, is that Marissa's body has also stiffened. She's the public one, with her charity meetings and boutique located on a busy stretch of Connecticut Avenue and annual Halloween bash at their home, which is always transformed into an elaborate haunted house.

Matthew sinks back into his seat. His anger flares quickly, but his control over it is impressive. "I've had a lot of time to think these past couple of days. I'm not sure I can truly forgive Marissa. But I want to give it a try. So, I'm on board with this. I've got nothing to hide."

Gratitude crashes across Marissa's face. "Thank you," she whispers.

"Let's talk about your families," I direct them. "Matthew, you mentioned in our first session that your mother died as a result of leukemia a few years ago. How was your parents' marriage before then?"

Matthew exhales. "Let's put it this way: I'm nothing like my father and I made sure to marry a woman who was nothing like my mother."

Marissa looks at her husband with wide eyes, almost as if he is dropping bread crumbs that lead to a place she has not been before.

"I have no idea why—or how—they stayed together." Matthew shakes his head. "They were toxic. If my father decided to get out the barbecue and grill some steaks, that would be the night my mother proclaimed she no longer ate red meat. If my mother bought my father a nice shirt for Christmas—she hated the clothes he wore, so she was making a point with the gift—he'd return it."

Matthew gives a half laugh containing no mirth. "My father probably would have liked to throw away the shirt, but he was too cheap for that."

"Cheap?" I echo. Matthew has succeeded in diverging from his father in at least this respect, given the opulence of his home.

"He only buys used cars, and after my mom died, he sold their house and moved into a one-bedroom condo downtown. He drinks Cluny and soda—" At my puzzled look, Matthew elaborates, "It's an inexpensive kind of Scotch. And his favorite restaurants are diners."

I take down a note. "Is your father remarried?"

"Yeah, to his work," Matthew says. "He's a lobbyist. That's pretty much all he cares about."

"He's good to Bennett," Marissa ventures.

"I'll give him that. It's the only reason my dad is still in my life."

I nod. "You mentioned you have a sister."

"Yeah, Catherine—we all call her Kiki. My dad was easier on her because she's a girl, but she didn't like being in our family any better than me. She moved to Colorado for college and never came back."

I wait for him to continue, but it seems as if he can't.

"Marissa's parents are still in love after forty years," Matthew says, adeptly redirecting the course of the conversation.

"Is that how you see it, Marissa?" I ask.

"Yes. They're like newlyweds. Still holding hands when they go on their early-morning walks."

"Do you see them often?"

"Every month or two. My parents live near a town called Chesapeake—it's about two hours away. My younger brother and his wife work with them running a gourmet food store. My parents come and stay with Bennett whenever Matthew and I travel, and we always visit them for a few days around Christmas, too."

"But," I prompt, because it's obvious there is one.

"The life I live, it's different." She gestures around the room, the sweep of her hand taking in the twelve-foot ceilings and grand stone fireplace and exposed beams, as well as all the fancy store-bought items within it. "My brother and his wife own one old truck, and they've never traveled out of the country. Same with my parents. They work really hard, and they don't have much to show for it."

"Does that make you uncomfortable?" I'm asking the obvious, because her body language tells me it does.

She begins to answer, but before she can say more, simultaneous chimes sound on the Bishops' phones. They both reflexively look down, then toward their front door.

"Are you expecting anyone?" Marissa asks her husband.

He shakes his head. He raises an eyebrow at me. "Is this something you set up?"

I didn't engineer this unexpected interruption, though it is the type of thing I might have done.

"Maybe the Girl Scouts are working overtime tonight," Matthew quips as he stands up and strides out of the room.

I look down at the name circled on my notepad. "What makes you think Natalie has a crush on Matthew?"

"Oh, it's just a feeling." Marissa frowns. "She calls to ask him for business advice sometimes, even though they're in completely different fields. She's a real estate agent. And she took him to lunch to thank him for writing a recommendation so her daughter could attend the same private school as Bennett—even though my name was on the recommendation, too. I see her sidle up to him at school functions and laugh too hard at his jokes."

I don't doubt Marissa's assessment. Women generally have good intuition about these things. And I've now got enough clues to track Natalie down without having to ask for her contact information, which would signal my intentions to the Bishops.

If Marissa strayed because of the distance in her marriage, perhaps Matthew helped create that space by reveling in the attention of another woman.

Matthew seems to have come around to the idea of therapy quickly. Too quickly?

I tuck away the thought to ponder later.

Matthew still hasn't returned. Marissa keeps looking in the direction of the front door, but it's several rooms away, and her view is blocked. Her fingers begin to worry the tassel on a throw pillow.

"Natalie is trouble," I tell Marissa in a low voice. "Don't give Matthew the opportunity to be alone with her. I know he wants to repair things, but he's vulnerable now."

"*Vulnerable?* That's not a word I'd ever use to describe Matthew."

An echo of my unspoken question from our first session rises in my mind: Is she scared of losing her husband or scared of him?

Taking people by surprise with blunt questions can be effective. So as casually as if I were inquiring about the weather, I ask, "Has Matthew ever been violent with you, Marissa?"

She blanches. "No, never! Why would you ask that?"

"No particular reason."

We fall silent as Matthew's footsteps approach the room. When he appears on the threshold, he's holding a vase filled with lush yellow roses.

He walks toward Marissa and puts them on the table beside her. "For you."

"Oh, they're gorgeous! Who are they from?"

He shrugs. "You tell me." His tone is flat.

The smile falls away from Marissa's face as she pulls the card from the little plastic holder. "There isn't any note. It's just my name."

"Maybe it's your *friend* from the gym." Matthew is standing over Marissa, just as he was in my office, but his fists aren't clenched. He's disturbed, but not enraged. I feel confident of this assessment.

"What? No—it couldn't—Matthew, they could be from anyone. It's probably a thank-you for some blazers I donated to Dress for Success last week." Her voice trails off as she seems to realize no charity would send an elaborate bouquet for a relatively small donation.

Matthew nods, though it's unclear if he buys it. "Sure. Maybe, Marissa."

He sits back down, and I ease him into a conversation about his job, Marissa's boutique, and how they juggle work and parenthood. Marissa clearly bears the brunt of the day-to-day chores of caring for Bennett, but she doesn't seem to mind.

When I glance at my watch, it's almost 9:45 P.M. I rise to my feet. "I can see myself out."

"Marissa knows I would never let a woman see herself to the door." Matthew gets up, and so does Marissa.

I walk directly over to Marissa, in the opposite direction from the front door. She stares at me, looking confused and more than a bit nervous. The sweet scent of roses perfumes the air around her.

"May I?" I don't wait for permission as I pluck the florist's card from her hand. Then I smile and exit the room.

———

Later that night, as I walk around my house checking that all my windows and doors are locked, I mentally plan my next steps: check out Natalie, call the florist, and visit Marissa's boutique when she isn't on the premises.

I'm not naive—I know the Bishops are still withholding important information. That's only natural. Everyone keeps secrets, I think as I stare through the bay window in my office out onto the quiet, darkened street.

Including me.

One of my biggest centers around a young woman named Finley Jones. She was the true genesis for my ten-session method. A few months after Paul died, back when I was a run-of-the-mill therapist sharing office space in Dupont Circle and squeezing in eight patients a day, an anxious young woman showed up for her initial appointment, claiming disturbing thoughts were disrupting her sleep and appetite. She was thin, with bitten nails and dark shadows rimming her gray eyes. Finley's presenting symptoms weren't uncommon; anxiety is rampant in our society. As we discussed her tumultuous relationship with her father and her insomnia, she didn't seem like the kind of person who'd upend my world.

Then she whispered, "My company is going to kill people."

My gut told me this wasn't paranoia, or delusions.

Can you tell me more? I'd asked, in the gentle therapeutic tone I utilized back then.

Finley was employed by a billion-dollar pharmaceutical giant as one of several assistants to the head of public relations. She didn't have a lofty title. She didn't have access. She didn't have the ear of company executives.

What she had was exquisite timing.

It was a Tuesday night, well past quitting time. Finley had met her old college roommate for drinks around the corner from her office, and before heading home, she stopped by the office to retrieve her gym bag. The twelve-story building was mostly empty, occupied only by the security guard, who greeted her as she flashed her ID, a few late-working employees scattered on different floors, and cleaning crews.

Finley headed down the dimly lit corridor to her cubicle, the blue-gray carpet swallowing the sound of her footsteps. Up ahead, her boss's office was illuminated; she could see him inside with another man she later identified as the chief compliance officer. But the lighting optics meant that they, looking out into a darkened hallway, couldn't see Finley approach.

As she bent down to retrieve her bag from beneath her desk—quietly, so as not to disturb their conversation—she heard her boss say, "Forty out of ten thousand? Jesus."

The words didn't make her blood run cold. But the way her boss spoke them did. Some deep-seated intuition told Finley this conversation was not meant for anyone to overhear.

Her instincts screamed at her to get away. But Finley felt physically frozen, rooted in her little cubicle just outside her boss's office.

She knew her company was developing a new migraine medication called Rivanux. Human trials were underway in India, where the drug would be manufactured, since production costs are far cheaper overseas. Phases One and Two of the trials had reportedly gone well.

Now they were in Phase Three, a much bigger trial, with ten thousand human subjects.

Forty out of ten thousand.

Finley kept listening. She stayed crouched in her cubicle, her legs aching from holding the deep squat, until the two men finally left, passing just inches from her hiding spot.

As she lay in bed that night, snippets of the conversation she'd overheard ran through her mind: *Hemorrhagic shock . . . Coma. . . . At least one percent already dead . . .*

Scrapping Rivanux would be an enormous blow to Finley's company. Stock prices would dip; shareholders would be furious. The ripple effects would include finger-pointing, layoffs, and stories in the pharma trade publications.

Finley returned to work, assuming that production of Rivanux would immediately be halted. Instead, a few weeks later, her boss emailed her a press release to proof.

The headline made her gasp: RIVANUX POISED TO WIN FDA APPROVAL. According to the release, the drug had performed exceptionally well during its trials, with only minor side effects.

As she stared at the words on the press release, Finley realized her company was engaging in a massive cover-up. She theorized that they must

have altered the data on the trials, knowing the FDA would never sanc-
tion a deadly drug.

My company is going to kill people.

As I watched Finley sink lower into her chair, her words ebbing into
a hoarse whisper, I knew what I was supposed to do: Maintain a proper
professional distance. Discuss Finley's feelings and fears. Encourage her
to explore the possibility of coming forward to the authorities.

That's exactly what I did, for the rest of the session. Though Finley
seemed to be telling the truth, I couldn't help wondering if she was ex-
aggerating. So after she left, I did a little research of my own. The head-
lines I saw left me equal parts terrified and enraged:

**Bayer and Johnson & Johnson are charged with downplay-
ing the life-threatening risks associated with Xarelto . . .
Merck pleads guilty and pays $950 million to settle liabili-
ties for misbranding the safety of the painkiller Vioxx . . .
Eli Lilly misbrands the antipsychotic drug Zyprexa for the
treatment of dementia and other disorders in elderly patients and has to pay millions in criminal and civil settle-
ments.**

And on and on, case after case. One article claimed that millions of
prescriptions for unsafe drugs had been filled in the United States within
the past two decades alone.

During Finley's next session—her second—I looked at the hunched,
scared twenty-six-year-old who'd stumbled upon an explosive secret and
realized that, even though a percentage of people who took Rivanux
would likely die, I wasn't sure she would ever report her employer.

She knew what could happen to her because it had happened to other
whistle-blowers: They'd start by creating a reason to fire her. Then they'd
discredit her—much like a prosecutor going after a defendant on the
stand. They could launch a social media smear campaign against her.
They could physically threaten her, or her family.

And perhaps they would follow through.

After all, Finley could cost her company hundreds of millions of dollars.

And her company had already shown that to protect its profits it would play fast and loose with the health and safety of individuals.

Finley wasn't strong enough to speak out and endure all that would follow.

So I did it for her.

I phoned the FDA's anonymous whistle-blower hotline and spoke to the man who answered, giving him all the details I knew. I trusted the system would do what it promised—provide anonymity—so I called from my cell phone.

I didn't reveal my name and I kept Finley completely out of it.

My second phone call was to Finley, so I could explain what I'd done.

Before I finished talking, she hung up on me.

Still, I felt a rock-solid surety in my decision: violating my professional oath by breaking the confidence of a client was the right thing, the moral thing, the *only* thing, to do.

Forty out of ten thousand.

If I hadn't called the FDA, pharma reps would have carried free samples into doctors' offices, urging them to pass the pills out to patients. Hospital aides would have placed the tablets into little paper cups and dispensed them. Husbands, wives, fathers, mothers, and even a few teenagers would have shaken the pills out of prescription bottles, washing them down with a swig of water or juice.

I thought back to Paul in his final days, the sun seeping through the blinds after another sleepless night for both of us, as I held a glass of water to his lips so he could take his pills, the ones that made his pain tolerable. I trusted that his drugs would do exactly what they promised.

Yet, a reputable company—one that made products ranging from baby shampoo to a sunscreen I'd used in the past—was knowingly manufacturing medicine that would make 4 percent of its users suffer terribly. And a subset of those people would bleed to death.

I couldn't have that blood on my hands.

The following Wednesday at 7:00 P.M. sharp, my doorbell rang. It was Finley, arriving for our third session.

She claimed her usual seat, but instead of curling up with her feet tucked beneath her, she sat up straight. Her eyes were bright and clear.

At first I felt really betrayed by you, but I've actually been sleeping well for the first time in ages, she said. *I feel different, somehow, since you took the decision out of my hands. Like this weight that was crushing me is gone. I've decided to start looking for a new job; I don't want to work for that company.*

In all the months—or years, in many cases—that I'd spent treating other clients, I'd never witnessed such a radical transformation.

I thought about all the times I'd forced myself to quash my instincts, often waiting in vain for my clients to find the path that was so clearly visible to me. Ever since I'd violated the code of my profession to uphold my personal morals, I'd been sleeping better, too.

I looked at Finley and made a snap decision. "Ready to change the rest of your life?"

We met seven more times. By the end of the last session, our tenth, Finley had decided to apply for a new job at a think tank, severed ties with the "friend" who kept flirting with her boyfriend, had the difficult conversation with her father that she'd been avoiding for years, and stopped biting her nails.

I had a new career path, and it was all based on what I'd learned from Finley, my first ten-session patient.

I'd also gained a powerful new enemy.

The pharmaceutical company must have cultivated a mole inside the FDA, because after my supposedly anonymous phone call, Acelia began sending me messages, loud and clear: they knew exactly who I was, and where I lived.

None of this made it into the *Post* article, which ran several months after I terminated the lease on my Dupont Circle space and set up shop in my home office. The piece focused on my academic credentials, my controversial method, the loss of my license and my subsequent successes, and anecdotes from clients who agreed to speak on the record.

The *Post* reporter who sat in my living room didn't ask about the security bars on my windows or the alarm code pad by my front door. He was so focused on his article that he didn't express curiosity when I asked to see his identification before allowing him into my home.

He missed the bigger story.

The first signal that Acelia was after me came one night when I returned home following an immersive session at a client's party and thought I detected the faint leathery scent of a man's cologne in the air. My doors and windows were still locked, and otherwise everything was exactly as I'd left it: a pair of running shoes splayed out next to my closet, the still-damp towel from my shower hanging from the hook on the back of my bathroom door, the book I'd been reading on my nightstand next to my water glass.

When I got ready for bed, I discovered one thing was amiss, however. A bottle of medicine stood on my dresser, partially hidden by a lamp.

I hadn't left it there. The drug was Synthroid, which I take daily to support my thyroid function. I always keep the bottle inside the medicine cabinet next to my moisturizer, since I swallow the pills first thing in the morning right after I wake up and brush my teeth. Synthroid is a prescription drug, the only one I possess. It wasn't difficult to figure out why the pharmaceutical company whose plans to release a new medicine that could be torpedoed by my knowledge had chosen to highlight the Synthroid's presence.

Acelia was letting me know they knew who I was and what I'd done. And that they could get inside my home without leaving a trace.

What they didn't know was who told me about the deadly trials in India. Acelia has tens of thousands of employees around the globe; I had no doubt they wanted to extract the name of the one they were seeking from me.

I began making sure every one of my doors and windows was locked, even the tiny windows in my attic, even when I ran out for a quick errand.

A few days later, while I was walking down my street on an unseasonably warm Sunday afternoon, gearing up for a run, a good-looking guy approached me with a wide smile. It was broad daylight. I could see my neighbor on his front porch. I felt completely safe. So I smiled back.

"I was wondering if you could help me," the man began, and for a moment I expected him to ask directions. "I'm thinking about buying a house nearby, but I heard there were some break-ins in the neighborhood."

He moved closer and put a hand on my arm. I stiffened and pushed it off.

"Do you really think it's safe?" he whispered.

"Get the hell away from me."

"All we need is a name."

Before I could scream or spray him with my can of Mace, he walked away.

I haven't seen that man since, but I know Acelia won't stop. They must be afraid that whoever told me could share the information about the faulty trial with others. And they're probably even more concerned that individual could be continuing to gather destructive information about Acelia.

I still went for my run that day; Acelia wasn't going to take that from me.

But as soon as I got home, I called the security company that sent me Derrick.

CHAPTER EIGHT

MARISSA

MARISSA PULLS THE PLUG from the drain and steps out of the bathtub. She towels herself off and massages a rich, buttery lotion—new to her store—into her damp skin. She slips on her terry-cloth robe and leans forward to wipe the condensation from the mirror. Matthew prefers her like this, with her hair pulled back and no makeup adorning her face. Perhaps it reminds him of the teenager he fell in love with, even though tonight she feels older than her thirty-eight years. She dots retinol cream onto her faint crow's-feet and smooths balm onto her lips.

She walks into the bedroom and pulls open a dresser drawer. Her hand hovers above her favorite soft cotton pajamas. Beside them rests a midnight-blue silky nightgown. It's Matthew's favorite. She slips that on instead, even though the lace itches the sensitive area beneath her collarbones.

She switches off the overhead lamp and lights a candle. Then she removes her phone from its charger. She reads through her recent text exchanges with Matthew. His replies to her queries—**Anything special you'd like for dinner? I could make salmon or steak tacos. . . . What time do you think you'll be home? . . . Do you need me to pick up anything at the pharmacy?**—have been brusque, when he has bothered to answer at all.

Her husband is one floor below her, probably watching television. She slowly taps out a new message to him: **I'd love it if you slept in our bed tonight.**

She stares at the screen. No response. She has no idea if he is ignoring her or simply hasn't heard the chime on his phone. She's about to replace her phone in its charger when three blinking dots form on her screen. He's typing a reply. Then the dots disappear, leaving an empty space beneath her invitation.

Her husband isn't ready to touch her yet, Marissa thinks as she blows out the candle and slides between the cool sheets. Avery promised there will be clarity about the health of her marriage in another couple of weeks, but right now, that's hard for Marissa to believe.

She closes her eyes and tries to meditate, but her racing mind resists. Tomorrow she needs to proofread the forty-page catalog for the auction at Bennett's school—a little task Natalie sprang on her—and talk to her accountant about her business taxes; it's hard to say which task she dreads more. She turns onto her side, facing the empty spot in the bed Matthew used to fill. Her sleep has been fractured for weeks, and now, every time she awakens in the middle of the night, Matthew's absence feels more pronounced.

She needs to do two other things tomorrow: First, call the florist to find out who sent those roses. Marissa has a suspicion, but she can't believe he'd be so brazen.

She also needs to pick up a pregnancy test.

She doesn't truly believe she could be pregnant, especially after she endured so many heartbreaking rounds of fertility treatments, but she needs to see a negative test stick to put her mind completely at ease.

The bedroom door creaks open and Matthew steps in. Soundlessly, she watches as he undresses, neatly hanging up his suit and tie in the closet and tossing his shirt in the hamper. Is he simply getting changed before returning downstairs? she wonders.

He walks over to the bed and stares down at her. Marissa feels pinned beneath his scrutiny. The light in the hallway is the only source of illumination in the room. It backlights him, so she can't see the expression on her husband's face.

"I've missed you," she whispers. As she speaks the words, Marissa realizes the deep truth they contain. It wasn't the barbed split that formed between them at the moment of her revelation that created her sense of loss, or even the pivotal moment when she succumbed to the tender touch of another man. The fissure began to form long ago.

He leans down. She inhales his familiar scent and closes her eyes. But instead of his lips touching hers, she feels the brush of fabric against her cheek. When she opens her eyes, Matthew is holding a pillow to his chest. A wild thought flashes through her mind: Is he going to smother me?

"The pillows in the guest room are too soft. Can you buy new ones?" Matthew strides back into the hallway without waiting for her reply.

Marissa can hardly be annoyed with Bennett for forgetting his saxophone when she herself didn't remember to bring an umbrella, she thinks as she hops over a puddle. She tries to shield her hair with her free hand until she reaches the entrance to Rolling Hills Academy even though she knows it's a lost cause. She pulls open the heavy glass door and greets the security guard manning the front desk, flashing her parent ID. He gives her a nod, clearing her to walk past the metal detector into the administrative office. Security is mostly invisible but tight at Rolling Hills, since several high-profile politicians send their children here.

"Hi, Joan," she calls to the school secretary. "Guess what my son forgot?" Marissa waggles the heavy saxophone case.

Joan laughs. "He's in Mrs. Tanaka's class, right? They don't go to music until after lunch, so you can leave it with me and I'll have him come down during recess." Joan, gatekeeper to the school, possesses an encyclopedic knowledge of Rolling Hills and its daily operations. "Oh, and I want to thank you again for the sweet baby gift! I gave it to Laurie and she sent me a picture of my granddaughter wearing the adorable hat and swaddled in the blanket. I hope you don't mind that I gave her your address. She wanted to write you a note herself."

For a moment, Marissa wonders if Joan's daughter could have sent the flowers. But no one would send a thank-you bouquet that cost almost as much as the gift itself.

The sender remains a mystery—at least for now. After Matthew headed off to the guest room last night, Marissa lay awake for hours, staring into the darkness. She used her phone to call up the florist's website, and she learned Bloom's hours were 10:00 A.M. to 6:00 P.M. But the yellow roses hadn't arrived at their doorstep until almost 9:30 P.M.

It was another question for the florist. She planned to call at 10:00 A.M. sharp.

"Please tell your daughter she doesn't need to write a note," Marissa assures Joan. "I remember how exhausted I was when Bennett was born."

Joan is opening her mouth to answer when the phone rings. "I have to grab this, but don't worry, I'll reunite Bennett with his sax."

Marissa waves goodbye as she exits the office. She peers through the glass door of the school entrance, hoping the rain is tapering off. But it's coming down even harder.

She's about to brave it and run to her car when she notices another parent approaching the building. The woman's face is shielded—*she* didn't forget her umbrella—but her distinctive walk and the outline of her hourglass shape in her cream-colored belted raincoat make her immediately recognizable to Marissa.

It's Natalie.

It isn't surprising that she has bumped into Natalie this morning; they often cross paths at the small school.

Marissa waits until Natalie reaches the door, then pushes it open for her.

"Thanks!" Natalie closes her pretty polka-dot umbrella as she steps inside. "Were you here to help with the auction class gifts, too? I'm getting the first-graders to paint their handprints on the rocking chair. It'll be so cute!"

"Oh, fun!" Marissa summons the energy to enthuse, even though she feels a little wilted in Natalie's presence. Marissa takes in Natalie's shiny black hair, perfectly made-up face, and impractical but gorgeous high heels. Natalie always looks good; her job selling high-end real estate probably requires it. But who appears so polished to spend a morning painting with a bunch of six-year-olds?

"I just had to drop off something for Bennett." Marissa runs her fingers through her own hair. She feels dampness and frizz; so much for her blowout.

"I've been meaning to check in with you." Natalie puts a hand on

Marissa's forearm and leans in, her voice lowering to a husky, confidential whisper. "Matthew told me the firm lost the Coleman account. You okay?"

Marissa blinks in surprise: Matthew lost one of his biggest clients?

Maybe it just happened. Perhaps he didn't mention it to her because he's barely speaking to her these days.

But why does Natalie know?

Natalie is watching her carefully, Marissa realizes. She forces her lips to curve up into a smile. "Yes, everything is fine," she lies.

"Oh, good." But something in Natalie's eyes confirms a suspicion that has been building in Marissa: Natalie wants her to feel uncomfortable about the history Matthew and Natalie shared.

Don't give Matthew the opportunity to be alone with her, Avery had warned.

Avery already seems to have Natalie's number. Maybe the marriage consultant knew of Natalie's existence even before her name came up during the session. Marissa was more than a little unsettled to learn that Avery was skimming through the details of their lives, but if Matthew is okay with it, how can she object?

Hiring Avery was risky. Marissa wonders, not for the first time, if it was the right move.

"Have a great day," Marissa tells Natalie, then pushes through the door and hurries to her car. Cold raindrops pelt down on her nose and cheeks, and she's shivering by the time she reaches her Audi.

She slides into the driver's seat, then twists around to grab the blanket she always leaves in the car—in case she gets chilly at one of Bennett's baseball games—and tries to dry herself off. She turns on the engine and watches the windshield wipers arc back and forth, taking an extra moment to gather herself before she backs out of the visitor's spot.

Perhaps business worries are contributing to the ruptures in her marriage. Matthew rarely discusses problems at work with Marissa. She'd like to put it down to a misguided sense of chivalry: he wants to protect her from any financial blips or unpleasantness. But she is complicit in the arrangement, too. She has always worked, from those early days at her family's store—named after their surname, Conner—to waitressing to help pay her way through college, to running her boutique. Still, her earnings pale in comparison to Matthew's. Even though she insists on handling some of the bills—Bennett's private-school tuition and her car, for example—he absorbs the bulk of their expenses.

Marissa glances at her dashboard clock: 9:48 A.M. Rush-hour traffic is over, so she should make it to Coco in twenty minutes. She'd rather not call the florist while she's on the road, but neither does she want to wait until she reaches her boutique, since she might be interrupted by Polly or a customer. She compromises by driving toward Coco and, as soon as the clock hits ten, pulling into a parking lot of a CVS.

She dials the number for Bloom and listens as it rings once, twice, three times. She's about to hang up and try again when a woman answers, sounding a little breathless. "Bloom Florist. This is Cathy, may I help you?"

"Cathy, hi, this is Marissa Bishop. I received the most beautiful arrangement of yellow roses from your store last night."

"I'm so glad to hear that."

"Yes, but there's just one little thing. I couldn't find a card, and naturally I want to thank whoever sent them. I was wondering if you could help me?"

"Of course, can you give me your name again?"

Marissa spells it out.

"Hang on just a second. . . ."

Marissa can hear the clicking of computer keys. She watches a mother enter the drugstore holding a wailing toddler in one arm and an umbrella in her free hand.

"Oh, hmm, this is interesting. The order came in online. I actually don't have the sender's name."

Marissa's stomach twists. "Wouldn't he have provided a credit card? Or she, of course?"

"Well, you see, they used a Venmo account. It was paid by @Pier1234."

Could Pier be a name, or does it refer to the structures by the water? Marissa finds a pen in her console and scribbles the handle down on the back of an old gas receipt that's floating in her purse.

"Wouldn't the person's name be on the Venmo account, though?"

"Not if they don't want it to be," Cathy replies. "Looks like you've got a secret admirer!"

Marissa closes her eyes briefly. "Thanks so much. They really are beautiful." She glances at the arrangement next to her on the passenger's-side floor, the water drained from the vase and the flowers' stems wrapped in a damp paper towel. Their aroma is filling her car, just as it filled the kitchen this morning.

She steps out of her car and enters CVS, quickly finding the correct aisle and picking up an early-pregnancy test, then she uses the self-checkout register before hurrying back to her car.

Not until she is walking into Coco, flowers in hand, does she realize she forgot to ask her other question: If Bloom closed at 6:00 P.M., why did the flowers arrive so much later? Calling Cathy back seems a bit nutty. Besides, it's possible the delivery service runs much later than the store itself.

"Good morning," Marissa calls out to Polly, who is stacking a pile of patterned cocktail napkins on a little table by the register.

"Morning!" Today Marissa's young assistant is wearing an emerald-colored dress accessorized with a woven leather belt. Marissa once told Polly green suited her perfectly, and ever since then, Marissa has noticed Polly's wardrobe slowly expanding with items in those shades. Marissa feels a tinge of guilt for the way she reacted to the window display; Polly's intentions are good, and besides, isn't imitation supposed to be a form of flattery?

"Ooh, those flowers are so pretty!"

Marissa smiles. "They're for you. Sorry I was snippy yesterday."

"Oh my gosh, are you serious? You didn't need to do that."

"I insist." Marissa hands Polly the arrangement. "Take them home after work. But they may be a little thirsty now."

Polly hurries off to fill the vase with water as Marissa pulls out her phone.

She stares down at the last unanswered text she sent Matthew, inviting him to bed. She'd placed the roses on the kitchen counter right before she'd gone to take her bath, but this morning, the arrangement was centered on the desk of the little office she used upstairs. Matthew must've moved them.

She slowly types a new message to him: **Hope you're having a good morning. Think I figured out who sent the flowers: They were a thank-you for all the work I'm doing on the school auction.**

Matthew will never verify it with Natalie; his pride won't allow that.

It isn't an outright lie, Marissa assures herself as her finger hovers over the little arrow that will send the text to her husband. In any case, she did it to save Matthew from any more pain. She loves him. She wants to repair their marriage; her heart is in the right place.

CHAPTER NINE

AVERY

I DON'T BELONG TO A GYM. I've always preferred to exercise in solitude: running and biking outside, lifting light weights at home, and stretching using my favorite yoga app. Yet here I am, exiting Pinnacle Studio with my umbrella in hand and a pass for a free one-week trial offer tucked in my bag. I won't be buying a membership, which I know will disappoint the chipper young man who just spent a half hour talking up the gym's special features and wide array of classes. I just need to get a feel for the place.

Marissa frequents the Pilates classes at this gym, which is located in almost a straight line down Connecticut Avenue from their home into northwest D.C. She likes to take them at least twice a week. It's not that I plan to spend hours at Pinnacle with the expectation that I'll bump into my new client chatting up the guy she slept with, but something I notice at this gym may inform the techniques I utilize in my sessions with Marissa and Matthew. And though it's highly possible Marissa might be avoiding her gym altogether now, I've learned that the people who seem straightforward can surprise you most.

In my new role as a ten-session fixer, I cast a lot of lines. Usually one gets a tug.

I wonder if Matthew is also tempted to check out the clientele at his wife's gym, since our inquiries seem to be overlapping this morning. When I called Bloom at 10:15 A.M., the woman who answered the phone laughed and said, "What's up with these flowers? You're the third person to call, and I can only tell you what I told each of them. The roses were ordered through a Venmo account and I have no idea who sent them."

Marissa and Matthew, I'd thought as I hung up the phone. They're the only other ones who would have phoned.

I pause at the street corner, taking a step back—to avoid getting splashed as a bus rolls through a big puddle, then cross with the light and reach my car. It's broad daylight, and I'm parked at a meter on the side of a busy road. Still, I reflexively check the back seat before closing my umbrella and climbing in.

I rub my hands together for warmth, then pull out my phone. There's one more thing I need to do before I head to the shelter to pick up Romeo.

I tap out a message to Marissa and Matthew: **Here's an assignment for you. Go on a date tomorrow night—alone. Pick a quiet restaurant. Reminisce about how you met, and what made you fall in love. Go back to those early days and try to relive them.**

They might dine at La Ferme's heated outdoor patio, or they could choose a different venue. But wherever they go, it won't be difficult to find them.

I put away my phone and merge into traffic, heading south, deeper into D.C.

Less than an hour later, I'm on my way home from the animal shelter with Romeo. He's riding shotgun, trying to wedge his snout through the window crack. His efforts are complicated by the plastic cone of shame ringing his neck.

"Sorry for the indignity. But the shelter has to neuter every dog before he's adopted."

From the look he gives me, I'm not sure that he accepts my explanation.

We idle at a stoplight on a tree-lined road, and Romeo gives a hoarse-sounding bark.

"You really showed that squirrel who's boss. Good boy."

His stitches should dissolve in a week or two, and in the meantime I've got a bottle of pain meds from the shelter's vet to keep Romeo comfortable. The trunk of my car is filled with his new supplies, and it just hit me that I'm going to be walking Romeo morning, noon, and night—even during storms like this one.

He bends down and tries to sniff my leather purse.

"Don't even think about it. You're already on thin ice."

When we get home, the rain has eased, so before we even go inside, I clip on Romeo's leash and we slowly stroll around my block. He wants to smell every shrub and tree and mark most of them. When a woman walking a golden retriever puppy passes by, Romeo shrinks against my legs. I stroke his head and tell him it's okay. We're almost back home when my phone pings with a text from Kimberly, one of my clients: **All good see you soon.** We'd tentatively scheduled an outdoor session at 3:00 P.M. but agreed to check in before meeting because of the weather.

Kimberly is a twenty-nine-year-old who initially sought me out because of a bad breakup. *I think about him all the time,* she confessed. *I can't stop checking out his Instagram. I even drove by his house the other night.* Her core issue wasn't the presenting problem. It rarely is. Kimberly had been sexually assaulted as a teenager and never received the help she deserved. She can't afford my usual fee, but I don't do this work solely for the money. Kimberly pays a fraction of what I charge clients such as the Bishops.

My strategy with Kimberly has been to begin gently, earning her trust and connecting her with a solid foundation of support networks. Now for our eighth session, which I've labeled The Test, we're amping things up by meeting on the trail in the park where the man grabbed her.

Romeo and I climb the front steps to my porch and I deactivate my home alarm. I hook his leash over a post and return to my car, making two trips to carry in his supplies.

After filling up his water bowl and giving him a chewy bone to work on, I set up his crate, placing a comfy pillow and a few toys inside.

"I'll be back in a bit." I give him a pain pill inside a piece of turkey.

He swallows it, but looks unconvinced.

"You're the master of the guilt trip," I grumble as I latch the door to his crate. But it's probably strange for him to be in such a quiet place after the constant noise of the shelter. I turn on some acoustic rock and grab my purse, then head back out the door.

All in all, it was a successful day, I reflect as Romeo and I amble down Connecticut Avenue in the chilly evening air, his leash in my right hand and my bag of spring rolls and *panang* dangling from my left.

Kimberly's session had gone well. At first she had been reluctant to even step onto the park's pathway, but in the end she did so of her own volition. And even though I let Romeo wander around the house while I typed up my notes and checked in with Cameron, my shoes remained unchewed.

My latest update from Cameron was also pleasing: Skylar had been released from the hospital and he'd resisted her pleas to drive her home. Apparently she'd taken an Uber.

As for my newest clients, the Bishops, Marissa had emailed to tell me she'd secured a babysitter for tomorrow night, and Matthew was making reservations for their date. She didn't reveal where they're going, but I'll park outside their home—using my late husband's car in case they recognize mine—and follow them to the restaurant. I'm curious about how they act when they think no one is watching.

Plus, I received another call today from a potential new client—my fourth since Monday. I'm at the point now where I need to turn away more business than I accept.

The contours of my life have changed so dramatically in the past year, and the freshness and unpredictability of my days typically imbue me with energy. But tonight all I want to do is flop on my couch with Thai food and a Netflix binge.

And I have to admit, it would be nice to have someone beside me to rub my feet and laugh with.

You wanted this life, I remind myself.

And I do. It's just sometimes, the paths not taken call to me. I'm considering texting Derrick when Romeo pulls me forward, lunging toward a piece of garbage someone left on the sidewalk.

I try to pull him away, but he resists, and for a moment I question the wisdom of getting a dog who can outmuscle me.

Then a deep voice calls my name: "Avery? Is that you?"

I spin around, startled.

My body relaxes when I recognize Skip, a guy I went out with a couple of times a few months ago. Skip is smart, kind, and easy on the eyes, but nothing sparked between us.

"Hey!" I call. His back is to Connecticut Avenue, where rush-hour traffic is still churning by. "What are you doing in such a hip neighborhood?"

He laughs and walks closer. "I had a meeting. I was just going to grab a burger when I saw you."

Skip looks a little thinner than when I last saw him, but otherwise his easy smile, broad shoulders, and blunt, appealing features are unchanged. Romeo doesn't seem to share my opinion; he's behind my legs, cowering, his plastic cone pressing against the backs of my thighs.

"Who's this guy?" Skip asks in a gentle voice. Instead of coming closer, he squats down. "Hey, buddy, it's okay. I'm a friend of your mama's."

"He's a little skittish."

"Is he like this around everyone?"

"Mostly just men. He's always been fine with me. But I don't really know much about Romeo, actually. I just adopted him today."

Skip grins. "Romeo?"

"He came with the name. And don't mention the cone of shame; he's sensitive about it."

Skip straightens up.

"So—" we both begin at the exact same time. We laugh in unison, too.

"What have you been up to?" he asks.

Skip moved to D.C. almost a year ago. He's a real estate developer, and the project that brought him here is the building of some luxury homes in Bethesda. I'd first met Skip at the bar at Matisse, a welcoming restaurant with a good wine list. I'd just had drinks with a friend. She needed to rush off to make dinner for her family, but I'd decided to linger over another glass of Chablis and the latest *New Yorker*. There was no one waiting for me at home.

The David Grann piece is terrific, Skip had said from the next stool over.

I'd lowered my magazine and glanced at him.

An hour later, my one extra glass of Chablis had turned into two, and Skip had pulled his barstool closer to mine.

As we stand together on the sidewalk now, I tell Skip work is keeping me busy, and he mentions that he finally finished renovating the main bathroom of the town house he bought in the Palisades neighborhood. He keeps his voice soft. Gradually, he edges closer until he's standing just a few feet from Romeo.

"He's had it tough, hasn't he? I see the scars. But he seems a little more comfortable around me already. He'll be okay. Just make sure you socialize him—not just with people but with other dogs, too."

I look down at Romeo. Skip is right; my dog is still cowering, but at least he's no longer trying to tuck his stubby tail between his legs. "Do you know a lot about dogs?"

"Some." His voice remains gentle and easy. "That collar you've got— you may want to swap it for a harness. It'll be easier on his neck, and on your wrist if he yanks."

By now the cold air is seeping through my coat, and I suppress a shudder. I make an impulsive decision and hold up the bag of Thai food: "It isn't a burger, but I'm willing to share. How about we keep the conversation going at my house and you can give me some more tips?"

Skip looks surprised, but recovers fast. "Sounds great."

We walk back to my place, our pace brisk, and as soon as we get inside, I uncork a pinot noir and pour us each a glass.

In the sharper light, I can see more changes in Skip. He's definitely thinner, and when he pulls off his knit cap, I notice his hair looks a bit shaggy, as if he's overdue for a trim.

The differences are more than superficial, though. His energy seems more intense. Edgier.

Skip fills up two glasses with water while I transfer the food onto plates, then set them out on the banquet table. Even though I don't know Skip well, it feels surprisingly natural to be with him again. When I go to scoop kibble into Romeo's bowl, Romeo jumps up, putting his paws on my stomach and nearly knocking me over.

"Down," Skip says, flattening out his hand and moving his palm toward the floor.

Romeo ignores him.

"Down," I repeat, mimicking the gesture and taking a step back so that Romeo's paws slip off me.

I look at Skip. "Guess we're going to have to learn some basic commands."

Skip nods. "A dog that size needs to know when to sit, get down, and stay. It could actually save his life."

"Really?"

"The streets around here are busy. You don't want to lose control of him."

I nod and take off Romeo's cone so he can eat. "You've already earned your dinner, Skip. Anything else?"

"Any bad habits he has—don't discipline him. It's not his fault. Redirect and reward him with a treat, since he's obviously food motivated."

I like Skip's approach. There's a lot I like about him, actually.

I wonder again why our relationship fizzled before it could ever start. Maybe it was timing. Or maybe it's because Skip is the kind of guy you get serious with, and I don't want to be serious with anyone right now.

We slide into the banquet and eat in silence for a minute while Romeo wolfs down his kibble, then he flops under the table by my feet with a satisfied sigh.

"He's doing really well with you around now," I observe.

The velvety wine and hot, spicy *panang* have chased away the chill I felt outdoors. It's also comforting to step out of my usual role and let Skip be the fixer with his concise directions about what I should and shouldn't do.

"So, give me an update on the houses you're building. They're in Bethesda, right? Has construction started yet?"

"It's good. Permitting took forever, but we break ground in two weeks. We've presold forty percent of them, so I'm happy. What about you? Any interesting new clients?"

Since I'm not a therapist, I'm not bound by the rules of confidentiality. Still, I'm circumspect in discussing the people who come to see me. Never using names or identifying details is one of my hard-and-fast rules.

"A few. I'm wrapping up with a young woman who kept getting her heart broken. She's in a better place now."

"Yeah?" Skip takes a big sip of wine. "You know, I was wondering—" He cuts himself off.

"C'mon," I prompt.

"I don't know, maybe you can give me a little advice, too?"

I shrug. "I can try. What's going on?"

"It's my sister. She's been dating this guy for a while now. I think he's bad news."

"How so?"

"I've been picking up signs that he's not the great person everyone thinks he is . . . and I'm worried about her."

"Anything specific?"

"I've got my suspicions, but nothing I can verify. Do you think I should say anything to her?"

"That's tricky. *Shoot the messenger* is a popular expression for a reason. She might resent you, even if you're pointing out what she subconsciously knows already. On the flip side, if what you're saying is accurate, something inside her will recognize it as truth. She won't be able to unhear your words."

Skip leans toward me, his expression intent, his half-eaten spring roll seemingly forgotten on his plate.

"It's a risk," I continue. "Your relationship might never be the same. Or you two might become closer."

He nods slowly. "Thanks. You're right, it is complicated."

He looks down at his plate, then back up at me. "Have you ever treated patients like that?"

"Like what? Your sister and her boyfriend?"

"I guess I'm grasping at straws." He gives a little laugh. "I was just wondering if you'd seen that dynamic before and how it played out."

I shrug. "Sure. Power struggles are common in relationships, but attempts at control raise that dynamic to a whole new level. Remember that woman I told you about who was living with a controlling husband?"

It wasn't a woman—it was Cameron. I'd shared the broad outlines of his case with Skip one night when we'd been trading stories about our lives. We'd also talked about my marriage to Paul, and Skip told me his real name was Steven, and that he'd earned his nickname as a boy because he'd been obsessed with sailing—Skip for "skipper."

Skip nods and takes a sip of wine. "Right, she's the one who was in IT?"

I'm impressed by his memory for detail. Skip's a smart guy, I think, watching his strong-looking fingers set down my delicate wineglass. I recall his telling me he'd gone to Dartmouth on a full academic scholarship after a friend's father had urged him to apply. *Without him I might not even have gone to college,* Skip had said modestly. We'd argued about whose college was better—Northwestern or Dartmouth—until I threw a cocktail napkin at him and he leaned in to silence me with a kiss.

I'd enjoyed kissing Skip.

"You said after ten sessions she was living on her own and was going to hire a divorce lawyer?" Skip prompts me.

"Yes. So even if your sister has been with this guy for a while, it's never too late to break free."

Skip nods and a faraway look comes into his eyes. We finish up our meals, but there's a shift in the air. Maybe he's more worried about his sister than he let on, because Skip isn't making as much eye contact as he was earlier, and he seems lost in thought.

I'm taking my last bite of *panang* when Skip begins to rub his temples. "You okay?"

"Yeah, just a headache. Sometimes it happens when I drink red wine."

"Oh? That's a bummer. I remember you always preferred red over white?"

"It's recent. I'm hoping it's just a phase."

I get up to refill his water. "Want some Advil?"

"Uh, sure, that would be great. Then I should probably get going. I have a ridiculously early meeting."

"Be right back." I head upstairs, feeling a tinge of disappointment with Romeo trotting behind me.

I can't help imagining what would have happened if Skip didn't have a headache and an early appointment, and the bottle of wine had turned into two, and we'd moved our conversation to the couch. I grab the bottle of painkillers out of my medicine cabinet and peek in the mirror, running my hand through my hair to smooth it. As I walk down the stairs, I wonder if I should invite Skip back in a week or two to see Romeo again. I wasn't ready for a relationship when Skip and I first connected, and he didn't seem to be either, but maybe things could be different now.

I reach the landing of the staircase, which affords me a full view of the entryway of my home, including my office.

Skip is no longer sitting at the banquet. He's stepping out of my office and closing the door behind him.

He looks up at me and freezes.

"What are you doing in there?" I can't restrain the indignation in my voice.

"Sorry—I was looking for the bathroom." The line rolls off his tongue, smooth and believable.

But the hairs on my arms stand up.

"The bathroom is just off the living room." I descend the final steps slowly, keeping my eyes locked on his.

My office is a sacred space. The only people who ever go in there besides me are my clients. My professional files are stored alphabetically in two tall cabinets. I keep all my financial information in my desk. A built-in safe contains my birth certificate, Social Security card, passport, engagement and wedding rings, and Finley's folder. It also holds my .38 pistol.

Skip has been to my house once before, when he stopped by after a day of meetings in Bethesda before we went to a concert at the Wolf Trap. I'm not 100 percent sure, but I'm reasonably certain he even used the bathroom on this level.

"Oh, yeah, right. Now I remember." He doubles back, heading toward it.

If Skip had merely opened the door and peeked in, he would instantly have noticed he was in the wrong room. But he went inside. What was he doing?

I peer into my office. Nothing looks out of place, and he couldn't have been in there for more than a minute, but I'm going to check more closely after he leaves.

Now I'm glad Skip provided the excuse for ending our evening early. I want him out of here.

When Skip exits the bathroom, I'm waiting with his coat. He shrugs it on, then leans down and tries to pat Romeo, who shrinks away. "Bye, buddy." Skip straightens and faces me. "I had a really nice night. We should do it again sometime soon. And don't hesitate to reach out if you have any more dog questions."

"Sure," I say lightly. I escort him to the front door, and before he's even off the front porch, I've closed and double-locked the door behind him. I turn and begin to walk toward my office, then I whip around again, this time to set the house alarm.

Maybe Skip's appearance—and sudden reappearance—in my life isn't a simple coincidence. I met Skip after I called the FDA and relayed the information Finley had overheard.

I step back into my office and riffle through my files, but they appear untouched. I check my other drawers, including the ones in my desk. Nothing seems to have been moved.

I glance at my safe, but there's no way Skip could have cracked the code; it's fingerprint activated. My laptop is in my bedroom, so he couldn't have installed spyware on it. I stand in the middle of the room and circle around slowly, considering the possibility that Skip had really been searching for the bathroom after all, then I spy the appointment calendar I keep on top of my desk. I log appointments on my phone, too, but I like having the physical reference as a backup. A striped ribbon that had been neatly nestled between the book's pages marking the current day is now askew, as if someone had flipped through the pages.

There's no good reason I can come up with for why Skip would be searching for details about my schedule.

I pick up the calendar and examine it closely. These days, surveillance techniques are so sophisticated that tiny cameras can be applied anywhere.

Nothing is affixed to my calendar, though. I search the entire room, running my fingers over every surface, checking the window blinds, and even peering up into the air-conditioning vent.

When I'm finally satisfied the room is clean, I sit down at my desk and review what I know about Skip. He told me he's a commercial real estate developer, and that he owns a town house in the Palisades neighborhood in D.C.

I log into my laptop and plug his name into a search engine. There are dozens of mentions of Steven Pierce. I click on one of the hits, an article that appeared in a local glossy magazine called *Washington Life*. Accompanying the brief piece is a spread of photographs from the Allison Gala at the Four Seasons Hotel last September. Skip appears in one, wearing a tuxedo and smiling directly into the camera, and the caption confirms his name and occupation.

I scroll through another dozen hits until I'm certain he checks out. Skip appears to be exactly whom he claims; I can't find a single loose thread. I finally stand up and walk out of my office, flicking off the light. But throughout the rest of the night, I can't stop seeing Skip standing in that doorway, like an intruder.

My heart tells me Skip is a decent guy.

My gut tells me to never go near him again.

CHAPTER TEN

MARISSA

MARISSA FINDS HERSELF HUMMING as she leans toward the bathroom mirror to apply a creamy lipstick, one that complements the rose-colored silk sheath she picked up at Coco's today. Her personal favorite of the many dresses in her closet is a black knee-length one, but Matthew prefers her in softer hues. He also loves how her legs look in high heels, so she slides into a pair of bone-colored pumps, even though she has been on her feet most of the day running errands and taking Bennett to a birthday party at an indoor trampoline park.

She desperately wants for tonight to go well. Matthew is still avoiding her, but Avery's instructions mean they'll have to talk over dinner. It's reassuring to have their agenda predetermined. Marissa spent most of her spare moments today sifting through memories, finding the ones that seem right to share. She's conscious of Avery's critique from their first session—*That's an Instagram post*—so she's doing her best to ensure the emotions contained in the remembrances are textured and honest.

The doorbell chimes as she reaches into her side of the closet for a wrap. Bennett's sitter, Hallie, must be here.

Unless it's another mysterious delivery, her mind whispers.

The sender of the roses never came forward, and after her initial call to the florist, Marissa decided not to pursue her inquiries further. Surely it ended there, she tells herself.

Marissa steps into the hallway and hears Matthew say something and Hallie respond with laughter.

Marissa exhales and heads back into the bathroom to spray a bit of Matthew's favorite perfume into the air and walk through the mist. She's almost as nervous for this date as she was before their first one, more than two decades ago.

She picks up her clutch and wanders downstairs into the family room, where Bennett and Hallie are ensconced on the couch, the board games Marissa set out on the coffee table ignored in favor of Bennett's Nintendo Switch.

As Marissa walks into the room, she catches sight of the back of their heads and freezes. Hallie has cut her waist-length hair; now it skims her shoulder blades. Hallie's hair is dirty blond and straight and shiny, just like Marissa's childhood friend Tina's used to be. Now it is the exact same length as Tina wore it, too.

A memory slices through Marissa: Tina flipping her hair as she stood on her bed and sang along, completely off-key, to Mariah Carey's "Vision of Love," while Marissa danced around and provided backup.

Hallie's voice interrupts the vision. "Hi, Mrs. Bishop!"

Marissa shakes off the memory. "Nice to see you, Hallie."

"I told Hallie I still had twenty-six minutes left today," Bennett says without looking up.

Marissa leans over and kisses Bennett's head.

"Funny how you forgot to do your math homework yesterday but can calculate every second of screen time you've earned." Marissa smiles at Hallie. "Twenty-six minutes. Then games or books."

"I got it, Mrs. Bishop." Hallie smiles, and Marissa is struck by the teenager's sweetness. Hallie usually pours herself a glass of milk, rather than the LaCroix or Diet Coke the other sitters prefer. And instead of watching those inane TikTok videos on her phone, she actually seems to enjoy the TV shows Bennett likes to watch.

"Bye, Bennett, bye, Hallie," Marissa calls as she heads into the kitchen.

"Bye, Mom!" Bennett calls back. Matthew should be standing by the door that connects the kitchen to the garage, his coat over one arm, scrolling through his iPhone as he usually does when he has to wait for her. But he's not there.

She frowns and circles back, making her way to the formal living room off the front door. It's empty, too.

She finds her husband in his office, seated in his favorite leather chair. At first she thinks he must be on a last-minute business call. Then she notices he's simply staring into space.

Dread infuses her body.

She steps inside, quietly closing the door.

Matthew is dressed for a night out, wearing dark jeans, a button-down, and his navy blazer. He holds what appears to be a gin and tonic, but the glass is completely full. She wants to walk over to him and sit on his lap, running her hand through his thick blond hair. She wants him to hold her the way he used to, pinning his strong arms around her so tightly it stole her breath away. For a moment she's tempted to try.

Then she notices he's not wearing shoes.

"Hey." Matthew looks up briefly before his eyes cut away, as if he can barely stand the sight of her.

"Matthew," she whispers, a plea in her tone. "Are you ready?"

"I'm not going," he says evenly, as if he's simply informing her that the moon is out.

Her heartbeat accelerates. "What do you mean? We have a reservation." As she speaks the words, she realizes how ridiculous they sound.

"I can't do it, Marissa." Matthew finally meets her gaze. "Every time I look at you . . . every single time . . . I just see you fucking that guy."

"But we told Avery—"

He lets out a harsh laugh. "Avery's not our boss. She works for us."

Tears prick Marissa's eyes. "Please, Matthew. Give this a chance. It's only dinner."

He leans forward, his expression tightening. "I drove by your gym today. I wanted to go inside and kill every single guy there. I lie awake at night imagining you with him. I just—" His explosive words abruptly cut off as he regains control. "I can't do this. Not tonight."

Marissa nods. Her throat is so tight it's difficult to speak. Her life until now has felt straight and true. She worked hard, married the man she loved, built a family she cherishes. She can't believe she risked everything so recklessly. So selfishly.

"I'm still going. I'll be thinking about you. About us."

She exits, closing the door quietly behind her.

The restaurant, Mon Ami Gabi, is a perfect mix of lively and romantic with its dark wood paneling, charming bar, and white-clothed tables. Marissa, seated toward the back, is surrounded by couples, most chatting comfortably but a few sitting in silence and barely looking at each other, as if they'd exhausted all their conversational topics long ago.

During the early years of their relationship, she and Matthew were in the first group—leaning in, laughing. When did they begin the slide toward the second one? There isn't a demarcation line she can point to; no triggering event that created the environment that made her susceptible to a one-night affair. She'd like to blame their marital drift on the busyness of everyday life, the demands of their jobs and schedules, the toll two miscarriages and her subsequent fertility treatments had taken on them. But the truth is, she knows couples with far more responsibilities and pressures who seem to have maintained strong emotional links.

She squeezes a wedge of lime into her Perrier, noticing a guy a few tables away reaching across the table to hold his date's hand. They're young and fresh-faced, and something about them—the creases in his shirt that suggest he tried to iron it himself, and the way the girl's hair has been styled to drape over one shoulder—tugs at Marissa's heart.

She looks at the empty chair across from hers and wonders what the other patrons think of her. All dressed up, alone, at a table for two.

The waiter delivers her appetizer—a steamed artichoke—and she thanks him. She plucks off one of the petals, dips the base into the butter sauce, and pulls the pulpy part through her teeth, grateful to have something to do.

Marissa knows how to expertly extract the tender, delicious heart of the vegetable; one of the signature dishes at her parents' store, Conner's, was a homemade artichoke dip. Growing up, she spent many afternoons at the big butcher-block table behind the counter, spreading open the petals of artichokes and twisting away the small, interior leaves to expose the fuzzy chokes. She'd blend them with spinach and cream cheese and garlic and pepper before sprinkling freshly grated Parmesan over the top and roasting it until the dish turned golden and bubbly.

The summer she turned fifteen was the first year Marissa had been allowed to work alone at the store during the slow periods, which came twice a day, as reliably as the tide, at midmorning and after dinnertime.

It was also the summer someone she loved died.

Not just *someone:* Tina, who for many years had been like a sister to Marissa. Tina had been killed by one of their high school teachers, an event so shocking and upsetting Marissa could barely eat or sleep for months afterward.

Marissa's throat tightens. Tonight was supposed to be about her and Matthew; why is she thinking so much about Tina?

She pushes away her plate and signals the waiter, asking for a glass of wine.

She reminds herself it was also the summer she fell in love, with Matthew. And it had been Matthew who had pulled her out of the darkness after Tina died.

Even though this evening isn't unfolding the way it was supposed to, Marissa intends to try her best to follow Avery's instructions. Otherwise, she'll feel as if she'll be giving up on her marriage.

Reminisce about how you met, and what made you fall in love. Go back to those early days and try to relive them.

At five minutes before the eight o'clock closing time of Conner's, on the tail end of a searing-hot August day, she stood alone by the cash register, listlessly flipping through a copy of *People* magazine. The bell over the door jingled and she looked up to see Matthew—a summer boy, and arguably the cutest one of all—walk in.

"Hey, Marissa."

She experienced a little jolt of surprise that he recalled her name so easily. His family had purchased a waterfront house just two years earlier, and Matthew, his mother, and his sister lived there during the summer months, with his father driving in from D.C. for the weekends.

"Hi," she replied.

He rocked back and forth on his heels, and she noticed that along with his collared shirt and khaki shorts, he wore a pair of blue-checkered Vans. "Do you have any ground coffee?"

"Sure. Right down that aisle." Marissa pointed, even though Conner's only had two aisles. "The beans are whole, but there's a little machine to grind them."

"Thanks. I don't want to face my mom in the morning if she's not caffeinated."

His nose was sunburned and beginning to peel, Marissa noticed, and his hair was so blond it almost looked white.

"My dad's the same." Marissa smiled, even though her affable father and Matthew's mother were nothing alike. Mrs. Bishop shopped at the store occasionally, always with special requests: She wanted Marissa to go to the back to get the freshest strawberries, even though the ones on the shelves had been picked just the previous morning. Or Mrs. Bishop would tell the butcher to reweigh the fresh turkey to make sure it was precisely two pounds, not one ounce under. She was the type of customer who never said "Please" or "Thank you." Marissa couldn't imagine what Mrs. Bishop would be like first thing in the morning, without coffee.

Matthew had inherited his mother's fair coloring and high cheekbones, but his manner was nothing like hers. Marissa stole another look at him as he walked over to grab a package of coffee.

"Uh, hey . . . this might sound a little stupid, but I've actually never used one of these."

"Oh, no problem!" Marissa hurried around the counter and went to stand beside him. "You just open up the top here and pour in the beans, put the bag underneath, then flip that red switch."

Matthew grinned. "Seriously? It's that simple?"

"You wouldn't believe how many people ask for help," Marissa fibbed. The directions for the machine were written out on a little sign right by it.

Matthew opened the silver bag of coffee and poured in the beans. When one fell out and skittered across the floor, he quickly bent down to scoop it up and tuck it in his pocket even though Marissa said, "Oh, don't worry about it." He pressed the red switch and the grinding noise erupted so loudly it made conversation impossible.

Marissa couldn't decide if she should stay there or walk back to the counter, and her indecision made the choice for her.

The machine cut off and Matthew sealed up the bag. The smell of the medium-roast grounds was strong, but not unpleasantly so.

"Need anything else? Cream, maybe?"

"Nah, thanks, that's it."

She walked back to the register, stopping at the door to flip the OPEN sign to CLOSED, and he followed.

While she rang him up, he looked around. "You work here alone?"

"Yeah." She felt a swell of pride. "I'm just about to close up."

For a moment she worried he might misconstrue her words and think she was trying to get rid of him, but he only appeared impressed.

He pulled a crumpled $10 bill out of his pocket to pay for the coffee, and when she gave him his change, their hands brushed together.

He looked down at his shoes, then directly up at her. Their eyes locked as Marissa, who'd felt limp and gray for most of the summer, as if she were the one who'd turned into a ghost when Tina was killed, experienced an awakening.

He picked up his coffee and tossed the bag from one hand to the other. She saw the Swatch watch on his left wrist, a scar on the underside of his jaw (from playing ice hockey, she'd learn), and almond-shaped icy-blue eyes.

"Want me to wait for you?" Matthew asked. "I could maybe walk you home?"

The waiter breaks into her memory, clearing away Marissa's appetizer plate and asking if she'd like another glass of wine when her scallops are delivered.

"No, thank you."

The young couple a few tables over get up and head toward the exit, the guy's hand hovering by the small of the woman's back but not actually touching it.

Marissa's eyes trail them. Just before they reach the maître d', they step aside to let another customer pass by.

Her heart leaps.

It's Matthew.

He strides to her table and leans over. He kisses her on the cheek, just as he did after he walked her home in the velvety August air on that long-ago night, when they were teenagers and on the cusp of something life changing. Back then, he was saying good night.

Right now, he is saying hello.

.

CHAPTER ELEVEN

AVERY

SUNDAY MORNINGS ARE SUPPOSED TO be lazy. If it weren't for Romeo trying to lick my face and bumping his cone against my cheek, plus the realization that I've scheduled an important 10:00 A.M. appointment, I'd roll over and go back to sleep.

Instead I flip onto my right side, draping my arm around my dog, and grab my cell phone from the charger. Two days in, and I've already broken the no-sleeping-in-my-bed rule.

There's nothing urgent to attend to. Just an email confirming the address of my meeting and a text from Derrick. **Fun night, babe. Wish I was waking up next to you.**

It *had* been a fun night, even if I'd arrived nearly half an hour late, explaining I'd had a client emergency. This was only a partial fib. I'd planned to be at Derrick's place in Adams Morgan by 8:00 P.M., but Marissa and Matthew's date night proved more complicated than I'd anticipated.

I'd needed to make sure the Bishops had followed my instructions and gone out together. And I'd wanted to observe the couple as they left their home, and again as they entered the restaurant. Would their body language change when they were in public versus in private?

It would be informative to compare my impressions with their recounting of the evening when we met for our third session.

The first surprise of the night came when Marissa drove to the restaurant alone. I followed her in Paul's old Mercedes, then double-parked with my hazard lights flashing, figuring Matthew must have had a prior commitment and was meeting her there. I hadn't used Paul's car in a while, and I swear when I first opened its door, I could still smell the faint scent of his cologne.

Twenty minutes later, Matthew still hadn't shown up, and I'd been flipped off by more than one driver who'd had to maneuver past me. Was it possible he'd driven to the restaurant before Marissa and I'd simply missed his entrance? I was tempted to call the maître d' and ask if the Bishops had arrived—I could pretend I wanted to send them a bottle of wine—then Matthew pulled up in his Land Rover and jumped out, handing his keys to a valet. But rather than hurrying inside to meet his wife, Matthew remained on the sidewalk. I leaned to my right and peered through the passenger-side window, trying to see what he was doing.

He was on his phone.

Matthew was late, and his wife was waiting. Was he trying to punish her, or was the conversation truly important?

After a full four minutes, Matthew finally tucked his phone into the inside pocket of his blazer and strolled into Mon Ami Gabi.

Now as I lie in bed, my fingers unconsciously stroke Romeo's back. It's soothing, but not just for him. Something about the steady, repetitive motion quiets the questions ricocheting through my mind.

All marriages contain secrets; of this I'm certain.

Marissa has revealed one. Is Matthew hiding something equally explosive?

I hope my 10:00 A.M. meeting will help me figure some of this out.

I haul myself up, throw on jeans and a sweatshirt, and brew a cup of to-go coffee. Then I grab my dog's leash and we head out into what has shaped up to be an unexpectedly sunny, mild day.

An hour later, I'm opening the door to a bedroom—but not my own. It's in a home on one of the most exclusive streets in Chevy Chase, just a half mile or so from Matthew and Marissa's place.

I take in the vaulted ceiling, gas fireplace, and blond hardwood floors. The walk-in closet is about the size of my first studio apartment in

Georgetown, and the bathroom is every woman's fantasy, with its deep, claw-foot tub and multi-jet shower.

"The tiles were handcrafted in Italy," murmurs the broker beside me. It's stunning. It should be, for $3.2 million, I think. It'll be tough to find a flaw.

My broker has been mostly quiet during our tour—she seems to want the house to speak for itself—but now she leads me back into the cheerful, newly renovated kitchen, where I know she'll ask questions designed to gauge my interest. I've already established myself as a serious buyer by telling her I'm prequalified and need to find something within the next month.

"So, where did you say you were moving from again?" she begins, leaning forward with her elbows on the kitchen counter. Her pencil skirt hugs her curvy hips, and her blouse is undone enough that I can see the tip of her blue lacy bra.

"Naples," I answer, because I have a little familiarity with the area from visiting my grandmother.

"Love it there! And it's just you and your son?"

"Yeah, his father and I divorced a few years ago. It was kind of messy."

"Say no more." She gives a knowing laugh, as if we were already girl-friends. She's good at her job; she's building rapport.

"Oh, are you divorced, too?" I ask, thinking, *Four years ago, but you're still friendly enough with your ex to wish him a happy Father's Day on social media.*

Natalie runs manicured fingertips through her shiny dark hair. She's every bit as alluring as Marissa indicated. "Yup. I have one child, too, Veronica. She turned six last month." *With a* Frozen*-themed birthday party,* I silently add.

"Oh, my Teddy is five! I don't suppose you have any advice about the schools here? That's next on my list, after getting a house."

"You have to get him into Rolling Hills. It's the best private school around. The teachers are amazing. They start Mandarin in the second grade. And they are building a new STEM building. Of course it probably won't be ready until after our kids graduate. . . ."

I nod, thinking, *Mandarin in the second grade?* "And the parents?"

"The usual—some helicopter moms, and a few cliques, but for the most part they're a good group."

"Hmm. What about the dads?" I give her a wink.

Natalie grins. "All the best ones are married. But you know what they say—every couple is just one big fight away from splitting up."

"Do they really say that?"

She shrugs. "I do."

As I suspected, Natalie is trouble.

I understand why Matthew was attracted to her—she's confident and sexy. She's as different from Marissa as a peacock is from a swan.

The question remains, Is Matthew still attracted to her?

When we met in my office during our first session, Marissa described the slowly developing rift in her marriage. I can't yet rule out the possibility that Matthew also had an affair—or is still having one—but has chosen to conceal it. The Bishops can't heal their marriage if one of them is still hiding a big secret.

I gently probe a bit more, but Natalie doesn't give up any details about her current romantic life. Instead, she asks whether I'm ready to put in an offer.

"It won't stay on the market long," she tells me.

I say I need to think about the house, and she hands me a card as we walk out.

As Natalie closes up the lockbox, she cocks her head. "You look familiar. Maybe we've crossed paths before. What did you say you do again?"

"Oh"—I glide down the front steps, toward my car—"I must just have one of those faces."

CHAPTER TWELVE

MARISSA

EARLY MONDAY MORNING, MARISSA HURRIES up the stairs to Pinnacle, her purse bumping against her side. After the rough start to her date with Matthew on Saturday night, the dinner had gone well.

At first she carried most of the conversation, but as the evening wore on, he added a few memories of the early days of their relationship: how he'd appeared at Conner's the evening after he'd first walked her home, and this time they'd headed down to the beach bonfire. He'd kept his arm around her, so everyone could see they were becoming a couple, and when he'd made a s'more, he offered her the first gooey bite. Marissa recalled how they'd once overturned a canoe as they paddled to a quiet cove on the lake for a picnic, and they both laughed as she described how the sandwiches she'd made had floated on the water. It had been, Marissa thought, far too long since they'd laughed together.

Matthew followed her home, his headlights glowing in her rearview mirror. Hallie had recently gotten her driver's license and didn't need a ride, which was a welcome change from previous evenings when she'd babysat. Marissa was grateful the mood didn't have to be broken by Matthew's going back out into the cold night again.

Matthew had slept beside her in their bed, and though they hadn't touched, she'd fallen asleep to the familiar sound of his breathing. On Sunday, Marissa, Matthew, and Bennett had gone to the zoo, watching the giant pandas chew bamboo and spending an hour in the Reptile House—Bennett's favorite exhibit. Matthew hadn't checked his phone even once, instead reading the little plaques that described the reptiles and discussing the facts with Bennett. As they'd exited the building, Matthew had opened the door for her and touched the small of her back as she walked through it.

Could Avery really be that good? Marissa had wondered. Two sessions and one date night in, and she and Matthew already seemed to be on the road to recovery.

Avery was worth every bit of her astronomical fee, which Marissa was paying for out of her own earnings. There was no better investment than the health of her marriage.

But last night, Matthew hadn't come to bed until after Marissa was asleep. And in the sharp light of this Monday morning, Marissa feels off-kilter; it's as if the magic of the weekend is already evaporating. She received a text from FedEx that the delivery of the hand-painted place settings she'd ordered from Portugal was delayed again, which meant the opinionated, difficult customer who planned to use them for a special dinner party would throw a fit. Then, as she was rushing out the door to get Bennett to school, he informed her that he'd failed his math test and she needed to sign the quiz. Plus one of her favorite bangles, the one with her and Matthew's initials engraved on the inside, was missing. She'd looked every place she could think of, even between the cushions of the couches and beneath her bed. She'd checked under the seats of her car and shaken out the contents of her purse.

Now Marissa approaches the gym's front desk. This is the exact time she used to frequent her Pilates class: Mondays and Wednesdays right after she dropped off Bennett and before she went to Coco. She watches as a woman with a towel draped over her neck heads toward the room where the Reformers are located.

Since her confession to Matthew, this is the first time Marissa has entered Pinnacle.

She stands behind a man at the front desk, who is asking for a new plastic tag for his key chain, awaiting her turn.

As the man turns away and Marissa steps forward to scan her own tag and gain access to the facility, she hears, "Hey, Marissa!" It's the gym manager—a handsome, muscular man in his early thirties. "Haven't seen you around recently."

"It's been crazy busy." She doesn't meet his eyes. The scanner doesn't work. "Come on," Marissa mutters.

"Sorry!" the front-desk clerk chirps. "The monitor's been acting weird lately."

The manager begins to walk over to help. Marissa takes a deep breath and tries again.

"There you go!" the clerk says.

Marissa smiles and rushes past her, tossing a wave to the manager as she hurries toward the women's changing room. She pays an extra fee to keep a permanent locker there, with her sneakers and toiletries. She inputs the code and her locker door swings open.

She shakes out each sneaker and checks her toiletries bag.

She closes her eyes and breathes a sigh of relief: The bracelet is tucked inside.

She's slipping it on her wrist when her phone rings. It's Matthew.

She considers letting it go to voice mail, but it's so unlike him to call during the workday that she wonders if something's wrong.

"Hello there."

"Hey, listen, I forgot what time we're seeing Avery tonight."

"It's in the family calendar. Seven P.M."

"Oh, yeah, now I remember." Matthew hesitates. "How's your day going?"

Is it possible Matthew called merely to hear her voice? It has been years since he's done that.

She clears her throat. "Good . . ."

A few feet away, two women begin to talk about the spin class they just took. "That was insane," the slim redhead says. "I don't think I'm gonna be able to walk tomorrow."

"Are you at Coco?" Matthew asks.

Does he recall that she goes to Pilates on Monday mornings? He admitted to driving by the gym and wanting to beat up every guy in it. Maybe this is a test.

"Uh, actually I'm at Pinnacle." She closes her eyes and quickly adds, "I'm canceling my membership."

She'll miss her classes and the convenient location, but she needs to put Matthew's mind at ease.

She waits a beat. "Matthew? Are you still there?"

"Ah . . . Okay." Her body sags in relief because his tone is fractionally warmer. "See you at seven."

Marissa opens the door to Coco and steps inside. No matter what else is going on in her life, this chic, intimate space feels like a sanctuary. Marissa was involved in every step of its creation, from consulting with the architect who drew up the plans to remodel the rooms—which formerly was an ophthalmologist's office—to choosing the reclaimed wood to wrap around the trio of beams that bisect the store. The lighting, the layout, the dove-gray paint on the walls—it's her vision, brought to life.

At first, she wasn't completely sure she could pull it off. Back at her parents' store, she discovered she had a knack for rearranging the display cases, but she had help—her best friend, Tina, had worked alongside her. Together, they'd come up with the idea of using little boxes to lift the trays of caprese and pasta salads, and bringing in springs of fresh herbs and pretty wildflowers to adorn the tuna steaks and deviled eggs. She and Tina had also bought inexpensive straw baskets to display tomatoes and zucchini and unshucked corn, and they'd convinced Marissa's parents to replace the tired laminated floor with inexpensive material that looked like stone tiles. Tina, who loved fashion and had an eye for color, had picked the stone; it was a shade of rust that Marissa wasn't sure would work. But Tina insisted it would, and it had. In another life, Marissa could still be working at Conner's—helping her brother, Luke, gradually taking over the reins from her parents, perhaps even branching out into a second location. She could have married a local boy and remained near the water. She wouldn't have Tina, but maybe she'd have started trying to get pregnant earlier and been able to have more children.

Marissa didn't have many regrets in life, but when she and Matthew began to drift apart, she found herself ruminating about her choice to be with him during the summer she turned fifteen, and how turning toward Matthew meant other doors had closed to her. But without Matthew, there could be no Bennett, which was unfathomable.

"Marissa! Hi! How are you!" Polly hurries toward her, an eager smile on her face.

"Fine. How was your weekend?"

"Oh, gosh, it was—well, first, do you want some tea? I just brewed some but it's easy to make more."

"No, but I appreciate the offer."

Something seems different about Polly this morning. Maybe it's that she looks a little tired.

Marissa begins to walk toward the back room.

Polly quickly moves to keep step with her. "Do you have a sec?" Polly tilts her head. It's her hairstyle that's different, Marissa realizes—she's never seen Polly wear a simple ponytail.

Marissa needs to light a fire under the supplier of the missing place settings, and attend to this month's bills, and email Bennett's math teacher to see if the poor test result is a one-off or if Bennett's truly struggling in the class. "Sure," Marissa replies, but her tone is brisk, and she keeps walking.

"So . . . nothing's really wrong, but . . ."

No sentence that begins this way can be good. Marissa inhales deeply, thinking, Get to it, Polly.

"It's just that there's a little bit of a rodent problem in my rental house." Polly wrinkles her nose. "I can't stand mice. The landlord sent out a notice last night that the exterminator was coming today and that the problem should be resolved soon."

"One of the hazards of city living. My first place here had them, too."

"Ick, I just keep imagining their scrabbly little feet running over my stuff, and I—" Polly shudders. "It grossed me out so much. So I hope you don't mind but I—I slept here last night."

Marissa stops walking and twists to face her. "Excuse me?"

"I'm sorry. I didn't have anywhere else to go." Polly bites her lip.

Could this be true? Marissa realizes that in the month or so that Polly has worked for her, Polly has never mentioned a boyfriend or a night out with friends. Her parents live in Milwaukee, and as far as Marissa can tell, they've never visited. None of Polly's girlfriends have ever popped into the store, and Polly's cell phone rarely rings.

"I wasn't planning to do it, but I was lying in bed and I knew I wouldn't be able to sleep. I brought my yoga mat and a blanket here, and I tidied everything all up so no one would ever know. . . ."

That explains the messy ponytail, Marissa thinks. Polly would have used the bathroom sink to freshen up, but she couldn't shower and style her hair.

The kind thing—the magnanimous gesture—would be to invite Polly to stay with her for a few nights until this is sorted out. Marissa has an empty bedroom at home. More than that, she has an entire finished basement that is almost never used with a sofa bed and separate walk-out entrance and full bathroom.

Yet she can't bring herself to make the offer. The idea of Polly drinking out of their glasses and asking Bennett about his day at school and running her big, eager eyes all over Marissa and Matthew's belongings is too much.

"Sure, you can sleep here, provided it's just a few nights. It would be a problem beyond that. I believe there's a city code that prevents retail establishments from being used as residential space unless you have a permit." The last bit could actually be true, Marissa thinks.

"Oh, thank you! I ran out and got a muffin this morning, so I bought one for you, too. Morning Glory, with raisins and carrots, so it's superhealthy. And if there's anything else I can do—if you need me to do errands for you, or if you want me to come in earlier or work later or anything—"

"No, Polly, it's fine." The store will open in fifteen minutes, and Marissa does actually crave a cup of tea. But she wants to make it herself.

Thankfully, Polly returns to the front of the shop while Marissa steps into the back room and brews tea, leaving the muffin in its little white bag since she had scrambled eggs with Matthew and Bennett this morning. She sips her tea while she attends to her email, cherishing the quiet.

A customer comes in immediately after Coco opens, saying she needs a birthday present for a friend, and Marissa helps her choose a luxurious box filled with a variety of aromatic body oils. Marissa asks Polly to gift wrap it while Marissa rings up the customer, then Marissa turns her attention to the FedEx and UPS boxes and padded envelopes that are stacked on a table in the back room.

Polly has organized the packages by size, with the smaller ones on top and an oversize cardboard box on the floor. Marissa unpacks the smaller boxes, then bends down to test the weight of the one on the floor.

Polly rushes to her side, calling, "Let me lift that for you."

"I've got it." The box contains throw pillows; it's less than five pounds. Polly remains, practically hovering over her.

Marissa sets the box on the table. She needs to clear the air or she'll end up snapping at Polly. "You seem a little anxious today. And while I appreciate you offering to help, I can make my own tea and lift boxes."

"Oh, okay. I just want you to know I'm here. You know, if you're tired or queasy or whatever . . ."

"I feel fine." Marissa frowns. "What's going on?"

"It isn't—" Polly cuts herself off, her face crinkling, as if she's trying to suppress her emotions.

Please don't cry, Marissa thinks.

But Polly does the opposite. She breaks into a huge smile. "I know I shouldn't say anything, but I saw the box when I took out the trash from the bathroom this morning!"

For a moment Marissa has no idea what Polly is referring to, but then everything seems to stutter to a stop.

Polly saw the Clearblue pregnancy test Marissa purchased from CVS on Friday. Marissa hadn't realized the lettering on the box was visible through the plastic bag.

Had Polly innocently noticed the box when she'd tossed out the bin's contents? Or could she actually be digging through Marissa's garbage?

At least Polly didn't go so far as to open the box and examine the actual test stick; if she had, she would have seen the result was negative.

Marissa is frozen, unable to form a reply. She stares at Polly's thin lips—coated in a light pink gloss that nearly matches a shade Marissa frequently wears—while her assistant prattles on.

Thank God she didn't invite Polly to stay in her home.

Marissa clears her throat. "It was a false alarm." She hopes the sorrow she injects into her tone will keep Polly at bay.

"Oh, no, I'm sorry. I shouldn't have said anything."

No, you shouldn't have, Marissa thinks, but she merely nods and asks Polly to take the empty boxes out to recycling. She watches as Polly disappears through the back door, her ponytail bobbing, and wonders when Polly crossed the line from eager and a touch overly solicitous into intrusive. As with the decline of her marriage, it's hard to pinpoint.

Even in this short time Polly has come to know too much about Marissa. Polly has also met Matthew a few times, and she spent a couple hours with Bennett one Saturday afternoon when Marissa brought him in to help with a big customer mailing. Polly knows about Marissa's past, since Marissa has often discussed growing up by the ocean and working at Conner's. Polly knows about Marissa's current business dealings, her tastes and habits, and even her mild allergy to soy. Now that Marissa is allowing her to sleep at Coco, Polly is stepping ever deeper into Marissa's world.

Then there's that text Polly may have seen. **I know I shouldn't say this, but I can't stop thinking about our night.**

Polly could become dangerous.

CHAPTER THIRTEEN

AVERY

THE DAY AFTER MY VISIT with Natalie, Romeo and I are enjoying a late lunch—a Milk-Bone for him and take-out sushi for me—when the sound of a bell softly jingles on my phone. It's an alert: someone has stepped onto my front walkway and is approaching my door.

I'm expecting visitors, so this isn't an unwelcome surprise. Lana called a little while ago to say that she and Greg wondered if they could stop by: "I really want you and Greg to meet. Plus he *loves* dogs! I showed him all the pictures of Romeo you've sent. . . ."

It was obvious from her tone that she's completely smitten, and I'm glad for the chance to check out Lana's new boyfriend.

I take my last bite of tuna sashimi, then head into the kitchen to put the little paper box in my recycling bin, atop a few other take-out containers. I should go grocery shopping, but after so many years of cooking and washing dishes and cleaning mushy vegetables out of the refrigerator, the ability to stroll through my neighborhood and pick up nearly any cuisine that appeals to me—a Greek salad; chicken tikka masala; a burger and sweet-potato fries on days when I feel like indulging—is too satisfying to give up.

I walk back toward the front door just as the bell chimes. After Lana and Greg's visit, I've scheduled a first session with a new client, a thirty-five-year-old woman who just learned her birth mother was actually her older sister. Then I'm meeting Matthew and Marissa for their third session, the one I call Escalation.

Even though I'm certain who it is, I check the peephole before I unlock the door. Romeo barks a few times from behind my legs as I welcome Lana and Greg inside, but when I shush him, he stops. I give Lana a hug, then turn my attention to Greg. He's thin and a little taller than my five feet six inches, with fair skin and a dusting of light stubble. His jeans are loose around his hips, and he wears a soft flannel shirt beneath his jacket.

"Nice to meet you. I've heard so much about you from Lana," he says.

Polite, I think. He and Lana look sweet together.

As soon as I take their coats, Lana drops to her knees, gushing, "Oh, you're such a cutie-pie! Even more handsome than your photos. Can we pet him?"

"Sure. He's a little nervous but very friendly."

Romeo immediately takes to Lana, rolling over to let her rub his belly. Greg approaches him gently, slowly crouching next to Lana, which bumps up my estimation of him a notch higher, until I recall that Skip was good with Romeo, too.

Romeo's stubby tail stops wagging when Greg extends a hand, but after a moment Romeo sniffs Greg's fingers and gives him a lick.

After everything Romeo has been through, he still loves humans. It's a little humbling.

"Do you guys want something to drink?" I ask. "I've got coffee and, um . . . water . . ."

"Do you have any green tea?" Greg asks.

"I'd love some, too," Lana adds.

"Just English breakfast," I reply. Lana once told me she thought green tea tasted like dirty socks. Clearly she's following Greg's lead.

"Sounds great."

Lana nods along with Greg's words.

"This is a really nice house," Greg comments as we head through the living area into my sunny kitchen.

"Thanks." I put the kettle on to boil and pull three mugs out of a cabinet. "I love it, too. It's a little big for me to be knocking around in by myself, but I can't see moving anywhere else. At least not for now."

"By *yourself*?" Lana lifts up Romeo's paw and waggles it at me, affecting a gruff voice. "What am I, chopped liver?"

I laugh and grab a small bottle of stevia, which I know Lana will want to add to her tea—unless Greg takes his straight.

Lana is too needy when it comes to men, so eager to please them that it threatens her own sense of self. I've spoken with her about it, but I make a mental note to schedule a dinner with her and broach the topic again.

"Lana, is this where you grew up?" Greg is sitting on the tiled floor, stroking my dog's back, so instead of serving tea at the banquet, I plop down next to him.

"Yeah—well, sort of. My dad bought this place right after the divorce, so I split my time between here and my mom's apartment."

"Where did you grow up, Greg?" I ask.

"Baltimore." He doesn't add anything else, and something about the way he states that one-word answer makes me wonder how happy his upbringing was.

"Does your family still live there?"

He nods. "My mom and sister do."

In other circumstances I wouldn't press, but this isn't just a casual introduction. I want to get a sense of the man my stepdaughter appears to be infatuated with.

"And your dad?"

Greg shrugs. "He walked out when I was five. Haven't had much contact with him since."

"That must have been tough. . . ."

"Avery, please don't start to analyze Greg," Lana says playfully. "She's a therapist," Lana explains to Greg.

Was, I think. But I don't correct her.

"Oh, hey, can I tell you about the dream I had last night?" Greg quips, then takes a sip of tea. "So, can I see your room? Do you still have posters of Justin Bieber and Zac Efron on the walls?"

Lana's eyes find mine. Neither of us has gone into her old bedroom in a long time.

Lana clears her throat. "After my dad got sick, we set him up in there. Then . . ."

Her voice closes up; she can't complete her sentence and tell Greg about the rest. Greg reaches over and gives her hand a squeeze, and we sit in silence for a moment. I break it to ask if either of them wants more tea.

"No, thanks." Greg says.

Lana quickly shakes her head, too.

We chat awhile longer, then Lana says they need to get going.

Romeo and I walk them to the door and I hand them their coats. Greg holds out Lana's for her to slip into as she smiles up at him. He seems like a decent guy and clearly cares for her. At least she seems to have chosen well this time.

I give them both a quick hug and stand on my porch, watching as they walk hand in hand towards Lana's Honda.

As Lana starts to unlock the door, I notice a woman with dark hair approach them. I can't make out what they are saying, but I assume she's asking for directions.

Then I recognize her.

I fly off my porch and race down the front walk, surprise and anger roaring through me.

The woman who is mere inches away from my stepdaughter wears jeans and a parka, rather than a blue hospital gown. She looks fit and healthy now that she isn't propped up against a pillow with an IV dripping fluids into her system.

It's Cameron's ex-wife.

I thrust my body between hers and Lana's. "Skylar, what are you doing here?"

Skylar smiles, and I notice the ease of her transformation—from a demanding ex-wife to a seemingly friendly acquaintance.

"Avery! Oh, my goodness, what a small world. Do you live nearby?"

Lana edges around from behind me. "You two know each other? So funny!"

"We sure do." Skylar laughs. "Turns out Avery treated my husband. He's almost like a different person now."

"That's great," Lana replies as Greg nods in agreement. They're oblivious of the undercurrent running through this encounter. Although Lana knows I lost my license a few months ago because I'd changed my therapeutic methods, she has no idea that the woman standing in front of her is the one who reported me.

"I wish we had time to chat," I say pointedly.

Skylar ignores my rebuff. "I've always loved this street. I was just telling your"—a crease forms in her brow as she looks from me to Lana—"niece, is it? Or—"

"I'm her bonus daughter, Lana."

Stop talking! I think.

"And this is Greg, my boy—"

"It's nice to see you again, Skylar," I interject. "Unfortunately they need to get going."

Lana finally seems to pick up on the edge in my voice. "Oh, right, I've got to run—I'm working a pirate pottery party at four o'clock!"

"A pirate party?" Skylar repeats.

Before Lana gives Skylar any more information, I reach out and pull open the car door, nudging her inside. Greg walks around to the passenger side and hesitates, looking at me over the roof, before he slides in.

Without a coat or thick sweater, the cold is seeping through my body. I suppress a shiver. "Why are you really here?" I say over the sound of Lana's Honda starting up.

I take in her features, studying her thin eyebrows and lined lips, as the friendly mask drops from her face.

From behind me, Lana toots her horn once as she drives off, and I instinctively flinch.

Skylar grins—a different smile from the one she displayed moments ago. "You know so much about me. I guess I wanted to learn more about you. Your daughter seems sweet."

Skylar doesn't scare me, but I don't like her knowing about Lana's existence. I've never mentioned Lana in any interview or to any of my clients, even before my work began to earn me dangerous enemies.

I take a slow step toward Skylar, until I'm so close I can see the pores beneath her foundation. I barely recognize my own voice as I bite off the words: "Do not ever go near her again."

My hands are nearly numb, but I'm prepared to wait her out on the sidewalk until she's the first one to walk away.

Then Skylar makes a move I don't expect.

She reaches into her purse. I stare at her hand fumbling in her large leather bag, then slowly beginning to slide back out. Adrenaline surges through my veins as my mind spins through scenarios: Could she be reaching for a weapon?

Then I see a flash of white.

She's pulling out a pack of tissues.

"Your nose is dripping and it's disgusting." She offers me one.

I ignore it.

She shrugs and tucks the packet back in her purse. "I'm parked just around the corner." Skylar begins to walk away. "See you around."

I remain on the sidewalk, staring after her, until she turns the corner and disappears.

I'm still trying to push aside the strange encounter with Skylar when I meet with Marissa and Matthew for our third session. Romeo is crated in my bedroom with toys and acoustic rock music playing—hopefully far enough away that my clients won't hear if he decides to complain about the situation.

Fifteen minutes in, my legal pad contains the following notes: *On the couch—close enough to touch again . . . Mon Ami Gabi: wine, mussels, steak au poivre . . . I could maybe walk you home . . . More eye contact; relaxed body language . . . Marissa almost touches his arm, then withdraws her hand . . . Overturned canoe, turkey sandwiches floating in the water.*

I watch as Matthew captures his wife's hand just before it returns to her lap. Their fingers twine together.

I add one more note on my legal pad: *It can't be this easy.*

"Sounds like everything went flawlessly . . . ?" I put down my pen and let my voice trail off so one of them will fill in the blanks. Neither has mentioned Matthew's tardiness, or that they drove to the restaurant in separate cars.

"Look, I'll be honest," Matthew says. "Initially I didn't think I could do it. But"—he twists to face his wife—"I'm really glad I did."

"Me, too." Marissa's eyes are soft.

We could easily fill the remaining thirty minutes stretching out their loving reminiscences, rebuilding the foundation of their marriage on the blocks of their past shared happiness.

That doesn't interest me, and as important, it's not an efficient use of our limited time.

Marissa and Matthew walked through my door with a presenting problem: Why did a seemingly perfect relationship fall apart?

Their marriage is a mystery, and my job is to piece together the clues.

But something more is at stake here than simply a relationship in trouble; I just don't know what yet.

I put down my legal pad and lean back in my chair.

The third session is Escalation. The basic blueprint is the same for all clients, but I change up my methods based on what I sense will provoke my clients at a fundamental level. Matthew is private; I can already tell he's used to operating on a superficial level, leading with his charm.

I need to strip off that veneer. "Is that why you were late to dinner, Matthew? Because you planned not to go?"

"Wait—what?" Matthew's eyes narrow and he withdraws his hand from Marissa's. He recovers quickly from being surprised, which I mentally note but don't write down. "How do you know that? Were you *spying* on us?" He's good at shifting the focus, too, but I'm not going to let him derail my questions.

I smile. "I'm not sure I would phrase it that way exactly."

Marissa becomes an unexpected ally: "Matthew," she says pleadingly.

He shakes his head and blows out a breath. "Fine. Yes, as I said at first, I wasn't sure I had it in me."

"And then . . . ," I prompt.

The pause he doesn't rush to fill means he's considering what to say next. Which might also mean he's debating whether to answer honestly.

People tend to extend more trust to individuals who are attractive; studies have proven this. Right now, as I take in Matthew's athletic body, classic features, and straight white teeth, I wonder how much he has benefited from this advantage. It's one that his wife must also enjoy.

"And then I decided to meet Marissa, and when I arrived at the restaurant, I got a work call, which further delayed me. I had to stand outside and talk to one of my partners for a few minutes."

Matthew could be covering himself while appearing to be forthcoming. He's an intelligent man. He probably deduced that I wouldn't be observing from a table or booth inside the restaurant because of the risk I'd be spotted, plus there was no guarantee I'd be seated near them. Therefore, he must suspect I'd been watching from outside—which meant I already knew about the phone call.

Not just intelligent, I think. He's sharp. A man who sees all the angles and can think quickly on his feet.

"A work call on a Saturday night," I say mildly. "Must have been important."

"It was." Matthew bites off the words.

Is he angry at me, or is it simply the call itself that's causing his abrupt tone?

"Is this about the Coleman account?"

At Marissa's abrupt question, Matthew's eyes widen.

Interesting, I think as I watch his body language. He didn't know she knew.

Marissa has blindsided him again.

Matthew is getting hit with a lot of surprises—first by me, and now his wife—but to his credit, he merely shakes his head no.

Marissa isn't ready to let it go, however. "I ran into Natalie the other day and she mentioned you lost the client."

Natalie, again. Why does Matthew's ex-girlfriend know more about his business troubles than his own wife?

Matthew inhales deeply. "Yes, we lost the account. But it's not that bad—we're looking to land two more clients this month."

It's important to see how a couple argue—do they fight fair, or are they more focused on being "right" than working through the issue? Does one withdraw while the other flares up (my bet is that Marissa does the former while Matthew does the latter)?

So I turn things up a notch again.

"Marissa, Natalie knew about this before you?" I wince. "Ouch."

Marissa folds her arms across her body. "I just feel like Matthew has been shutting me out. We haven't been close in—well, in a while. Yes, I admit it hurts that he confided in Natalie." Marissa's perfectly poised, even in the midst of her anger and pain.

"*I* didn't tell her." Matthew looks at me, then turns toward his wife.

"So who did?" I probe.

Matthew shrugs. "I have no idea. She probably heard it from one of her clients. Natalie likes to gossip."

Marissa's face softens.

I speak before she has the chance. "Matthew, why would one of Natalie's clients tell her about *your* business?"

A beat of silence.

"She's right, Matthew, that doesn't make sense," Marissa says slowly. Her eyes glitter, but before I can determine whether it's from anger or tears, she blinks and the moment is gone.

"I don't know. There was an item in the trades—maybe she read it." He pauses. "Or look—honestly?—maybe it did slip out when I bumped into her a few weeks ago at that school thing."

"International Night?" Marissa interjects.

Matthew nods. "I can't remember any reason why it would have come up. But, come on, let's get real. Even if I told Natalie, that hardly compares to Marissa cheating on me."

His zinger lands; she shrinks a bit in her seat.

Given that the betrayal is still fresh in his mind, I can't expect Matthew to fight fair.

Still, he has proven that he comports himself fairly well under pressure. Now it's Marissa's turn.

"True," I muse. "Even if Matthew did confide in Natalie—even if he goes out to lunch with her later this week and flirts with her and relishes the memory of what she was like in bed—it wouldn't come close to the way you betrayed him."

Marissa's lips press tightly together.

"Do you think Natalie still wants you, Matthew?" I ask.

He smiles. He *likes* the question.

"Of course she wants him." Marissa's color is high; we've hit a nerve. "She never stopped wanting him."

"She's single, right?" I ask.

Matthew frowns. "How did you know that?"

"Just a hunch," I say lightly.

"We set her up with one of our friends last summer, but it didn't go anywhere," Matthew replies. "I don't think she was that into him."

"Because she's into *you*," Marissa says sharply.

Matthew rolls his eyes at his wife.

Over a decade of marriage, and he hasn't learned that an eye roll practically guarantees a marital fight? Maybe he's spoiling for one.

"Natalie still wants Matthew? How can you tell?" I urge Marissa on.

"We had dinner together after we fixed her up—the four of us. But it was like Matthew was the only one at the table. It's always like that with her."

"Come on, Marissa. That's ridiculous."

They're on the cusp. Then Marissa gathers herself.

"I admit it; I'm a little jealous. . . . And, yes, Matthew is perfectly free to have lunch with whomever he wants." Marissa bows her head. "I know we're not here because of Natalie."

It's as if she took a pin and popped a balloon; the swelling pressure in the room immediately evaporates.

"Marissa, I've never given her any reason to think she has a chance with me." The annoyance is gone from Matthew's tone.

"I know. And I'm sorry. I'm having an issue at work myself, and I'm a bit out of sorts."

Matthew claims Marissa's hand again. "What is it?"

"Polly"—Marissa glances at me—"she's my new assistant, and I'm thinking about letting her go."

I casually lift my pen and write down the name.

"What? I thought she was doing a great job."

"It's complicated." Marissa's fingers are moving; she's gently massaging Matthew's hand. "We can talk more about it later. I'd love your advice, actually."

Well done, I think, watching Marissa smile at her husband. Marissa defused their fight and owned her issues. She snatched her husband back, luring him away from the tantalizing words I dangled about his imagining Natalie in bed.

She was almost too perfect.

CHAPTER FOURTEEN

MARISSA

MARISSA ENVISIONED A DIFFERENT SORT of evening after the conclusion of their third session with Avery. She thought she and Matthew would enjoy a late meal at home, perhaps dining by candlelight. She'd purchased fresh salmon fillets and sweet potatoes, something she could assemble quickly while they sipped a glass of wine.

But Matthew had said he needed to return to the office for a couple of hours. So after paying Hallie and putting Bennett to bed, Marissa ate leftover spaghetti at the kitchen island.

She finishes wiping down the counters and turning on the dishwasher as rain begins to patter down softly in the night. Marissa cracks open the window above the sink; her skin feels dry, and she welcomes in the natural humidity.

She pours another two inches of red wine into her glass, then dims the lights and walks into the living room. Matthew won't be home for another hour or so. He'd called to say good night to Bennett and had told Marissa that he wanted to have breakfast as a family in the morning. *I love you,* Marissa had told him.

Sending you a hundred kisses, Matthew had replied just before he'd hung up.

She'd cringed, grateful he couldn't see her face.

Those words were the precise ones her husband had uttered on the phone on that *other* night, when he'd been in New York on business—just a few hours before she acted so recklessly, so thoughtlessly, so hurtfully, that she imperiled her marriage.

Marissa steps into the family room and places one hand on the back of the light gray sectional sofa.

She lifts up her wineglass, then tips it, splattering the dark liquid onto the middle cushion. She watches as the last drops slide out of her glass and join the widening puddle.

It looks like a bloodstain.

She walks unhurriedly back to the kitchen, grabbing a wad of paper towels, and after giving the stain a moment to set, she dabs at it.

The replacement couch—the one she ordered the morning after Avery conducted a session in this room—won't arrive for another week.

Tomorrow she'll show the ruined cushion to Matthew, lamenting that they won't even be able to donate it to Goodwill.

There are downsides to this plan. Matthew might be annoyed by her carelessness. He's the one who insists they only serve white wine and champagne for their indoor parties. Plus, she feels guilty about ruining a practically new piece of furniture, but Matthew would certainly question her if she said she simply wanted to redecorate.

It will be an enormous relief to have this sofa gone. She imagines the heavy-trash-receptacle collectors hoisting it up and feeding it into the crushing jaws on the back of the machine; the wood and metal frame splintering and the cushions collapsing.

Erasing the physical link to that night, but not her traitorous memories of the illicit hours she'd spent on it with the man she'd invited into their home.

You are even more beautiful now than you were as a teenager, he'd said, holding her eyes above the rim of his wineglass as he'd taken a sip.

Those words had sent a charge through Marissa; they'd filled a space inside her that she hadn't even recognized as being empty.

Stop! Marissa had laughed, leaning her head back on the sofa. She was in faded jeans and an old, oversize sweater, clothes she'd worn to Bennett's Cub Scout meeting that night. Her hair was up in a twist, and the light makeup she'd applied that morning had probably worn off. She hadn't planned to have anyone over that evening.

Bennett was asleep upstairs. Matthew was in New York, and she'd had a long day.

It's true, he'd said, flushing slightly as he fiddled with the slim woven white rope Bennett had been given by the scoutmaster to practice his square knots.

More wine? She'd leaned over for the bottle on the coffee table and topped off his glass.

They'd been talking for nearly an hour, and the bottle he'd brought was nearly empty.

He reached out with his strong fingers and ran one over the faint scar on the back of her hand, creating an electric path on her skin.

She'd suppressed a shiver.

I remember when you got this, he said.

She hadn't been touched that tenderly in so long.

He spoke her name softly, like a gentle invitation. His expression was filled with longing.

An invisible force seemed to pull them toward each other.

Just before their lips met, she closed her eyes.

It was breathtakingly intimate and passionate, Marissa thinks now as she stares down on the scar on her hand. And she'd never regretted anything so much in her life.

Marissa walks away from the ruined couch, toward the built-in bookshelves. She stands in the precise spot Avery had and also extends her hand to grasp a photo. Not the one of her and Matthew as teenagers on the dock, though.

Marissa chooses the one next to it. Her wedding photo.

She pulls the silver-framed image close as her eyes skim over the faces of her mom and dad; her brother, Luke; and Matthew's parents and sister, Kiki. Her two bridesmaids and Matthew's matching groomsmen flank the family members.

Marissa's eyes fix on one man in the photograph, the guy with the broad shoulders and hazel eyes. He was always around, casting fishing lines off the long wooden pier, tossing a beer to Matthew at bonfires, game for any water activity, and pulling a first-aid kit out of his Jeep to bandage up the back of Marissa's hand when she sliced it on an oyster shell by the water's edge.

There was never a man from the gym.

This is the secret she still keeps: the man in the wedding photograph is the person with whom Marissa betrayed her husband.

PART
TWO

CHAPTER FIFTEEN

AVERY

JUST A MAN I MET at the gym, Marissa had said during our first session.

It's 9:45 A.M. right now, the time of day Marissa usually departs Pinnacle Studio and heads to Coco to open the store. I arrived early for Pilates and have been lingering on a mat, stretching, since the class let out. Pinnacle is quiet; the prework rush is over. A few guys lift barbells in the weight room, and another is tearing up the treadmill. The friendly manager, who came over to introduce himself yesterday when I was bending over the water fountain to get a drink, is in his office chatting on the phone.

They all seemed like possibilities at first. But nothing is clicking.

The manager told me his husband taught a HIIT class that I had to try. The weight room guys—who barely look thirty—seem hyperfocused on their routines. And the runner doesn't even shift his gaze when an attractive woman in a crop top and leggings saunters by in front of his treadmill.

It's more than that, though. I've gotten to know Marissa, and my gut tells me she isn't the kind of woman to have a one-night stand with a mere acquaintance.

I'll bet anything she's still holding a big secret or two.

I hurry into the locker room and shrug on my light jacket—the first hint of spring is in the air, which I was especially grateful for on my early-morning walk with Romeo—then wave goodbye to the front-desk clerk (a college-age guy with a tattooed neck; Marissa would never go there) and push through the door, scanning my surroundings as I head back to my car.

As I pull into a parking spot across the street from Coco, I imagine I am Marissa Bishop: I've risen with the sun to make breakfast for my family in our luxurious kitchen. I've exercised and showered, and now I'm dressed for the day—let's say in a casually chic pair of dark-rinse jeans, suede ankle boots, and a fitted blazer. I'm about to enter my charming boutique—my favorite creation, after my son—where I'll chat with customers and select new inventory from vendors around the world. I'll likely run out to pick up a salad for lunch, and during slow moments I'll catch up on paperwork.

It's not the kind of life I'd ever want, but I know it's an enviable one for many women.

I've chosen this time of day to visit Coco because during our session last night, when I posed questions designed to better understand their daily routines, Marissa lamented that the upcoming school auction was infringing on her finely calibrated schedule. *My cochairs want to meet after drop-off tomorrow, but that means I'll probably get to Coco late.*

Matthew had pointed out that although Marissa was feeling increasingly annoyed by Polly, this was another reason to keep Polly employed, at least for a little while longer.

Polly should be here alone. It will be simple enough to say I'm searching for a present for my stepdaughter.

I stroll down the sidewalk, past a coffee shop and a dry cleaner's, my ears filling with the rush of cars passing by on Connecticut Avenue. I spot the royal-blue logo of Marissa's store painted on its glass-front windows and step inside, triggering a bell that jingles merrily. A young woman who must be Polly is talking to a male customer toward the back of the store. They're partially obscured by a pillar.

"Be right with you!" Polly calls, and her customer—tall, blond, wearing a dark suit—turns around.

It's Matthew.

I take a step closer to them just in time to see Matthew grab what appears to be a document off a glass table.

"Avery? Long time no see. What are you doing here?"

It's almost comical, the way he's hiding the paper behind his back—like a little kid caught sneaking a cookie.

"Hi, Matthew." I move closer to him with each word. "I suppose I could ask you the same question?"

"You two know each other?" Polly's head swivels between us.

Instead of answering her question, Matthew responds to mine. He uses his free hand to lift up a bouquet of red roses from the table. "Thought I'd surprise Marissa. If anyone is going to give my wife flowers, it's me. Unfortunately I forgot she has some auction thing at the school."

Marissa mentioned her committee meeting just last night, but Matthew has a lot on his mind.

I take a closer look at him. He seems tightly wound, as if he just drank a triple espresso; his body appears rigid and his jaw is clenched.

"Hi, I'm Polly. Marissa's assistant. Can I help you find something?"

She seems a bit hyped up, too. I can practically see the jittery waves radiating off her.

I wonder what I've interrupted and whom the flowers are really for. I take measure of Polly, just as I evaluated the men at the gym: young, skinny, big teeth, a voice that's a bit high-pitched—I can't see Matthew being interested.

As I reach this conclusion, Matthew releases a sigh. "Polly, I don't think Avery is here to shop. . . ." He turns to me. "Am I right?"

I nod. There's no point in lying; Matthew knows I've been probing aspects of his and Marissa's lives outside of my office.

Matthew says to Polly, "Avery is a—well, a therapist—who is helping Marissa and me."

His candor surprises me—especially since I'd recommended the Bishops keep my involvement in their life quiet for now. Plus, most guys wouldn't freely admit they're in counseling, and given my true title, Matthew didn't even need to explain my role in the Bishops' life at all.

Polly simply stands there, her hands clasped in front of her. She doesn't seem terribly surprised by the news, or by Matthew's having shared something so highly personal.

I fervently hope no other customers enter the store now. I need to understand the strange energy coursing around Matthew and Polly.

"Actually, Avery, maybe it's a good thing you showed up." Matthew slowly pulls the document from behind his back. It's an ordinary white piece of paper, the kind everyone uses to stock printers.

"Polly found this note slipped under the door this morning when she opened up."

Matthew places the single sheet on the table, and I look down at the words. They're typed in a large, bold font: **I'm not letting you go so easily. . . .**

I glance over at Polly. "Do you think it was meant for you?"

She shakes her head. "I was just telling Matthew that no one I know would have left me a note like that."

I look at the flowers in Matthew's hand, remembering the yellow roses that were sent anonymously to their home.

"You open and close the shop, right?"

Polly blinks, probably finding it curious that I know her schedule.

"So you left here at what—six P.M. yesterday?"

"Actually, last night . . ." Polly clears her throat and looks at Matthew. "I slept in the back room. Marissa knows—there's a mouse problem at my house."

"You spent the night *here*?" I ask.

Matthew doesn't appear shocked by this; Marissa must have explained Polly's situation to him.

"Yeah, I went out and got dinner, then watched a movie on my laptop until about eleven. I did a walk around right before I went to sleep because there's this mannequin head that was kinda creeping me out and I wanted to put a jacket over her"—she gives an embarrassed giggle—"and I know the note wasn't there then."

So it was delivered later last night, or early this morning.

"Look, it's obviously for Marissa." Matthew's fist tightens as he crumples the paper, just as he crushed the plastic cup in my office during our first session. "That guy from the gym—"

I interrupt, "Have you told Marissa about the note?"

Matthew shakes his head and smooths out the note.

"I could call her," Polly offers.

"Please hold off." I touch Matthew's sleeve. "Why don't we talk privately?"

Polly lingers, not taking the hint, and I'm struck by the thought that instead of being on the fringes of the Bishops' life, as she should be, she's actually deeply entangled in it. As is Natalie. And perhaps others I don't yet know about.

I lead Matthew outside the shop. We stand on the sidewalk, facing each other.

"Start from the beginning. Tell me what happened this morning."

Matthew rocks back on his heels. "I had a breakfast meeting at our country club. It's just a few miles from the house. So I was driving to work later than usual, and when I stopped at a light, a guy was walking up and down the median strip, selling flowers from a bucket. Gotta be a rough job. So I bought a dozen. Figured I'd drop them off here, surprise Marissa."

I study his body language, but it tells me nothing. One of his hands is down at his side, and he's gesturing with the other.

Matthew claimed he'd forgotten that Marissa had a school meeting. Normally, at this time of day, she'd be just arriving here from the gym. I haven't run into her during any of my workouts, so I assume she's avoiding the place. But Matthew may not know that.

Was he trying to spring a trap on his wife, appearing at her shop unannounced to see if she'd resumed her routine at Pinnacle?

"When I rang the buzzer, no one answered. I started to unlock the door—I've got an extra key—thinking I'll leave the flowers on her desk. Then I see Polly coming toward me, and after she let me in, we both saw the note on the floor."

I stretch out my hand. "May I have it?"

He frowns, but gives it to me. I study the message again. The words could lend themselves to different meanings—romantic, passionate, committed—but given the circumstances, they feel ominous.

"Look, Matthew, even if this"—I shake the paper—"is from that guy, it doesn't mean that Marissa is still interested in him. The note actually implies the opposite."

Matthew nods. "Yeah, I suppose. I mean, Marissa does seem like she wants to work things out. I can't see her stringing him along."

It's as if the crux of the Bishops' problem—a seemingly straightforward infidelity—is growing tentacles that keep ensnaring new complications.

There's a lot I need to do, fast: talk to Polly one-on-one. Explore the exact nature of Matthew and Natalie's relationship. Confront Marissa with my near certainty that the man she slept with was not just some guy from the gym.

"You told Polly not to say anything to Marissa. What are we supposed to do, just pretend this never happened? Because that's not going to work for me."

I hear a faint hitch in his voice. He sounds like a man who loves his wife and feels battered by emotions.

It's a good thing the Bishops came to me. There's no way they could have navigated this alone.

I'm about to answer Matthew when I catch a glimpse of Marissa hurrying down the block. Her head is down as she taps on her phone, so I take a moment to study her. With her oversize dark sunglasses and the silky floral scarf tied off-center around her neck, she looks effortlessly stylish. She passes a homeless man on the corner, then lifts her chin.

She stops in her tracks, her eyes widening, as she spots Matthew and me. Then she continues walking, at a slower pace, until she reaches us.

"Perfect timing," I announce. "Our fourth session begins now."

The gentle beauty of the March morning feels incongruous to the tense mood enveloping the three of us as we walk in silence up Connecticut Avenue, toward Chevy Chase Circle. The sun is warm and welcoming on my face, and the gentle breeze holds the smell of the hyacinths lining the window boxes of a café we pass. We reach the circle and carefully make our way through the crosswalk, entering the little plot of land straddling the line that divides D.C. and Maryland. The circle once held a majestic fountain that spouted water high into the air, but now it's broken, and just the concrete base remains, surrounded by azalea bushes and trees. Cars and trucks whip through the triple lanes that surround the little oasis; it's like being in the eye of a hurricane. Instead of sitting down on one of the benches, we remain standing in an asymmetrical triangle, facing one another.

"What's going on?" Marissa asks.

I hand the note to Marissa with the briefest of explanations: "This was slid under the door of your shop sometime between eleven P.M. and nine thirty A.M."

I take in her expression as she reads it: shock, then dread.

"Matthew." She swallows hard and her fingertips begin to play with the scarf around her neck. "I don't know what to say."

"So you assume this is for you, and not Polly?" I ask.

Marissa flinches. "It could have been, of course. But Polly isn't dating anyone and she hasn't ever mentioned a man pursuing her."

Her rationale for her assumption is smooth and logical. But Marissa's reaction to the note was raw and unfiltered, and that told me more. She immediately knew it was meant for her, and not by a process of elimination.

"Marissa, you answered several important questions for me during our first session," I say. "If there's anything you haven't revealed, we need to know it right now."

She shakes her head. "I swear. It was just that one time. It's over. I don't know why he won't—"

She cuts herself off. Was she going to say, *Won't leave me alone?* I wonder. Which begs the question, *What else has he done?*

"Maybe it's over for you, but obviously not for him," Matthew interjects sharply. "Read what he wrote: *He's not letting you go!*"

"Matthew, let's—" I begin.

"C'mon, Avery, with all due respect, look at the facts here. This guy knows where my wife works. He probably knows where we live. He could be dangerous."

"He's not dangerous," Marissa interrupts.

"How do you know that? He's just some random guy, right? I mean, how well could you really know him?"

Matthew's tone is sincere. I wonder how long it'll be before he starts to suspect Marissa hasn't told us the entire truth.

If anyone is going to give my wife flowers, it's me.

Matthew's phone pings and he pulls it out of his pocket. "Fuck it. I'm late for a client meeting. He flew in from Switzerland. You know what would be almost as bad as losing you, Marissa? Losing my job. I gotta go."

Marissa wipes her eyes as Matthew retraces his steps, back toward Coco.

I study her as she stares after her husband. I've never seen Marissa like this: her mascara is streaked, and her face looks pale and a little hollow, as if she has dropped a few pounds she can't afford to lose.

"Are you ready to tell me what's really going on?" I ask her.

A puzzle I've been wrestling with is how the opportunity for infidelity presented itself to Marissa. The natural intersections in her life for her to meet men are few. Coco caters to women, and all but one of her vendors are all in other states or overseas. Her son's private school, where she's involved as a volunteer, hasn't any eligible candidates—no handsome soccer coach or intriguing male teacher. I've checked. Even the math tutor she just hired is female.

Natalie mentioned some good-looking dads at Rolling Hills, but Marissa wouldn't risk entangling her son in something as sordid as a fling.

Other than Marissa's boutique and Bennett's school, her present life revolves around Matthew. Which leads me to conclude that the man she slept with is almost certainly from her past.

I wait for her to speak, but she just shudders and wraps her arms around herself.

For most of my clients, the fourth session—Revelation—means finally acknowledging lies. Either ones they've told themselves, or lies other people have convinced them to believe. Marissa's revelation, one that should hit her hard, is that she is betraying not only her husband, but herself and me, by continuing to conceal the truth. That's something I won't stand for.

"Marissa, this isn't working," I say crisply. "I'll send you a final bill for today. Good luck."

I turn on my heel and walk away.

CHAPTER SIXTEEN

MARISSA

Marissa watches as Avery stands at the head of the crosswalk, waiting for a break in traffic to venture across the busy lanes of traffic, and out of Marissa's life forever.

Her head throbs and a wave of dizziness passes through her. Last night, she woke abruptly at 3:00 a.m. and lay there until dawn, while Matthew slept beside her, unaware. She nibbled on a half piece of dry toast this morning and drank too much coffee.

Her secret is a rough, tight knot in her stomach.

She can't continue like this.

"Wait!" she calls out.

Avery doesn't turn around.

"Avery, please!"

Maybe it's the tone of Marissa's pain-filled cry that captures Avery's sympathy, because she pulls back the foot she was about to plant in the street.

Avery twists to face Marissa and studies her for a moment, then walks back.

"It wasn't a man from the gym. That guy doesn't exist," Marissa blurts.

Avery nods. "He's from your past, right? Someone you met at college, or maybe your hometown."

The color drains from Marissa's face. "How did you . . . ?"

"Matthew knows him, too." Avery says this as a statement, not a question.

Marissa wraps her arms around her waist and begins to shiver. "Yes," she whispers. "We've known each other forever."

Avery exhales. "You should have told me. We've wasted so much time working under a false pretense."

"I'm sorry. Please, you have to help me. I'll do anything to fix this."

"What else have you lied about?" Avery asks abruptly. "Did you sleep with him more than once? Maybe it went on for a couple weeks. Or longer . . . ?"

"No!" Marissa cries. She feels as if she were on the witness stand, being cross-examined. And she's guilty, she knows she is, but only of that single infidelity.

"He's always had a thing for you. You like the attention. Maybe you led him on, flirted behind Matthew's back. But now he's hooked on you, and he's a problem that won't go away."

Nausea fills Marissa's throat. How can Avery know so much? Marissa *had* liked the attention, but she never flirted, either in or out of Matthew's presence. And not because she didn't have the opportunity. The man she'd cheated with had been woven through most of their lives: When she was just a kid, he'd taught her to bodysurf the waves. They'd shared beers on sandy blankets, and he and Matthew used to race each other out to the floating dock. On her wedding day, he'd worn a tuxedo and stood beside the other men, and when Bennett was born, he sent a gigantic stuffed dog from FAO Schwarz. She has sat across from him at dinners dozens of times—and, yes, she has looked up and caught his longing eyes lingering on her face.

And just weeks ago—on the night this sordid mess all began—he phoned to say he was in the neighborhood, and a few minutes later she opened her front door to see him standing on her stoop with a wide grin and a bottle of Malbec tucked under his arm.

"He wasn't ever my boyfriend," Marissa tells Avery now. "But . . . he was my first kiss."

His lips had felt warm and soft on hers. She'd caught the scent of the wintergreen Life Savers he'd always loved before she drew away. It was over in a moment, yet it felt as if it had the potential to change everything.

But then Tina had been killed and the whole world seemed to turn upside down. It didn't take long for their high school English teacher to be arrested—everyone agreed, after the fact, that he'd always been creepy—and afterward, the connection Marissa had felt seemed to evaporate. "If Matthew finds out, it will kill him." Marissa can hardly bear to say the words aloud. "I'm not hiding it just to save my marriage. It's to protect Matthew. How could he ever recover from that?"

A screeching noise erupts, and both women whirl around in time to see a small brown car narrowly avoid rear-ending a delivery van.

"This circle is a nightmare," Avery observes. "Accidents happen here all the time."

Marissa reaches for the arm of a bench and eases herself down. She's so light-headed she could faint. Avery knows everything now, and there's no predicting what she'll do. She could call Matthew at this very moment and blurt it out.

Matthew wouldn't come home tonight, or ever again. He'd divorce her; Marissa feels certain of that.

"Here's what we'll do," Avery finally says, and Marissa holds her breath. "You can keep this one secret for now, but this"—Avery points to the note still in Marissa's hand—"has to stop. Tell him you need to see him."

"Won't that only encourage him?"

"It will be a brief meeting. He'll get the message loud and clear."

Marissa briefly closes her eyes as her body sags in relief. "Thank you."

"Text him now. One line: Can we meet today?"

Marissa pulls her phone from her purse and types the message.

Almost immediately, three dots appear on her screen. "He's texting back."

She waits, holding her breath, then reads the reply: **I'm in L.A. all week. How's Friday night or anytime over the weekend? I'll clear my schedule.**

"Clear my schedule," Avery repeats, shaking her head. "He really does have it bad for you. Obviously you're not going to meet him over the weekend because you'll be focused on your husband. Text him back and tell him you'll see him at noon on Monday at the coffee shop down the street from your store."

Marissa frowns, her hand hovering over her phone.

"What?" Avery prompts.

"It's just that he's in California . . . but I guess he must've pushed that note under my door before he left."

"Probably on his way to the airport early this morning."

"Noon on Monday at Java Nation," Marissa repeats as she types the message. The appointment feels like both a reprieve—because it's almost a full week away—and a punishment.

"Between now and then, do not reply to any texts he sends. Do not answer the phone if he calls."

Marissa nods.

"Put him completely out of your mind. And let me know if he does try to contact you."

"But what am I going to say when I see him?"

"That's what you've hired me for."

Marissa has barely stepped inside Coco when Polly rushes to her side, bombarding her with rapid-fire questions: "Who would have left that note? . . . Should we keep the door locked during the day? . . . Do you think it's safe for me to sleep here?"

Marissa massages her temples. "I have no idea. . . . I don't think it's necessary. . . . That's up to you. . . ."

"It was the craziest thing!" Polly puts a hand to her chest as Marissa begins to walk away. "I heard the buzzer, and even though it was a little early, I went to open the door. Right after I saw Matthew through the glass, I noticed the piece of paper. Matthew almost stepped on it when I let him in."

The anonymous note is clearly the most exciting thing that has happened to Polly in a while. Her cheeks are flushed and her eyes are bright.

The throbbing in Marissa's head worsens.

"I put Matthew's flowers in a vase," Polly calls unnecessarily, as Marissa has already hurried into the back room and spotted the roses.

Their sickly sweet smell permeates the small area. Marissa appreciates Matthew's gesture, but the flowers look a little wilted and brown around the edges. They're not nearly as lush as the bouquet she received just a few days ago.

Her hand shakes as she uses a box cutter to slice open UPS packages and takes out cotton sweaters that just arrived from Santa Monica. She'd ordered them weeks ago, thinking their bright stripes would be perfect for spring. But now the jaunty colors seem garish, and she wonders if her judgment is off.

"Do you want some tea?"

Marissa starts at the sound of Polly's voice. "I'm fine." Marissa doesn't glance up. Why can't Polly take a hint?

Marissa's phone pings and she snatches it out of her purse. She'd texted Matthew as she retraced her steps from the Chevy Chase Circle back to Coco: **Hope your day goes well. . . . I love you.**

It's just an email from Natalie. In the hour or so since the conclusion of this morning's auction meeting, Natalie has already sent along the minutes and created a spreadsheet with action tasks assigned to each committee member. Marissa is supposed to ask her vendors to donate additional goods for the event, even though the school already has more than 150 pieces for the silent bidding.

This is Natalie's first time on the benefit committee, and she has made it clear that she wants to set a record for profits. Marissa closes the email without reading it through to the end.

Marissa is searching for a missing invoice for her accountant and fighting the urge to check her phone again when Polly pokes her head into the room. "You sure I can't pick you up a salad or a sandwich?"

"No. Thank you," Marissa replies in a tight voice.

"Well, if you need anything, I'm just up front. I'm going to start wrapping the bridesmaids' gifts for the Webster wedding."

Marissa can sense Polly's presence; her young assistant is hovering in the doorway. "I was just thinking. About that message. It's so creepy! Should we call the police?"

"No!" Marissa's tone is knife sharp. She spins around to face Polly. "Actually, Polly, I do need something."

Polly's face lights up.

"I need you to answer a question for me. Why did you show that note to Matthew?"

"Uh . . . like I said, he was right there when I saw it—"

Marissa cuts her off. There's no reply Polly can give that will better the situation. If Polly were a different sort of person—thoroughly professional and discreet—Matthew might not ever have known about the note.

Her husband is smart. He could very well be working his way to the same conclusion Avery already reached about the sender.

"You have no idea what you've done," Marissa's voice catches on her last word.

"I'm so sorry, Marissa, but I—" Polly's lower lip is trembling and her eyes shine with tears.

Marissa can't manage Polly's feelings now. She can't even be around her for another minute.

The intrusions, the borrowed earrings, the mimicry. It's too much.

"Why don't you leave for the day," Marissa snaps. "Actually, don't come in for the rest of the week. I'll pay you for your usual hours."

"What?" Polly looks utterly stricken.

"I think you should take some time off."

Polly begins to babble. "I didn't mean to—"

Thankfully, Marissa's ringing phone cuts her off.

It's a client who wants to place a special order. "Hold on just one second and let me get to my computer," Marissa says into the phone. She mutes the call. "Polly, I'll be in touch soon."

Before Polly can say another word, Marissa turns all of her attention back to her caller.

The first few hours without Polly are like a holiday. Only two customers stop by, so Marissa has the luxury of sipping tea and straightening every last shelf, drawer, and surface in her shop. She hadn't realized how pervasive Polly's presence was in the shop; how *watched* Marissa felt. Alone with her thoughts, she begins to formulate what she'll say to Matthew tonight. She'll suggest another date night this weekend, so they don't lose the progress they've made.

But the moment Marissa checks the calendar on her computer, her hard-fought peace vanishes. Matthew's overseas client will be here all week, and Matthew will be working late every night. Bennett has a baseball game at three today that Marissa planned to attend. Plus, she has a dental checkup on Thursday, and there's another auction meeting Friday morning. The only options Marissa has are to cancel everything, to shut down the shop while she's away, or apologize to Polly and ask her to come back.

Marissa looks around her tranquil, gorgeous store. She's tempted to hang a little sign on her door explaining the hours have been adjusted, but that's a guaranteed way to upset customers. She needs Polly here this week. Marissa will blame her irritability on the events of the past few days. Polly will probably understand: the pregnancy disappointment, Marissa's lack of sleep, the ominous note . . . But Marissa will simultaneously step up her search for a permanent replacement. She has already reached out to a few friends to see if they know anyone who might be looking, but she hasn't received any promising replies. Marissa takes a moment to craft an email to the career placement center of George Washington University, asking if she can post a listing.

Then she dials Polly's number. It goes straight to voice mail: "Hi, this is Polly. I'm out and about. But if you leave your number, I'll give you a shout."

Even Polly's rhyming message irritates Marissa, but she simply asks Polly to please call her back as soon as possible.

Marissa helps a young man choose a cashmere blanket for his girlfriend and a woman on her lunch break select gorgeous bookends for her secretary. Even though the woman shops at Coco every few weeks, Marissa can't recall her name. If Polly were there, she'd prompt Marissa. Polly made it a point to learn all of the details about their frequent customers.

Ringing the woman up, Marissa glances at the name on the credit card. "Bye, Carole," Marissa calls out as her customer exits the store.

Then Marissa dials Polly again. Still no answer. This time, Marissa doesn't leave a message.

Marissa glances at her watch: Bennett's game is at St. Albans's field.

She wants to send Matthew pictures of their son playing, not only because he'd love to see them, but also as a reminder of all they've built together.

But she can't man the store *and* attend the game.

Polly still hasn't phoned back. And Matthew hasn't texted.

Marissa reaches for her laptop computer and searches her email files until she finds the résumé Polly submitted when she applied for the job. She lives near American University, just off Massachusetts Avenue.

The cursor blinks on Marissa's computer screen as she calculates time and distance, mentally reorganizing her afternoon. Polly probably went home, even given the rodent issue. She'd mentioned to Marissa that she would be stopping by her house every day to shower and grab a change of clothes. Perhaps she's in the shower now, which is why she isn't answering her phone. If Marissa closes Coco and leaves immediately, she could get to Polly's, convince her assistant to come back, and still make it to the field in time for the second inning.

She removes her coat from the hook inside her office, flips the store's OPEN sign to CLOSED, and types the address into Google Maps. It's a seventeen-minute drive, according to the app.

Marissa makes it in fifteen.

She pulls up to the curb outside the small brick rancher and looks at the house. Polly is a major player in Marissa's world, but this is the first time Marissa has entered Polly's orbit.

It's a pleasant-looking place. The yard has recently been mowed, and though the home is modest, the screened-in porch must be nice to sit in during the bug-filled summer evenings. Marissa hurries up the front walk and presses the doorbell.

She can hear music playing inside—the folksy jangle of the Grateful Dead—then an unfamiliar female voice calls, "Who is it?"

"I'm looking for Polly Walker. Is she here?"

The door opens, revealing a young woman with frizzy brown hair and glasses. "Sorry, who are you?"

"Marissa Bishop."

Clearly the housemate has no idea who Marissa is. "Polly works for me."

The woman pushes her glasses up on her nose as she examines Marissa more closely.

"Oh, right, at the real estate company? Anyway, she's not here. Sorry."

Behind her Marissa can hear laughter and then a male voice shouts, "Is it the pizza guy?"

"Nah, someone for Polly," the woman calls back. Then she turns back to Marissa. "Maybe she's in class?"

Had Polly once mentioned she was taking a design course? Marissa can't remember. She knows so little about her assistant—she didn't even remember Polly once had a job in real estate—even though she has asked Polly about her life from time to time. But Polly, so seemingly artless in some ways, is adept at always turning the conversation back to Marissa.

"Please tell her I stopped by and would love for her to call. And if the exterminator isn't finished, she can stay at the store tonight."

"Exterminator?"

The words die in Marissa's throat before she can utter them. *For the mouse problem.*

There is no mouse problem, she realizes with a start. Polly fabricated that story.

The question filling Marissa's mind is, Why?

CHAPTER SEVENTEEN

AVERY

"SO, HOW ARE YOU HOLDING up?" My primary care physician, Dr. Hernandez, fixes me with warm brown eyes. I've been seeing her for years, since I was in grad school. She guided me through a cancer scare—the lump in my breast was benign—as well as my thyroid issue and has seen me transform from a single woman, to a married one, to a widow. Now I sit in her private office, with a view of the Potomac River and a vase of irises on her uncluttered desk, for my annual wellness visit.

Dr. Hernandez is in her early sixties, and wears a slim gold band on her ring finger. A photograph of her with her wife is on her desk, and I sometimes wonder if her life is as serene and well-ordered as it appears.

"Pretty well," I say.

"Are you still taking the trazodone? Do you need a refill?"

"I'm okay."

The truth is I never even picked up the prescription she gave me shortly after Paul's death. I know Dr. Hernandez meant well when she suggested the antidepressant. *It'll help with your sleep and anxiety.*

Like everyone else, my doctor assumed Paul's death would upend my world. And it did, but not in the way she anticipated.

My feelings about Paul are complicated, though their jagged edges have softened with time. I am grateful I never told Paul I was planning to move out, so I could at least spare him that emotional pain, even if I couldn't rid him of his physical suffering. And I will never regret caring for him during those final months.

Before Paul got sick, I'd drafted a different ending for us; I assumed that after the bumpiness of our divorce, we'd become friends. I didn't know if either of us would remarry, but we'd always be linked by our years together, and through our love for Lana. I could see us consulting on patients, and perhaps sharing holiday dinners now and then.

But we don't always get to write our own stories.

Paul was robbed of his second act. But I can't deny that I'm enjoying mine.

Maybe it sounds selfish, but I sleep better these days, alone in my bed, than I ever did by Paul's side, even before he got sick. The vibe in my house is no longer dictated by his mercurial moods.

Most of all, I find relief in not having to be accountable to anyone. I can book a client for any hour, get a massage during dinnertime, spontaneously meet a friend at 8:00 P.M. for cocktails—then stay out even later if I meet someone interesting.

When my husband died, my life opened up. It isn't the right thing to say, which is one of the reasons why I've never said it to anyone.

"Uh, I actually haven't been taking it," I tell Dr. Hernandez. "I adopted this dog, Romeo, and that's really helped. The extra exercise and companionship."

My implication is that I adopted Romeo shortly after Paul's death, rather than just last week. I don't enjoy misleading Dr. Hernandez, but it's easier this way.

"Okay . . . how are you eating?"

"Pretty well. I'm not getting my seven servings of fruits and veggies a day, or whatever they recommend, but who really does that?"

She smiles. "It's nine. Just do the best you can. What about drinking? How many units of alcohol would you say you consume per week?"

"Five or six." I watch as she types the information into her laptop. "Actually, it's probably more like ten or so. Does everyone undercount when they come in here? You should probably just double whatever people say to be safe."

This gets her to laugh.

"And before you ask, yes, I occasionally smoke a joint or take a gummy. But that's it. No hard drugs."

"A little pot won't hurt, as long as it's not too often." She finishes typing and looks up at me. "Anything else you want to discuss?"

This is the part I've been dreading. "Yeah, when you're running my blood work, would you mind just adding on a test for any STDs?" I force myself to look Dr. Hernandez in the eye as I fib, "There was this one guy. . . ."

I'm not going to tell Dr. Hernandez I've been with a few men since Paul died. People feel comfortable with the image of a grieving widow; they're far less generous when someone strays from the confines of that perception.

"Avery, this is a doctor's office, not a courtroom." She puts a hand on my shoulder. "As long as you're taking care of yourself, I'm not here to judge."

Not for the first time, I'm struck by the thought that I could be friends with Dr. Hernandez under other circumstances.

After the physical exam, I check out at the front desk, then step out of her office and walk down the short corridor to the elevator and press the call button. It's late morning, and though several other medical professionals occupy space on this floor, I'm the only one waiting.

I pull out my phone to check my email, still looking down at my screen when the elevator arrives.

I step inside and press P3, then type a response to a client who wants to switch her appointment time later this week. Just as the doors begin to close, a man's arm shoots through them, forcing them back open. I hadn't even noticed him in the narrow hallway.

I tuck my phone back into my purse and step aside to let him choose his floor. He avoids eye contact with me and doesn't even seem to glance at the button panel. Instead, he merely moves to the far corner.

There's a 25 percent chance we could have parked on the same level, since the lot only has four. Still, I shift my body so I can see him in my peripheral vision. He's wearing a suit and tie with an overcoat, but he doesn't carry a briefcase.

Something is off; he's staring at me now.

It all happens so quickly that before I can act, the doors close, sealing the two of us together. I mentally kick myself: Like many women, I've placed my desire to be polite ahead of my need to protect myself. I should simply have stepped out of the elevator and waited for the next one.

My body prepares for a threat. I edge forward until my hand is by the control panel. If he tries anything, instead of pressing EMERGENCY STOP, which would trap me, I plan to push the buttons for every single floor, as well as the one labeled EMERGENCY CALL.

We reach P3 and the doors slide open. I exhale the breath I've been holding.

The man waits to exit until I step out. Many guys do this; it's considered gentlemanly. Still, I don't like having him behind me again.

It's a bright day outside, but the underground lot is dim and shadowy. The parking attendant who'd handed me my ticket on the way in is several stories above us, well out of earshot.

I walk toward my BMW, adrenaline thrumming through my body. In the distance I can see there aren't any other vehicles parked near mine, so the man should be heading in a different direction. But unless I turn around, it's impossible to tell. The tapping of my heels on the cement is amplified in the subterranean lot, and I can't hear any other noises. Right before I reach my car, I steal a look behind me and my pulse explodes.

He's just a few feet away. He has been keeping pace with me this whole time.

That crisp, expensive-looking suit and his blank gaze—they unnerve me. This man is targeting me; I'm done being polite.

I whip around to face him. "Can I help you?" I ask, aiming for the fiercest tone I can muster.

His voice is so low I can barely make out his words: "Just give us the name."

He's from Acelia. They still think I might give Finley up. But I never will. I fumble in my purse for my fob, chastising myself for not having it out earlier, keeping my eyes glued on the man. He could be carrying a gun, its shape concealed by his overcoat.

"You volunteered information. Who told you?"

My hand gropes inside my purse again, feeling my wallet and makeup bag and phone—and, finally, the hard metal edge of the can of Mace attached to my key chain.

"It can be very simple, or you can make it complicated."

Adrenaline floods my limbs. If he is going to come after me, he'll do it now. I have a plan for that, too—I'll blast him in the face with Mace, then hit the alarm button on my fob. I'll go down fighting; there's no way I'll let him abduct me from my own car.

I suck in a shallow breath, my body tense.

He remains immobile. "We won't stop. And it can get much worse."

I back up until I feel the edge of my fender, then in one furious, fluid motion, I unlock the driver's-side door, slide inside, and instantly lock it again.

He stares at me through my window, still expressionless. But he hasn't made a move toward me.

I reverse out of the parking space, nearing sideswiping him, then speed up the circular ramps. When I reach the attendant, I'm about to tell him about the strange man. But what crime can I report the guy for? Getting on an elevator with me and riding it to the same level?

It takes a while for my body to unclench. The thought of going home and curling up with Romeo is tempting, but I've got a full day, and I'm not going to let Acelia steal it from me.

As I wind my way through the streets of D.C., heading toward Maryland and the café I want to scope out before Marissa's meeting with her ex-lover, a thought strikes me.

How did that man know where to find me today?

Is there a tracker on my car? Could they have hacked my computer? A wave of dizziness engulfs me and I pull over to the side of the road.

I flick on my hazard lights and crack my windows to let in the cold, bracing air. It's after noon and I haven't eaten anything today or even had coffee—standard procedure before an annual physical—which is making it difficult to think clearly.

Perhaps they simply followed me here, I think.

It takes me a moment to come up with another possibility.

The words *Dr. Hernandez* and *10 a.m.* were in the appointment book I keep on my desk, the book with the striped ribbon.

The one I'm now certain Skip checked out when he came to my place on Friday night.

CHAPTER EIGHTEEN

MARISSA

MARISSA WATCHES THE SPINNING, dipping baseball arc into center field, then bounce roughly against the grass.

She breathes a sigh of relief as Bennett scoops it up. It's the bottom of the second inning, but neither team has yet scored, and she got here in time to see Bennett make a good play. Matthew hasn't replied to her text, Marissa had to shut down Coco for the afternoon, and she has no idea what to do about Polly, but at least this one thing is right in her world.

She continues walking toward the bleachers, waving at a cluster of parents, as she watches her son twist and hurl the ball to second base, his aim straight and true.

Her heart gives a little leap. Bennett is really improving in baseball.

"Good job!" she calls, starting to applaud.

Then she stops.

The thin, light-haired boy who made the play isn't her son.

Maybe Coach Santo put Bennett in a different position, she thinks. Marissa missed last week's game, but Bennett told her he'd played well. She peers into the distance, trying to make out each player's face. It's hard to tell who's beneath the identical red baseball caps, but she finally spots Bennett. He's hunched on the dugout bench next to a boy with a cast on his arm.

"Marissa!"

She lifts her head at the sound of her name. It takes a moment for her to place the mom who waves her over. It's Carrie, whose son Lance plays first base and opts to wear his older sister's hand-me-down pink cleats, a detail that endears him to Marissa.

"Come, sit. Ooh, I love your jacket." Carrie gives Marissa a quick, hard hug.

Her warmth takes Marissa by surprise; Marissa unexpectedly feels on the verge of tears and is grateful for her sunglasses. Marissa hasn't made any close friends at the school, but she has always had the impression that Carrie is funny and kind. Marissa has a faint recollection of Carrie's once suggesting they grab lunch. Marissa never followed up on it, though. It feels like another in a long list of her mistakes.

"It's good to see you," Marissa says, squeezing into the crowded row.

Carrie has a big snack bag between her feet, with sliced oranges in a giant Ziploc and individual packets of trail mix studded with pretzels, raisins, and bright M&M's. Marissa's stomach growls and she realizes she has barely eaten today.

"Is Bennett okay?" Carrie asks.

A player from the opposing team hits a pop fly, and the pitcher makes a diving catch, ending the inning. The parents applaud—one man who, Marissa surmises, is the pitcher's father stomps his feet against the bleachers—and the players run in to end the inning.

"I thought so," Marissa tells Carrie. "Maybe I should go check."

A woman seated in front of them turns around, her glossy blond ponytail swinging against her shoulder. She frowns, but no creases form in her perfect skin. "I wasn't here last week, but Jacob says he didn't play then either."

"Hi, Dawn," Marissa says, trying to keep the resignation from her tone. Dawn is also on the auction committee—Marissa sat across from her at this morning's meeting—and she seems to be one of Natalie's many hangers-on.

Marissa turns to Carrie. "Is that true? Did Bennett sit out last week?"

Dawn stays twisted around, clearly more interested in the scene behind her than the one playing out on the field.

"Uh, I think so," Carrie says softly, ducking her head.

Marissa's stomach clenches as she recalls the conversation with Bennett after his last game: *I got on base twice,* he'd said, and Matthew had congratulated him and tousled his hair.

Why would Bennett lie? Is he being bullied again, or is Coach Santo punishing Bennett because he did something wrong?

With Dawn's gaze fixed upon her, Marissa tries to hide her distress.

"I'm sure it's no big deal," Carrie says, patting Marissa gently on the knee. "He probably just isn't feeling well. I think a little bug is going around."

"Yeah, that's probably it," Marissa says, grateful for the excuse Carrie has lobbed her.

For the rest of the game, Marissa tries to catch Bennett's eye, but he's so focused on the field that he never turns around. Or at least he's pretending to be. She's so tense that when her cell phone gently buzzes with a text, Marissa flinches, as if the sound were a gunshot.

She hopes it's from Matthew. But she doesn't want to pull out her phone here, with the other parents so close-by, in case the message is from the wrong man.

She cheers along with the crowd when Lance hits a triple, and she groans softly when another boy overthrows the ball to the catcher, letting in a run, but her reactions are a beat off, and her mind is consumed by what she should do when the game ends. She'll talk to Bennett first, then call Coach Santo tonight or tomorrow, she decides.

Bennett isn't a natural athlete, something all the private coaching and encouragement in the world can't make up for. But he possesses something more rare and, in Marissa's eyes, far more valuable. Once, during a baseball game, a player on Bennett's team hit a grand slam during the final inning, winning the game. While all the other boys on his team ran toward each other, whooping, Bennett walked up to the pitcher of the opposing team, who was crying, and tried to comfort him.

Bennett's tender heart is perhaps his greatest gift. Now, as Marissa stares at her son's thin shoulders and slightly bowed head, hers aches for him.

She helps Bennett collect his things after the game, then, as they walk to the car, Bennett crouches down and peers into the grass.

"What is it?"

Bennett points. "A honeybee."

"Oh, I see it now." Marissa carefully steps over it.

Bennett remains in a squat, watching the insect.

"Come on, sweetie." The temperature has dipped in concert with the sun, and she's eager to talk to Bennett.

"It shouldn't be out here alone."

"What do you mean?"

"Honeybees cluster around the queen in their hives in the cold weather. That way they stay warm."

"Why do you think this one is out?"

Bennett shakes his head. "He must be confused. He left the hive too early."

"Maybe if we leave him here, he'll find his way back."

Bennett looks around, at the wide-open grounds, clearly taking in that no beehive is nearby.

"Do you want to bring him home with us?" Marissa doesn't like insects, but she could use her portable coffee mug to contain it, if that's what it takes.

Bennett merely stands up. "No. I think we should leave him. He doesn't belong inside."

Bennett sighs heavily, and Marissa wraps an arm around him as they continue walking. At the car, Marissa pops the trunk so he can put his baseball bag and backpack away. He buckles himself into the back seat—he still uses a booster, since he's small for his age—and Marissa turns off the radio, giving Bennett a chance to start the conversation.

As she winds through the streets toward home, she keeps glancing in the rearview mirror at Bennett, who is picking around the raisins from his bag of trail mix to get at the pretzels and M&M's. He has taken off his baseball cap, and his hair is sticking up in the back.

A parenting book Marissa once read suggested a car ride as an ideal time to have difficult talks with boys, claiming that they feel less vulnerable opening up when they can avoid direct eye contact.

She asks as casually as she can, "So . . . you want to tell me why you didn't play today, sweetie?"

"My stomach hurt." Bennett pops another M&M's in his mouth.

"Seems like it's better now," she replies gently as she turns onto Wisconsin Avenue.

"Um, yeah . . ."

"And last week?"

Bennett doesn't answer.

"Jacob's mom says you didn't play then either."

"I hope the honeybee is okay."

"I hope so, too." Marissa lets the baseball games drop for now.

When they get home, Bennett runs up to his room to feed Sam, his gecko. He desperately wants a dog, but Matthew is allergic, so the little green creature is the only pet in the house. Marissa takes tortillas, a bell pepper, cheddar cheese, and cooked chicken out of the refrigerator to assemble quesadillas, then pulls out her phone. She has three texts: The first is from her mom—who has recently discovered emojis—and its four lines are filled with hearts, kisses, flowers, and a random broccoli floret. The next is from Polly, asking if they can talk. And the third comes from Matthew, telling her that he'll be out late with his client.

The reply to her mother is easy; Marissa shoots back a row of hearts. Polly is more complicated. Marissa finally suggests a coffee before the store opens tomorrow. Now that Marissa is no longer going to Pinnacle, her mornings have more give. Polly responds immediately: **Of course! See you then!** Marissa considers asking Polly if she is sleeping at the store again, but decides to let it go. The last thing Marissa wants is to spark a long exchange.

Marissa turns her attention back to the most important message, Matthew's, trying to glean the subtext. He didn't respond that he loved her, too, but neither was he curt, and he did write, **Sorry, babe.**

She thinks about telling him she'll wait up for him, or asking him to check in with Bennett, who has migrated to the family room. But in the end, she simply writes, **Ok. Good luck!**

Marissa sets down her phone and pours herself a glass of Sancerre. She closes her eyes and takes a sip, thinking that the first taste of morning coffee and the first one of evening wine have to rank up there with the world's greatest pleasures.

She unwraps the block of cheese and begins to grate it. Her chest feels tight, and she tries to match her inhalations and exhalations to the back-and-forth motion of her hand.

She has almost filled the small bowl when Bennett shrieks, "Mom!"

Marissa's knuckle scrapes against the grater. "Shit," she mutters. A tiny drop of blood is on her finger, but at least Bennett isn't there to remind her about the curse jar.

"Mom!" Bennett yells again. "I can't find my Cub Scout rope!"

Cub Scout rope? She has no idea what he's talking about. Then it comes to her—at the last meeting, all the Cubs were sent home with a white, foot-long length of rope to practice their knots.

"Isn't it in one of the baskets by the TV?" Marissa calls back.

She remembers Bennett attempting to tie square knots in the family room, chewing on the inside of his cheek the way he always does when he is concentrating.

Even now she can still hear the instructions he'd memorized:

Loop on top, rabbit runs up through the hole, back around the tree, down the hole again.

"No! I looked!"

"Sweetie, I'm making dinner, so—"

"I need it *now*!" Bennett's voice hitches.

Marissa hurries into the family room and sees Bennett sitting in the middle of the rug, all of his toy bins emptied around him.

"It isn't anywhere!" Bennett is on the verge of tears.

Marissa sinks to her knees and sorts through the puzzles, Marvel action figures, *Star Wars* lightsabers, and board games. She and Bennett peer under the chairs and the couch that Marissa deliberately stained. They even remove all of the cushions. But the rope is nowhere.

Finally Marissa says, "We'll have to get another one."

"But my test is tomorrow!" Bennett begins to cry, his face reddening.

"Honey—"

Bennett's wail drowns her out. He throws a Harry Potter wand across the room, barely missing a lamp.

"Bennett!" Marissa can't recall her mild-mannered son having a tantrum like this since he was a toddler and grew overtired at the Sesame Place Theme Park.

She reaches over and enfolds him in her arms, feeling his body shudder with sobs.

"I was supposed to be practicing. I'm going to fail."

"Oh, sweetie, it's okay." She repeats the words as she rocks her son, attempting to soothe herself along with Bennett. She has tried so hard to conceal from her son the turbulent emotions she has been feeling, but clearly he's absorbing some of the stress swirling inside their home.

She wishes Matthew were here, to join in their hug and then maybe run out to Home Depot to pick up another rope.

But Matthew will hardly see Bennett this week. Marissa will be the one to take Bennett to Cub Scouts again, and while some moms are always at the meetings and events, most of the boys are there with their fathers.

Bennett has never complained about this; still, Marissa wonders if it could be contributing to his pain.

Matthew made it to the pinewood derby last year, but it was the scoutmaster who'd helped Bennett build his little wooden race car. Matthew simply doesn't have the time to take Bennett to Nationals games or nature centers or attend every school conference. Bennett must be missing a feeling of connection to Matthew, too.

Maybe fractures exist not only in her marriage, but in their family.

Instead of trying to put on a happy facade—the equivalent of a curated Instagram post—she should be more real with her son. That's what Avery would recommend.

"I've been a little stressed lately, too. . . . You know how sometimes you and Charlie get into arguments, and then you make up?"

Bennett nods. "Yeah, like when he tried to feed Sam a Froot Loop, which could have been really dangerous."

"Yes. Well, Dad and I have been arguing a little, but we're doing better now."

Bennett grows perfectly still, and Marissa wonders for a moment whether she's made a mistake. Maybe this is too much information.

Then, in a small voice, Bennett asks, "Is that why he was sleeping in the elephant room?" It's Bennett's nickname for the guest room, which has a big painting of a majestic elephant on the wall.

"Yes."

"Are you going to get divorced like Olivia's parents?"

"Of course not. Daddy and I love each other very much. And we both really love you."

Marissa remains on the floor, holding her son, knowing that despite everything else demanding her attention, nothing matters more than this.

Bennett sniffs. "Okay . . . Then can you tell Dad I don't want to play baseball?"

"You don't want to play baseball?"

Bennett has played since Matthew signed him up for a T-ball league when he was five. He complained about going to practice sometimes, but Marissa assumed he had a good time when he got there.

Bennett shakes his head. "It isn't fun."

"If you don't like baseball, you don't have to play baseball," she finally says. "I'm sure Dad will understand."

She knows Matthew won't be happy about it, though. He lettered in three sports in high school and played club ice hockey and baseball in college. It's only natural that he hoped their son would inherit that physical prowess and enjoy being on teams.

But Bennett isn't built that way, emotionally or physically. He's his own person.

And he's certainly intuitive enough to know that Matthew will be disappointed.

Marissa hugs her son tighter. "I have an idea. How about we order pizza for dinner? Then maybe I can find something else for you to practice knots with."

Bennett squeezes her back, his thin arms locked around her waist, then lets go. "I love you."

"Love you more." She kisses the top of his head. "Should we go pick toppings? You want pineapple and anchovies, right?"

"Ewwww!" Bennett pretends to throw up, then gets to his feet.

As he and Marissa walk back into the kitchen, Marissa spots the Transformers watch that Bennett left on the end table next to the sofa. She hesitates. Something about the way the fabric wristband is splayed across the wood table jars her memory, and it hits her: that's the exact spot where she last saw the Cub Scout rope, on the night when Matthew was in New York and her life began to unravel.

"Mom?" Bennett calls, and Marissa is reminded that she has also betrayed her son.

Bennett is already sitting on his favorite stool at the granite island, clicking away on Marissa's laptop—it's a little frightening how adept he is with technology—and has called up the website for his favorite pizza place.

Marissa steps into the kitchen, expecting him to ask what size pie he should select or whether he can get a Sprite with dinner. She's prepared to give him anything he wants.

But the question that comes from her son surprises and saddens her. It will reverberate through her mind the rest of the evening, fighting her attempts to sleep until, finally, at a little after 11:00 P.M., she takes a Xanax to quiet her brain.

Bennett asks, "If you and Dad do get divorced, can I live only with you?"

CHAPTER NINETEEN

AVERY

THE FAINT ODOR OF COOKED meat hits me when I walk into my house, as if someone is eating a hamburger in my kitchen.

I stand motionless in the doorway, my eyes roaming over the items littering the hallway and living room: torn paper towels, eggshells, an empty carton of Greek yogurt, and a mushy speckled-brown banana peel I threw away yesterday.

For a split second, I worry someone has broken in again. Then I identify the culprit.

Romeo stares up at me, his tail thumping against the wood floor, part of the grease-stained Five Guys foil wrapper from last night's takeout stuck to his plastic cone.

"Are you kidding me?"

His tail raps harder as I sigh and begin to clean up. In the kitchen, I discover the built-in drawer holding my trash and recycling bins is wide open. Either I forgot to shut it tightly, or my dog has figured out how to open it.

"My little Dumpster diver, you were doing so well out of the crate. What happened?" I scold Romeo as I wipe down the floor. He licks my hand and looks suitably ashamed.

I have no idea what he is digesting, and I don't want another unwelcome surprise from him, so I change into my workout clothes, clip on his leash, and take him for a long walk. It feels a bit like I'm rewarding Romeo's bad behavior, but I remember Skip's advice to go easy on him.

I no longer trust Skip, but he did seem to have a way with my dog.

Every few minutes, I spin around and check the street behind me, and I scrutinize the faces of people who pass me. I don't intend to let Acelia's henchmen catch me unawares again.

When we get back to the house, I reset the alarm, then settle in to work, keeping Romeo in my office with me. After paying a few bills, conducting a Zoom session with a client who had to unexpectedly leave town to care for her ill mother, and returning a few other calls, I turn my attention to drafting emails to send to Matthew and Marissa separately. Our next session is Devastation. I need the Bishops to be in a positive frame of mind when they come to see me on Thursday, because experiencing an abrupt drop in emotions—such as the dip in the roller coaster that comes after the slow climb—will strip away more of their superficial gloss.

I craft my message to Marissa first, thinking about what I want to accomplish.

When he learned of his wife's betrayal, Matthew's ego suffered a major blow. Marissa needs to offset some of that damage. I type this instruction: *When you next see Matthew, bring up something that makes him a great husband. Be specific.*

Then I follow up with a message for Matthew. Marissa feels unseen in her marriage; this is one of the top reasons a woman will stray from her husband, and why it's so important for Matthew to make a course correction.

When I spoke to Matthew alone during our first session, I took him back to the early days of his relationship with Marissa in the hopes of recapturing some of those positive feelings.

Given the bomb Marissa had just thrown into the room, it took a while for Matthew to be able to say anything positive about his wife. But when he did, it was such a stunning, raw declaration that I still find myself replaying it in my mind. The sentiment Matthew expressed is one of the reasons why I'm eager to help the Bishops find their way back to each other.

I send Matthew the following instruction: *You told me the first time you kissed Marissa, it was like glimpsing the ocean for the first time. The next time you see her, tell her this.*

Before I can hit SEND, my cell phone rings and Lana's photo appears on my screen. We spoke earlier today, while I was driving to Dr. Hernandez's office, so I'm surprised she's reaching out again.

"Hey, sweetie—"

"Avery! Oh my God—my car—I just left work—I can't believe someone—"

"Slow down. Are you hurt? Were you in an accident?"

"No, no." She lets out a huffing sound. "My tires! Someone let the air out of them—all four. They were that way when I got to my parking spot. Who would do that to me?"

I suspect I know exactly who: Acelia.

The parallel is clear: someone came after me in a parking garage today and now they're messing with my sweet, guileless stepdaughter in a different parking lot. Fury courses through my body.

"Where are you now?" I'm glad it's still daylight out.

"I'm right by my car. I tried my mom, but she didn't pick up. Greg's at work so he can't talk."

"I'm glad you called me. I'm going to get in touch with AAA, and I'll come wait with you."

"Okay, thanks. I'll be here."

I frown as I grab my purse and slip on my sneakers. I don't want her alone in a parking lot even for a short time.

"Actually, is there somewhere else you can go? How about that sandwich shop you like?"

"Why?"

"I'm hungry," I lie. "Order us two of those veggie things and I'll meet you there."

An hour later, Lana's tires have been refilled and she's at Greg's place—where she plans to sleep tonight—and I'm driving home, clutching my steering wheel so tightly my knuckles are white. Skip must be the key to all of this. He knows I have a stepdaughter since Lana phoned once when he and I were together, and although I don't recall mentioning where she worked, he could probably find out. And who else would know about my doctor's visit? I never mentioned it to a soul.

I'm tempted to call Skip and let loose, but I tamp down on that instinct. If Skip is weaving some complicated web, he's already several steps ahead of me, and acting impulsively is the worst thing I can do.

I mentally review what I know about him: He's forty, never married, and a commercial real estate developer. He's the youngest of three, went to Dartmouth, and lived in California before moving to D.C. There's no obvious tie between him and Acelia. But I can't shake loose the idea that if I dig deeper, I will find one.

Maybe it's time to call the police. I also know a former cop who now works as a private investigator; I used him on a case a couple months ago.

I step harder on the gas, trying to catch the tail end of a yellow light. Part of the reason I'm so enraged is because I genuinely liked Skip. My instincts told me he was a decent guy, and I'm not usually so off base when it comes to sizing people up.

He's making me feel like a fool.

The light turns and I slam on my brakes, the nose of my BMW edging into the intersection. A woman walking a white poodle glares at me as she maneuvers around my car.

Get a grip, I order myself sternly, as I would a client.

My front windshield begins to fog up so I turn on the defrost and try to swipe away some of the cloudy film with my sleeve, but my thin Lycra top is ineffective. I reach into my center-console glove compartment, where I usually keep a few paper napkins. I don't see any, but there's a pack of tissues.

I pull one out and stare at it, remembering how Skylar plucked a tissue out of her handbag and offered it to me.

I shake my head as I realize my mistake.

I've been focusing on the wrong parallel.

A car honk from behind me jolts me, and I shift my foot off the brake, driving more carefully now.

What happened to Lana's car wasn't a message from Acelia to let me know they could get to my stepdaughter. Someone else was behind it.

You know so much about me. I guess I wanted to learn more about you, Skylar had said.

Cameron's ex must be the one who let the air out of Lana's tires; it seems like exactly the kind of spiteful act she would perpetrate.

I turn down my street corner and park in front of my house, but I don't immediately cut off the engine. My mind is operating clearly now that the muddy swirl of my emotions is falling away.

I need to do two things, fast: confirm Skylar did this to Lana, and find a way to make sure she never comes near my stepdaughter again.

I consider a few options before I find the right one. The genesis for my idea is right there on my phone screen, in a message Derrick texted shortly before I left the house: **Hey babe, u free tonight? Job just cancelled.**

Derrick and I pull up outside Skylar's house in a suburban Silver Spring neighborhood shortly after 7:00 P.M. The modest, single-story brick structure is on a dead-end street filled with nearly identical houses. While the other homes have nice details—a rope swing hanging from a tree in one front yard, and pretty landscaping in another—Skylar's place looks a little tired and worn since I was here last fall. The grass in her front yard is patchy, and it's the only house on the block with a garbage can languishing at the curb.

Cameron used to tend to the lawn and lug the garbage bins up and down the driveway on trash day, along with everything else he did, such as the grocery shopping and cooking. Now that Skylar is living alone, it's on her to keep up with the household chores.

"Thanks again for doing this," I say as Derrick opens the driver's-side door of his van, the one with the name of his security company emblazoned on both sides. I slide into the back so I can peek out the tinted window.

Derrick climbs Skylar's stairs and rings the bell. He's in his work uniform—crisp dark slacks, a button-down shirt, and a jacket with his first name and his company's logo embroidered beneath his left shoulder. Skylar opens her door and peers out at Derrick. I wonder if she's having the same reaction I did when Derrick showed up on my doorstep, looking more like a Nike model than a tech guy.

I can't hear them talking, but I know what Derrick is saying. We crafted his lines together. He's reassuring Skylar that this isn't a sales call, and confiding that his company sent him to see her because she might have information about a crime. With his husky voice and warm eyes, I have no doubt that Skylar will be seduced into believing Derrick.

Skylar steps out of her house, joining Derrick on the stoop. He gestures toward the truck, and she glances at it, nodding.

Derrick keeps talking, telling her that his company would prefer this conversation to be confidential, and I see her smile. He has that effect on people. She tosses her hair back and leans in closer to him, and I can't help thinking about a fish being reeled in.

I can tell the moment he delivers the punch line: *We have you on video letting the air out of the tires of a silver Honda in the parking lot near the Uptown Theater.*

Skylar's hand flies to cover her mouth.

Gotcha, I think.

She shakes her head, trying to deny his words, but Derrick keeps talking, telling her it's a misdemeanor and that the car's owner is considering whether to forward the video to the police as well as suing for towing and court costs. Derrick knows what to do next. He drills in, informing her that the vehicle's owner can and will legally disseminate copies of the recording to Skylar's neighbors, her boss, and everyone she is connected to on social media if Skylar ever goes near the car or its owner again.

I see Skylar's body crumple into itself, like a balloon deflating.

A different video marked the beginning of my trouble with Skylar. Now this nonexistent one will end it.

Derrick walks away as Skylar stares after him. For a brief moment, I actually feel sorry for this lonely, miserable woman.

Later that night, I lie in bed next to Derrick. His muscular arm is draped over my bare stomach, his breath as warm and rhythmic against my neck as his body had been moments before.

"Mmm, that was incredible," I say. "I told you I'd make the visit worth your while."

His fingertips stop tracing circles across my still-sweaty skin, and I wonder if he's drifting off to sleep.

I prop myself up on an elbow and catch a glimpse of the digital clock on his nightstand. Almost midnight; time to get going.

I climb out of his bed and reach for my lacy bra.

"You know, before tonight I didn't even know you had a stepdaughter."

"Oh," I reply, thinking, *And she's about the same age as you.*

Derrick has only been to my place twice—during our initial meeting, when he installed motion detectors and glass-break sensors and a couple of panic buttons, and a few days later, when I called the number on the business card he'd given me and invited him over for a drink. A photo of Lana is on my mantel, but Derrick probably didn't notice it.

"Look, Avery . . . I'm glad I could help you out tonight."

I pause, balancing on one leg, my other foot sliding into one of my high heels. "But?"

"It's just—sometimes I feel like all we have is *this*. . . ." He lifts his hand and gestures above the bed.

"But isn't *this* pretty good?" I give a little laugh, then grab his fingers and kiss them.

"It's been a few months. And I like you. I know we both said it was okay to see other people. But . . . maybe we shouldn't."

"C'mon, you're ten years younger than I am." At twenty-six, he's actually fifteen years my junior. "You can't really think—" I stop myself when I see the hurt on Derrick's face. The air between us feels heavy and tight, something I've never experienced before.

"Let's talk about this more tomorrow. I really have to go. My poor dog has never been left alone this long."

"Okay." Derrick gets up to walk me to the door, naked. I love his sense of chivalry, and his uninhibitedness.

I'm just not in love with *him*.

CHAPTER TWENTY

MARISSA

MARISSA AWAKENS INTO DARKNESS so thick and heavy it's like black velvet. Her body and mind feel sluggish, the result of the two glasses of wine plus the Xanax she took last night.

She rubs her gritty eyes, then reaches over to Matthew's side of the bed. But instead of touching his warm body, she feels the covers tightly pulled up against the mattress.

Did her husband not come home last night?

Pulling herself upright, she blindly fumbles for her phone on the nightstand, nearly knocking her glass of water onto the floor.

Eight thirty-two A.M.

She blinks hard, certain her eyes are playing tricks on her and that the eight is really a six. But the slim white numbers don't change.

In a panic, Marissa leaps out of bed, calling, "Bennett! We're late for school!"

She races down the hall and flicks the switch by the door of his room, cringing as the bright overhead light sears her eyes. Sam, Bennett's gecko, scampers across his cage, making a rustling sound.

"Bennett, come on! I overslept, so—"

She hurries closer to his bed, then realizes the lump beneath the rumpled covers is Mr. Rainbow, his stuffed bear.

Her heart stutters.

Her son is gone.

She spins around in a circle, yanking at doorknobs, praying he is in his bathroom, or getting clothes out of his closet. But those spaces are empty, too.

She calls her son's name again as she hurries downstairs, her bare feet padding soundlessly against the thick carpet.

What is *happening*? Where is her family?

She skids into the kitchen, crying out as her hip bangs against the hard, unforgiving edge of a countertop.

The kitchen is just as she left it last night—the sink is empty, the countertops are smooth and gleaming, and the empty pizza box is folded in the recycling bin.

But Bennett's backpack is missing from the hook by the garage door.

Marissa sucks in a deep breath, fighting a rising swell of fear, then she pivots and stares at the coffee maker next to the refrigerator.

It's full of rich-smelling, freshly brewed coffee.

Beside it is a note, written on a Post-it: *You looked so peaceful I didn't want to wake you. B and I are getting bagels on the way to school.*

Marissa closes her eyes as relief courses through her, wondering how she blotted out so much: Matthew's arrival home last night, and the sound of his alarm going off at six thirty this morning—as it did every weekday. He would've taken a shower and changed and roused Bennett, while she slept on.

But Marissa *never* sleeps late—all too often, she wakes around 4:00 or 5:00 A.M., her mind churning. During the increasingly rare occasions when she does manage to catch a full night's rest, she always jolts awake at the sound of Matthew's alarm.

She looks at Matthew's note again. This isn't a complaint about her husband, but she can count the number of times Matthew has taken Bennett to school on both hands, and that includes his spontaneous drive-in last week. And he's been so busy at work, which makes the gesture seem all the more loving.

Is it possible that her husband has truly forgiven her?

He wouldn't if he knew the full story, Marissa thinks as a wave of dizziness passes through her.

Marissa takes a glass from the cupboard and fills it with cold water, drinking it straight down. She is parched and has the faint beginnings of another headache.

She needs to get a grip.

With the first bracing sip of strong black coffee, she feels the stirrings of clarity in her mind. She begins to form a plan: no wine for the rest of the week, and certainly no Xanax. She'll eat well and get in some cardio so that her body will be naturally relaxed at bedtime.

She needs to talk more to Bennett, too, so maybe she'll pick him up right after school—now that he is quitting baseball, there is no need for him to stay for practice. She'll take him out for his favorite frozen yogurt at the place where you can choose from dozens of sugary toppings. Polly will cover the store—

Polly. Marissa wants to scream. She is supposed to meet Polly in— Marissa glances at the clock on the microwave—exactly four minutes.

Marissa runs back upstairs and grabs her phone, typing a quick text to Polly: **So sorry! Had an emergency this morning and I need to reschedule coffee.**

She hesitates, then adds, **Can you open the shop? I'll be there ASAP and we'll sort everything out.**

She holds her breath until the reply comes in a moment later: **Sure! I'll be happy to!**

Out of all the unpredictabilities in her life, at least Polly's eagerness has remained a constant.

When Marissa arrives at Coco a little later, Polly is assisting a woman looking for a hostess gift.

"The great thing about Le Labo candles is that even though they're a little pricey, they really last," Polly says. "I personally love the Palo Santo Fourteen. It's slightly spicy, but not cloying. Plus there's a hint of sage to banish away negativity."

Marissa watches as the woman leans down and sniffs it.

"Mmm," she murmurs. "You know what? I'm going to get Julia one and I'll also take one for myself."

Marissa has to admit that Polly is a good sales associate; her memory for detail is impressive.

One would think Polly had a lot of experience in retail, but when Marissa hired her, Polly's résumé listed only one sales job, at an Anthropologie in Bethesda. Her other position had been as a nanny for a family with three girls in Potomac.

So why did Polly's roommate think Marissa was Polly's boss at a real estate company? Her roommate could have muddied the details—there was the loud Grateful Dead music and the aroma of pot wafting from the house—but still, the inconsistency nags at Marissa.

After Polly finishes ringing up her customer, Marissa approaches and puts a hand on Polly's back, feeling the sharp edge of her shoulder blade.

"I'm sorry," Marissa begins.

"No." Polly spins around to face Marissa. Her fair complexion is mottled with red splotches, and she can barely meet Marissa's eyes. "I'm the one who should be apologizing! I lied to you. I don't really have a mouse problem."

Marissa feigns surprise. "Oh?"

Polly traces an invisible line across the wood floor with the tip of her shoe. "The truth is, it's boy trouble. My roommate, Keith . . ."

Was Keith the one who shouted, *Is it the pizza guy?* Marissa wonders.

"Long story short, I like him. But he's not into me. He has this new girlfriend and I—I just needed a few nights away."

Marissa nods. When she was Polly's age, she was on the cusp of being engaged to Matthew, but she recalls the angst her friends felt over guys back then.

"Why didn't you tell me the truth?" Marissa asks quietly.

"I guess I was embarrassed." Polly swallows hard. "I mean, you've probably never been rejected by anyone. Look at you! You've got this gorgeous husband *and* a secret admirer."

Not so secret, Marissa thinks, her stomach clenching. How is it that Polly can have Marissa softening in sympathy, then tensing in annoyance a moment later? She and Polly simply don't gel; they never have.

Marissa clears her throat, then adds, as if it were an afterthought, "Polly? Your roommate said something strange. . . . She mentioned she thought you worked at a real estate company?"

Polly shakes her head. "Yeah, she gets a little confused sometimes, especially when she parties. . . . She's thinking of a place I temped at for a couple weeks."

Marissa supposes Polly's explanation makes sense.

"So we're good?"

Marissa nods. "We are."

One task on her to-do list is complete, so Marissa heads to the back room to research stationery distributors. Several customers have recently asked if Coco has cards to go along with the gifts they have purchased. Marissa scrolls through various websites, bookmarking a few possibilities. She sends emails to the suppliers, inquiring about pricing and availability, then considers Avery's instruction to think of a genuine compliment for Matthew. It shouldn't be hard to do, but Marissa wants her words to come from the heart. The catch is, with Matthew working late all week, when will she find the right moment to deliver them?

She texts Avery about her dilemma and is reading Avery's reply when Polly pokes in her head. "Hey, I just had a thought! I wonder if you checked the security camera footage if you could see who left that note."

Drop it! Marissa wants to yell. "I already looked yesterday. It was too dark to see anyone clearly."

Now they're even, Marissa thinks. She and Polly have each lied to the other.

"Okay, although I wonder . . . ?"

Before Polly can say another word, Marissa interjects, "Hey, you know what would be really helpful? Could you run out and get us some more packing tape? Maybe grab us a couple coffees, too—my treat."

Marissa craves the caffeine—she was too rushed to gulp more than a few sips this morning, and her head still feels a little foggy—but she craves a break from Polly even more desperately.

As soon as Polly exits the store, Marissa begins riffling through the files in her desk trying to find the paperwork for the alarm system she had installed years ago. She'd completely forgotten about the system until Polly had brought it up.

As with most discussions involving technology, Marissa zoned out while the nice man conducting the installation explained the system to her in mind-numbing detail. She's never once looked at Coco's video footage, and she can't even recall the name of the alarm company. After sifting through files containing her company's taxes, vendor bills, and inspirational tear sheets, she finally finds the Visionex manual in a thick folder labeled *Miscellaneous,* which serves as a catchall for all the papers Marissa suspects she will never look at again, but feels as if she should save.

The red-and-black logo seems familiar, and Marissa thinks she recalls seeing the app on her phone, sandwiched between Bennett's *Angry Birds* and *Minecraft* game apps. Sure enough, it's there, and she easily logs on using their family's catchall password, the four numbers on a phone's keypad that correspond to the name of Bennett's gecko, Sam B (*B* for "Bishop"). The app is surprisingly user-friendly. All she has to do is select the date and scroll through the footage. She starts with Monday at 6:00 P.M.—closing time for the shop—and leans back in her chair as she stares at the image of Coco's front door.

At 6:02, Polly appeared, her image softened through the glass, and locked the door from the inside. Marissa figures out how to speed up the footage—it's similar to fast-forwarding a television show—pausing it only when she glimpses movement.

People passed by frequently during that first hour, but as the night wore on, fewer pedestrians crossed the sidewalk in front of Coco.

Then, around 10:00 P.M., after a lone jogger with a headlamp moved in and out of the frame, the foot traffic ceased.

At 11:28 P.M., someone approached the store.

Marissa leans forward in her chair, holding her breath. It was a man—a big guy in a bulky coat with a hat pulled down low.

He walked slowly, holding a folded piece of paper, the white rectangle standing out starkly against the backdrop of his dark jacket.

As the man came closer to the boutique, he glanced up and down the block. Even though Marissa is certain of the visitor's identity, her body grows warm and perspiration prickles her skin.

The man took a final step toward Coco and bent down to slip the note under the door. It turns out Marissa hadn't lied to Polly after all; it really was too dark to make out his features.

Marissa exhales the breath she didn't know she was holding and is about to exit the app when she sees that the figure slowly lifted his head. He stared directly up at the camera, as if he realized he was being watched. For a moment, it appears as if he sees Marissa. She gasps and her phone slips from her damp hands.

She *does* recognize the person in the video; she walks by him a couple of times a week. The face staring up at her, creased with wrinkles and partially covered by a scruffy salt-and-pepper beard, belongs to Ray, a homeless man who often sits on a bench along Connecticut Avenue, with his rotation of funny cardboard signs: BET YOU A DOLLAR YOU'LL READ THIS; MY EX-WIFE HAD A BETTER LAWYER; and TOO OLD TO MODEL, TOO HONEST TO STEAL.

Ray left the disturbing note?

It makes no sense at all.

The most substantive conversation they've had is when Marissa has offered to pick him up a sandwich on her way to grab lunch. She knows he favors turkey-and-cheese subs and Orange Crush soda, and that he served in the Vietnam War.

Marissa passes the hours in a haze of distraction, managing to wait on customers and clear dozens of emails out of her in-box, but constantly checking the clock. Finally, at 3:15 P.M., she tells Polly she needs to pick up Bennett from school. But instead of heading to her car, she rushes down Connecticut Avenue, toward Ray's favorite bench.

Sure enough, she spots him wearing the same oversize coat she saw in the video. This time the sign by his feet says, in perfect block letters, SAVING UP TO BUY A BABY GIFT FOR HARRY AND MEGHAN.

"Hey, Ray." Marissa tries to control the waver in her voice.

"Hey, Coco lady." He gives her a little salute.

"I like your sign." She digs a $5 bill out of her wallet and places it in the cup by his side. The best way to do this, she decides, is to be direct. "Ray, I saw some video footage of you by my store late at night."

"Yeah." He seems unsurprised.

"Who gave you that note to put under my door?"

"Some dude. Why? What did it say?"

"Nothing important. Do you remember anything else about him?"

"He was taller than me. I couldn't really tell what he looked like—he had on a coat and hat, like everyone."

Marissa wraps her arms around herself. "Did he tell you his name?"

"Nah. He just handed me twenty bucks and told me to slide the paper under your door. Didn't know why he couldn't just do it himself, but I wasn't complaining. He waited until I got back and thanked me."

Ray lifts his hand to cover his mouth as he coughs, and Marissa does a double take.

His blue leather gloves look expensive, and new—in stark contrast to the worn coat and old boots Ray is wearing.

She gapes. "Those gloves—"

"Oh, yeah." Ray looks down at them. "Guess he knew I was cold. He took them off his hands and gave them to me. Nice, right? They're probably from one of those fancy stores on Wisconsin Avenue—those places you can't even go in if you don't have a gold card."

Marissa does know; the gloves were purchased from one of those very stores. The man who came to her house when Matthew was away was wearing them—they were, he told Marissa, his favorite pair, because she'd bought them for him for Christmas.

"I think they're lined with cashmere."

"They are," Marissa whispers as she backs away.

CHAPTER TWENTY-ONE

AVERY

I awaken to Romeo's scratchy tongue licking my cheek. When I open my eyes, the morning light is shining through the slats of my blinds. I must have forgotten to set my alarm when I got home from Derrick's late last night—or, technically, early this morning.

I roll over and let out a little groan as I recall how we left things.

I don't want to give him up, but neither do I want to lead him on. He deserves more than I can offer right now.

As usual, it's easier to help my clients solve their problems than tangle with my own.

I brush my teeth and dress quickly, and as I'm clipping on Romeo's leash, my phone pings with an incoming text: **I'm sorry to bother you, but with Matthew working late all week I'm finding it impossible to compliment him in person before our next session.**

Come on, I think impatiently. How is Marissa going to fix her marriage if she can't even manage to connect with her husband for a few minutes this week? It's Wednesday, and I'm seeing the Bishops tomorrow night. If the two of them haven't even been in a room together, it'll be tougher to make progress in our session.

Marissa's creative and thoughtful—I saw evidence of those qualities in her artfully arranged boutique, and in her social media posts, such as the Instagram snapshot of the Scary Berries she made for Bennett's class Halloween party (strawberries decorated to look like pumpkins, ghosts, and monsters that must have taken a ridiculous amount of time to construct).

She needs to channel some of that ingenuity into this assignment.

What about a surprise visit to his office? I type. **Bring him a special treat before you pick up Bennett.**

Three dots indicate she's replying. But the message doesn't come through until Romeo and I are partway down the block.

The text that finally appears is a single word: **okay.** It makes me wonder what she erased before hitting SEND.

I pull Romeo away from the staring match he's conducting with a squirrel, deciding that while Marissa visits her husband, I'll pay a surprise visit of my own.

A few hours later, I walk down the sidewalk toward Coco, passing the same man on a bench Marissa walked by the other morning. He holds up a sign that makes me smile: SAVING UP TO BUY A BABY GIFT FOR HARRY AND MEGHAN.

I tuck a few dollars in his cup and continue, pausing in front of Coco to take in the charming window display: two mannequins appearing to enjoy a luxurious-looking picnic. Instead of pulling open the door, I peer through the glass. Polly is there—alone, just as I'd hoped. She's standing in the middle of the store, staring at herself in a wall mirror as she ties a silky floral scarf around her neck. She frowns, unties the scarf, and reties it, this time a bit off-center.

It's exactly how Marissa wore her scarf yesterday.

I watch as Polly gives her reflection a satisfied nod.

She must feel my eyes on her because she spins around. I immediately pull open the door, causing the bell to jingle.

Polly greets me with a wide smile. "Hi! Welcome to . . ." She squints. "Avery?"

She memorized my name—just as I did hers the moment I wrote it on my yellow notepad during my third session with the Bishops.

"How are you?" I walk deeper into Coco. No customers are milling around—just like the last time I visited—and for a moment, I wonder how Marissa turns a profit.

"I'm good, thanks. Um, Marissa isn't here. She had to run out for a bit."

"Oh, no worries. I just stopped by because I left my sunglasses here yesterday."

"Are you sure?"

"Almost positive. Mind if I look around?" I don't wait for permission as I glance behind the counter where customers are rung up, my eyes scanning the shelves, which hold tissue paper, bags imprinted with Coco's logo, and glossy white boxes. "So, how long have you worked here?"

"Oh, just about a month."

"Where are you from?"

"Um, Georgia originally." She's clearly uncomfortable with my intrusion—I see her flinch when I pull open a drawer that contains scissors, tape, and other odds and ends—but she doesn't try to interfere. The air of authority I've put on is suppressing her desire to stop me.

"Hmm? No accent?" I move to a table and shift aside a mannequin head, wondering if it's the one that frightened Polly on the night she slept at the shop.

"I only lived there until I was nine. Then my family moved to Milwaukee."

I catch sight of the three-digit price tag on a simple woven bracelet. Now I get how Marissa turns a profit.

"What made you move to the East Coast?"

"School. I went to American University."

"Ah." I reply. Polly is too close to me; I can see the tiny freckles on her nose. I flash to the way she stood next to Matthew yesterday. At the time I read a strange intimacy into their body language, but now I'm wondering if she's just someone who doesn't get the concept of personal space.

I keep peppering her with questions while I examine the room.

Polly finally asserts herself. "I'm happy to scour the store for you, but maybe you left your sunglasses somewhere else?"

I give her a wide, innocent smile. "Let me just check this last area. So, have you always been interested in retail?"

"Uh, well, I'm—"

I finally hear the noise I've been waiting for: the jingle that means the front door is opening.

"Hell-o!" a woman calls out in a cheerful voice. "Marissa? Polly?" She steps into view, and it's almost comical to watch the struggle play out on

Polly's face: she needs to greet the customer, but she doesn't want to leave my side.

"I'm just going to use the restroom," I tell Polly, walking toward a door that I assume leads into the private area of the shop. "Then I'll get out of your hair." I can't resist adding, "Cute scarf, by the way."

Polly finally detaches from me to do her job, and I swiftly survey the small back room. It's filled with UPS boxes and racks of clothes and a long table with two chairs. On the wall are several hooks. A coat is hanging from one, with a leather purse looped beside it.

Bingo.

"Oh, these trays are so fun!" Polly's customer trills. "Are they John Derian?"

Take your time, I think as I creep over to the purse and unzip it.

It's a big hobo-style bag, but everything is organized: wallet, makeup case, keys. I open the wallet and pull out Polly's driver's license, using my phone to snap a picture of her full name and address. There's nothing else of interest in her wallet, so I move to the inner pockets of the bag. One contains AirPods and a tin of Altoids.

Tucked behind the Altoids is a plain legal-size white envelope. Slowly I slip it from the bag as Polly chatters away, explaining John Derian's decoupage technique.

The envelope isn't sealed. I lift the flap and peek inside, glimpsing a rough-looking sheet of paper, full of creases that someone tried to smooth out before folding the paper into thirds.

I slide it out, and as I unfold it, I realize it wasn't just crumpled up—it was also torn into jagged pieces, before being taped back up. As if someone wanted to destroy it, but then reconsidered.

I know what it is even before I see the typewritten message, the one everyone assumed was meant for Marissa: **I'm not letting you go so easily. . . .**

"Perfect! If you can give me just a minute, I'll ring this up for you," I hear Polly say, her voice growing louder as she approaches the back room.

I snap a quick picture of the note, then return it to Polly's bag and step toward the door just as it opens.

"Everything okay?" Polly asks me.

I meet her gaze. "You know what, it turns out I had them in my bag all along." I shrug and lift up my aviators.

I walk out of the shop without another word, feeling Polly stare after me.

It's easy to reconstruct the events that led to the note landing in her possession. Marissa had it yesterday while we spoke by the broken fountain. She returned to Coco after our conversation. I can see her tearing up the paper, then crumpling the pieces in her hand and throwing them into the trash, while Polly surreptitiously watched. Polly must have taped the letter back together before concealing it in her purse.

I reach my car and climb inside, but I don't turn on the engine yet. Marissa is probably with Matthew right now, and I don't want to disturb them, so I send her an email instead of a text, requesting that she send me Polly's résumé as soon as she can.

I just bombarded Polly with a dozen questions, partly to keep her off-balance and partly to learn more about her.

I've got another one, but instead of asking Polly, I'm going to find the answer myself: Who are you, really, and what exactly are you up to?

CHAPTER TWENTY-TWO

MARISSA

MARISSA APPROACHES THE LOBBY of Matthew's office building holding a small white bag from his favorite bakery, and a cardboard tray loaded with two hot drinks.

Dustin, the guard who has manned the security desk for nearly three decades, hurries to open the door for her. "Hey, Mrs. Bishop. Nice to see you again."

"You, too." She realizes it has been ages since she's seen Dustin, which means she hasn't visited Matthew at his office since . . . the annual holiday party? No, one of the Bishop, Simms & Chapman partners hosted the last celebration at his home, so it has been even longer than that. It must have been Matthew's birthday in May, nearly a year ago, when she met him here before going out to dinner at Marcel's.

She and Matthew used to occasionally meet for lunch in Lafayette Square. Marissa would pick up sandwiches from Balducci's, and they'd spread out on a blanket. But they haven't enjoyed a picnic together in ages. Marissa also used to come downtown once in a while to meet Matthew for drinks on the rooftop of the W or the bar at Old Ebbitt Grill, but lately, life has seemed too busy. No, not just lately, Marissa mentally corrects herself. It has been years.

Avery's instructions had at first mildly irritated Marissa. Now she has the eerie sense that Avery can see more deeply into the dynamics of her marriage than Marissa herself.

"I thought I'd bring Matthew—and you—a little treat." Marissa hands

Dustin one of the lattes from her tray. It's a tiny bribe, designed to soften him up for the request she's about to deliver.

"Aw, that's so nice of you. Exactly what I needed." Dustin reaches for his phone. "I'll let him know you're here."

"Actually, would you mind just letting me up? I'd really love to surprise him."

Dustin hesitates. Ever since an employee at Bishop, Simms & Chapman was fired and subsequently caught trying to break into the building, security has been tight. Visitors now go through a metal detector, and Dustin has an emergency button beneath his desk.

Marissa smiles, hoping Dustin sees her for what she truly is: a wife eager for a few stolen moments with the husband she loves.

He returns her smile. "Of course."

Marissa's stomach flutters as she enters the elevator and presses the button for the sixteenth floor. Her visit feels a little illicit and daring. She already knows the words she will say to flatter her husband, and the napoleon in the bakery bag will be a sweet reminder of their trip to Paris, during which Bennett was conceived.

The elevator doors slide open and Marissa steps into the lobby of Bishop, Simms & Chapman. The gorgeous space has floor-to-ceiling windows and bold, colorful artwork adorning the walls. Marissa helped select those pieces, as well as the onyx-and-cream color palette for the office.

Marissa waves to the receptionist, who is busy on a call, then walks directly to Matthew's corner office, which is on the far side of the floor, with a stunning view of the Washington Monument. As she approaches, Marissa sees that Matthew's office door is closed and his secretary, Ginny, is bent over her computer, typing intently. Only when Marissa gets closer does she realize the dark-haired woman isn't Ginny after all.

Their coloring is similar, but their features aren't, and this woman is at least ten years older.

Maybe Ginny is out sick, or on vacation, Marissa thinks as the woman lifts her head and looks at Marissa with a questioning expression.

Now that she thinks about it, Marissa vaguely recalls Matthew telling her Ginny had gotten a new job and moved on. And Marissa's sure he told her about his new assistant, but she can't remember him mentioning her name. Although perhaps this is simply another detail that Marissa has forgotten in the blur of the last few months. Still, what kind of wife doesn't know the name of her husband's assistant?

She'll have to fake it. "Hi . . ."

"Mrs. Bishop!" The dark-haired woman rises from her chair. Marissa is impressed; the woman must recognize Marissa from the photo Matthew keeps on his windowsill, which was taken on their wedding day. "How nice to finally meet you in person!"

Just as the silence begins to awkwardly stretch out, Marissa sees the bronze signage affixed to the cubicle wall: RENEE HAMMERMAN. "It's a pleasure. Please, call me Marissa."

"I'm so sorry I didn't know you were stopping by. I would have come to the lobby to meet you."

"It's actually a surprise." Marissa nods toward her bakery bag and tray. "I figured Matthew has had a tough few days, so . . ."

"He'll be thrilled! Matthew talks about you all the time!"

Marissa can't suppress the questioning tone in her voice. "He does?"

Renee's desk phone begins to ring, and she hurries to pick it up. "Matthew Bishop's office, please hold." Then she turns back to Marissa. "I'm sorry, it's a madhouse here today. Matthew is in his office with Mr. Simms. Should I interrupt him?"

Marissa hesitates. Spencer Simms is one of Matthew's partners. He's sharp and impatient, with a terrific sense of humor. Marissa and Matthew have gone out to dinner with him and his wife, Jean, several times, and while Marissa likes him, he can be intimidating.

Matthew has made it clear he has a crazy week, plus he has that important client in town. He'll be working late. Marissa begins to wonder if Avery got this one wrong; perhaps Marissa's visit will be an inconvenience.

"Oh, I don't know." She feels guiltily aware of the blinking light on Renee's phone. "What do you think?"

"Let me slip him a note. I think they should be wrapping up soon. And his next meeting isn't until four, so this actually could be a good time."

Marissa sits down on a chair outside Matthew's office and begins checking her emails as Renee deals with the caller. There's one from Avery, asking if Marissa has a copy of Polly's résumé, and if so, could Marissa send it as soon as possible. She frowns. The request seems odd, but Avery must have a good reason for it. Marissa knows exactly where in her in-box the résumé is, since she just searched for it herself. She hesitates for a moment, then forwards it.

Marissa tucks away her phone as Renee passes by on her way to dis-creetly knock on Matthew's door. A moment later, Matthew's door opens wider, and Spencer and Matthew exit the office.

"Marissa!" Matthew exclaims, striding over to kiss her on the lips. Far from being annoyed, he's acting as if her visit is the highlight of his day. Marissa can't recall Matthew ever kissing her in his office before. "What are you doing here, babe?"

"Special delivery," Marissa jokes, lifting up the white bag and coffee.

Matthew turns to Spencer. "Aren't I the luckiest guy to have my beau-tiful wife bringing me treats on a random Wednesday?"

"You really are," Spencer agrees. "Nice to see you again, Marissa."

"You, too. I hope I'm not interrupting."

"Nope, but even if you were, it would serve me right for calling Matthew on a Saturday night and making him late to your dinner date."

Of course Matthew had been truthful about the call; Marissa can't believe she doubted him even for a moment.

Spencer frowns as a man down the hallway waves to catch his atten-tion. "Sorry, gotta run." Spencer begins walking away hurriedly.

Matthew reaches for Marissa's hand. "Renee, can you hold my calls?"

She smiles. "Of course."

Matthew leads Marissa into his office and closes the door. The gener-ous, sun-splashed space is just as she remembered it. Matthew's glass desk and leather chair are positioned against a far wall, while the coffee table, love seat, and chairs that make up his sitting area are closer to the door.

"Sit down, sweetie."

Marissa claims a spot on the love seat, leaving room for him to join her. "What's in the bag?"

"You'll have to see for yourself."

He peers inside: "Mmmm . . . it's like you knew I needed a sugar fix to get through the rest of the day."

A ringing sound cuts through the room, and Matthew frowns and hurries to his desk, picking up his cell phone. "I'm going to mute it."

Marissa nods and her gaze drifts behind Matthew, toward the stunning view.

Her eyes widen. The black-and-white wedding photo that used to stand alone on the deep windowsill is now surrounded by a cluster of family pictures: one of Marissa and Matthew on the back of a camel in Egypt, another of Marissa in a black dress and Matthew in a tuxedo holding Harlequin masks over their eyes, and several of Bennett, including a baby photo in which he's clutching a giant bagel with both hands, this year's school picture, and one of him in his baseball uniform. The biggest photo of all is of the three of them, posed in front of their fireplace for their annual holiday greeting card.

Marissa experiences a flash of shame. She felt abandoned by her husband—even ignored at times—but all the while, he was surrounding himself with images of their family while he worked.

Maybe he felt as lonely as she did.

Now here he is, walking back toward her, looking at her with so much love, just like when they were first dating. He is so handsome he takes her breath away.

"I know you're really busy. But I missed you and wanted to see you."

He sits next to her and reaches for the napoleon, offering her the first bite.

She takes a small taste, then he brings the pastry to his mouth and takes a more generous one.

"Delicious," he says. "You know, these always remind me of our trip to Paris."

Marissa feels her eyes unexpectedly prick with tears. "Matthew, I want you to know how much I love you." But instead of giving the compliment she rehearsed on the way over, she speaks from her heart. "Marrying you was the best decision of my life. You are the strongest, smartest man I've ever known. I don't know when things between us began to shift, but I want more than anything for us to feel connected."

A tiny cloud of whipped cream is on the side of his mouth. When he leans forward and kisses her, deeply, she tastes the sweetness on his lips.

A little later—after Matthew has walked her around the office to say hello to a few of his colleagues, keeping his arm around her the entire time; and taken the elevator with her down to the office lobby; and seen her safely to her car—Marissa finds herself so lost in thought at a stop-light that she doesn't notice when it turns green.

The words Matthew murmured in her ear as they said goodbye fill her with a warm glow; it's as if she were floating home: *The first time I kissed you, it was like glimpsing the ocean for the first time. All these years later I still feel the same way.*

CHAPTER TWENTY-THREE

AVERY

NOTHING ABOUT POLLY is adding up.

After I rifled through Polly's purse, I decided to remain in the area. Luckily, I'd tucked my laptop into my bag before leaving home, so I was able to work in the coffee shop down the street from Coco, giving me a chance to check it out in advance of the Monday meeting between Marissa and her old friend.

According to the résumé Marissa forwarded to me, Polly worked as a nanny and as a sales associate at Anthropologie prior to her job at Coco. When I talk to the mother of the young girls Polly babysat for, she verifies Polly's employment, saying Polly was a devoted babysitter who really seemed to love the kids. Then I call Anthropologie, pretending to be the owner of another local boutique, but the manager isn't available. Rather than leave a message, I decide to try again later. People tend to be more candid when they're caught off guard.

I keep envisioning Polly trying on the floral scarf and tying it exactly as Marissa had worn it. It wasn't just the off-center bow that caught my attention. The way Polly tilted her head and held her body as she stared in the mirror—she transformed from a slightly awkward, anxious young woman into someone who was confident and assured. It was as if she wanted to *be* Marissa.

I take a sip of my espresso and continue typing, detailing everything I can remember about Marissa's assistant. Polly slept at Coco the night the mysterious note was pushed under the door, practically guaranteeing she'd be the one to find it. Instead of waiting and giving it to Marissa or simply calling her, Polly showed the note to Matthew.

After Matthew shared the note with me, my focus was on him and Marissa. The anonymous message thrust them toward the edge of a new crisis, one that I'm working to reel them back from.

Polly was in my periphery then. Now I bring her into full focus.

She was flustered when we all clustered around the note, her cheeks flushed and her eyes bright. Agitated . . . or perhaps a little thrilled?

It's common for perpetrators to visit the scene of the crime, to crave involvement as their misdeeds play out.

Marissa, Matthew, and I assume we know who wrote the message, which could be interpreted as longing, determined—or slightly sinister.

But maybe we all got it wrong.

What if *Polly* wrote the message?

I run through possible scenarios in my mind. Polly is secretly in love with Matthew, and trying to cause trouble in the Bishops' marriage. Or, she could be obsessed with Marissa.

I set aside my questions about Polly and spend a couple of hours attending to other work, glancing up when a man takes a seat at the table directly next to mine, even though a number of empty tables are scattered around the coffee shop. I straighten my back and brace myself in case he's from Acelia, but he simply pulls out his phone and begins playing an online game of Scrabble.

My week is busy: Sandra, my client who recently learned her older sister got pregnant with her at the age of fifteen and their parents pretended Sandra was their baby, is coming to see me tomorrow morning for her second session, Disruption. She's a smart, articulate legislative assistant for a Democratic congresswoman. She is a challenging client, the kind I like best. I'm also meeting with a few prospective new clients, and I need to write the speech I'm giving at Georgetown University next week.

But nothing is pulling at my attention as much as meek, awkward Polly and the complicated lives of Matthew and Marissa Bishop. I'm acutely aware of time ticking by as I order another espresso, decaf this time, and a packaged cheese-and-fruit tray to nibble on. At 5:45 sharp, I pack up my laptop. Coco closes at 6:00 P.M., and I want to make sure I'm nearby when Polly leaves.

A little later, I'm several cars behind Polly's white VW Rabbit, heading toward Dupont Circle. The gentle rain that began earlier this afternoon has picked up in intensity; my wheels splash through a pothole, spraying up an arc of water.

I know from Polly's résumé that she lives near American University in D.C., close to the Maryland line. We're heading in the opposite direction, deeper into the city.

Could she have also fabricated her address? I wonder.

My tank is full of gas, I fed and walked Romeo before I left the house, and I'm riding a caffeine wave. I can track Polly as long as I want. I've followed plenty of people since I embarked upon the new phase of my career, and I'm certain she'll be simpler than most.

Polly swings around the circle and continues down Massachusetts Avenue. We're moving against the flow of rush-hour traffic, so we make good time. When Polly turns the corner of Fourteenth and H Streets, I momentarily lose sight of her. Then I see the tail end of her car disappearing into an underground parking garage.

This area is filled with office buildings, restaurants, and a few bars. Ford's Theatre is within walking distance, and so is Chinatown. She could be going anywhere.

I follow Polly into the garage—it's fairly empty, since most commuters have headed home by now—and find a parking spot close, but not too close, to the one she selects. I wait until she gets into the elevator, then I leap out of my car and sprint up the stairs to street level.

The sidewalks aren't crowded, and even under an umbrella, Polly, who's wearing a turquoise jacket, is easy to spot.

She walks about a block, then takes her phone out of her bag and stares down at it. I can't tell if she's checking her messages or writing one. She tucks it away, then takes a few more steps and enters a small bistro with a red awning emblazoned with the name Giovanni's. I walk to the cover of the awning and hesitate, trying to decide whether I should go in, too.

There's no good reason for her to drive all the way downtown, passing dozens of restaurants, simply to have a meal. She must be meeting someone here.

When I asked Polly if someone she knew could have written her that note, she claimed she hasn't dated anyone recently, so it isn't a boyfriend. Maybe a friend then, or a Tinder date. I glance around; every square inch of real estate is claimed, with tall office buildings pressed together like commuters on a crowded subway. The one directly across from me is more elegant looking than its neighbors, with large glass windows dominating its facade. My attention is caught by a middle-aged, dark-haired woman who exits the building and stumbles when one of her heels snags in a sidewalk crack.

I watch as she steadies herself, then I glance back at the restaurant. I pretend to scan the menu that's posted in the window while I look through the glass for Polly, but I can't see her.

For the first time, I begin to question my decision to follow Marissa's assistant. I'm not going to learn the reason why she came here by simply standing outside in the rain. But if I go in, there's a good chance she'll spot me.

I'll deal with that complication if it presents itself, I decide. I pull open the heavy glass door and step inside. Luckily, the bistro is half-full, and the lighting is dim. It's an upscale place, the kind you don't frequent on a saleswoman's salary, adding to the mystery of why Polly came here.

I scan the bar, but I don't see her among the half dozen or so patrons claiming the polished wooden stools. I make my way to an empty one on the side, which gives me a better view of the restaurant's floor, and its patrons.

Polly is seated at a table for two toward the center of the room, chatting with a waiter. I angle my body so that I'm slightly blocked by a pillar, but she never even glances my way.

"What can I get you?" the bartender asks, pulling away my attention.

"Tequila on the rocks with a few limes." Mindful that I'm driving tonight, I add, "And a water, too, please."

"You got it. Want to see a menu?"

"Sure." If Polly is staying for dinner, I will be, too.

Polly must have ordered a glass of white wine because the waiter delivers one to her on a tray. She takes a sip. Even from a distance, I can see she's wearing a bright shade of lipstick and her hair looks freshly brushed.

Polly glances at the door, and so do I, just in time to see the brunette in heels from across the street walk in. She strides directly to the bar, step-ping into an empty space a few feet down from me. But she doesn't claim a stool. She simply looks at the bartender while he prepares a martini in a silver shaker, apparently waiting to get his attention.

Polly is still sipping her wine, but she has now pulled out her phone. I'd give anything to be able to see the screen.

". . . to drink?" I catch the tail end of the bartender's question to the dark-haired woman.

"Actually, I'm picking up a take-out order. For Matthew Bishop?"

The name sends a shock wave through my body.

Don't react, I warn myself, quashing my instinct to whirl around and stare at the woman.

This intersection of Polly and Matthew can't be a coincidence.

"Sure." The bartender checks the paper receipt stapled to a brown pa-per bag by his register, then carries the bag to the woman. "Medium-rare burger with lettuce, avocado, and tomato?"

"I think so." The woman hands over a credit card.

"Don't worry, it's his usual." The bartender smiles at her as he swipes the card through a machine. "Matthew must be busy tonight; usually he comes in himself."

"Yeah, he was just walking out when he got a call from overseas." The woman signs the receipt.

"Tell him Jimmy says hi. And I'll have his Scotch waiting for him next time he comes in."

I catch sight of the credit card as the woman tucks it back into her wallet. It's an American Express corporate card, but I can't see the letter-ing that identifies the company.

I don't need to, though.

I pull out my phone to confirm what I already know: Matthew's com-pany, Bishop, Simms & Chapman, is located in the elegant building di-rectly across the street.

I move a few feet to my left, so that Polly's view of me is almost com-pletely blocked by two men who are at a high-top table near the edge of the bar area. Before I wasn't too concerned about her spotting me; now it's vital that I stay concealed.

I watch the dark-haired woman as she disappears through the door,

my mind scrambling to sort the information I've just gathered into a co-
hesive narrative: Matthew must be a regular here on nights when he
works late. He probably sips a Scotch at the bar, chatting with the amia-
ble bartender, while he waits for his food to be prepared. Then he brings
his styrofoam container back to the office and puts in a few more hours.

But tonight, he sent someone else—an assistant, or a junior
colleague—to retrieve his dinner.

His routine changed at the last minute.

I observe Marissa's assistant take another sip of wine, wondering when
she'll realize that Matthew isn't going to wander into the restaurant tonight.

What was Polly's plan? To pretend to "bump into" him and invite him
to join her at her table?

It might have worked.

Although I can't believe for a moment that Matthew would ever be
attracted to someone such as Polly; she may be operating under a delu-
sion. Or her motives for this attempted encounter could lie elsewhere
entirely.

I wait for another twenty minutes, until Polly signals for the check.
I watch as she slides her wallet out of that hobo bag. The taped-up note
must still be tucked inside.

Polly tucks some cash in the leather folder and exits Giovanni's.

When I follow a moment later, I take a final glance at her table, watching as the waiter clears away the wineglass. Polly didn't even bother to
finish her drink; the lipstick-stained glass is still half-full.

I stand by the exit to the parking garage, shielded by a railing, and
watch as Polly's VW Rabbit exits. She turns north, heading back in the
direction of Maryland.

I'm not surprised. There's no reason for her to remain downtown.

How disappointed Polly must be, I think. She has to feel as if her evening was wasted.

Mine, though, has gotten a lot more interesting.

CHAPTER TWENTY-FOUR

MARISSA

MARISSA POURS HOT WATER into her mug of tea and settles on the love seat in the family room. Her gaze drifts to the new couch, then her eyes jerk away. She's grateful the replacement has finally arrived, but it looks so much like the original piece that it still unsettles her.

She'll get a few throw pillows, she decides, to mix things up. Matthew won't mind; he leaves the decorating to her.

It has been a long day, beginning with her oversleeping and awakening muddy headed, and culminating with Bennett's Cub Scout meeting. At least that had gone well. On the coffee table now rests Bennett's blue uniform with its adorable ascot—"It's a neckerchief, Mom!" she can almost hear Bennett chiding—a travel sewing kit, and the badge Bennett earned tonight for tying knots.

Even though he'd had to practice with an old bungee cord that she'd cut down to the size of the missing white rope, he'd easily passed his test.

Usually, this time of night awards Marissa a sense of peace: her son is tucked snug in bed, the house is clean and orderly, and she finally has a few moments to herself.

But something feels off.

Maybe the room is haunted by the memory of the act she committed here. She shakes off the thought and picks up the sewing kit, but it takes her three tries to pass the blue thread through the eye of the needle. She wonders if anyone will notice that her stitches aren't smooth and even.

A crack of thunder seems to shake the house. Marissa looks at the silvery rain streaking down outside, wishing Matthew were home. He tends to drive too quickly, and he'll be exhausted when he finally leaves the office tonight, which is a bad combination on wet roads.

She snips the end of the thread and ties a knot, then stands up and walks to the staircase, folding the shirt as she climbs it. She enters Bennett's bedroom and hovers on the threshold for a moment, letting her eyes adjust to the dim glow of his night-light. His giant FAO Schwarz dog is in one corner, leaning against a bookshelf that's filled with the Harry Potter and Percy Jackson series.

Marissa places the shirt on top of his dresser so he can see it first thing when he wakes up. Then, even though she is tempting fate, she walks over to her son and presses her lips to his forehead. She closes her eyes and inhales deeply. Even if she were blindfolded and a hundred little boys were lined up, she could recognize Bennett simply by his smell.

"Mama," Bennett murmurs as he rolls onto his side and instantly falls back asleep.

Long ago, Marissa had read a newspaper article about a teenaged girl who was flying a small airplane. The instructor was seated next to the girl, and her father was in the back. The plane crashed, and all three died. One detail of this tragedy stood out to Marissa: the father was found with his arms wrapped around his daughter. Even at the terrifying moment of his death, his fear was dwarfed by his need to protect and comfort his child.

Marissa looks down at Bennett, thinking that she understands the ferocity of that kind of parental love.

He is wearing his favorite Spider-Man pajamas, which he won't give up even though the cuffs extend only to his forearms and the bottoms barely reach his shins. Marissa pulls the covers up more securely around him, then eases away and heads back downstairs.

In the distance, she hears the wailing of a car alarm that must have been triggered by the storm. She wraps her arms around herself, wondering if she should turn on the gas fireplace and curl up with a book or maybe take a hot bath. She can't seem to get warm.

She puts on a soft fleece that she keeps in the hall closet and picks up an Anita Shreve novel she's forever been meaning to read, but her mind is too jittery to process the story.

Every minute that passes brings her closer to the Monday meeting in the coffee shop. Avery seems so confident that she knows what to do, but what if she's wrong?

Marissa's eyes flit to the sofa again, seeing herself as she was that night: her back arched, her lips parted, her body set aflame by the slow touch of strong hands.

Enough, she orders herself, reaching for the remote and selecting a mindless comedy.

She watches two episodes while simultaneously scanning Instagram and replying to a few work emails, then turns off the downstairs lights and rechecks the house alarm, as she does every evening. Crime rates are surprisingly high in their neighborhood, and although most are simple car break-ins late at night, there is an occasional home invasion, and last year two armed men held up the neighborhood pharmacy where Marissa buys vitamins and gets prescriptions filled.

Marissa has just finished smoothing on her favorite night serum and climbed into bed when the home phone shrills. She's tempted to let it ring. Only two categories of people call the house phone: telemarketers, and her parents, who prefer landlines to cells.

But telemarketers are prohibited from calling after 9:00 P.M., she remembers.

Her parents, who open the store at 7:00 A.M., go to bed early. If they're calling now, something must be wrong. She throws off the covers and hurries to the side table where the phone rests in its charger.

It isn't her parents: caller ID shows a 202 area code, which is for D.C.

"Marissa?"

The female voice is familiar, but Marissa can't immediately place it.

"This is Renee Hammerman." Matthew's new secretary, the woman Marissa met just today.

"Hi, Renee. Is everything okay?"

"I'm sorry to call you so late at home, but I'm still in the office and need to speak to Matthew briefly. I wouldn't bother him unless it was urgent."

"Wait, isn't he there with you?"

In the pause that follows, Marissa feels her skin prickle.

"No, he left about forty-five minutes ago. . . . I keep trying his cell, but he isn't answering."

There's no traffic at this time of night, so the ride home should be twenty minutes, tops. Even if he'd stopped for gas, Matthew should be here.

Unless—Marissa clutches at the thought—he was hungry and picked up something on the way. Typically when he works late, Matthew gets takeout from Giovanni's, the restaurant across from his office, and eats at his desk. But maybe his routine changed.

She shares this thought with Renee, but Renee immediately replies, "I actually picked up his dinner because he had to jump on a call."

Marissa grabs her cell phone off her nightstand and hits the button to dial Matthew. "Renee? Hold on a second. . . . I'm trying him now."

When it goes to voice mail, she taps out a text: **Where are you? Please call me.**

Maybe Matthew had gone to meet a client unexpectedly, though it would be highly unusual for him to not let her know.

"I can't reach him," she tells Renee. "Can you explain exactly what happened when he was leaving?"

"He told me he was heading home and emailed me a final electronic document to format and send. He said to make sure to get one of the security guards to walk me to my car, and that I should come in late to-morrow. When I was reading through it, I realized he hadn't signed one of the pages. I've been trying to reach him, but like I said, he's not an-swering his calls or texts." Renee hesitates. "Which we both know isn't like him," she concludes with a nervous laugh.

"Let me keep trying him. I'll call you back."

The rain seems to be falling even harder, pounding down relentlessly, as she stares at the tiny image of her smiling husband in the circle at the top of her phone screen. The line rings and rings and then goes to voice mail. She sends him another text: **Getting worried. Please call me ASAP.**

A certain kind of wife would figure her husband had simply forgot-ten to charge his phone. Another might assume her husband had stopped off at a bar to meet some buddies and couldn't hear the ringer over the loud music. A third might suspect her partner was with another woman.

But Matthew never lets his phone battery dip below 50 percent. He also doesn't have a group of drinking pals. And despite Marissa's own infi-delity, she does not believe Matthew would exact revenge. Especially after the connection they shared at his office just this afternoon.

There has to be some logical explanation, but the only one that comes to mind is even worse than the final scenario she conjured.

She hurries downstairs, her phone in hand, and checks the family room, in case Matthew slipped inside while she was getting ready for bed. Maybe he's slumped on the couch, decompressing after a long day. But all the lights are off and the house is still. She peers out the window, futilely searching for a glimpse of his headlights coming up the driveway.

With every minute that ticks by, her worry grows.

She calls Renee, who answers midway through the first ring.

"He's still not home."

"Maybe he stopped to run an errand or something. . . ." Marissa can tell from those few words that Renee is uncomfortable; she hasn't been working for Matthew long so she can't know him well, and perhaps she has mentally run through the same scenarios as Marissa.

"Why don't you head home. I'm sure the document can wait."

"Thanks, but I'll stay a little longer."

"I'll let you know as soon as I hear from him." Marissa hangs up.

Because she can't sit still, she flicks on some bright lights and begins to pace, doing a loop through the family room, formal living room, kitchen, and dining room.

Any minute now, she tells herself, Matthew will walk in and stretch out his arms to envelop her. He'll apologize for worrying her and promise it won't ever happen again.

She looks down at her screen, hoping—praying—to see the three dots that indicate Matthew is typing a response to her calls and texts. Marissa enters Matthew's study and stands still for a moment, forcing herself to think harder. Maybe the explanation is the simplest one. Renee said Matthew had forgotten to sign a document. He probably remembered this on his way home and is driving back to the office right now.

But even as Marissa considers this, she knows it can't be. Even *if* Matthew had driven all the way home, he would've made it back to the office long before now. Plus she's fairly certain he could simply use DocuSign.

In any case, this still doesn't explain why he's not answering his phone.

Where is he?

She wraps her arms around herself, suppressing a shiver; she's wearing only a camisole and pajama bottoms, and the house is so cold.

She's walking through the dining room when she hears the joyful, welcome noise—a faint scraping.

Matthew is turning his key in the front-door lock. He must have had car trouble and taken an Uber home; that's why he isn't coming in through the garage. Perhaps he left his phone in his car—it all makes sense now! She runs to the door and reaches for the handle, her movements swift and reflexive, propelled by an enormous wave of relief. Just before she throws open the door, she realizes there was no chime on her cell phone to alert her to a presence at the door.

She peers through the peephole.

She steps back, shaken to her core.

The stoop is empty.

Did she imagine the scraping sound because she so desperately wanted to hear it, or was it simply the wind, rustling through the bushes and shaking the trees?

The storm is still raging, increasing in strength; her husband is somewhere in the dark night, amid the sheets of rain and driving wind.

Marissa texts Renee and again urges her to head home. **I'm sure everything is fine,** Marissa types, but her hand is trembling so badly that she needs to backspace and retype the word *fine*.

Then she begins to call hospitals. There are several in the area: Georgetown, Sibley, GW, Suburban . . .

But no one will give her any information. All the hospitals refuse to confirm or deny whether a Matthew Bishop has been brought in.

"It's the law," one of the operators explains, her voice sympathetic yet firm.

Marissa dials 911, and the dispatcher puts her through to the local police precinct. The officer who answers the phone is kind and tries to be reassuring, but clearly he doesn't consider this an emergency.

She can't help it; she breaks down. "I know my husband. Something terrible has happened."

"I'm sorry, ma'am, but there's—"

His sentence is interrupted by the clicking of another call.

She looks down at caller ID, and in block letters Marissa sees the information she has been dreading: GEORGETOWN HOSPITAL.

She quickly accepts it, ending her call with the police.

"Mrs. Bishop?" a man asks.

"Yes, yes, this is she," Marissa blurts.

"This is Dale Whitaker, I'm a nurse here at—"

Before he can finish, Marissa blurts, "What happened to my husband?"

Marissa's legs give out and she sinks to the hardwood floor as she listens to the efficient yet soothing voice of the ER nurse informing her that Matthew was brought into the hospital by ambulance earlier that night.

A car accident, Marissa thinks. She knew it: the rain, his speeding . . .

Her body begins to shake uncontrollably. Matthew would have called if he could have. He must be seriously hurt.

But he's alive, she tells herself. He has to be, or wouldn't the police show up at her door to relay the devastating news?

Marissa wipes her eyes and braces herself for the words that will come.

Whatever happened—if Matthew broke a half dozen bones and totaled his car or crashed into another vehicle and injured its driver—they'll face it together.

She's so certain she knows the origin of the incident that brought him to the ER that it takes her a moment to process the nurse's words:

"Your husband was assaulted and lost consciousness. He's awake now and is going to be fine, but we're monitoring him overnight."

"Assaulted?" Marissa gasps. "By who?"

"I don't have any information on that."

Marissa is racing upstairs to her bedroom to pull on jeans and a sweatshirt. She can't—won't—process the words now. She only needs to get to Matthew.

"I'll be there as soon as possible," Marissa says breathlessly. "Can you please tell him I'm on my way?"

She's slipping on her sneakers before she realizes she can't leave Bennett home alone. If he woke up, he'd be petrified not to find her here.

It's almost midnight. The fastest solution would be to ask a neighbor for help. She looks out the window at Louise Johnston's house across the street. The Johnstons have two children, and Marissa once watched their five-year-old daughter when their son had to be rushed to the doctor because he'd shoved a marble up his nose and they couldn't get it out. But the Johnstons' home is dark, and Marissa doesn't want to wake them at this hour. The only house she can see with a light on is owned by Max Carrey, or, as Bennett calls him, Scary Carrey. He is clearly not an option.

Hallie is a junior in high school and probably asleep. She needs to be up for school in another six or seven hours, but Marissa taps out a text to her anyway. There's no reply.

Marissa has no one else.

If only her parents lived nearby, Marissa thinks, or if she had a close friend to call for help.

Matthew's father, Chris, lives just a few miles away, but Marissa knows her husband would be furious if she called him. Matthew has made it clear through the years that he never wants help from his father. She scrolls through her contacts, rapidly dismissing possibilities, until she gets to the *W*s. *Polly.*

Bennett doesn't know Polly well, but he has met her. Although he'd be startled to find his mother's assistant here in the middle of the night, he wouldn't completely freak out. Plus, Polly got a stellar reference from the family she worked for as a nanny last year.

With any luck—and she definitely could use some tonight—Bennett will stay asleep.

I wouldn't ask unless it were an emergency, Marissa begins her text. **Matthew was injured and is in the hospital–could you come to the house and stay in case Bennett wakes up?**

Polly's response comes so swiftly it is as if she were staring at her phone when the text landed: **On my way.**

Before Polly's VW comes to a stop in the driveway, Marissa is in her car, pulling the seat belt across her body. She waves at Polly and watches to make sure Polly gets inside the front door Marissa left cracked open, then she presses down the gas pedal. As her windshield wipers swoosh fervently back and forth, her heartbeat keeps pace.

Who would want to hurt Matthew?

Perhaps that disgruntled employee, the one Matthew fired last year. Or maybe it was a random attack; someone could have seen Matthew pull up at a stoplight, the engine of his expensive car idling, and decided to carjack him. If Matthew tried to resist—and knowing her husband, he might have—it could have turned violent.

Between the heavy rain and her damp eyes, Marissa can barely see the road. When she approaches a stoplight on Macarthur Boulevard just as it turns yellow, she is tempted to accelerate through it. At the last second, though, she slams on the brakes. The only thing that could make this night worse would be getting into an accident of her own.

She finds a spot in the visitors' lot and hurries toward the hospital entrance, holding her coat over her head to shield her from the rain.

She gives her name to the employee at the front desk and shows her driver's license, and a moment later a nurse appears and escorts Marissa to Matthew. Navigating past the curtained partitions, Marissa hears the beeping of cardiac monitors and a patient loudly calling for more ice.

In all of their years together, the only time she and Matthew have been in this hospital together was when Bennett was born.

How lucky they have been.

The nurse parts the curtain to Bed Six, revealing Matthew lying on a gurney, an IV needle buried in his forearm. He's wearing a blue hospital gown, his bare feet are sticking out from beneath the sheet that's draped around his lower body, and a white bandage is on his forehead.

But his eyes are open, and he's smiling at her.

"Hey, babe," Matthew says as she steps toward him.

"I'll leave you two alone," the nurse says. "Just press the call button if you need me."

Other than the bandage and some dried blood by Matthew's hairline, he looks the same. He looks like *her* Matthew.

Although Marissa swore she wouldn't, she begins to cry again.

"It's okay. I'm fine. Just a few bruises."

She holds his hand with both of hers, soaking in the warmth of his skin. "I'm just so relieved. I thought . . ."

"Shhh. I just wish I could've gotten a swing at the other guy." He mock punches with his free hand.

With those motions, his torso shifts, and beneath the gaps in his gown, Marissa sees eggplant-colored marks on his ribs.

She gasps. "Why would someone do this to you?"

"No idea." Matthew shakes his head, then grimaces. "I keep wondering the same thing. One minute I was about to get in my car, and the next I'm on the ground with some asshole kicking the shit out of me."

Marissa winces, trying to block out the image of her husband being hurt.

"It's not that bad." Matthew pulls his gown closed. "I thought I could make it home. But, well, guess I was wrong. I passed out and crashed just as I was exiting the garage."

"I don't understand. Was he waiting for you in the parking garage? Did you see him?"

"I didn't get a look at his face. He came at me from behind."

A terrifying thought sears through Marissa's mind. "Your keys! Did he take your wallet and keys?"

The assailant could have their address and be breaking into their house right now, sliding the key into the lock while Bennett sleeps just one floor above. She fumbles for her cell phone, but Matthew's voice stops her.

"No, that's the strangest part." Matthew looks bewildered. "He could've easily grabbed my wallet, my watch . . . anything. Even the car. But it's like the only thing he wanted to do was beat the crap out of me."

CHAPTER TWENTY-FIVE

AVERY

I'M SO LOST IN THOUGHT it takes me a moment to register that the mail-man on the sidewalk in front of my house is trying to get my attention.

Ever since Marissa phoned to tell me what had happened to Matthew, I've been sitting in a chair on my porch, pen and notebook in hand, dia-gramming the strange events surrounding the Bishops.

We're five sessions in, and for the first time I worry that my ten-session method might not work for these clients.

"He gonna be okay if I bring this up there?" the mail carrier asks, nodding at Romeo, curled by my feet basking in a patch of sunlight.

I want to reply, *He's more scared of you than you are of him,* but some-thing holds me back. I didn't get Romeo for protection, obviously, but I don't need to advertise that my big, muscular dog is as aggressive as a cannoli.

"I'll come and get it," I call as I stand up.

The mailman hands me a few envelopes and a catalog, which I tuck under my arm as I head back up the steps, my mind still considering and discarding potential connections.

I sit down, placing the mail beside me on the side table, and reach for my notebook again. I stare at the jumble of words, my eyes flitting across the page—*Coco, Polly, yellow roses, anonymous note, attack* . . .

Clearly Polly didn't carry out the assault. She isn't strong enough to overpower Matthew; besides, he is certain the perpetrator was a man, Ma-rissa told me.

But Polly's presence near Matthew's office just a few hours before the incident is more than strange. It's highly significant. I just don't know how yet.

I stretch out my foot and absently rub it against Romeo, who rolls onto his back, his tail thwacking against the wood porch floor.

The biggest question in my mind is the identity of the man who hurt Matthew.

Marissa mentioned that both she and Matthew suspected the assault could have been conducted by a disgruntled employee, and they'd relayed their suspicion to the police. I imagine the parking garage has video cameras, too, which could aid in identification.

I rub my temples and stand up, bringing my empty coffee mug and the stack of mail into the kitchen. Maybe caffeine will help.

While my coffee brews, I flip through the mail: catalog, bill, junk, bill . . . and an envelope with the return address for LifeLine, the agency that handled Paul's life insurance policy. Probably just a follow-up, since they already sent Lana the generous settlement. I slide my finger under the seal and remove the letter.

I scan the document quickly at first, then my eyes widen: *medical fraud . . . investigation . . . misrepresentation . . .*

My hand begins shaking and I almost drop the sheet of paper.

It sounds as if the insurance company thinks I had something to do with Paul's death.

I sink onto a counter stool, rereading the letter, this time more closely.

Then I reach for my cell phone and call my lawyer.

I expected the Bishops to cancel their session tonight; after all, Matthew was released from the hospital only this morning.

I was hoping they'd reschedule. My lawyer, Sylvia McColaugh, did a little digging after I scanned the letter from LifeLine and sent it to her. She scheduled a Zoom call with me for 5:00 P.M., right after I'd gone for a long hike with Romeo, hoping to simultaneously burn off some of my physical stress and shake loose some new ideas in my mind.

But any relief I'd found during my walk through Rock Creek Park evaporated the moment I saw Sylvia's frowning face on my phone screen, her big green eyes further magnified by her glasses and her white curls a halo around her head.

It's not great, she'd said, forgoing pleasantries and cutting to the chase, which is one of the reasons why she keeps my business. *They're opening an investigation into Paul's death.*

Before I could ask why, she told me, *They received an anonymous tip that you euthanized Paul.*

An anonymous tip.

The irony isn't lost on me. My call to the FDA whistle-blower hotline was supposed to be anonymous, but it wasn't. Neither is this one to LifeLine.

Acelia is demonstrating that they can swing a sledgehammer and aim it at any chinks in my life.

Sylvia told me to sit tight, and that she'll circle back when she has more information. *You get any more letters or calls, a cop comes to your door, anything—you phone me immediately. Don't let them in, don't say a word.*

After I hung up, I filed away Lifeline's letter, then popped a CBD gummy and soaked in a hot bath while I listened to Joan Armatrading on my AirPods. But I couldn't stop seeing images of Paul during his final weeks, especially this one: me sliding into his bed and cradling him in my arms while he took his final breaths. He was so frail by that point; he barely weighed more than a child. I held him for a long time, until his body was no longer warm. As the sun rose, I dialed Lana's number so she could come over and say goodbye. Then I set into motion the arrangements Paul and I had discussed: a cremation, a celebration of his life at a local pub with the music and food and drinks Paul loved best, and toasts given by Lana and his closest friends. I mingled for a few minutes, then hid in a back room. I couldn't give a toast, for the same reason why I couldn't read the sympathy cards and letters.

I don't care what all those people will think if they learn the insurance company is investigating me, but I am concerned about Lana's reaction. What if she believed the claims? It would break her heart and possibly destroy our relationship.

And what if I'm found guilty?

I cast aside the worry for now, pulling myself out of the bath to get dressed in anticipation of Marissa and Matthew's arrival.

This, our fifth session, is Devastation, the point at which my clients reach rock bottom and fear they won't succeed. But in this case, I'm the one who is beginning to worry they won't succeed. The Bishops' case is outside the lines; so many unseen forces are competing with my techniques and conspiring to harm them, too. I can't repair their marriage until I uncover the truth—about each of them and their motivations, as well as the complicated people in their orbit.

My doorbell chimes at 7:00 P.M. sharp, and I welcome them into my office. Marissa looks pale and exhausted and seems so jittery I'm tempted to offer her a gummy from my stash. Matthew, by contrast, appears robust and intently focused. If it weren't for the bandage on his forehead, I'd never know he'd been brutally attacked less than twenty-four hours ago. He keeps his arm around Marissa as they sit side-by-side on the couch, as if he wants to protect her from whatever their future holds.

I begin, "It's been quite a twenty-four hours, hasn't it?"

They both assume I'm referring to theirs, which is my intention.

"So, I think Marissa filled you in on everything," Matthew says. "The only new information is that the employee I had to let go—the guy who tried to get into the building with a gun last year—had a clear alibi. And the police reviewed the footage from the garage, but the attack happened in a blind corner. They saw a guy hanging around the garage before I was hit, but they couldn't see anything else."

"I see." I ask for the fired employee's name, which Matthew freely gives, and I jot it down in my pad. "Do either of you have any other thoughts on who would want to hurt Matthew?"

Marissa fixes her gaze to the floor and fiddles with her wedding band.

Matthew shakes his head. "I've been thinking about that all day. Must've been a random attack. Maybe he thought he heard someone coming and didn't have time to rob me."

Marissa's eyes rise, and I can read the raw fear in them. We're both wondering if the man she slept with, the one who can't let go so easily, is behind it. She shakes her head, almost imperceptibly, her expression pleading.

I can almost hear her thoughts: *It wasn't him. . . . He's out of town. . . . Don't say anything. . . .*

I'm not going to break the promise I made to her by letting Matthew know she slept with one of his old friends, but I am planning to pull Marissa aside after the session. I can't wait until Monday to start checking this guy out; I need a name.

Marissa clears her throat and changes the subject. "There's one other thing I can't stop thinking about. When I got home from the hospital, I couldn't find Polly at first."

"Polly?" I put more emphasis on her name than I intended.

"Yes, my assistant at Coco. I asked her to come to the house because I couldn't leave Bennett alone. I told her he'd probably sleep through everything, and that she could nap on the couch."

Polly had a busy night trying to keep tabs on the Bishops, I think.

"I finally found her in Bennett's room." Marissa gives a little shudder, and Matthew pulls her in even closer. "She was sound asleep, leaning against his big stuffed dog. . . . Something about it made me deeply uncomfortable."

"I can imagine," I comment. "What did you do?"

"I woke her up and motioned for her to come into the hallway. She claimed she heard Bennett whimpering and went to check on him. He hadn't woken up, but she said she decided to stay close. Just in case."

"She heard him whimpering from one floor below?" I ask.

Matthew frowns. "Marissa, there's no way she could have . . ."

"So what was she really doing up there?" I interject. "There's Bennett's room and the master bedroom and what else?"

"Just a couple of guest rooms," Marissa replies. "One I use as a little office, but I don't store a lot there. Most of my work things are at Coco."

Which Polly has full access to, I think.

"Your bedroom." I tap my pen against my pad. "Anything missing or moved in it?"

I haven't seen the master bedroom in the Bishops' house, but I imagine it's similar to areas on the first floor, which means it looks like a spread out of a design magazine.

"I'm not certain." Marissa hesitates, then frowns. "I'm pretty sure our closet door was open and I always keep it closed, but I left in such a rush . . ."

"We don't have anything in there but clothes and shoes," Matthew says. "There's nothing of real value in the bedroom."

"Matthew, all my jewelry is there. And I left my watch and the necklace out on the dresser."

Matthew's phone buzzes, and without looking at it, he reaches into his pocket to silence it. "Sorry."

I'm pleased his priorities are where they should be right now.

"But nothing's missing, right?"

Marissa shakes her head.

"Look, there's an old axiom that the simplest explanation is usually the correct one," Matthew continues. "Bennett has nightmares now and then. It's possible that Polly came upstairs to sneak a look around and really did hear him whimpering. There's no other good reason for her falling asleep in his room."

Marissa nods slowly. "You're probably right. I can see her taking a peek at our bedroom—she's intrusive like that—but it's probably nothing more than her curiosity and lack of boundaries."

Matthew clears his throat. "There is one more thing. Polly called me yesterday, right after she closed up Coco. She said she wanted to talk."

Marissa stiffens, but I speak before she can. "About what?"

I see Matthew caressing Marissa's shoulder, as if he's trying to soothe her. Their roles have shifted during our time together since the first session, I realize. At first, Matthew was enraged and Marissa seemed equal parts frightened and placating. Since then, he's displayed admirable qualities, such as forgiveness and protectiveness, while Marissa seems a little more fraught, not to mention deceptive, considering she's still lying to her husband about whom she cheated with.

Matthew continues, "Polly told me she was worried about you, Marissa. She said she was driving downtown and asked if I could meet her."

Aha, I think. Polly's puzzling visit to Giovanni's.

"And you didn't tell me any of this?" Marissa's tone is dangerously quiet.

Matthew shakes his head quickly. "I'm sorry."

The question that came to my mind during my first session with the Bishops surfaces again, but this time the order of the players shuffles: Is Matthew fearful of upsetting his wife—or is he fearful of *her*?

"I never saw Polly. I got an important work call and couldn't leave the office, so I texted her to say I'd call her on my drive home. I was going to tell you about it, but obviously I never made it out of the parking garage. . . . Anyway, she phoned me and left a message while I was in the hospital."

Matthew reaches into his pocket and pulls out his phone. He touches the screen a couple of times, then Polly's reedy voice fills the room: "Um, hi, Matthew. . . . So, I've been waiting for you to call, but it's getting late. Anyway, I just wanted to tell you I'm really worried about Marissa. She doesn't seem like herself—I'll explain more when we talk. Okay. Bye."

Matthew puts his phone away again. "I haven't called her back."

Marissa's lips are tightly clenched. "This is outrageous. I'm firing her tomorrow."

"Marissa, I get it, she's weird and she clearly idolizes you," Matthew replies. "But, look, with everything that's happened lately, I don't want you alone in that shop. Fire Polly, but can you at least wait until you hire someone new?"

Marissa exhales. "Fine. I actually just got a few résumés from promising candidates who go to GW. Hopefully one of them will work out."

Even though I'm growing ever more intrigued by the mysterious happenings churning around the Bishops, and I have my own suspicions about Polly, I can't lose focus on the reason why I was hired. We need to use our sessions together to do the internal work of repairing their marriage. If someone on the outside is trying to wrench the Bishops apart, that's for me to explore on my own time.

"Let's shift gears," I tell them. "Marissa, when you first got the call from the hospital, how did you feel?"

Marissa slumps and closes her eyes briefly.

"It was awful. I was really worried that he—"

"Talk to Matthew directly, Marissa. 'I was really worried that *you* . . .'"

Marissa turns to face her husband. They're so close that the tips of their noses are just inches apart. "Matthew, I was really worried that *you* wouldn't make it." She swallows hard and her voice trembles. "That we wouldn't get a second chance. I've hurt you so badly, and I was terrified I lost you just when it seemed like we were finally finding each other."

Even though Marissa's words sound a bit Hallmarky, I believe they are sincere. She truly wants a deeper relationship with Matthew; something more than a curated Instagram marriage. If Marissa had had that connection with her husband in the first place, she would never have sought it with another man.

Maybe it's the naked yearning on Marissa's face or perhaps it's my earlier remembrance of Paul's final moments, but I feel my throat tighten, as it always does when I'm about to cry. I look down at my notepad and pretend to jot something down.

"Marissa," Matthew begins.

Then Marissa's phone buzzes with an incoming call. She looks at her purse, then back at Matthew. Her face twists as she says, "I'm so sorry. Bennett is over at his friend Charlie's house and I need to grab this. Just in case."

She lifts the phone to her ear and listens for a few seconds as her expression morphs. A minute ago, she was gentle and vulnerable. Now, a kind of darkness has come into her eyes. Her moods seem to shift like a body of water on a windy day.

"Wait, I'm here with Matthew. Let me put you on speakerphone. Can you repeat that?"

She lays her phone on the coffee table and a deep voice begins, "We need Matthew to come to the station. We have a suspect in custody and want Matthew to try to identify him in a lineup."

CHAPTER TWENTY-SIX

MARISSA

MARISSA PAUSES AT a stop sign, taking an extra moment to ensure the cross street is clear before she presses down on the gas pedal.

She's so worn-out that even the extra cup of coffee she gulped this morning barely made a dent in her exhaustion, and though she's cutting it close in getting Bennett to school on time, she is careful to drive under the speed limit. The last thing they need is another accident.

Back at home, Matthew is still asleep. True to form for her hard-charging husband, he overdid it yesterday afternoon by going to the office for a couple of hours and retrieving his car from the garage, then meeting her at Avery's for their fifth session. Marissa had suggested postponing it, but Matthew insisted he was fine.

He might have been, but the visit to the police station, even though it was brief, seemed to put him over the edge. She couldn't recall the last time Matthew had taken a sick day, but he was doing so today.

Matthew couldn't identify anyone from the lineup. *I never saw his face,* he explained to the police detective. It appeared to be a random attack. Yet Marissa couldn't stop thinking about how Matthew's assailant ignored his expensive watch and wallet filled with cash and credit cards.

The attack felt personal.

"Mom?" Marissa looks in the rearview mirror and sees Bennett playing with his Rubik's Cube, twisting around the colorful pieces of plastic. "Can we have pizza tonight?"

Bennett's timing is exquisite; ordering out has never sounded so appealing.

"You know what? Maybe not pizza again, but we can definitely get takeout. Let's check with Dad, too. He's going to rest at home today."

Bennett nods. "'Kay."

She tries to gauge his tone, but it's hard to decipher how he feels. Bennett knows Matthew got hurt—there was no hiding the bandage on Matthew's forehead—but they'd simply told their eight-year-old that his father had been in a minor car accident. Revealing Matthew had been assaulted would only have worried Bennett, even though Marissa is sure he would have loved to hear about Matthew's going to the police station and looking through the one-way mirror at suspects in a lineup.

"I'm going to be late," Bennett frets.

"No, you won't. We've got ninety seconds until the bell, and we're just about there." Marissa pulls into the loop that will take them to the South Entrance, where the third-graders disembark and shake the hand of the lower-school principal.

Then she sees Natalie's familiar figure striding toward the main entrance.

"Damn it," Marissa mutters, suddenly remembering the auction meeting she's supposed to attend this morning right after drop-off. Luckily Bennett is too focused on his puzzle to mention the curse jar.

"Okay, sweetie. Time to get out," she nudges. "Don't forget your lunch box!"

"Love you." Bennett slides out of his seat.

"Love you, too." She feels the truth of the words down to her bones.

She drives to the visitor parking lot and finds an empty spot, then glances in the rearview mirror and swipes on some lip gloss. She looks down at her leggings and faded sweatshirt and shrugs. They'll have to do, even though they don't fit the unspoken uniform of Rolling Hills mothers. Wearing exercise clothes to a parent-run meeting is acceptable, as long as it's an appropriate brand and doesn't have mysterious stains, such as the coffee dribbles Marissa sports on her right cuff. She rolls up her sleeves to hide the dark marks and fluffs her hair, wishing she had time to put on mascara and concealer. She feels so washed-out.

She hurries past the construction site of the new STEM building, toward the lower school. Since she wasn't planning to even enter the building this morning, she has forgotten her parent ID at home. The guard gives her a temporary pass to affix to her sweatshirt, and Marissa strides down a hallway lined with photographs of Rolling Hills students dating back to its first class in 1924, toward the library's small conference room, where the auction committee is meeting. Just her luck—no other members are in sight.

Just before she reaches the library, her phone vibrates. She checks the screen: it's Avery. Marissa declines the call. Through the closed conference room door, she can hear the muted sound of chattering, followed by Natalie's throaty laugh.

Marissa's stomach tightens as she enters and the heads of the nine other committee members swivel toward her. But instead of stepping into the room, Marissa makes a swift decision: She isn't going to endure an hour of discussion about the incredible items the other committee members have procured for the live auction—a private tour of the Washington Monument, dinner for six at the Inn at Little Washington, a chance to feed the Amur tigers at the National Zoo—while Natalie presides over it all.

"Morning." Marissa keeps her hand on the doorknob. "Sorry to interrupt. I just wanted to let you know I won't be able to join you today, after all."

Natalie rises to her feet unhurriedly, smoothing her yellow pencil skirt. She has paired it with a patterned silk blouse and alligator-print heels. Her amber-tinted sunglasses rest atop her head, pushing back her shiny dark hair. Marissa wonders if Natalie actually took the time to match the lenses with her outfit.

"Are you sure?" Natalie asks.

"You're already here," Dawn adds in the same judgmental tone she used during the boys' baseball game three days ago.

Marissa forces herself to smile. "Unfortunately, there's been a bit of an emergency, and I need to get"—at the last moment she decides to swap out the word *home*—"to my store."

"Oh, can't that eager young assistant of yours cover the shop for a bit?" Natalie pushes.

Marissa feels an intense surge of dislike. She doesn't need to justify her decision to anyone, and she's not even going to bother responding to Natalie's last question.

"I'll see you all soon!" Marissa says cheerfully, closing the door.

As she drives back home, she tries to shake off her dark mood, the result of her brief encounter with Natalie. Marissa is glad she didn't give Natalie any indication the crisis involves Matthew being injured. Knowing Natalie, she'd probably swoop over with a hearty lasagna or casserole—one loaded with meat and cheeses and calories, the kind that most men can't resist—then make a point of checking up on Matthew.

Marissa realizes her foot is pressing down harder on the accelerator, and she eases up. She swears she can feel her blood pressure rising. Ever since Natalie moved back to town, Marissa has tried to be a good sport. She looks the other way when Natalie places a hand on Matthew's sleeve or leans in a bit too close to talk to him. She pretends to not notice when Natalie keeps her eyes fixed on Matthew, all but ignoring Marissa.

Those small aggressions have been piling up, though, and Marissa has finally reached her limit.

Avery would probably tell Marissa to be direct, to cut away the veneer of false friendship and voice her frustration. The thought is oddly liberating. Marissa will relish telling Natalie off.

But for now, her most important task is to get home and check on her husband.

She slips into the house quietly. The kitchen is exactly as she left it, with Bennett's plate and empty orange juice glass in the sink. Marissa slides a coffee pod into the Nespresso maker and brews a cup, then carries it upstairs.

Matthew is propped up in bed, checking his phone.

"Hey"—she walks over to kiss him—"you're supposed to be resting." She gives him the coffee.

He takes a grateful sip. "I am resting. I'm still in bed. How much more relaxed could I be?"

He sets his coffee on the nightstand and lifts up the covers, patting the empty spot next to him. Marissa smiles and slips in beside him. Careful to avoid his bruised ribs, she lays her head lightly on his bare chest. His arms tighten around her.

"Marissa, I wanted to say this yesterday in Avery's office before we got interrupted." His deep voice is serious; beneath her left ear, she can feel the sure, steady beat of his heart. "I've done a lot of soul-searching these past few days. I want to be a better husband to you. And dad to Bennett. When I woke up in the ambulance, it was all I could think about. My regrets . . ."

Marissa quashes the impulse to shush him, to tell him he's a wonderful husband and father. She remains silent because his words contain truth.

"I'm going to be around more. I promise." Matthew kisses the top of her head. "Starting now."

"I would really love that." Is it possible, Marissa wonders, that all the horrible things that have happened will actually make their family stronger? She has been so achingly lonely in her marriage. If she is brutally honest with herself, as Avery has urged her to be, that feeling didn't just sprout up in the months leading up to her terrible indiscretion. It has existed throughout her relationship with Matthew, this sense that only a tenuous, gossamer tie links them, and that something as fleeting as a strong gust could blow them apart.

She shivers involuntarily and snuggles closer to her husband, soaking in the warmth of his body. She can hear her phone buzzing on the nightstand, but she ignores it. If Bennett's school is trying to reach her, they have the home number.

"So, what's Bennett's schedule after school today?" Matthew asks. "Boy Scouts? Baseball? I was thinking I could pick him up."

Marissa doesn't correct him by saying it's Cub Scouts, not Boy Scouts, and that they always meet on Wednesday nights. "Actually, he's free this afternoon."

"Fantastic! I know what we can do. I'll take him to the batting cages. I can see how my little slugger is doing."

Marissa hesitates. "There's something I need to tell you. Maybe this isn't the right time to mention it, but Bennett wants to quit baseball."

"What?" Matthew sounds shocked. "He loves baseball! Didn't he tell us he got on base twice last week?"

"He was lying," Marissa says softly. "He didn't want to disappoint us." Disappoint *you*, she silently clarifies.

Matthew doesn't immediately reply.

"I'm sorry I brought it up," Marissa finally says. "We don't have to talk about it now."

"No, it's okay." Matthew clears his throat. "You know, I've actually been thinking about *my* dad a lot lately."

In the pause that follows, Marissa holds perfectly still, barely breathing. She can't distract Matthew from what he may be about to say.

Matthew *never* wants to discuss his father, whom Marissa calls by his first name, Chris, because she has never grown close enough to him to use the term *Dad*. Even though he lives twenty minutes away, Matthew sees him only twice a year, on Christmas Eve and on Chris's birthday. Marissa and Bennett visit Chris more often, and Chris and Bennett also spend time together alone on occasion, going to a movie or bowling. Although Chris can be brusque to the point of rudeness around Matthew, he is unfailingly gentle with Bennett.

Still, her husband would clearly be happier if he and his dad had no relationship at all.

Marissa has long since given up trying to get Matthew to talk about it. *It is what it is. You know I don't like all that processing BS,* he would say whenever she tried in the past.

"I did so many things I thought would impress him," Matthew says now. "And it was never enough. I got good grades. I played sports. I married you," he concludes with a little half laugh.

Marissa has witnessed this subtle dynamic over the years. It's almost as if Matthew's father disdains Matthew for being *Matthew*—classically good-looking, savvy, a natural athlete, and born with the proverbial silver spoon. Marissa has always sensed that Chris somehow doesn't respect Matthew's innate gifts. As if he wanted his son to have to work harder, to struggle more.

As *he* had.

Marissa waits for Matthew to keep talking, but he seems lost in thought. Finally, she says carefully, "I wonder if the way he grew up . . . affected his relationships."

Matthew's father was the oldest of four in a blue-collar family and worked part-time throughout high school to help his parents pay the bills. Chris didn't have time to play on sports teams or join the SGA or hang out at the diner with the other students. He didn't attend school dances because he didn't own a suit and figured no girl would want to go with a guy in a shabby blazer. When his father fell ill, Chris got his GED and began working full-time as a delivery boy for a D.C. lobbying firm, ferrying important documents all over town on his old three-speed bike, but managed to earn his college degree by taking night classes. By the time Chris turned thirty-two, he owned his own lobbying firm, and plenty of women were clamoring to be by his side, even though he still favored sturdy, well-worn clothes. He chose Matthew's mother, a Mount Vernon College graduate from a well-heeled family. He and the blueblood debutante were obviously an abysmal match.

"He hated the way my mother spent," Matthew says now. "The clothes. The trips to the salons. Our summer place. He would have bought a little fishing cottage, but she insisted on that big house."

Marissa's hand strokes slow circles on Matthew's arm, an echo of the movement she makes on Bennett's back when their little boy is upset.

"Don't most parents want their kids to have a better life than they did?" Heat fills Matthew's tone. "I work my ass off! I deserve a nice house, a good car. . . ."

"Of course you do." Even though Matthew got a huge running start in life—the best schools, his college tuition fully paid for, and a pedigree that guaranteed doors would open to him in business—she can understand his anger.

Marissa thinks back to the first and only time Chris visited them in their new home. Dinner had gone fairly well; Marissa made sure to have Chris's brand of Scotch, Cluny, on hand, and she served steak and baked potatoes, which was his favorite meal. The conversation never flowed easily, though. Then Chris went out to his car. Although by then he could have bought a fleet of fancy foreign models, he drove an old Buick LeSabre. It refused to start; the engine repeatedly sputtered but wouldn't catch in the cold night air. Matthew went inside to call AAA, and when he came back out, Chris had the hood up and had gotten a toolbox out of his trunk. He was so focused on tinkering with the carburetor he merely grunted, *No,* when Matthew asked if Chris wanted Marissa to make him some hot tea.

After standing around for a few minutes, Matthew went back inside. By the time the tow truck had arrived, Chris had fixed the problem.

You can't outsource everything in life, Chris had said. *Though I guess you're used to having other people clean up after your messes.* He'd picked up his tool-box and closed the hood. The slam seemed to echo through the night.

Matthew had never again invited his father over.

"Bennett's not going to feel the way I did," Matthew says now, his voice fierce. "If he doesn't want to play baseball, he doesn't have to play baseball. We'll do whatever he wants this afternoon."

Marissa lifts herself up and kisses Matthew.

"I love you," she whispers.

He kisses her back, deeply, as he pulls her closer.

CHAPTER TWENTY-SEVEN

AVERY

I THRUM MY FINGERTIPS AGAINST my steering wheel, keeping watch out my window, while I speculate about the man who hurt Matthew.

When the Bishops rushed out in the middle of our session to go to the police station last night, Matthew promised to fill me in on what happened. I got a text from him a few hours later, letting me know he couldn't identify anyone in the lineup, and that the police didn't seem to have a real suspect.

As of now, it appears to be a random attack.

Still, I've decided not to wait until Monday to learn about the man Marissa slept with.

I reach for my cell phone and dial Marissa's number. It rings a few times, as it did when I called earlier this morning, then goes to voice mail again. Last time I didn't leave a message. Now I do, asking her to phone me back as soon as possible with the name of the person we discussed at the Chevy Chase Circle. Enough is enough. I need to check him out.

The front door of the house I'm watching opens, but the person who steps out isn't the one I'm waiting for. It's a tall, gangly looking guy with longish hair. He shifts his backpack higher up onto his shoulders and walks past me, never even looking in my direction. I shift in my seat and exhale, then glance at the dashboard clock: it's a quarter past nine.

I should have pushed Marissa to tell me more that day about her infidelity when we stood in the middle of the traffic circle, but she seemed so broken and afraid that I merely told her not to worry, and that I'd handle everything. I regret this tactic now.

I'm beginning to wonder if Marissa emotionally seduced me—the way she probably seduced the man she slept with. And the way she must have seduced Matthew, too, all those years ago. Not overtly through her sexuality, as Natalie would, but with a subtle vulnerability. Marissa is gorgeous and fragile with her soft voice, delicate frame, and long-lashed cornflower-blue eyes. Her magnetism is quiet, but undeniable. Even Polly fell under her spell.

What if there never was another guy? Perhaps she's been stalling because there is no name to offer up.

Marissa has already created one major fabrication—saying she slept with a near stranger from her gym—and it's entirely possible her lies didn't end there.

But what would be her motivation?

From early on, I've sensed the Bishops are more complex than my typical clients, and I'm still not convinced Marissa is the only one hiding something.

Matthew's swift acceptance of me and my methods seems almost too compliant. Plus there was that phone call outside Mon Ami Gabi, and the revelation that he told Natalie, not his wife, about the lost business account.

Like his wife, Matthew seems almost too perfect.

If either—or both—of them is playing a game, I'm several moves behind, and I desperately need to catch up.

My day is jam-packed, with appointments stacked up: a meeting with my accountant to answer his many questions about my taxes, a visit from the mobile vet to give Romeo his Bordetella vaccine, and sessions with three clients, including a brand-new one. But one way or another, I'm going to get to the bottom of this.

There's just one thing I need to attend to first.

As if on cue, the front door of the group house opens, and Polly steps out, blinking in the bright morning sunlight. As she walks toward her VW Rabbit parked at the end of her walkway, she scans her phone.

She is so absorbed that she doesn't even notice me until I am nearly by her side.

"Hey, Polly," I say casually. "Got a minute?"

She starts, then looks from side to side, as if seeking an escape route. "I have to get to work."

"You have some time. I'll be quick."

Discomfort spreads across her face. She's clearly trying to come up with a reason to say no, but she must not be able to think of one.

It's chilly and the wind feels fierce. Polly is wearing the same light-weight turquoise jacket she had on the other night. As she shoves her hands into her pockets, I notice her nose is already beginning to redden.

"You're cold. Why don't we sit in my car and talk? Or yours, if you'd rather."

I'm hoping she'll choose her car because you can learn a lot about someone by checking out their personal spaces when they don't have advance warning. She hesitates, then as another gust of wind hits us, she uses her key fob to unlock the doors to her vehicle.

The passenger seat is clear, unlike in my car, and everything is well organized, just like her purse: a blue hair scrunchie is wrapped around the gearshift, a stainless-steel water bottle is tucked in the cup holder, and a pack of disinfecting wipes is in the console.

Polly starts the engine and a Britney Spears song blares. She quickly reaches for a knob and turns off the radio.

I wait for her to begin the conversation. A moment later, she does: "What did you want to talk to me about?"

"I know strange things have been happening around Coco. Like the creepy note you found. I need you to tell me what else is going on."

I speak with authority, hoping Polly will succumb to it, as she did when I searched Coco. But maybe she learned from that experience.

"I'm sorry, but I'm not really sure I can tell you anything. I mean, not without permission."

"Marissa's permission? Polly, she is in *danger*. Matthew told me you called him to say you were worried about her. Do you really think I'd be here if the Bishops didn't want my help?"

"He told you that?" Polly looks surprised.

"Yes, he also told me you drove all the way down to Giovanni's restaurant to try to see him."

"Okay." Polly shifts in her seat. "So, I didn't think it was a big deal at first, but twice in the past week a guy has called and asked for Marissa. When I asked who it was—Marissa taught me to do that before handing the phone to her—he hung up."

"Any idea who it could have been?"

"No, I didn't recognize his voice. And there have been a few hang-ups, too. Like someone keeps calling because they hope she'll answer instead of me."

I play the devil's advocate: "Could be a telemarketer."

"I don't think so." Polly is practically bristling; she has a lot invested in her role in Marissa's life, and Polly doesn't like me downplaying the drama she feels she's a central part of.

"Is that all?" I keep my tone a little bored.

Polly takes the bait: "There's actually video footage from the store that night when someone put that note under the door. . . ."

"There is?" I can't believe I didn't think to ask the Bishops about this. Or that they hadn't mentioned it.

"Yes, and here's the thing. I asked Marissa about it, and she told me she checked the footage, but the camera angle was off and it was too blurry to see anything."

I reflexively glance at the purse on Polly's lap, wondering if the note is still tucked inside.

"But . . ." Polly's voice drops and she leans closer to me. I suddenly have an image of her as a young girl in a school classroom, whispering into the ears of other children, spreading rumors and sowing discord before smiling innocently up at the teacher and offering to wipe down the cafeteria tables after lunch. "I checked the video, too. I called the company and asked them to email us a copy of the recording from that night. They sent it over to the store's account, which of course I check every day. Anyway, I thought maybe I'd see something Marissa missed. . . . And I did. I saw the guy who left the note."

"Did you recognize him?" I ask urgently.

Polly nods proudly. "At first I couldn't place him, but then I realized who he was."

Get to the point, Polly! I want to scream.

"He's this homeless man, Ray, who usually sits on a bench down the street from our shop. He always has these funny signs. Do you think he's the one who is obsessed with Marissa? I know she buys sandwiches for him sometimes."

I blink hard, trying to sort and categorize what I've just learned. If I trust the information Polly has given me—and it should be easy enough to verify—I've just learned something crucial: Matthew and I aren't the only people Marissa has lied to; she blatantly deceived Polly about the contents of the video camera. Marissa must have known for days who put the note under the door.

Anger sweeps through me; she conned me. Again.

The theory I've been playing around with—that Marissa never actually had an affair—could be bolstered by this new information.

Perhaps Marissa asked the homeless man to leave the note. Maybe she is arranging for the calls Polly has been answering at Coco. Marissa could even have sent herself flowers, timing their arrival so that Matthew and I would be there to witness it.

If Marissa created this elaborate scenario to try to cast herself as a victim and get attention from her husband—or for some other, more sinister reason—she has succeeded, I think, remembering how Matthew held his arm around her protectively during our last session.

One percent of the population is composed of psychopaths, and most of them aren't the homicidal criminals we envision. We've all encountered them: people who seem charming and charismatic, but who lie without remorse and manipulate and deceive. And female psychopaths can be particularly adept at manipulation.

I think back to the moment the Bishops first entered my home, looking like the couple who had everything. I've spent the past few weeks trying to get to know them intimately, yet they still feel like strangers.

Then I look over at Polly. "Have you told Marissa you saw the footage?"

Polly shakes her head.

"But you drove all the way downtown to tell Matthew?"

"He's worried about her. Like really worried . . . I just felt like I should tell him."

Polly is studying my face, nakedly eager for our conversation to continue now.

"Is that all?"

"Isn't that enough?" she cries.

"Actually, there is one more thing. How did you enjoy working at Anthropologie?"

Polly has a terrible poker face. Her flush extends to include her ears.

Or maybe she's a brilliant actress.

"Look, I didn't really have a job there, okay? Please don't tell Marissa. The truth is, I had stopped working as a nanny and I was temping when I walked into Coco and I never wanted to leave. It's sophisticated and elegant and everything. . . ." Polly looks down at her lap and her final words come out as a whisper. "Everything I'm not."

I breathe in deeply, wondering if she's talking about Coco, or the woman who owns the boutique.

"I'll let you get to work now." I open the car door, but before I step out, I decide to toss her a bone. Polly could be useful in the future. "It was very smart of you to check the camera."

She smiles, and I straighten up, shutting the door and watching her drive away.

I learned a lot about Marissa during the past couple of minutes. She has plenty to answer for, and I deliberately didn't tell Polly I am also heading to Coco, because I don't want Marissa to have any warning of my impending arrival.

But I learned something about Polly, too.

Every time I inhaled, I smelled a delicate, floral perfume—subtle, but distinctive enough that I recognized it.

It's the scent Marissa wears.

CHAPTER TWENTY-EIGHT

MARISSA

MARISSA DOESN'T ARRIVE at Coco until almost eleven, and even Polly's usual barrage of questions or the news that Avery stopped by unexpectedly right after the store opened, hoping to catch Marissa, can't erase Marissa's smile. Her chin is slightly red from rubbing against Matthew's unshaven stubble, and throughout the day she finds her hand rising to touch the tender skin, as if to seal in the memory.

Lovemaking with Matthew felt different this morning. Powerful, raw, fierce—Marissa can't put her finger on the exact word to describe it, but those come close.

Matthew's eyes had been closed; he'd seemed to lose himself completely in the physical act, not even feeling the pain of his injuries. At the very end, he'd opened his eyes and stared into hers. *You're mine,* he'd whispered.

Polly touches Marissa's shoulder. "Marissa?"

Marissa pulls herself away from the reverie. "Yes, what is it?"

"I was just saying a few gift certificates came in for your school benefit."

"Great. Put them in the back room along with the rest of the auction items. I need to get them to . . ."

Her voice trails off before she completes the final word in her sentence: *Natalie.* Marissa frowns, watching as Polly picks up the gift certificates. Polly is asking if Marissa wants her to order more tissue paper inserts for the shopping bags, since they're down to a few hundred sheets.

Marissa nods, but it's a different question, one that was asked by Natalie earlier this morning, that Marissa is focused on:

Oh, can't that eager young assistant of yours mind the shop?

As far as Marissa knows, Natalie has been to Coco exactly once, and it was more than a year ago. She was in the neighborhood, Natalie had explained as she'd greeted Marissa with a kiss on the cheek that left a smudge of coral lipstick. Natalie wandered through the store, taking it all in with an appraising eye, and left without purchasing a thing.

At the time, Marissa's assistant was a woman in her midfifties, a mother of twins who'd decided to return to the workforce after her children left for college.

Natalie would never refer to her as *young*. She must have been talking about Marissa's current assistant.

But how does Natalie know such specific details about Polly?

Marissa's breath catches as she recalls Polly's roommate asking if she, Marissa, was Polly's boss at the real estate company.

Natalie is a real estate agent.

Could Polly have temped at the same company where Natalie works? Do they actually know each other?

The skin on Marissa's arms prickles as she watches Polly open the store's laptop, using the password Marissa provided her, and begin updating the spreadsheet containing customers' contact information.

Polly seems to feel Marissa's gaze and looks up. "Oh, I forgot to tell you Janice Henderson called yesterday and asked me to let her know when we get in more size-eight swimsuits. I was just making a note of it."

"Great." Marissa casually walks into the back room, but keeps Polly in her peripheral vision.

Polly has access to most of Coco's business information. She knows every inch of the shop; she has even slept here. She has slept in Marissa's home, too!

Marissa's heart is pounding. She forces herself to draw in a few even, slow breaths as she thinks back to the circumstances of Polly's hiring. Polly had wandered into the shop a month or so ago, all fresh-faced and sweet-seeming. It was a slow Monday morning, and Polly had knowledgeably discussed a few items Marissa sold, favorably comparing Coco's hand-blown glass vases to the brand carried by Anthropologie. As Marissa was ringing up the picture frame Polly selected, Polly had said almost wistfully, "It would be a dream to work in a place like this. You don't happen to need any help, do you?"

A few days later, Polly showed up for her first day at Coco. Marissa had verified the first job on Polly's résumé, a nanny position, but the manager at Anthropologie didn't return Marissa's call, so she let it go.

"Marissa?" Marissa flinches at the sound of Polly's voice.

Polly pokes her head into the back room, and Marissa studies her carefully. Polly is wearing her hair pulled back into a twist today—a style Marissa occasionally favors—and has on an ivory sweater sold by Coco, which Marissa gifted to Polly because a customer got a lipstick stain on the inside collar while trying it on.

"Oh, there you are," Polly continues. "I was just wondering if there's anything special you need me to do now, or . . ."

"You can rearrange the shelves by the standing mirror." Marissa conjures this up to keep Polly tucked away in a far corner of the shop. "The Sundry T-shirts are selling well, so make sure they can be easily seen."

Polly nods, and as she heads off to tackle the task, Marissa's composure returns. It strains credulity to think that Natalie would send Polly to work at the shop and keep tabs on Marissa. What would be the purpose? If Natalie has her sights set on Matthew, there are far less complex ways to try to entice him.

Still, something about Polly is fishy. Marissa has arranged to interview on Monday morning the best candidate from the résumés she has received. She'll tell Polly to run a few made-up errands to get her out of the way.

If the applicant is as promising as she seems, Marissa will give Polly her official notice on Monday afternoon. Maybe Marissa will do it right after her meeting at the coffee shop, so that Monday will feel like a day of clearing away the tainted, stressful pieces of her life, and beginning anew.

Marissa checks her watch at a little after 3:30 P.M. Matthew would have picked up Bennett by now, and they're probably on their way to whatever it is they decided to do. Maybe they'll get ice cream or go to the zoo again.

Even though Marissa came in late, she's tempted to leave early. She can order something yummy from DoorDash for dinner and set out Monopoly or Scattergories, so everything is waiting for her two guys when they walk through the door. It would mean giving Polly free rein of Coco, but by now Polly has surely seen every square inch of the shop.

Still, Marissa plans to take the store's laptop with her. She finishes tracking down a special order and checking out a new handbag company based out of Austin, then begins packing up just as her cell phone rings. She expects it to be Avery, since they've been playing phone tag today, but Matthew's photo flashes on the screen.

"Hey, babe," he says when she answers. Marissa can tell she's on speakerphone; she hears Bennett giggling in the background. "We've got a little surprise for you."

"Oh, really?" Marissa's voice sounds tight and strained, so she makes an effort to lighten it. "What are you two cooking up?"

"You're going to the spa!" Bennett shouts.

"The spa?" Marissa echoes.

"We booked you a massage at the Red Door," Matthew confirms. "Can you get there in thirty minutes?"

Marissa can't disappoint them, not when they're so clearly excited. "Oh my gosh, that sounds amazing!"

"Dad just bought me that Blaster Faster rocket. The one that goes up seventy-five feet!" Bennett's voice is pure joy. "We're going to Candy Cane City to launch it."

"Take a video?" Marissa asks. "I'd love to see."

"Yep. And let's just order in dinner when you come home," Matthew tells her. "Make it a lazy night."

"Love you both!" Marissa cries, but she can't tell if they hear her before Matthew disconnects the call.

Marissa tucks her cell phone into her bag and reaches for her light spring coat. She knows it's ridiculous to complain about getting a massage, but she feels a deep tug toward her family right now. She only wants to be with Matthew and Bennett; it's a longing that is imbued with urgency.

So much has happened lately. It's natural that she is nervous and jittery, she tells herself.

But it's more than that.

She's scared.

Marissa closes her eyes and conjures an image of Bennett's smiling face: his wide blue eyes, the freckles that dance across his nose, his gap-toothed smile. Her son isn't in danger; he's going to a public park on a sunny afternoon, where there will doubtless be other kids and parents and nannies.

Besides, Matthew would never let anything happen to Bennett, Marissa tells herself. With that thought, she finally exhales.

CHAPTER TWENTY-NINE

AVERY

By the time the sun begins to set, I still haven't reached Marissa. She didn't show up at Coco this morning—I didn't even get a glimpse of Ray—which made going there a complete waste of time.

"Yeah, she texted me to say she was coming in late. You should have told me you were planning to come by, I could have saved you the trip," Polly had said with a bit of an edge, as if she was happy I'd been inconvenienced.

When Marissa did call me back, I had my hands full, literally, consoling Romeo while the vet administered his shot, and I couldn't pick up, so she left a message simply saying she was sorry we'd missed each other. But she didn't provide the name I'd requested.

Then I received an urgent text from a client who'd had an altercation with his new boss, and I spent the next hour talking him down. When I finally got the chance to phone Marissa back, her voice mail came on, and a moment later she texted, **With a customer. Sorry!**

I can understand why Marissa would rather not text or email the name of the guy to me—a paper trail could come back to haunt her if Matthew has access to her accounts—but there's no reason why she couldn't have left the information on my voice mail, as I specifically instructed.

But she hasn't.

Now it's early evening, and I've got a few minutes before my last appointment of the day: a new client who told me she is grappling with an enormous betrayal, which is likely another case of infidelity.

I reach for my phone again. My call goes straight to voice mail, as if Marissa has turned off her cell.

It feels a little too convenient that her mysterious lover has been out of town all week, and suddenly Marissa seems to be avoiding me.

I wonder again if she is playing me.

I want to throw the coffee cup I'm holding against the floor and watch it shatter.

As soon as my final session is over, I'm heading over to the Bishops'. I'm going to corner Marissa tonight.

Romeo pads into my office and looks at me, his expression concerned, as if he has intuited my irritation. He nudges his cold nose beneath my palm, and I stroke his head, which is finally free of the cone, since the vet told me I could remove it.

I stand up and Romeo follows me as I enter my living room. I open the back door to let him out into the fenced yard, tossing his favorite squeaky toy hot dog onto the lawn. He bounds off to get it, but refuses to drop it at my feet, so we have a little rough-and-tumble game of tug-of-war that I probably need more than he does.

When my new client, Rose DeMarco, rings my doorbell at 6:00 P.M. sharp for her first session, Romeo is upstairs in his crate and I'm ready for her.

I peer out the peephole, noticing she looks better than the photo on her driver's license—then again, most of us do. I never used to ask clients to send me identification in advance of our first session, but thanks to Acelia, I can no longer afford to let anyone in my house that I haven't checked out.

I open the door and welcome Rose inside, showing her to my office and indicating the coatrack, where she hangs her navy blue belted jacket.

I take my usual chair, and Rose settles herself on the middle cushion of the couch across from me.

"So, what brings you here today?" I begin.

I know already from verifying the information on the driver's license she scanned and sent to me that Rose is twenty-seven and lives in Adams Morgan. Through my own digging, I discovered she works as a history teacher at a private girls' school in Bethesda, which makes it surprising that she can cover my fee, but perhaps she comes from family money.

Rose crosses her legs at the ankle. She's wearing a below-the-knee skirt and flats, and her permed, shoulder-length hair and shapeless patterned sweater aren't doing her any favors.

"I've experienced a terrible betrayal, but I have a feeling you can help me find the solution."

"That's what I do best."

What usually comes at this point is a long pause. When clients first meet me, they need to take a minute to compose their swirling thoughts and lay out their confession in a succinct way. Trying to summarize the problem that has likely consumed many of their waking hours—for weeks, months, or even years—can be a big challenge.

But Rose doesn't hesitate. "Someone discovered my very private information and shared it with the worst possible person."

I wait for Rose to elaborate, but she doesn't.

"Was it a boyfriend who betrayed you?" I imagine compromising photos posted on the internet.

"No."

"A friend? A family member?"

Rose shakes her head twice.

"We could save a lot of time if you just tell me who did it."

"A colleague," Rose says evenly.

It's not what she says that makes me put my notebook down in my lap, freeing my hands. It's the way she says it.

The room is perfectly still; Romeo is upstairs in his crate. There's no audible ticking of a clock or faint waft of music or distant honking from rush-hour traffic.

It's as if Rose and I are suspended together in a glass globe.

I choose my next words carefully. "What makes you think *I* can help you?"

"I have a strong hunch." A bead of sweat rolls down the side of Rose's face, but she doesn't make a move to wipe it away. "In fact, I think you're the *only* one who can help me."

I casually place my hands on my chair's armrests, fighting my body's instinct to clench. I need to appear relaxed and unconcerned.

"The only thing I was wondering about is your fee."

I mentally begin compiling facts: Her skin is pale, and she has no birthmarks or scars or freckles on her face—unless she has covered them up. Her eyes are hazel, but those could be colored contacts. It's impossible to tell her body shape beneath her clothes.

I play along for the moment. "My fee is nonnegotiable. If we decide to work together, I'll need to be paid up front."

"That won't be a problem. I already know I want to work with you."

And I've already decided we aren't going to work together, I think, mentally willing myself to memorize the precise sound of her voice.

"But if you do help me the way I think you will, I'm going to be so grateful I'll want to pay you a lot more."

I shift again in my chair, casually moving my left hand an inch lower on the armrest. "I don't allow secrets in this room, Rose. Tell me why you're here or this session is over."

My index finger finds the smooth button on the underside of my chair's armrest, but I don't push it. Not yet. Rose's clothing doesn't contain any visible pockets, and her hands are clasped on her lap. Her purse is down by her feet. Her posture is unthreatening.

Still, I don't take my eyes off her for an instant.

Despite the thermostat in my home being set at seventy degrees, another bead of perspiration rolls down her cheek, leaving a faint glistening trail.

I wonder what her real hair color is, beneath the wig that is making her head sweat.

If I passed her on the street, I wouldn't give her a second glance. She blends in: medium height, medium weight; there's nothing striking about her. Which is probably exactly why she was chosen to come see me.

"I didn't come here under false pretenses. I'm being straight with you." Rose's eyes stay fixed on mine. "Like I told you, I experienced a huge betrayal by a colleague. This person has caused a lot of trouble for me . . . *and* my company. You know who it is. So how about it, Avery? Can we work together?"

Her words are so deliberate. To an outsider, they'd probably appear strange but innocuous. I force myself to smile. "I don't think my methods are a good fit for you, *Rose.* Why don't you see yourself out."

This is it; the moment when everything could shift.

But Rose merely gets to her feet, reaching for her coat and slinging her purse over her shoulder. "If you change your mind, you've got my number and email address."

Which are connected to a burner phone and untraceable electronic address, I'm certain.

I don't reply. She cocks her head and gazes at me. "You've got such a pretty face." She looks around my office. "And such a nice house. Sometimes we don't realize how grateful we should be until we lose everything."

She smiles and slips on her coat.

Despite her implicit threat, I'm certain Rose came here not to harm me, but to try to strike a deal—money in exchange for the name of who gave me the information. Still, it's difficult to remain seated while she disappears into the hallway.

A moment later, I hear the sound of my front door shutting and her footsteps going down the outside stairs. Only then do I take my finger off the panic button that alerts police and my alarm company I'm in danger.

I walk to the window and watch Rose disappear down the sidewalk, blending into the dark shadows.

I wonder what she really looks like beneath her plain disguise. She must resemble the real Rose DeMarco, who probably has no idea that her identity was borrowed for tonight. Acelia must have searched for an innocuous-seeming local woman who wouldn't raise any suspicion in me, creating a copy of her driver's license and sending a fake "client" who looked enough like Rose that I'd open my door.

But as with everything else Acelia has done, no real harm resulted and the details are murky enough that I can't report this incident to the police without appearing paranoid.

What I can do is to implement a new policy: I'll only meet new clients in public places.

I walk into my hallway and activate my alarm system, staring at the logo on the code box. It's the same logo Derrick had on his work shirts.

Derrick protected me well, I think. It was he who suggested installing the panic button on my work chair.

I'm gripped with the urge to call him, but even as I'm pulling out my phone, I realize how unfair that would be.

Derrick would provide me with comfort. I'd repay him with pain.

I slide my phone back into my pocket and go upstairs to let Romeo out of his crate.

CHAPTER THIRTY

MARISSA

MARISSA LIES ON THE massage table, willing herself to relax, while a woman with salt-and-pepper hair pulled back in a bun works on the knots in Marissa's lower back. Beneath the notes of the classical music through the salon's speakers, she hears the incessant thudding of her heart. The padded cushion against her face makes it hard to breathe.

"How is the pressure?" the masseuse asks.

"Fine," Marissa manages to whisper.

But surely her rigid body tells a different story.

What is she doing here? She should have trusted her instincts and skipped the treatment and gone home. Or better yet, driven straight to Candy Cane City to meet Matthew and Bennett. She berates herself for letting down her guard. Someone is trying to hurt them. Matthew has *already* been hurt. They aren't safe.

"I'm sorry." Marissa abruptly twists onto her side, pulling the sheet around her as she sits up. "I suddenly don't feel well. I need to go."

The masseuse begins to apologize.

"It isn't anything you did," Marissa assures her hastily.

Finally, the woman exits, and Marissa puts on the terry-cloth robe and slippers the spa provides its clients.

When Marissa first entered the room, the last of the day's sunshine was creeping through the slanted blinds, a fractured bit of brightness. Now there's only darkness. She feels light-headed and disoriented.

Marissa pushes out the door into the hallway. She hurries into the locker room to retrieve her purse, her cell phone, and other belongings.

A woman is putting her things in the locker immediately above Marissa's, blocking the way, so Marissa waits, her stomach coiling tighter with each passing second. Finally, the woman steps aside and Marissa moves forward, tapping in her usual four-digit code. The locker door swings open and Marissa immediately pulls her phone out of her purse.

There's nothing except another missed call from Avery. She knows Avery wants the name of the man she slept with, but there is no way Marissa is leaving that information on voice mail.

A sign on the wall announces the use of cell phones in the locker room is prohibited, and an attendant is nearby, setting out fresh towels, but Marissa can't stop herself: She curves her body to block the view of the attendant and calls Matthew's cell phone.

It rings several times, then goes to voice mail.

She instantly tries again, but Matthew doesn't pick up.

He's probably playing a video game or watching TV with Bennett, she tells herself. The phone is vibrating right next to him, on the end table by the couch. He just can't hear it.

She knows she isn't behaving rationally, but her premonition is so strong, she can't help herself:

Call me ASAP, she texts.

She waits, her body frozen, but there's no response from her husband.

Just as on the night he was attacked.

Marissa yanks on her clothes, then pulls on her boots and coat, leaving her hair twisted up in the terry-cloth scrunchie the masseuse offered her. She doesn't even glance in the mirror; her movements are quick and jerky, fueled by the certainty she needs to get home. She flies out the door of the spa and takes the stairs down two flights, rather than waiting for the elevator. She hurries to the parking lot and slips behind the wheel of her car, barely waiting for the attendant to accept her ticket and raise the electronic gate before she races through it.

At the first stoplight, she calls their home phone, even though all the ringers are turned off downstairs so they aren't bothered by telemarketers.

No one answers.

When the light turns, she swerves into the lane to her left, then back to her original one, trying to jockey ahead in the traffic-filled streets a few inches at a time, just like the drivers she normally complains about.

Matthew and Bennett are safe at home, she tells herself, repeating it like a mantra. She'll walk through the door and Matthew will look up at her and smile, while Bennett chatters excitedly about his new rocket. They'll devour the tacos and guacamole and chips Matthew picked up for dinner, then they'll all snuggle on the couch and watch a movie. It will be a perfect night.

That's an Instagram photo, she hears Avery's voice chide. But it won't be, she assures herself, because she and Matthew are changing. Because their marriage finally feels as if it is becoming the union she used to only pretend it was.

"Matthew and Bennett are safe at home," she repeats aloud. She's so close to them; in another few blocks, she'll turn off the main artery, into their neighborhood.

She continues winding her way north, passing the treacherous circle that divides D.C. and Maryland, then turning down a quieter road.

Everything is as it should be on her street, she realizes. There are no sirens. No flashing blue-and-red lights from police cars or ambulances. No cluster of gaping neighbors in front of their home.

Her body finally unclenches a bit when she sees Matthew's car in the garage. He must have left the door open for her, but she leaves her car parked on the driveway apron, not taking the time to fit it into the enclosed space.

Marissa grabs her purse from the passenger's seat and slams the car door, then begins to hurry toward the house. She can't fully relax, not until she lays eyes on her family.

A loud honk sounds behind her, and she whirls around. Bright headlights shine in her eyes, and she instinctively raises her hand to shield them.

Then she hears her name being called: "Marissa!"

CHAPTER THIRTY-ONE

AVERY

WHEN NEW CLIENTS COME to me with a confession, it's often camouflage for their actual issue, which exists below the surface of their conscious lives. It lurks in a place that feels too hazy and perilous for them to enter alone—if their mind allows them to be aware of it at all.

I reach for my phone and replay the message Marissa left me this afternoon: "Hi, Avery. I'm sorry we keep playing phone tag. I know you are eager to catch up and I'll be . . . Sorry about that. . . . Anyway, I'm sure we'll talk soon."

Her message wasn't entirely directed at me; she briefly spoke to someone else midway through it, probably pulling her phone away reflexively for a moment.

I close my eyes. Marissa was walking down a busy street, probably Connecticut Avenue, near Coco, judging by the background noises.

Her aside was a bit muffled, but I play the message again, focusing intently on the words she spoke between "I'll be" and "Sorry about that" to confirm I've heard them correctly.

"Oh, hi, Ray."

The name isn't terribly common, but I heard it just this morning, when I went to visit Polly. He's the homeless man Polly recognized on the video, the one who pushed the note under Coco's door late at night. He wasn't near the store when I stopped by earlier, but he must have returned by the time Marissa left me a message.

Something has always bothered me about that letter, as it has about the delivery of those roses.

Both acts were supposedly anonymous.

Yet both seemed designed to engender witnesses.

If the man who seems obsessed with Marissa wanted to leave her a note, why didn't he simply put it in an envelope with her name on it, ensuring her privacy? Or for that matter, send her a text or an email, rather than print out a single line on a sheet of white paper and arrange for it to be delivered to Coco?

I stand up from my desk and walk across the room, Romeo trailing at my heels. I'd let him out of his crate as soon as the fake Rose DeMarco left, and although I refuse to be shaken by her visit, I can't pretend that my dog's presence isn't comforting.

We head to the kitchen, where I give Romeo a rawhide bone and check to make sure he has fresh water.

Marissa should be home for the night by now.

And one thing I've learned in my work, which was proven again only this morning with Polly, is that people tend to be more forthcoming when you catch them off guard.

I leave on plenty of lights for Romeo and double-check that the house alarm is set while he's busy gnawing on his treat.

"Back soon," I call to him as I head out my door, toward the Bishops' house and our sixth session.

Traffic is in full force, but I'm not in any rush. I stay in the middle lane of Connecticut Avenue, thinking about what I know of the Bishops.

If I were my own patient, I might accuse myself of avoiding my lurking issue: the escalating threat posed to me by Acelia. *Avoidance, suppression, denial*—a lot of clinical terms could be applied to my actions, since I'm heading to the Bishops' right now instead of trying to process the intrusion I just experienced.

I'm not going to allow Acelia to take up any more of my mental real estate, though. That monstrous company wants me to be cowering at home, fearing what it might do to me next.

But even though I'm confident they've researched me thoroughly, they must not know this about me: I've never liked bullies.

I pass through the circle that straddles the D.C.-to-Maryland line, braking hard to avoid a pickup truck that doesn't seem to understand the concept of yielding. I honk, and when the driver gives me the finger, I fire one right back at him.

I reach Marissa and Matthew's street a few minutes later. It's like turning into a different world: Only blocks away is a city filled with noise and bustle; I drove over three potholes on my way to get here and passed a bus shelter that held a half dozen weary-looking people. Here, graceful three-story homes are set back from the road, buffered by well-tended yards and expensive cars. It's quieter, and the roads are perfectly paved.

As I pull up in front of Marissa's house, I spot her getting out of her Audi in the driveway. I honk, and my headlights pass over her. She turns around and lifts her hands to shield her eyes.

"Marissa!" I call.

"Oh, Avery!" She puts her hand to her heart. "You startled me."

"Good timing." I pull in behind her car. "I'm glad I caught you alone. Mind if I park here? I'll be quick."

She glances at her house, then back at me. "What is it?" Nervous energy is radiating from her; I can tell she's distracted.

"I was hoping we could talk." Remembering my conversation with Polly, I suggest, "How about we sit in your car for a few minutes?"

Marissa shakes her head, almost imperceptibly. "I'm sorry—no, I just—I—I need to go inside first."

It's the first time I've ever spoken with her that her words have emerged choppy and unpolished. Marissa's hair is piled up in a scrunchie, and a smear of mascara is under her left eye. One of her pant legs is caught inside her high-heeled leather boot, and the other one hangs free.

My poised, glamorous, *perfect* client seems to be falling apart.

This will be our sixth session, Confrontation.

For Cameron, it meant finally standing up to his wife, Skylar. For Kimberly, whose parents minimized her rape, it meant writing them a letter detailing how they'd failed her.

It's not lost on me that I literally had to confront Marissa to arrange this meeting. I'm the architect of my method, but the contents of the Confrontation session, more than that of any others, tend to surprise me.

"I'll come inside with you." I begin walking up the steps toward the front door. I expect her to protest, but her expression fills with gratitude. She seems so distraught that I have to quash the instinct to offer her my arm to hold on to.

"Did something happen today?" I ask just before we reach the door.

My question seems to take her by surprise. "No. Not that I know of."

She slides her key into the lock and pushes the heavy wooden door open and rushes inside. I hear a Dave Matthews song playing and, over it, Matthew's loud, animated voice. He seems to be in the middle of telling a story.

"Are you sure you're okay?"

"Matthew! Bennett!" Marissa calls sharply, ignoring my question.

She doesn't even take off her coat or slide her purse off her shoulder. She hurries down the hallway, toward the sound of Matthew's voice.

I'm right behind her.

"Hey, sweetie!" Matthew comes out of the kitchen, holding a glass of red wine. He's in khakis and a black crew-necked sweater, with a fresh-looking small white bandage on his forehead.

"Avery!" he adds when he spots me a second later. "This must be the night for surprise guests."

Like Marissa, he seems startled but not displeased by my unexpected arrival.

Matthew walks over to Marissa, who seems frozen in place, and plants a quick kiss on her lips. "Bennett's upstairs playing *Minecraft* on the Xbox. Come on in, ladies."

Before we can move, however, another man emerges from the kitchen, also holding a glass of wine. Unlike Matthew, he's dressed more casually in faded jeans, a hoodie sweater, and Nike running shoes.

I glimpse his face and my stomach plummets. Dizziness engulfs me.

The scene unfolding in front of me is surreal. Different parts of my life are colliding and merging, like the shards of a kaleidoscope, in a way that makes absolutely no sense.

The Bishops' other guest greets Marissa first, bending down to kiss her cheek, giving me a desperately needed moment to try to collect myself.

Then he straightens up, and his eyes meet mine.

I know those eyes well.

I also know the feel of those lips on mine.

"Avery, this is one of our closest friends," Matthew says. "Meet Skip."

PART
THREE

CHAPTER THIRTY-TWO

AVERY

THERE'S NO WAY MARISSA and Matthew just happen to know Skip; his presence can't be a simple coincidence. A bigger, more ominous force has brought us together tonight.

I want to freeze this moment and study all the players. I want to pull out my yellow legal pad and scrutinize my notes. I want to take these people aside, one by one, and interrogate them.

But I can't do any of that; I have a hunch it would not be in my best interests.

I smile and choose my words carefully. "Hi, Skip."

As his big hand closes around mine, I notice his fingers feel cold, and before his eyes skitter away from mine, I glimpse concern. Or is he merely wary?

My simple, ambiguous greeting has supplied him with a choice. He can pretend it's our first meeting, or he can acknowledge we already know each other.

"Nice to meet you, Avery."

So this is how he wants to play it.

A dozen questions erupt in my mind. Before I can decide which one to ask, Marissa heads for the staircase, her coat on and purse still slung over her shoulder. "I'll be right back. I want to check on Bennett."

We all turn to look at her as she practically runs up the steps. There's a moment of silence after her abrupt, awkward departure.

Matthew breaks it. "How about a glass of wine, Avery? Come on, we've got a bottle in the kitchen."

One thing I know for sure: Matthew is the only one of us who seems at ease.

Matthew didn't explain to Skip how I'm connected to him and Marissa, even though he was forthcoming with the information to Polly. Perhaps Skip already knows that the Bishops have hired me—either of the Bishops could have ignored my advice and mentioned it to him. The metropolitan D.C. area can be a small town in some ways, and it isn't inconceivable that I would know someone in the Bishops' circle.

But if Skip doesn't have something to hide, why would he keep it a secret that we'd been on a few dates, and why does he look so deeply uneasy?

Skip stands aside to let me follow Matthew, then falls into step behind me. The hairs on the back of my neck rise; I don't like not being able to see Skip.

I'm not walking into a trap, I remind myself. I didn't tell anyone I was coming here—I didn't even know it myself until a little while ago—so there's no way Skip could have engineered this meeting. Matthew and Marissa couldn't have, either.

I exhale and enter the kitchen. It's as gorgeous as I remembered, with its built-in appliances and glass-fronted cabinets. A bowl of mixed nuts is on the island, next to a half-full bottle of Malbec and a red, white, and blue plastic rocket. Matthew pours a generous amount of the ruby-colored wine into a balloon glass and hands it to me.

"Had some quality father-son time with Bennett this afternoon." Matthew gestures to the toy. "That thing is a lot better than the bottle rockets I had growing up."

"Nice." I take a sip of wine, feeling its warmth ease down my throat, then turn to Skip. I decide to take control of the conversation. "Do you live in the neighborhood, Skip?"

I already know he lives in the Palisades—at least, that's what he told me when we met at Matisse. I want to see if that information fits what the Bishops know about him.

"Not too far away. I've got a place in D.C.," Skip replies, avoiding my eyes. I'm trying to read his energy, but I can't decipher it. He seemed so straightforward and solid when I first met him. Then, when I caught him coming out of my home office, he seemed a little jittery and off. Now he's acting guarded and cagey. But I detect nothing in his affect that feels threatening.

"Skip's house is fantastic," Matthew adds helpfully. "He just finished renovating it." Matthew seems oblivious of the prickly undercurrent linking Skip and me.

So far Skip's biographical data aligns. Yet I feel as if the more time I spend in Skip's presence, the less I know about him.

He is the missing link in a chain I never knew existed, an invisible stitch affixing me to the Bishops.

I swiftly review the timeline in my mind as Matthew tops off Skip's drink, then his own.

I called in my supposedly anonymous tip to the FDA, then I met Skip. Several weeks later, Marissa reached out to me. In between my encounters with Skip and the Bishops, Acelia began unleashing their intimidation tactics. All of these events seemed independent at first. Now I wonder if hidden connections exist, like the sticky threads of a nearly invisible spiderweb.

"Do you live nearby?" Skip turns my question around on me.

"Cleveland Park," I tell him, as if he weren't eating Thai food at my kitchen table just last week. I look back and forth between him and Matthew. "So, how do you guys know each other?"

As Matthew opens his mouth to answer, Marissa enters the room. The smudge of mascara is gone from beneath her eye, and she has smoothed her hair. But one pant leg is still tucked inside her boot, and she looks wrung out, even worse than when she exited her car a few minutes ago.

"How was your massage?" Matthew leans over to give her another quick kiss.

"Amazing." But Marissa doesn't seem like a woman who has just spent a blissful hour getting her body kneaded with lavender oil.

"A massage?" I wonder if this is why I couldn't reach her.

"Marissa's been under so much stress lately, I thought she deserved a break." Matthew lifts up the bottle of wine. "Pour you a glass, babe?"

Marissa stares at the bottle for a beat, then shakes her head. "I'm going to stick with water and rehydrate."

"That makes sense," Matthew says as Marissa takes a glass out of the cabinet and fills it with water.

It's only because I'm watching Skip so intently that I realize he is staring at Marissa with an equal intensity.

She tilts back her head, exposing her long, graceful neck, as she takes a long sip of water. She must feel Skip's eyes on her because she turns to him.

"How are the new town houses coming along?" She glances at me. "Skip is a real estate developer."

I nod, pretending it's new information. This, too, fits with what Skip has told me.

"Really well," Skip says.

"You still thinking about letting Natalie handle some of the sales?" Matthew asks.

Natalie *again*? I think.

Skip nods—a little curtly. I can't read Marissa's face because at the mention of Natalie's name, she turns around again and opens the refrigerator door. Then she closes it without removing any items.

"Shall we move this party to the living room?" Matthew says easily.

Matthew lifts up the wine bottle and his glass in one hand and the bowl of mixed nuts in the other. We all trail Matthew into the room where I held my second session with the Bishops. Something is different about this space. At first I'm not sure what it is, then I realize the sectional couch is darker and smaller than the one that used to be here. As before, Matthew claims a chair facing the couch, and since I'm right behind him, I get to pick next. I choose the only other chair in the room, the same place I sat last time.

That leaves the gray sectional for Marissa and Skip. They sit a few feet apart, like strangers who enter the same elevator together and immediately put a healthy distance between them.

I make sure I'm the first one to speak. I need this question answered: "So, you were about to tell me how you guys all know each other."

"Marissa and Skip were friends first." Matthew leans back and perches his right ankle and foot atop his left thigh. "They actually grew up in the same town." He names an area on the Eastern Shore.

"I've heard it's lovely." I've never been, but Paul had friends who owned a vacation home there and often traveled from D.C. for the weekend.

"My parents bought a summer place there when I was fifteen," Matthew continues. "Skip was quite the entrepreneur even then. He had a little fishing boat and ran a charter business. My dad still talks about the snapper he caught with Skip before dawn on Saturday mornings while the rest of us were sleeping."

"Hey, some of us had to work during the summers," Skip chimes in. "Right, Marissa?"

She nods and smiles weakly.

"But we all had fun together at night," Matthew says.

"That's true. Those beach bonfires . . . man, I miss them." Skip looks only at Marissa when he replies.

It sounds idyllic. I wonder, though, if like everything else in the Bishops' life, the pretty memories are layered over something murky.

Skip's dynamic with Matthew seems to hold hints of one-upmanship. Maybe that began when they were young.

"So when did you two become close friends?" I ask.

Something passes between Skip and Matthew—their eyes briefly meet, then flicker apart. Marissa's empty glass of water clinks loudly against the stone coaster as she sets it down.

"When I was sixteen. Skip's much older than me—he was seventeen." Matthew winks, apparently ribbing his friend.

Then Matthew smiles at his wife. "The same summer I fell in love with Marissa."

Before anyone can reminisce further, Marissa quickly stands up, smoothing the front of her pants. "Would anyone like some water? I'm going to get another glass."

"Why don't you fill up the pitcher?" Matthew suggests.

She nods and exits the room quickly.

"I'll go help." Skip shoots a look at Matthew as he rises. It almost feels like a rebuke, as if carrying in a pitcher of water and a few glasses is too much for Marissa.

"You've kept in touch since you were teenagers?" Now that the shock of seeing Skip has passed, my adrenaline has dipped back down to a normal level. I need to maximize every second I get alone with Matthew by pulling as much information out of him as I can.

"Yup."

I glance at the bookshelf to my left, the one that holds the photo of Matthew and Marissa with their wedding party. I have a copy of it on my phone and make a mental note to study it later in case Skip was a grooms- man.

"What about Skip's wife?" I lob. "Are you and Marissa close with her, too?"

"Skip isn't married. I guess he hasn't found the perfect woman yet."

"Unlike you."

Matthew smiles, a proud, proprietorial smile. "Yeah, unlike me." He leans forward. "You know, it's a shame he hasn't dated anyone seriously in a while. He's the one I set up with Natalie, but they didn't click. He's a great guy. And I know he really wants kids."

I cast back in my memory for what Marissa had said about the setup: that Natalie wasn't interested in Skip because she wanted Matthew. What a strange gathering *that* must have been.

Marissa returns with a stack of three glasses, followed closely by Skip, who holds a cobalt-blue water pitcher. Instead of letting Marissa fill up a glass and give it to her husband, Skip does so.

Marissa sits back down—a little farther from Skip than before, and closer to me—and crosses her arms around her waist.

"Thanks, buddy." Matthew is still the picture of ease.

"How are things going at Coco?" Skip asks, turning toward Marissa.

While she answers, I look at Matthew. If he is at all bothered by the way Skip is attending to his wife, he doesn't show it.

For the next twenty minutes or so, the conversation ranges from the killer arm of the new pitcher of the Nationals baseball team to the weather to the top executive at Howard University who is considering a run for Congress. I join in enough to make it seem as if I were a full participant, nodding at the correct moments, and laughing along with everyone else when Matthew cracks a joke about politicians.

All the while, I'm cataloging clues being revealed in body language, word choices, and vocal tones. Earlier tonight, all I wanted was to get Ma- rissa alone. But I no longer need the information I came here to retrieve.

Marissa's sudden intake of breath causes my head to twist.

She's staring at a stack of children's games on the coffee table. They look brand-new in their plastic packaging.

"Bennett talked me into buying those when we were at Child's Play," Matthew comments. "We thought we'd have family game night."

Marissa nods, but the motion seems mechanical. If she was anxious before, now she seems completely spooked.

I look at the games: Pictionary, Scattergories, and a kid's version of Truth or Dare cards. What could possibly have triggered that reaction in her?

Marissa lifts a shaking hand to her mouth to conceal a yawn.

The gesture seems fake. She's clearly trying to end the evening, but is it because of her discomfort with Skip, or something else?

Every single person here is concealing something, I realize. The velvety, expensive wine, attractive decor, and friendly conversation can't mask the truth: ugly, explosive secrets are swirling around inside this room.

Still, I pretend to take the hint. It's time to break up this little party; I want to talk to Skip alone.

"I'm always wiped out after a massage, too," I tell Marissa. "And I must be keeping you all from your dinner. Thanks for the drink."

I stand up, assuming Skip will do the same. Especially since Matthew indicated earlier that Skip was a surprise guest, too.

Skip remains on the couch, sipping his wine, the red wine he'd supposedly developed a recent allergy to. "Nice to meet you, Avery."

Marissa looks at me, and I can see anguish in her eyes.

I need to decide if I'm going to save her from this situation or leave her to flounder.

The last thing Marissa wants is to be left alone with her husband and his old friend.

The one I'm now certain she betrayed Matthew with.

CHAPTER THIRTY-THREE

MARISSA

MARISSA FEELS AS IF she is struggling through a swamp; the air around her is heavy and oppressive, and her limbs are leaden.

She knew something horrible would happen tonight. And it has.

First Avery confronted her outside her home demanding to talk. And then when she pulled open the door, there stood Skip. Skip, whom she wasn't supposed to see until Monday, when Avery would provide her with the magical elixir to fix everything.

Skip's presence in her house—beside her on the couch, close enough for her to smell his aftershave—is almost too much for her to bear.

Does Matthew suspect?

She steals a glance at her husband, who is telling a joke about politicians, gesturing with both hands and smiling broadly. This is their *home*. They created it together, not only with bricks and mortar, but by building layers of memories. They chart Bennett's growth on the door of his closet in different-colored markers every year. They play board games, assemble puzzles, and watch movies in this very room; they've shared tears and hurt feelings and hugs.

All the work they have done to create and repair not just their marriage, but their family, will be shattered in an instant if Matthew knows.

She feels the heat of Skip's gaze on her again. He's acting so strangely. Why did he follow her into the kitchen and insist on carrying out the pitcher? Matthew had said Skip was a surprise guest. Why in the world would he pop by without an invitation?

I know I shouldn't say this, but I can't stop thinking about our night.

She blinks hard, and the image of those printed words disappears, only to be replaced by these: *I'm not letting you go so easily.*

She tries to track the relaxed banter, but her mind is churning.

She takes a sip of water as Matthew tells the punch line and Avery and Skip laugh; Marissa has missed another beat.

She watches Matthew lift his glass of wine and drink from it. Skip must have brought the same Argentinean Malbec over as he had the night she slept with him; she recognized the label when Matthew offered it to her.

Why won't Skip just leave them alone?

Her gaze drifts to the coffee table, where three children's games are stacked up. Pictionary, Scattergories, and a card game.

Truth or Dare for kids! Reads the description on the box. *Pretend to be a dog! Do you believe in ghosts? Do a crazy dance!*

Marissa's body is trembling. She can't be here for another minute; she has to get Skip and Avery out of her house, now. At last there is a break in the conversation and she fakes a yawn.

It's unlike her husband to miss a cue such as this; normally Matthew would find a way to gracefully end the evening. But he merely leans forward and grabs another handful of nuts.

Avery takes the bait and stands. She looks from Matthew to Skip and then to Marissa. She hesitates for a moment.

Marissa's throat thickens; she swallows back the surge of nausea. *Don't leave me alone with them!* she wants to cry out.

Matthew begins to rise. He is a chivalrous host, of course he will show Avery out. And Marissa will be left alone with Skip.

But before Matthew can get to his feet, Avery says, "Actually, Marissa, can we chat for a second?"

Marissa nods and follows Avery into the entryway. She has no idea what Avery wants from her. Why did *she* drop by tonight uninvited?

Before Marissa can say a word, Avery begins, "When I leave, tell Matthew and Skip you don't feel well. That you are having some sort of reaction to the oil the masseuse used. That you need to excuse yourself. And then go directly upstairs."

"But what about Bennett? What about dinner?"

"Marissa, your husband is a capable man. He'll figure it out. Besides, once Skip leaves, you will have a miraculous recovery and can recapture your family night."

Marissa nods. "Okay."

Avery leans in closer, her voice a whisper. "I know he's the guy."

Marissa rears back. Is it that obvious?

Avery looks directly into Marissa's eyes, seeming to take measure of her. Does Avery suspect what else Marissa is hiding?

"I'll need to see you tomorrow for another session."

Marissa swallows hard and nods. "Of course. I can make myself available whenever you'd like."

Avery nods crisply, as if that were a given. Marissa feels a rush of relief; Avery not only showed up at the best possible moment—almost as if she intuited how desperately she would be needed—but she has also provided Marissa with an out tonight.

Avery points toward the family room, where the two men await. "Now go."

Marissa leans her head back against the hard porcelain tub, wishing the hot water would melt the coldness inside her. Downstairs, Matthew and Skip are probably still chatting, and she has no idea what Skip's agenda is in showing up here tonight. He'd said he would be in LA until Friday evening, so he must have come straight here from the airport.

Regardless, they had an agreement—to see each other on Monday at the coffee shop. Why would he change that plan without telling her?

Matthew had said he'd put a frozen pizza in the oven for Bennett for dinner, which means he'll need to leave the living room to heat up the oven and pop in the pie, then again to take it out and call Bennett down to dinner. Those interruptions to his conversation with Skip might finally prompt Skip to leave.

Marissa uses her toes to turn the tap down to a trickle and sinks lower into the water. The anonymous bouquet, the ominous note, Skip's uninvited appearance tonight . . . none of it seems true to character.

These actions, taken together and under the circumstances, feel almost malicious, designed to inflict distress. While Skip would never be called a saint, in all the years she has known him—since she was seven and Skip was nine!—she can't think of a single time he acted deliberately cruelly. The only hurtful instance she can recall occurred when he seemingly rejected her after their kiss, during the summer that seemed to be on all of their minds tonight.

Now that Avery knows the truth about Skip, Marissa can finally tell her the full story about the summer she kissed Skip but ended up as Matthew's girl.

Marissa closes her eyes, getting the narrative straight in her head. The details remain so vivid that the scenes spring forward, fully formed.

The rhythms of that season had shifted: Her parents deemed her old enough to close up Conner's, so several nights a week Marissa ate dinner early at the kitchen table, then went to relieve her father. After she locked up the store, she would sometimes wander down to the shore to meet up with the other teens.

The night she saw Skip with new eyes began as just another warm, languid evening. The moon was tucked behind clouds, so she used the small flashlight on her key chain to make her way down to the water, her flip-flops squeaking slightly with every step. Once she got closer to the beach, the light of the bonfire helped guide her, and she could hear the Red Hot Chili Peppers blaring from a boom box.

There was often alcohol—pilfered from parents' liquor cabinets or bought from the bored clerk at the Stop 'n Save—and sometimes a little pot, too. Marissa occasionally sipped a wine cooler, but never drank more than one.

"Hey, Marissa," Tina called out. "C'mere, we're about to start Truth or Dare." Tina's speech was slurred, the way it always got when she was buzzed, something she'd been doing a lot more of that summer.

"Seems like the party started early tonight," Marissa called back, but by then Tina's attention was on twisting another can of Bud Light out of the plastic six-pack ring. Marissa and Tina had been best friends through eighth grade, sharing clothes and makeup, stickers and secrets. But right before high school began, Tina's father moved away and Tina's mom seemed to completely check out of parenting. Tina appeared to grow up overnight. Instead of wanting to be with Marissa, Tina started cutting classes, partying, and hanging out with some of the older kids. She already had a reputation, although no one knew how true the rumors were.

As Marissa drew closer, she saw Skip standing there, a smile curling the edges of his mouth, holding firewood logs. His arms were flexed under the weight, and she could see the outline of his biceps beneath his old T-shirt. His face being partly in the golden firelight and partly in shadows made him look both familiar and somehow brand-new.

She smiled back, feeling a strange flutter in her stomach.

Skip lifted up a log and tossed it on the fire, sending up a shower of sparks, then used a big stick to pull apart two pieces of wood, allowing more air to mix with the flames.

Out of the corner of her eye Marissa watched him work, struck by his physicality, his strong shoulders and biceps flexing as he lifted and pulled. Then he'd turned and smiled at her with a boyish grin that let her know he'd caught her watching.

When she claimed a seat, she felt another flutter when Skip came to sit beside her.

"I'll go first," Tina cried, jumping to her feet. "Someone give me a dare!"

The game progressed predictably: kids usually accepted dares—running into the surf fully clothed, shotgunning beers—but a few selected truths.

Then it was Marissa's turn. Usually Marissa picked truth, partly because she didn't have any big secrets, and partly because the dares got edgier as the game wore on.

But tonight, something pushed her to say, "Dare."

"Kiss one of the guys next to you," a girl giggled.

Marissa pretended to hesitate, as if she were considering which boy to choose. She took another sip of her wine cooler for courage, then turned toward Skip. She leaned forward and closed her eyes. His lips were soft and he smelled like suntan lotion and the Wintergreen Life Savers he always carried in his pocket.

The whole interaction lasted less than five seconds, but for Marissa, it changed everything.

As the game continued, she was acutely aware of Skip—Skip, the boy

she'd known forever!—just inches away. She swore she felt his aware-
ness of her, too.

Tina also seemed to sense it.

Marissa detected the heat of Tina's glare. Marissa had a hunch Tina
liked Skip, but Tina seemed to like lots of guys. Skip wasn't hers to claim.

Besides, the sting of Tina's abrupt withdrawal from Marissa's life hadn't
abated.

Tina abruptly stood up, even though it wasn't her turn. "I dare myself
to take off my shirt!" Guys hooted and cheered as Tina slowly lifted her
top, first revealing her pale, soft stomach and then her bright pink bra.

Marissa could barely fill out an A cup, and for a moment she was as
awestruck as the boys by Tina's lush body. It hadn't been that long ago
that Tina and she had stuffed socks in their training bras, giggling as they
admired themselves in Marissa's bedroom mirror.

A few of the kids clapped as Tina did a little shimmy. She stumbled
briefly before catching her balance again.

"Dare you to take off your bra!" shouted Jimmy Parsons, one of the
rough boys, who was a year ahead of Marissa. Instead of laughing and
sitting back down, Tina slowly reached back with both hands, but she
wasn't looking at Jimmy. Her eyes, outlined in a bright turquoise, were
staring straight at Skip.

Marissa heard the quick intake of breath of the guy on the other side
of her.

The tenor of the evening changed instantly, as if the darkness just beyond them had seeped into their circle of firelight.

"Do it! Do it!" Jimmy chanted.

"Do it!" several other guys joined in.

The boys' energy was palpable; it felt to Marissa as if a pack of wolves
had picked up the scent of a rabbit. Tina was too impaired and too desperate for attention—even the wrong kind of attention.

Marissa jumped up. "Hey, Tina. Why don't you have some water?
Maybe it's time to go home. . . ."

"Who are you, the hall shark?" one of the guys yelled, bringing up
the nickname of the school monitor who kept tabs on the students.

"C'mon, man." Skip reached over and gave him a gentle punch on
the shoulder.

"We've all seen her tits anyway," Jimmy said, leering. "It takes one beer to kiss her, two beers to touch her, three beers to undress her, and four beers to fuck her!"

More hooting and hollering came from the other boys, and Marissa watched as Tina crumpled, as if the words were stones raining down on her.

"Screw you!" Tears streaked down Tina's face. She grabbed her shirt and began to run.

They all watched her go, then Jimmy said, "I didn't even get to what she does after five drinks!"—which made everyone laugh, except Marissa and Skip.

The laughter must have carried to Tina. As Marissa watched Tina slip as she struggled to run in the soft sand, Marissa found herself thinking about how before Tina's parents divorced and the two girls would have sleepovers, Tina used to fall asleep snuggling a stuffed monkey. How utterly alone she must feel, Marissa thought.

"One of us should get her home," Marissa whispered to Skip. "Make sure she's all right."

Skip looked at her in surprise. "Yeah?"

Marissa nodded. The thing swelling between her and Skip—it could wait.

"Do you want to go, or should I?"

"Let's both go," Marissa decided.

But that had been the wrong call: Of all the things Marissa regretted in life, this topped the list. She should have chased after Tina alone and hugged her and invited her to stay over again. Maybe then Tina would have been safe.

Seeing Skip and Marissa together had only upset Tina more. She'd lashed out at them, then run away again. By the time Marissa unlocked her front door later that night, her parents were sound asleep. She slipped upstairs quietly, put her clothes in the hamper, and brushed her teeth.

She lay awake for a long time, though.

The next morning, she awoke much later than usual and headed into the kitchen. Both her mother and her father sat huddled at the small table whispering, which made no sense, because who was manning the store?

They lifted their heads and stared at her. She'd only seen them look that way—so pale and stricken—once before, when her maternal grand-mother had suddenly died of a heart attack.

"What is it?" Marissa had gasped.

"Sweetheart." Her mother's voice caught. "We have some terrible news. Tina . . ."

Her mother didn't continue—maybe she couldn't—and Marissa felt her heart pound. Dread infused her.

"Tina was found dead," Marissa's father finally said. "The police think she was murdered."

Marissa's legs buckled.

Everything changed again, seemingly in an instant.

The whole town went on high alert. No kids were allowed out alone, even in the daytime. Marissa's father closed up the store in the eve-nings while she stayed home with her mother and Luke. Details and rumors seeped out: Tina had been beaten to death. No, she'd been suf-focated. Her body was found on a pile of rocks near the water. She'd been raped—or maybe she'd had consensual sex. She'd been discovered by an early-morning fisherman, but had likely been killed around ten the pre-vious evening, shortly after she'd left the bonfire.

The police questioned all the kids who'd been at the beach that night, including Marissa, who told them about Truth or Dare, Tina's drinking, and how she and Skip had gone after Tina and tried to console her, but she'd resisted, calling Marissa a bitch and physically lashing out at Skip and scratching his forearm, so they gave up.

Skip walked me home afterwards, Marissa had said.

The detective nodded and jotted something down in his notebook.

So we were the last ones to see her alive? Marissa had whispered. Marissa's father had placed a hand on her shoulder; he'd told the police there was no way they were going to talk to his teenaged daughter without him being present.

The police detective had regarded her, expressionless. "Other than the killer."

The phone rang all the time, bringing news from friends and neigh-bors, and Marissa's father carried home more information from the store's customers. A timeline emerged: Most of the kids stayed at the bonfire, continuing the games and drinking. After he walked Marissa home, Skip had apparently gone to Matthew's house, which seemed odd to Marissa, since he and Matthew weren't close, and Skip had watched a movie with Matthew. Matthew's mother verified this, saying she'd brought the boys a bowl of popcorn and cans of soda. Everyone had an alibi, and besides, no one thought one of the teenagers was a murderer.

A suspect emerged quickly: the English teacher at the high school, who'd always seemed a little creepy. Four days later, everyone in town breathed a collective sigh of relief when the teacher was arrested for Tina's murder after he gave a full confession. The police found pictures of Tina and some of the other cheerleaders, taken surreptitiously at their practice, on his camera.

A memorial service was held for Tina, but after the tears and the high school choir's rendition of "Amazing Grace," it seemed as if she was quickly forgotten, as if the tide that had erased the traces of her footprints that night had also washed away memories of Tina herself. The beach bonfires resumed, though no one ever suggested playing Truth or Dare.

By August, the paralyzing fog around Marissa finally yielded to a more manageable grief. She'd barely left the house, other than to lay flowers on Tina's grave—pink and purple bouquets, because those were Tina's favorite colors—but now Marissa began to venture out again, and to resume working at the family store.

Skip seemed different, though. Marissa hoped he'd seek out her company; more than that, she'd counted on it. But he never did. When she bumped into him, he was both friendly and remote.

She told herself she'd imagined the spark between them. She had kissed him, not the other way around.

Then, in mid-August, Matthew came into Conner's to buy his mother coffee beans.

Now Marissa looks down at the wedding band on her finger, then plunges her head down into the warm water. Seeing those words on the card game—*Truth or Dare*—brought back so many memories.

Including the one of that first kiss. The spark she'd felt for Skip had never gone away. It had merely lay dormant until Skip's second kiss reignited it a few weeks ago.

But she loves her husband. She made a choice long ago to commit to Matthew.

Marissa's head breaks the surface just as Matthew knocks on the door.

"Sweetie? You okay in there?"

"Yes, thanks."

"Skip just left."

Marissa mentally wills a message to Avery: *Thank you.* "I'll be down in a minute. I'm feeling better now."

CHAPTER THIRTY-FOUR

AVERY

GABE'S DELI IS a Washington, D.C., institution. Nestled between a copy shop and an upscale sneaker store, it's a hole-in-the-wall, but the food is anything but ordinary. Gabe, the owner, has reimagined classic comfort dishes—mac 'n' cheese, meat loaf, and chicken noodle soup—with a healthy twist. The ingredients are farm fresh, organic, and wholesome.

The cashier by the front door, who doubles as a hostess, tells me there's a waiting list for a booth, but a few counter stools are open.

I glance around the restaurant and thank her. The counter will do just fine.

"Guess that bowl of nuts didn't fill you up either," I comment to Skip, who is tapping a message into his phone on the next stool over.

He looks startled, but recovers quickly. He must realize I followed him here when he left the Bishops. Maybe he even expected it on some level.

"Hey, Avery."

I thank the waiter who slides a glass of water in front of me, and since I feel that I have to order something, I tell him I'll have a grilled cheese.

"I guess you've got a few questions for me." Skip swivels on his stool to face me.

I take measure of him. Like Marissa, Skip seems a little ragged. He still needs that haircut, and the bright overhead lighting reveals a few lines in his face that I don't remember seeing before.

"Let's start with this one: What the hell is going on?"

Skip glances at his phone, then tucks it away. "Fair enough. I'll just lay it out: I'm the one who sent Marissa to see you."

I ran through a lot of outlandish premises in my mind on the drive here, but this isn't one I considered.

"That article about you in the *Post* magazine. I emailed it to Marissa and suggested she make an appointment."

A friend forwarded it to me a while back. It's the reason I sought you out, Marissa had told me in our second session. So Marissa, who seemed so innocent at first, had lured her husband to the counselor her lover had suggested. For a woman who claims she has no more secrets, she sure conceals a lot.

"When?"

"About a month ago, maybe a little longer."

"So right after you two slept together." I stare straight into his eyes as I deliver the words.

"She told you about us?"

I cut him off; I'm the one asking questions now. "I'm not saying I don't believe you, but this doesn't make sense. Why in the world would you want the Bishops to come see me and try to fix their marriage when you're obviously in love with Marissa?"

Skip's eyes look hollow. "I didn't expect Marissa would bring Matthew. I figured she'd go to the sessions alone."

It still isn't computing. "And then what would happen?"

"You'd make her realize she needs to leave Matthew."

I want to laugh, but Skip's expression is so bleak I don't.

"Skip, Marissa loves Matthew. She wants to repair things with him. I can't make her realize anything she doesn't believe. That's not how this works."

Skip opens his mouth, but before he can reply, the waiter moves to our end of the counter and tells Skip his order will be ready soon. "Sorry for the delay, the kitchen's really backed up tonight."

When the waiter moves away, Skip leans closer to me. "Look, you were asking about the summer when Matthew said he fell in love with Marissa. But *I* loved her first. I was her first kiss—did she ever tell you that?"

I shake my head. I'm beginning to feel sorry for him.

"There's always been something between me and Marissa."

That makes me sit up straighter. "So that wasn't the first time you slept together?"

"No, no, it was. Just that once. I meant that—"

"That you've always loved her." Skip, the man who has never married and may have difficulties with intimacy, given that I don't know of any long-term relationships he has had. He only went out with Natalie once, and even though I felt a connection to him and thought it might turn into something more, it was fleeting.

"I just want what's best for her. And Matthew isn't it."

"You need to let this go, Skip. Don't send Marissa flowers or call her again. And for God's sake, don't leave her anonymous notes."

"I don't—"

Skip cuts himself off as the waiter comes over again, this time holding four to-go bowls. He sets them on the counter in front of Skip, then begins stacking them in a paper bag with Gabe's logo on the front. "Want saltines?"

Skip thinks for a second, then nods. "Please."

The waiter sticks several little packets into the bag.

"Actually, do you have any extra?"

"Sure." The waiter adds another handful. "Anything else?"

"That'll do it, thanks."

"Careful, the soup's pretty hot."

I look at the bag. "Four bowls of soup?"

Skip nods. "Yeah. Marissa doesn't feel well. I'm bringing them back for her."

The roses, the note, the phone calls, and now this? Skip isn't in love. He's obsessed. He glances at the bill the waiter has left on the counter and pulls out two twenties, leaving them beneath his water glass.

"Skip, don't you think Matthew is capable of taking care of his wife? He doesn't need you to be the delivery boy."

Skip flinches. He doesn't react with anger, though. He looks at me levelly: "Did you notice how tired Marissa looked? Matthew didn't even care that she was going to carry that heavy water pitcher or go upstairs without dinner. She can't skip meals like that."

His demeanor is at odds with his words; Skip is acting as if it were perfectly natural for him to be the primary person looking out for Marissa's well-being.

Skip reaches for the handle of the bag. "When Marissa was pregnant with Bennett, the only thing she could keep down was Gabe's chicken noodle soup." It's such a specific detail. How many other nuances of Marissa's life has he cataloged through the years?

Now that Skip has Marissa's dinner in hand, I'm going to lose him. He's like a missile, being guided straight back to her. I wonder if he'll leave the soup on the doorstep or ring the bell and try to go inside again.

How long until Matthew catches on? I wonder.

My plan for the Monday meeting at the coffee shop won't work now; there isn't anything Marissa will be able to say to convince Skip to let this go. He wants Marissa for himself—by his own admission, he has wanted her for twenty-five years—and based on his actions tonight, he isn't going to stop.

I'm so caught up in my thoughts that it takes me a moment to process the layered meaning of Skip's words: . . . *when Marissa was pregnant with Bennett.*

"Skip, you don't think Marissa is pregnant—"

"Yes, I do." He stands up, his expression resolute. "And I'm almost positive it's my baby."

CHAPTER THIRTY-FIVE

MARISSA

MARISSA SCANS THE GROUP gathered at North Chevy Chase Park, searching for a familiar face. Matthew would hate this, Marissa thinks as one of the boys in Bennett's Cub Scout troop, wielding a stick like a spear, runs past her through a muddy puddle, screaming, "Ka-ya!"

Or at least the old Matthew would have. Maybe the new one, who'd played Scattergories with her and Bennett for two hours last night and woke up early to make Bennett "Daddy pancakes" (substituting M&M's for Marissa's usual berries and chia seeds), wouldn't have minded at all.

After Skip finally left their home and Marissa rejoined her family, it was as if the world tipped back onto its correct axis. Though Marissa still felt unmoored and shaky, Matthew and Bennett were filled with stories about their rocket launches, including Bennett's excited description of Matthew hoisting Bennett "twenty feet high!" into a tree to retrieve the toy when it got stuck. By the time they'd all gathered around the game, Marissa had felt calm enough to nibble a slice of pizza and join in the laughter.

The only off note came when Skip sent a group text to Matthew and Marissa to let them know he'd left some chicken soup on their doorstep for Marissa.

The gesture seemed completely over-the-top, but Matthew merely read the message, then looked at Marissa and shrugged. "That's nice of him. Guess he was worried you were really sick." Then he'd wrapped an arm around Marissa and pulled her closer.

This morning Matthew had seemed genuinely disappointed to miss the prep for the great outdoors event, but a crisis had erupted at the office and he needed to go in for a couple of hours.

That wasn't unusual; Matthew often worked on weekends. What was different was his promise to make it up to them.

"I'm all yours as soon as I get back," he'd said as he shrugged on his coat. She'd glanced at Bennett, then followed Matthew into the garage, hesitating as she carefully chose her next words: "Would it be okay with you if I invited Chris to the Cub Scout thing?"

The event, with its focus on tent building and wood whittling, would be the perfect bonding opportunity for her handy father-in-law and his grandson. Plus it would be nice for Bennett to have a male relative there, since so many boys came with their fathers.

"Bennett hasn't seen him since they went to see that last Spider-Man movie," she'd continued.

Matthew didn't look up as he opened his car door. She held her breath, hoping she hadn't shattered their new equanimity, as he seemed to come to a decision.

"Sure," he'd said quietly. He met her eyes over the roof of his car. "You know, I've been thinking maybe we could invite my dad over for dinner again sometime. Not for a special occasion or anything."

Was it possible that Matthew was changing the tenor of all the significant relationships in his life? She'd read about it in books and seen it in movies: A character who had a medical scare or near-death experience completely reevaluates his or her life. It was fairly common; she just never thought it would happen to Matthew.

My infidelity with Skip might actually have saved my husband, Marissa had thought in wonder.

Now Marissa watches Chris supervise Bennett as her son lays out tent stakes and poles and shakes out a bright blue tarp.

"Lay it shiny side up, buddy," Chris instructs Bennett.

If it weren't for the way Chris treated Matthew, Marissa might actually like her father-in-law. As it is, her feelings toward him are mixed.

"Okay, Gramps," Bennett replies. "So the shiny side should face the shiny sun."

"That's right. Now find the big pole that's going to hold up the tent. . . . No, not that one. It's the one to the left. . . ."

Bennett lifts up both of his hands to see which index finger and thumb form the letter *L,* a trick he learned from a teacher.

Out of the corner of her eye, Marissa spots a familiar figure approaching the park. She stiffens. "I need to get something from my car," Marissa tells Chris. "Would you mind watching Bennett for a bit?"

Chris waves her off, and Marissa hurries to intercept the new arrival.

Chris's presence today serves a dual purpose: bonding with Bennett *and* affording her the chance to slip off, unnoticed.

The voices of the group fade as Marissa walks farther away, toward the wooded area by the playground equipment.

A few parents are pushing kids on swings or soaking in the sun on benches, but no one takes any notice of Marissa as she passes by, to where Avery waits.

"Thanks for meeting me," Marissa begins. Seeing Avery here brings the tumult of last night rushing back, and Marissa's stomach twitches.

"We've got a lot to cover, so talk fast." Avery folds her arms. "What happened after I left?"

Marissa fills Avery in on everything: her soak in the tub and the memories of that summer, the games, and the soup delivery. From her position in the park, Marissa can't see Bennett or Chris. She is gripped with the same irrational fear she felt right after her massage, the one that compelled her to rush to Bennett's side.

He's fine, she tells herself. He's with Chris. And Chris knows how to handle himself. At seventy, he has the strength of many men half his age. Chris doesn't go to a gym or play golf or tennis, but whenever there's manual labor to be done—fifty-pound bags of mulch to spread around his yard, or a dead tree that needs to be cut down—he works unceasingly until the job is complete.

Because Avery doesn't react when Marissa tells her about the soup delivery, Marissa keeps talking nervously. "I know I shouldn't have lied to you about Skip, but I never thought he'd become . . . such a big problem." Marissa realizes she is wringing her hands together, and she forces herself to stop.

"What is it? No more secrets."

Marissa clears her throat. "The note that was slipped under Coco's door . . . I reviewed the security camera footage and recognized the person who delivered it."

Marissa can't see Avery's eyes beneath Avery's dark sunglasses. It's impossible to know how she is feeling.

Avery fired her as a client once before; now that she knows Marissa has been keeping more information concealed, will she walk away again?

Marissa is in too deep; she has to keep going. No more secrets. "It was a man named Ray. He's homeless, and he often sits on a bench down the street from my store. I talked to him and he told me someone had paid him to do it."

"Who?"

"Ray didn't get a name."

"And?" Avery snaps.

"And in addition to paying Ray, he gave Ray his gloves. I recognized them because they're the same gloves I bought Skip for Christmas."

"How do you know they're the same pair?"

"They're blue leather. They're very distinctive."

Avery is silent for a moment. "Did you ever doubt it was Skip who left that note?"

Marissa shakes her head. "No. The moment I saw it, I knew."

Marissa wishes Avery would remove her glasses so she could gauge her expression.

"I'm going to ask you something really personal now," Avery finally says.

Marissa nods. She resists the urge to look back and crane her head to try to glimpse Bennett through the trees.

"Are you pregnant?"

"*What?*" Marissa gasps. "No! Why would you think such a thing?"

"You're sure?"

"I'm positive." Marissa is not going to explain the details of her cycle to Avery, but she can say with 100 percent certainty this is true. Marissa's cell phone vibrates in her pocket, but she ignores it.

"Well, I have a feeling someone suspects you are."

Who? Marissa begins to ask, but the word dies on her lips. The image of the opaque CVS bag, the one that contained her pregnancy test, bursts into her mind. "Polly! Did she tell you I was?"

"Why would Polly think that?"

"After Skip and I—well, I knew the odds were very slim, given my fertility issues. But I had to make sure. So I picked up a test and used it at work. The result was negative. But then Polly started acting strangely. She wouldn't even let me pick up a pillow. I finally got it out of her that she saw the kit in the trash can."

By the time Marissa is finished recounting the story, Avery is shaking her head. "So you explained to your overly solicitous assistant that you aren't pregnant?"

"Yes. And she appeared to believe me. Did she tell you otherwise?" Marissa's heart is pounding; she is so angry that if Polly were here, she'd not only fire her on the spot, she'd have trouble restraining herself from slapping Polly across the face.

"Have Polly and Skip ever met?"

"Polly and Skip?" Marissa feels dizzy under the onslaught of questions. She doesn't want to be here, trying to untangle the horrible mess she's created. She should be with her son, watching him pitch a tent for the first time. If only she hadn't answered her phone that night when Skip had called, saying he was in the neighborhood. If only she'd said she was tired, instead of telling him to stop by, that Matthew was out of town but she'd love to catch up. If only she hadn't drank half the bottle of wine he'd brought . . .

Marissa forces herself to consider Avery's question. Marissa needs to make sure the information she gives is true. "No. Polly hasn't worked for me long. Skip has never been to the store during that time. At least that I know about."

The sun dips behind a cloud. The young-looking father sitting on the bench stands up and collects his children, leaving only a woman pushing a baby in a stroller back and forth. The baby is crying, a tired, drawn-out sound that borders on a whine. His noises are drowning out the faint voices of the Cub Scouts, and Marissa quashes the urgent desire to run back to Bennett.

Avery shifts topics. "Polly said someone has been calling the store and hanging up when she answers. It's pretty obvious who the mystery caller is. Is it possible that he didn't hang up once? That he and Polly spoke?"

Marissa shrugs. "I have no idea. Truly."

She feels her cell phone vibrate in her pocket again. "Sorry." She pulls it out and stares down at the notification: another missed call. There's no name for the contact—Marissa erased it weeks ago—but she recognizes the number as Skip's. Marissa's chest tightens. "It's him again."

"Don't answer. Until I figure out how to handle Skip, I don't want you to talk to him."

Marissa turns the screen so Avery can see it. Along with the missed call is a text: **Just checking in to see how you're feeling.**

"Why is he so worried about—" Marissa's hand flies to her mouth. "Oh my God," she whispers as the realization hits her: Avery's personal question, Skip's overattentiveness, Gabe's chicken soup. "Skip thinks I'm—"

A child's shriek cuts through the air.

Just as Marissa could pick Bennett from a lineup based on scent, she can recognize his cry even from this distance.

"Bennett! I've got to go!" She races back toward the makeshift campground.

In the time she's been gone—how long could it have been? Seven minutes? Ten, tops, she assures herself—a medley of tents have been constructed, and the Scouts, in their identical uniforms, are swarming around. Where is her son? she thinks frantically.

Finally she spots the back of Chris's hunter-green jacket. He is huddled with a few other adults, including the troop leader. Bennett is in the center of the group.

"Bennett!"

He turns around. He is pressing a handkerchief to his thumb.

"I don't think he needs stitches, do you?" she can hear the leader asking as he opens a first-aid kit.

Marissa's pulse slows; Bennett isn't badly hurt. He isn't even crying. "What happened? Sweetie, did you cut yourself whittling?"

"This is going to sting just for a second, okay?" the troop leader, peeling back the handkerchief, tells Bennett.

Marissa leans over and puts her hand on Bennett's shoulder. She wants to take him in her arms, but the other children are watching, and she knows Bennett is trying to keep his composure.

The leader pours a bit of iodine on the cut, then begins to bandage it up. "Next time you'll use a regulation pocketknife, right?" The troop leader winks at Bennett.

"I don't understand. Bennett has a regulation knife."

Chris clears his throat. "He was using mine."

Marissa sees the pocketknife on the grass. Its blade is longer, and likely much sharper, than the one used by the Scouts. Chris reaches over and picks it up, using the palm of his hand to fold the blade back in.

She quashes a surge of irritation. Naturally Chris would give Bennett a bigger knife and expect him to know how to use it; it's the sort of thing Chris did to Matthew all the time growing up. Matthew had once told her that while he was still in elementary school, his father expected him to take over mowing the vast lawn of their home. *Luckily, my mom hired a mowing service to come once a week while my dad was at work,* Matthew had said, laughing. *He never knew.*

Now Marissa straightens up and the other parents begin to drift away. That's when Marissa sees Avery has joined them. She has finally removed her sunglasses and appears to be taking everything in.

"Why don't we skip whittling for today," Marissa suggests to Bennett. "You can make up the lesson when your thumb feels better."

"He's fine," Chris interjects. "Better to get back on that horse."

Bennett picks up the stick and winces.

Marissa's jaw clenches, but her tone remains cordial. "I think we should call it a day. Why don't we take Bennett out for some ice cream?"

"Ice cream?" Bennett's face lights up.

Chris shakes his head. "Can't believe his dad didn't teach him how to at least *open* a pocketknife."

In the frozen moment that follows Chris's harsh words, Marissa witnesses the troop leader avert his eyes, and Bennett's face turn crestfallen. Avery, as always, seems to catalog every detail.

Anger swells inside Marissa.

The old Marissa would have swallowed her ire. She would have glossed over the moment, pretending it had never happened, to save face in front of the troop leader and other parents. Her need for pleasing appearances would have trumped her need for authenticity.

No more, she thinks as she glares at Chris. Matthew isn't the only one who is changing the tenor of all of his relationships.

When Marissa speaks, her voice is lower than usual. "Don't you ever talk that way about Matthew again."

Surprise briefly flashes across Chris's face.

"Come on, Bennett, you can show me how to take down the tent." Marissa deliberately excludes Chris, shifting her body so that her back is to him.

As they walk away, she thinks, my infidelity with Skip might actually have saved me, too.

CHAPTER THIRTY-SIX

AVERY

I'M UNLOCKING MY CAR DOOR when footsteps crunch against the ground behind me. I spin around to see Marissa's father-in-law, nearly close enough to touch.

Chris is built like a wrestler, broad and compact. His thick white hair is buzzed short, his skin is weathered, and he wears a hunter-green windbreaker and well-worn khakis. Aside from his light blue eyes, he looks nothing like his tall, polished son.

Chris smiles tightly.

I feel instantaneous dislike, and not just because of the way he insulted Matthew a few minutes ago.

He extends his hand, and after a moment I take it and feel the rough calluses on his palm. "I'm Chris Bishop. What was your name again?"

Again. A strange choice of words; it's as if in his mind we've already been introduced. The moment almost feels like a mirror image of last night, when Skip pretended we'd never met.

"Avery." I decide not to offer my last name, although I'm not exactly sure why.

He nods, his eyes intent. "You're friends with my daughter-in-law?"

I'd said goodbye to Marissa, but since she was busy with Bennett, I hadn't lingered. Chris must have been watching her closely to have observed our brief interaction.

"Friend of a friend." It's my default answer when I see a client in public. I pull my hand away from Chris's and open my car door.

"Nice to meet you."

I experience a brief flash of déjà vu. Those were the exact words Skip uttered to me last night, even though he and I were far from strangers.

Although I've done a little research on Chris as part of my work with the Bishops—I know the name of his lobbying company, and where he lives—I haven't considered him worthy of much attention.

Now I wonder if I should take a closer look at him. The mother-daughter dynamic gets a lot of coverage, but the father-son relationship is equally complicated. In my years as a therapist and now as a consultant, I've learned that if a son has a strained relationship in his present life, it's not unusual for it to be traced to a past dysfunction with his father.

I watch as Chris climbs into a LeSabre parked across the lot from me. I wait a few minutes, wanting him to drive off first. But even though I see clouds of exhaust coming out of his tailpipe, indicating the engine is on, the vehicle doesn't move.

Perhaps Chris is making a phone call.

I decide to make one, too.

Marissa had said Matthew was at his office, but I dial Matthew's cell number anyway, thinking that it's still probably the most efficient way to reach him.

It rings three times and I wonder if he really had a work emergency or—and this could be me projecting—if it was merely an acceptable ex-cuse to avoid the rambunctious Cub Scout event.

Then he picks up, sounding a bit out of breath.

"Hey, I'm glad I caught you." I watch Chris's car out of my rearview mirror as I speak. It still isn't moving. "I know you're at the office, but I was hoping we could chat."

"I'm really crazed, Avery. Can this wait?"

"It won't take long. It's about something that came up last night."

Matthew hesitates.

"I'm actually downtown already," I fib. "How about we meet at Giovanni's for a quick coffee?" I name Matthew's regular take-out place, the restaurant where I saw Polly.

When he doesn't immediately reply, I say firmly, "It's important."

Matthew gives a little laugh. "Okay, you caught me. I lied to Marissa; I'm not actually at work."

You've got to be kidding me, I think.

"I'm at the Wharf. If you really need to talk now, come here."

Typically, in the cases I take on, I act as a funnel for clients: their problems seem overwhelming and chaotic at first, but as we chip away at their situation, their issues distill into manageable entities.

With the Bishops, it's the opposite.

For our seventh session, Exposure, I'm splitting the time between Marissa and Matthew.

The Wharf is set on the Potomac River, and in the summer it's usually full of tourists and residents alike. There's everything from restaurants to shops to a Ferris wheel. Today, some people are milling around, but it's too early in the year for the crowds. The area Matthew directed me to is quiet; a dozen vessels ranging from catamarans to big sailboats line both sides of a long wooden pier. Most of the boats are winterized, covered up to protect them from the elements until warmer days arrive.

A few men are working on the edge of the dock, and another is tinkering with something on his sleek-looking cigarette boat. I stand at the spot Matthew directed me to—an outdoor bar called the Watering Hole, which is closed now—and see him waiting for me by the end of the pier, standing with his back to the Potomac. I walk toward him.

He looks boyish, with his wind-ruffled hair and wide, open smile. It's as if a weight he has been carrying around is finally slipping off his back.

"Surprise!" he says, then does something that truly takes me off guard: he opens his arms and envelops me in a brief, hard hug.

When he releases me, he turns and gestures to the boat behind him. It's beautiful, with its glossy wood detail against the gleaming-white fiberglass hull.

"You bought this?"

Matthew shakes his head. He can't seem to stop grinning. "But it's mine for the weekend. Tomorrow is our anniversary. Twelve years. Marissa thinks we're going to some fancy restaurant. But I'm bringing her down here for a catered dinner and moonlight sail. Want to take a look?"

He motions for me to kick off my shoes and step aboard. "Picture a table for two right here, with poached lobster and champagne from the year we were married." He gestures. "I've got a playlist on my phone, songs that mean something to us. Blankets in case it gets cold. And I've arranged for Bennett to spend the night with his friend Charlie. She's going to love it, right?"

"I would imagine so." But I'm beginning to wonder if this is what Marissa truly desires.

"Let me show you the rest."

We climb down six steep, narrow steps into the cabin, where there's a bedroom, bathroom, and living room. The spaces are tiny, but everything is beautifully appointed.

"Can I get you anything? Marissa loves these grapefruit seltzers, or there's orange juice. I just stocked the fridge."

"No, thanks." I take a seat on the curved banquette.

Matthew sits opposite me. "So, I'm seeing you twice in two days. Last night was fun, right?"

I wouldn't categorize the evening as fun exactly, but I nod.

"I'm glad you had a chance to meet Skip. He's been an important part of our lives forever. He knows a lot about boats and he's actually helping me arrange all this." Matthew sweeps out his arm.

I think back to the yellow roses ordered through the anonymous Venmo account @Picr1234.

I need to tread carefully as I peel back the protective layers in Matthew's mind, the ones that keep him from recognizing the truth about his good friend and his wife. Exposure is a delicate process.

"So you and Skip are close?"

Matthew shrugs. "Yeah, I mean he and Marissa are like brother and sister. Their parents have been friends forever. So I guess I inherited him."

Matthew's tone is affectionate. Does he truly not see that Skip is in love with his wife?

I don't want to lead him to the conclusion I've already formed; it'll be more powerful if Matthew recognizes it for himself.

I've been working with Marissa about acknowledging the ugly underbelly of the different situations and relationships she navigates. Matthew has been complicit in creating a beautiful but vacant picture of their life together. His anniversary dinner is the equivalent of a dieter buying a treadmill: A splashy statement that will do absolutely no good unless the gesture turns into a routine.

What I'm about to learn is whether Matthew is ready for some fundamental changes. "I can tell Skip really cares about Marissa."

The tiniest off note is in my tone, but it's up to Matthew to choose whether he wants to hear it.

He nods and begins to speak. Then he cuts himself off and turns to face me. "You sound like there's something else you want to say." His buoyancy is vanishing; the smile has dropped from his face.

I can't bring up the supposed pregnancy or the soup because then Matthew will know I've talked to Marissa or Skip.

But I don't have to because Matthew didn't really think there was something else I wanted to say. He meant there was something *he* wanted to talk about.

I let the silence stretch out until he breaks it.

"Okay, here's the truth about Skip."

I hear a creaking sound, as if the boat is rubbing against a piling, but I don't take my eyes off Matthew.

"Last night, after you guys left, he texted that he'd brought Marissa some soup. At first I thought, that's nice. You know, good old Skip, always looking out for his friends."

Baby waves rock the boat, making a gentle slapping sound each time they hit. In the distance, what sounds like a Jet Ski cruises by, the roar of the motor swelling and then fading. Matthew's gaze grows unfocused; it's almost as if he were talking to himself now.

"I didn't get the soup off the porch right away. We'd already eaten and Marissa was feeling better. I went out there when Marissa was putting Bennett to bed."

As I picture Matthew treading onto his front porch in the darkness and spotting the carrier with Gabe's logo, I hear something. It sounds as if it's coming from the deck where Matthew plans to serve his romantic dinner.

A footstep? I glance up, toward the mouth of the stairs, but don't see anyone. Sound travels over water, I remind myself. Maybe the noise is coming from farther away. Still, I shift my body to have a clear view of the stairs. Matthew is so lost in the memory of last night that he doesn't even seem to notice.

"The bag was heavy, and when I looked inside, there was a hell of a lot of soup. After I put it all away and went upstairs, Marissa was already asleep. I guess the massage really conked her out. Normally I'm out when my head hits the pillow, but last night I lay awake. I kept thinking about something Natalie once said." Matthew's leg begins to jiggle, then he stills it.

"After I set her up with Skip and we all went to dinner, she told me it was obvious Skip had a crush on Marissa. I figured Natalie was jealous. She's always been jealous of Marissa."

I wait for more. I know there's more.

"But. . . . Skip went all the way to this restaurant in Silver Spring and bought her four bowls of chicken noodle soup." Matthew shakes his head. "Who does that?"

"Someone who . . ."

". . . *really* cares about my wife," Matthew finishes the sentence, echoing the words I lobbed earlier with a heavy emphasis on the word *really*.

Matthew is easing his toes into icy water; he's not ready to fully plunge in yet.

Matthew twists to look directly at me. "So what should I do?"

Our boat rocks again; through the small windows above the banquette I see the cigarette boat putter by. I watch as it glides out into the open water and accelerates, sending up a spray of water.

"When you've been married awhile, it can feel nice to know you're attractive to someone other than your spouse," I tell Matthew.

"I'm not blaming Marissa for the way Skip feels."

"I'm not talking about Marissa. I'm talking about you."

He blinks.

"Natalie has feelings for you. Skip has feelings for Marissa. And neither of them has any place in your marriage."

Matthew nods slowly. "I get it."

I stand up, feeling a little claustrophobic in the tight space. I keep my feet apart for balance as another, slightly bigger wave rocks the boat.

We could dig deeper, but I'm overcome with the desire to end our talk—I want to get off this boat. But Matthew isn't done. For a guy who was furious at his wife for tricking him into coming to see me, he sure has embraced the process wholeheartedly.

"I'm gonna let you in on a little secret: Skip was Marissa's first kiss. It was right before she and I started dating."

Marissa has already told me this, but I feign surprise.

Matthew looks down at his hands and clears his throat. It's the most vulnerable I've ever seen him. "Last night, the main thing that kept me awake was thinking about that summer. I've never told this to anyone, but sometimes I wonder if all that drama hadn't happened, maybe Skip and Marissa would be together instead of us."

"Drama?"

"One of Marissa's friends was killed."

I don't give away that I already know this information. Tina was murdered more than twenty years ago. So why does her death keep coming up?

"Why would you think that?" I ask.

"I'm pretty sure Skip liked Marissa, even back then. But after the murder—well, to hear Marissa tell it, Skip started acting strangely. I guess it really threw him, that this girl he'd known for his whole life had been killed by one of their teachers."

I want to sit down again, to encourage Matthew to continue to be open. But a deep-seated instinct is keeping me on my feet, instead of trapped behind the banquette.

"What about you? Were you upset?"

"Honestly, a little. I guess mostly because of the realization that something like that could happen. We all hung out at the beach, but I never got to really know her. She wasn't my type. She could be a little wild." Matthew hesitates.

Again, I wait.

"Tina actually had a thing for Skip. That's what Marissa says. The night she died—" Matthew cuts himself off.

"What happened the night she died?"

Matthew shrugs. "Look, I'm not really sure. You know how people are—everyone had crazy theories about what happened to Tina. But the truth came out. And Marissa and I ended up together, so . . ." He spreads out his hands, as if it were the end of the story.

It isn't for me, though. I'm about to dig for more when I spot a blur of motion out of the corner of my eye.

"Matthew, is someone else on the boat?"

"Huh? No, not that I know of."

By the time he's finished answering, I'm at the stairs.

I scramble up the first two, then my foot slips on the third narrow wedge of wood and I have to grab the railings hard to keep from falling. I climb the rest of the way a little more slowly and land on the deck, blinking as direct sunlight hits my eyes. I spin around, trying to look in all directions, but for a few moments I'm blinded. When my vision returns, I scan my surroundings, but all the bobbing boats obscure clear sight lines. I glance at the vessels on either side of us, thinking that someone might have hopped into one. But they appear to be empty.

Then I see a man jogging off the end of the pier and heading toward Pearl Street. He's moving at a good clip, and his back is to me.

Matthew comes up to join me. "Look. No one else is here."

Someone *was* though.

I strain to catalog details about the man, but he's too far away.

The wharf is even quieter now; the men who were working must be taking a lunch break. If someone was creeping around our boat, it must have been him.

I point. "Did you see that guy when you first got here?" I turn to Matthew.

He is watching me with a concerned expression. Behind him is a vast, open expanse of water. "I don't see anyone."

I turn back again and realize the man must have already turned the corner or disappeared into one of the few open restaurants.

I slip on my shoes and reach into my purse for my sunglasses. "I've got to go. How much longer are you planning to stay?"

"I'm actually about to go, too. I just need to take care of a quick thing here, then I'm going to pick up a few more items for tomorrow night and head home."

"One more question. Do the police have any more leads on who might have attacked you?"

Matthew shakes his head. His bandage is gone now; the only evidence of his assault is a faint bruise near his hairline. "Not that I know of. Since I couldn't identify anyone out of the lineup, they weren't able to make an arrest."

I say goodbye and walk down the pier, taking in deep breaths of the cold, fresh air.

As I head up the ramp and pass over the retaining wall, I think about various scenarios: Someone could have followed me here. I already know, thanks to the man who came after me in the garage and the fake client who entered my home, that Acelia employs far-reaching ways to get to me.

Or maybe Matthew was the target. Someone could have crept onto the boat hoping to find him alone.

I'm still not convinced that random attack against Matthew *was* purely random. Anyone can be hired to do just about anything to us. Even Ray, the homeless guy who hangs out near Marissa's store, was paid to deliver a threatening note.

I take a final look behind me. Matthew is still standing there, watching me go. Or maybe he's just taking in the air, too.

I'm passing by the Watering Hole when I spot a small white object in the path the jogger just traced. It's probably nothing. Still, I veer left and pick it up.

It's a slip of paper, folded in half.

It's a bit crumpled, but it looks too pristine to have been here for longer than a few minutes.

When I unfold it, I see the name and address of a restaurant called the Whistler Bar & Grill printed on top. It's in D.C., on Sixteenth Street. Lower down, in the middle of the receipt, two charges are listed:

Cluny and soda, $6.99. Then again: Cluny and soda, $6.99.

It's the brand of cheap Scotch that Matthew said his father drinks.

CHAPTER THIRTY-SEVEN

MARISSA

"Now go wash that chocolate mustache off your face before it becomes permanent," Marissa teases Bennett as she unlocks the door leading from the garage to the kitchen.

"You're home!" Matthew calls out, getting up from a stool at the granite island, where he has been reading the newspaper. He's wearing jeans and an old sweatshirt and his cheeks look a little ruddy. He seems relaxed and happy; Marissa supposes he solved the work crisis.

"How was the Cub Scout thing?" Matthew ruffles Bennett's hair. Before Bennett can answer, Matthew spots the gauze wrapped around Bennett's finger. "What happened to your hand?"

Bennett glances over at Marissa, then down at his sneakers and shrugs.

"What happened?" Matthew repeats, this time asking Marissa.

Marissa walks around to the other side of the island and sets down her purse on the stool next to the one Matthew just vacated so she can avoid her husband's eyes. "Just a little cut."

The last thing she wants to do is to explain to Matthew that his father had given their eight-year-old an adult-size pocketknife. Not when it seems as if Matthew's icy feelings toward Chris are just beginning to thaw. Plus, she knows this admission will inevitably lead to questions about how Marissa, who should have been by their son's side (but was instead a couple hundred yards away talking to Avery), allowed it to happen.

"It's not a big deal. I didn't even cry," Bennett chimes in.

Marissa looks at Bennett's sweet face and feels bile rise in her throat. She and Bennett have formed an unspoken alliance; they're complicit in a lie.

Kids are perceptive. They model what their parents do, not what they say. What is she teaching her son?

She isn't being a good role model for him at all, especially not today, when she's seething with anger toward Polly and trying to put on a happy face for her family.

Marissa promises herself she will clean this up later and explain the full story to Matthew, but in the moment she merely nods. "He's okay."

All she can think about is getting to Coco and confronting her big-mouthed, interfering, *infuriating* assistant; she can't be drawn into a long discussion now or she'll crack under the pressure of her mood.

"So what's on the agenda for this afternoon?" Matthew asks.

"Look, do you guys mind if I run out for a bit?" Marissa gives Matthew a wink. "I want to pick up something from the store to wear tomorrow night."

"No problem." Matthew turns to Bennett. "So, should we start your dinosaur diorama or finish *Star Wars*?"

"*Star Wars!*" Bennett shouts.

"I'll be back before Princess Leia and Han Solo get trapped in the trash compactor!"

Matthew waves her off as Bennett runs into the family room and grabs the remote control. "I got this."

Marissa smiles as Matthew settles down next to Bennett, slinging an arm over the back of the couch. She picks up her purse and heads out through the kitchen door, into the garage.

The smile immediately vanishes from her face.

She drives directly to Coco, not hitting a single red light, making it to the store in near-record time and instantly finding a parking spot, as if the fates are on her side, propelling her forward.

She yanks open the door to Coco and spots Polly by the sunglass display with a customer. Polly gives Marissa a little wave, as if everything is business as usual. It takes every ounce of her self-control for Marissa not to storm over.

"Your face is a soft oval shape, so you can get away with oversized frames. The aviators would also look really good on you. Let me get you a hand mirror," Polly offers as the customer picks up a few pairs.

Marissa waits, fuming. But her hot wash of fury is finally cooling. It isn't that she is considering forgiving Polly for everything. If Polly really did tell Skip she thought Marissa could be pregnant, as Avery had seemed to insinuate—and who else would have given Skip that idea?—then simply firing Polly won't be enough.

The anger that made Marissa feel out of control is morphing into something more powerful, more dangerous: an icy, finely honed rage.

"I love both pairs on you!" Polly enthuses to the customer. "Ooh, do you want to try these Gucci ones, too? They're iconic."

Marissa's senses feel heightened. She is acutely aware of Norah Jones's smooth, rich voice playing over Coco's speakers, and the tangy apricot scent of the lit candle on the nearby table.

Yet Marissa's focus has never felt more acute. It's as if she has tunnel vision; all she can see is Polly, with her shiny rose-colored lip gloss and tucked-in-the-front shirt, chattering with the customer and occasionally shooting Marissa a quick look, seemingly delighted by her boss's attention.

I want to erase you from my life, Marissa thinks.

"Would you like to step outside to see which you prefer in the natural light?" Polly suggests.

Marissa smoothes her hair and walks over to the customer. "I personally would go with these polarized ones. They're perfect on you. And I think you'll find you can see everything more clearly."

Marissa locks eyes with Polly as she speaks. The obsequious grin falls away from Polly's face, and her expression turns to confusion.

Finally the customer selects the pair Marissa suggested, and as Polly rings her up, Marissa glances around to make sure no other customers are present. She glimpses herself in a full-length mirror: still in the cropped camo pants she wore to Bennett's Cub Scout event—they're a little baggy on her now—and with a smear of mud on the side of one of her old sneakers.

A few weeks ago she would never have considered coming to her store dressed like this. Today she simply doesn't care.

"I hope you love them!" Polly calls as the customer exits, setting the bell over the door jangling merrily.

Marissa walks over to face Polly and jabs a finger at her, stopping just an inch or two away from Polly's chest, as she unleashes her first question: "Why are you gossiping about me?"

Polly's face crumples. "Wha—what are you talking about?"

"Come on, Polly. Drop the act. You told my friend Skip—"

A familiar voice coming from the rear of the store interrupts her. "How *is* Skip?"

Marissa spins around, feeling disoriented. Coco was empty, save for her and Polly. Marissa is certain of it. Even the curtain of the dressing room was drawn open. The only place someone could have been in is the back area, which is off-limits to customers.

Natalie is strolling toward her, holding two large shopping bags with Coco's logo.

"Hello, Marissa."

Marissa blinks a few times, feeling a little dizzy.

Natalie is acting as if she has every right to be here; she sauntered out of the back room and greeted Marissa as if she were the owner of Coco and Marissa were someone who'd just wandered in off the street.

"What are you doing here?" Marissa's voice is shaking.

"I came to pick up the auction items." Natalie lifts up the bags. "We were all supposed to drop them off at the school yesterday. Remember?"

Marissa finds her backbone: "Obviously I didn't remember or else I would have done it!"

Natalie smiles, seemingly pleased she provoked a rise in Marissa. "Look, it's okay." Her tone is sugary sweet and a touch condescending. "You seem like you've been under a lot of stress lately, so I decided I would just come get them myself. No biggie."

Marissa watches as Natalie sets down the bags and runs her hand over a faux-fur throw draped over the back of an accent chair. The gesture seems oddly proprietary.

Marissa whirls back around to face Polly. "What is wrong with you? You let a stranger into the back of my store?"

Before Polly can answer, Natalie, her full lips curving up into a smile, steps closer to Marissa. "Marissa, I don't know why you're getting so bent out of shape. I'm not a stranger to Polly."

Natalie smiles at Polly, who gives her a tentative smile back.

Marissa feels as if her head is going to explode. Natalie and Polly know each other?

"In fact, I'm the reason Polly is working here."

Marissa's legs feel wobbly. This can't be true: She vividly recalls the first time she met Polly. Polly wandered into Coco, gushing about how much she loved the store. Polly knowledgeably discussed the hand-stitched detail on the decorative pillows and the thread count of the luxurious bedsheets. She asked if Marissa had ever considered hiring an assistant. Marissa's former employee had just left for another job, a higher-paying one, at Saks.

Polly's timing was impeccable.

"You two are friends?" Marissa's head swivels between the women.

But even before she finishes asking the question, she knows Natalie is telling the truth. Natalie had offered up a clue. Why did Marissa never follow up on it?

"I wouldn't have let just anyone in the back, but I knew you had all the auction stuff there, and I was with that customer when Natalie showed up," Polly explains.

"I've got to run." Natalie scoops up her bags and heads toward the door. "See you soon!"

Marissa watches her go, then twists back to look at Polly.

Polly appears on the verge of tears. "I'm sorry," she blurts.

Marissa isn't swayed by Polly's meek act—if it is an act. Marissa's phone vibrates in the side pocket of her camo pants but she ignores it. There is no one she wants to talk to at this moment other than Polly.

"Natalie suggested you work here?"

"No, that's not how it happened. I was temping for the real estate agency where she worked before I started here." Polly's words come out in a rush. "My dad's old college roommate is a bigwig there—he hired me. I was a receptionist, and it was only for a couple weeks. They really didn't need me, he was just doing my dad a favor."

That would be a plausible reason for leaving it off her résumé, Marissa concedes.

"But I didn't know Natalie well at all. She was mostly out showing houses. I just saw her a few times when she stopped by the office. I figured it was a total coincidence when she showed up today."

Marissa's phone buzzes again, just once, tickling her thigh. She folds her arms across her chest. "Go on."

"But Natalie acted like she expected to see me here. She gave me a hug, as if we were friends, and said her daughter went to the same school as Bennett. She told me she'd come to pick up the auction items. I thought you knew she was dropping by."

Marissa almost believes Polly. *Almost.* But there's a giant hole in her assistant's story. "If you and Natalie barely knew each other, why would she tell you about the job opening here?"

"She didn't. That's the strange thing." Polly looks bewildered. "My dad's friend—I think he's Natalie's boss—anyway, he's the one who told me to apply here. I had no idea you and Natalie knew each other."

Marissa sinks into the accent chair, her mind whirling.

Natalie must have told her boss that Polly could be a good fit for Coco. It's possible she knew Marissa's old assistant had moved on; Marissa had asked a few other moms at the school if they knew anyone who might be interested in working at Coco, and perhaps word had spread to Natalie.

But why wouldn't Natalie have ever mentioned this connection to Marissa?

Polly clears her throat. "Are you mad I let her take the auction stuff?"

Marissa bites back a harsh laugh; Polly's query is so off the mark, it's ridiculous. "Let's go back to the question our mutual friend Natalie interrupted: Why have you been gossiping about me to Skip?"

Polly spreads out her hands. "I don't know anyone named Skip. I swear it, Marissa."

Liar or cunning actress? Marissa thinks again. Natalie could be the link between Skip and Polly. Hadn't Skip just said last night that Natalie might be involved with the sales of his town homes?

"I could never do anything to hurt you, Marissa. The truth is, I haven't just been looking after the store. I've been trying to look after *you*."

Marissa wants to scream. "I don't need you to look after me!"

Polly wipes her eyes. "Please don't be mad at me. It isn't my fault!"

Marissa grits her teeth. The promising candidate from GW is coming in on Monday, she reminds herself; Marissa will hire her even if she's less than ideal. Anyone would be better than Polly.

The store phone rings. "I'll get it!" and Polly turns.

"No!" The word comes out harshly. "Polly, we're not done talking." Marissa rises and walks to the checkout desk, thinking, If Skip is the one who kept trying my cell and is now calling the store, I will completely lose it.

The number on caller ID flashes. It's her home line. She snatches up the receiver. "Matthew?"

"Hey, I tried you on your cell but you didn't pick up. Were you in my home office earlier?"

"No, why?"

"The cleaning woman wasn't here, was she?"

"No, she never comes on Saturdays. What's wrong?"

"Did you leave the window behind my desk open?"

"Of course not." Marissa rarely goes into Matthew's first-floor office—the last time she did, it was just before their date at Mon Ami Gabi—and she would certainly never leave the window open. One of Matthew's prized possessions is a small original Picasso sketch that his mother gifted to him when he graduated from law school. It hangs between the two windows in the room. If moisture got through to it, the artwork could be damaged.

"I just went in there to grab my laptop because Bennett wanted to look up dinosaur pictures for his diorama. The window was open a couple inches."

"Oh my God. Did someone break in while we were all out?"

"My laptop was on my desk and everything else seemed the same. Hang on, let me check upstairs."

Marissa holds her breath as she hears Matthew's quick footsteps thudding. "Nothing looks different in the bedroom. Your jewelry is still in the drawer. I'll check the rest of the house just in case."

"I'm coming home."

Polly is staring at Marissa, clearly riveted by the half of the conversation she can overhear. Marissa slams down the receiver to the store phone and doesn't bother bidding Polly goodbye; Marissa runs straight out the door.

She dials Matthew from her car. "Matthew, that guy who assaulted you—could it be him?"

"No way," Matthew says firmly.

Marissa slams on the brakes as she approaches a red light. She's driving too fast; she needs to get herself under control.

"Why? Why couldn't it be him?"

"C'mon, Marissa. The police said it was probably a random attack. I was just in the wrong place at the wrong time."

Marissa's breathing sounds ragged even to her own ears. "But he didn't mug you. And whoever broke in didn't take anything. Someone is obviously after something!"

"We're safe, babe. No one messes with me or my family."

The steel of his voice grounds her. Matthew is a fighter, she reminds herself. "Where's Bennett?"

"He's in the kitchen. He's fine."

Marissa blinks hard against the tears spilling down her cheeks. "Almost there," she whispers.

Marissa holds on to the vision of Matthew and Bennett together, looking at pictures of dinosaurs, for the rest of her short drive.

She hurries into the house and finds them together at the kitchen island, just as she'd imagined.

"Mom's home!" Matthew shouts, his voice surprisingly joyful. He must be trying to normalize things for Bennett. Marissa gives them each a quick, hard hug, then bends down to get a closer look at the image Bennett is considering on the laptop.

"It's a *Coelophysis*," he explains. "They were in the Triassic."

"He looks fierce."

Bennett nods. "He's a carnivore."

The kitchen seems exactly as she left it. Surely if someone had broken in, she'd be able to sense an intrusion?

But maybe she's giving herself too much credit. She misjudges people all the time. She underestimated Natalie's animosity toward her, and she still can't get a handle on Polly. And she never thought Skip would become so—she shies away from the word, but it's the correct one—obsessive.

Bennett is looking up at Marissa with a solemn expression. Her intuitive son probably senses her stress.

Even though Matthew assured her nothing was taken, Marissa wants to see for herself. "I'm just going to run upstairs for a second. Be right back."

She checks the bedroom first, then her office and the guest rooms. Bennett's room is last.

Everything is as it should be: one of his dresser drawers is open—Bennett never remembers to shut them—and his blue comforter is stretched neatly across his race-car bed.

At the far end of the room, the closet door is shut. Marissa stares at it, feeling goose bumps rise on her arms.

Surely when Matthew made sure nothing had been taken, he also ensured no one was still inside the house. He said he'd check.

He must have looked in all the closets.

A thought enters her mind. It's irrational, yet she can't ignore it: What if Matthew somehow overlooked this one?

She's tempted to call downstairs to ask him, but their home is solidly built, and noise doesn't travel easily between the floors. Plus her mouth is now so dry it feels as if it would be difficult to form words.

She could run downstairs and ask Matthew to check with her. But that seems like an overreaction.

She steps farther into the room, her feet sinking into the thick carpeting.

She reaches the door and puts her hand on the knob, but she can't bring herself to turn it.

So many horrible, jarring things have happened to them lately.

She can't help but think she set this all in motion; their lives were so simple before she cheated on Matthew with Skip.

No one messes with me or my family, Matthew had vowed. Marissa is certain he meant those words with everything he had.

The thought gives her the strength to fling open the door.

The sudden motion makes a few of Bennett's shirts flutter on their hangers, but otherwise everything is exactly as it should be.

The rush of relief she feels is so intense that Marissa wants to sink to the floor, but she forces herself to head back downstairs.

Bennett and Matthew are just as she left them, their two blond heads side-by-side, now considering different dinosaurs from the Jurassic era.

"C'mon, nothing beats the king!" Matthew is saying. "The *T. rex* could crush a car in its jaws!"

"I still like the *Brachiosaurus* the best." Bennett's voice is small.

"Which one is the *Brachiosaurus*?"

Bennett turns the screen so Marissa can view it. "His neck is really long, like a giraffe's. It was tough for them because they're so big, but they were herbivores. They probably had to spend almost all of their time finding food. And they couldn't defend themselves well."

Of course her sensitive boy would tilt toward an equally gentle creature.

"Marissa, we've got a few cardboard boxes in the basement, right?" Matthew pushes back his stool. "I'll go grab one for your diorama base."

Marissa takes a glass from a cabinet and fills it with water, then gulps it down.

When she turns around, Bennett is back to studying the computer screen, chewing on the inside of his cheek, as he always does when he is concentrating. Then he sticks his left hand, the one without the bandage, into the pocket of his jeans. He pops a small object into his mouth.

Marissa looks more closely at her son. Bennett isn't chewing on the inside of his cheek. "What are you eating, sweetie?"

He ducks his head.

"C'mon, silly. I saw you." Marissa sticks out her tongue.

Bennett laughs and does the same. A round, white candy is on his little tongue.

Bennett already had ice cream today; he knows a second sugary treat is against the rules. Plus, where would he even get candy?

As if to answer her unspoken question, he pulls a roll of Life Savers out of his pocket. Wintergreen Life Savers, the kind Skip has carried around ever since she's known him.

Marissa stares at it for a beat. "Did Uncle Skip give those to you last night?"

It's exactly the kind of thing Skip would do; he's always been kind to Bennett. And people without kids don't always think about the effects of sugar on young children.

Bennett shakes his head. "I found them."

"Bennett!" Marissa stretches out her hand, and Bennett puts the half-eaten roll in her palm. "Where? At the park?"

"No, Dad's office."

Matthew comes into the kitchen, holding a big cardboard box. "What's going on?"

"Bennett found these." Marissa holds up the candy.

Matthew shrugs. "Guess Skip dropped them last night."

Marissa forces a smile, even though the sound of Skip's name makes her stomach clench.

"So can I have them?" Bennett asks.

"No!" Marissa and Matthew say in unison.

"Maybe a few after dinner," Matthew concedes. "But only if you eat something green. Like a pile of broccoli taller than a tree!"

Matthew tickles Bennett, who laughs and squirms away.

Marissa's fingers close around the hard roll. A thought comes to her. It's so insane she almost doesn't ask the question.

Then she does. "Were you and Skip in your office last night?"

Matthew pauses in flattening out the box. "Huh? No, we just hung out in the living room and kitchen."

He looks at her quizzically, then appears to grasp the reason for her question. "Oh, maybe Skip wandered in there for some reason when I ran upstairs to tell Bennett his pizza was ready. Maybe he had to make a private call or something."

Marissa nods. "That must be it."

As Matthew reaches for a ruler and he and Bennett begin discussing how big to make the cardboard base, Marissa glances in the direction of Matthew's office.

If someone wanted to break into the house, the office, which faces the leafy side yard, would seem like the easiest entry point.

Enough, Marissa tells herself sharply. She isn't thinking straight; her mind isn't reliable right now.

Skip has no connection to the open window in Matthew's study. Skip was a guest in their home last night—*not* an intruder this morning.

If he wandered into the office last night and dropped the roll of candy, it was because he bent over to tie his shoe or something, not because he was wrestling with one of the windows.

Matthew reaches over and begins to massage Marissa's neck. She can feel the tightness of the cords under his strong fingers. "You okay, babe?"

"I didn't sleep well." It isn't a fib; although she fell asleep shortly after climbing into bed, she awoke in the middle of the night and tossed and turned until she finally rose at a little after 5:00 A.M.

"Why don't you take a nap? Bennett and I will tackle the dinosaurs."

She doesn't want to leave her little family. She yearns to be here, in the cocoon of the kitchen, shaping warm clay in her hands as the three of them create an imaginary world.

"We can't have you stressed and tired for tomorrow night. And I can't wait to see you in whatever you picked up from the store." Matthew's voice drops to a low whisper: "And get you out of it."

Marissa briefly squeezes her eyes shut. She doesn't have any outfits Matthew has never seen.

She could tell Matthew a partial truth about why she rushed off to Coco, filling him in on the disturbing Natalie-Polly connection. But she is not going to spend her anniversary talking about Natalie.

She'll have to come up with a plausible-sounding reason for wearing something she already owns to their special dinner, she thinks.

An excuse. A fib. Smoothing things over for the sake of appearances.

I should just call it what it is, she thinks. I'm lying to my husband.

Something I've learned to do well.

CHAPTER THIRTY-EIGHT

AVERY

I'M IN LUCK. The Whistler Bar & Grill opens at noon on Saturdays. I need to confirm what I strongly suspect—that Chris Bishop, Matthew's father, was sneaking around the dock while Matthew and I spoke. The question is, did Chris go to see his son—whom he's supposedly estranged from—or was he following me?

I've already determined that the Whistler is four blocks from Chris's office on Sixteenth Street, in northwest D.C.

If the axiom is true—like father, like son—it's possible Chris also stops in at a regular place after work for a meal or a couple of his favorite drinks. And men talk to bartenders the way women talk to hairdressers.

I know I can't simply barge in and act all nosy about one of their customers. That's why I ran a few errands first.

Now I sit in my car, parked at a street meter outside the bar, assembling my props. I pull out the flimsy fake-leather wallet I just purchased at CVS—it seems like something Chris might actually own, given his predilection for cheap options—and remove all the cash I have in my own billfold, a grand total of $24, tucking the money inside. The wallet looks a little pathetic, even if it's one I'm claiming to have found in a nearby parking lot, so I contribute an old metro card of mine, a business card I picked up the other day for a new nail salon in my neighborhood, and a few random receipts I grabbed out of a trash can at CVS. I just have to hope whomever I hand it off to won't examine the contents too closely.

Which leads me to the final items—ones I hope the bartender *will* take a good look at.

What sort of grandfather would Chris be without a few family photos?

It was easy to buy a USB cord at CVS and use it to attach my phone to the photo-printing machine at the back of the store. I made prints of photographs I already have, the ones I surreptitiously snapped with my phone when I was standing in front of the Bishops' bookshelf during our second session.

It took a bit of cropping and filtering, but I ended up with reasonable facsimiles of the black-and-white wedding shot of Marissa and Matthew surrounded by their wedding party, as well as an image of Chris, Matthew, and Bennett—three generations of Bishop men—standing in front of a Christmas tree.

I maneuver the prints into the clear plastic inserts in the wallet, then check my appearance in my rearview mirror. I'm still in the jeans and black jacket I wore to meet Marissa in the park and Matthew on his boat, but I've tied my hair back in a knot and I'm wearing glasses with non-prescription lenses and cherry-red frames, which I also purchased at the drugstore, for $14.99. If someone were to describe the way I look right now, the glasses would be the main thing they'd remember.

I step out of my car and walk toward the restaurant, bending the wallet back and forth in my hands so that it seems more worn. It's still a little too new looking, so just before I reach the door of the Whistler, I drop it on the sidewalk and grind my heel into it.

I scoop it back up, pull open the door, and blink as my eyes adjust to the dimly lit restaurant. It's a dive—old dark-wood furniture, dust motes swirling through the few beams of sunshine streaming in through a dirty window, with the smell of old beer spills and even older cooking grease.

A half dozen or so customers are at tables and booths. Two servers stand behind the long wood bar, talking. One is a youngish-looking man with a mustache, and the other a middle-aged woman with bleached-blond hair.

Women typically have better memories for faces than men, so I claim an empty barstool closer to the female server.

"Get you something, hon?" she asks.

"As long as I'm here, I'd love a Michelob. But I actually came by for another reason."

She flips off the cap and puts the bottle in front of me, then narrows her eyes. "I'm trying to figure out if you're the type who wants a glass."

By way of answer, I tilt up my beer and sip from the bottle.

"So what's the other reason?"

The bartender with the mustache is listening to us, but I don't blame him. Not much else is happening in this run-down place.

I lay the wallet next to my beer.

"I found this in the parking lot of a CVS. I wanted to return it, but there's no ID. The only thing I could find was a receipt from here." I pull out the receipt and hand it to her.

"Let me see." She pulls up the reading glasses on a chain around her neck and peers through them. "Yeah, that's us. Hmm, two Cluny and sodas."

"There's a few family photos, too. Maybe you'll recognize him. . . . Or her. The owner of the wallet."

I tap on the wallet, indicating the plastic sleeve with the photos.

"Fancy," she mutters as she looks at the wedding portrait. Then she flips to the one in front of the Christmas tree. "Son of a gun. That's Chris Bishop. Now don't we look all festive!"

I take another sip of beer, trying to strike the right affect. Interested, but not overly. "So you know him?"

"Oh yeah. He comes in here pretty often. I've probably served him hundreds of Clunys over the years."

So it *was* him. I bet Chris followed me from the parking lot of the park to the boat; I left immediately after my phone call to Matthew, and Chris's LeSabre was still in the lot. I was so intent on moving forward toward Matthew's surprising destination, I never looked back.

Maybe Chris was tracking me before that, too—from the Cub Scout gathering on the grass to my car. He acted strangely when he introduced himself. If he recognized me from the *Post* article or other interviews I've done, why wouldn't he simply ask?

Perhaps his curiosity was piqued when he saw me interacting with Marissa. He could rightly assume she's one of my clients.

But there's no universe in which a normal reaction to that discovery would result in his following me. Why not simply ask his daughter-in-law?

"Thanks for dropping this off. I'll get it back to him." The server flips back to the wedding photo, then notices the cash. "I should pocket this to make up for all the one-dollar tips he's left over the years."

Keep her talking, I think to myself. "Oh, one of those," I say, grateful I've got an emergency twenty in my makeup bag so I can leave a generous tip when I get my bill. The last thing I want to do is pay with a credit card and leave a clue for Chris.

"He's all right. Bit of a loner."

The other server, who has inched closer to us, interjects, "Not last time he was in, Darlene. I'm actually the one who served him those Clunys. Chris met someone here."

"Really?" She frowns.

I let my gaze drift away. Their conversation will be more uninhibited if I appear to disengage.

"Yeah, I think it might have been his son."

"I didn't even know he had kids till I saw those pictures. He never mentioned a son."

Before I came here, I cross-referenced the date on the receipt. It was the same night I had my second session with the Bishops, the one we arranged for at 9:00 P.M. in their home because Matthew said he had a work event. But the time on the receipt was 8:17, so Matthew could easily have had a drink with his father first.

And when Matthew opened the front door for me, I smelled alcohol on his breath.

"Want to see a menu, hon?" Darlene offers.

This conversational topic has played itself out; I can tell she's ready to move on.

But I'm not. I point to Matthew standing beside his father in the wedding photo and look at the male server. "Was he here with this guy?"

"Coulda been." He shrugs.

I flip to the more recent photo of Matthew with his dad and son. "Him?"

Darlene shoots me a strange look.

"No, definitely not that one."

Goose bumps appear on my skin. It's as if my body knows what is coming before my brain recognizes it.

One person has been woven through every single one of my sessions with the Bishops. Sometimes he's invisible, sometimes he surfaces at unexpected moments. He's linked to both Matthew and Marissa. To Natalie. Possibly Marissa's assistant, Polly. And to me.

He isn't just the stitch connecting me to the Bishops. He's the whole damn spool of thread.

I slowly flip over the photograph again, aware that Darlene is staring at me with sharp eyes. "Him."

The male server looks down at the wedding picture, tracking to where my index finger is pointing. I've singled out another tall, smiling, light-haired man in a tuxedo—not the one next to the beautiful bride, but one on the periphery of the image.

Electricity shoots through my body. I'm getting closer to the axis of the mystery; I can sense it.

Darlene clears her throat. "Maybe I ought to find Chris's phone number and tell him about the Good Samaritan who came here to drop off his wallet."

I ignore her and keep my eyes on the male server, barely breathing.

"Yeah," he finally says. "I think that's him."

My finger is pointing to Skip.

CHAPTER THIRTY-NINE

MARISSA

MARISSA HAS EXPERIENCED THIS SENSATION of absolute dread and fear only a few times before.

It happened during two of her pregnancies, when her doctor's face fell while administering her sonograms. And another time, when she momentarily took her eyes off Bennett at a county fair and he was swallowed up by the crowd until she located him fifteen minutes later at the petting zoo.

This afternoon, when Matthew suggested she take a nap, her mind had been too fractured to quiet. Instead, she'd reached for her laptop resting on the nightstand. The Natalie-Polly connection was haunting her, and she needed to get to the bottom of it. She'd plugged Polly's name into the search engine, along with Natalie's. But nothing had come up. So she'd added the name of the real estate company where Natalie worked. Still nothing. She'd stared at the computer screen for another minute and had been about to shut the lid, but then her fingers had begun moving again, trembling as they'd typed in the name of another woman who has been haunting her. Her old best friend: Tina Lennox.

She wasn't sure what she was looking for exactly. What new information could there be to see? No baby announcement. Or Employee of the Month recognition. There would be no wedding photograph. Not even a mention of a high school graduation. Tina's life ended before it could really begin.

The first few items that appeared were familiar to Marissa: a couple of old Associated Press stories and a few longer ones by *The Baltimore Sun.* Marissa had clicked on Tina's yearbook photo, the one all the newspapers ran, and stared at it for a long time. For the photo, Tina had worn the yellow sweater that she and Marissa had decided was the prettiest one Tina owned, and her hair was curled.

Then Marissa noticed a few new mentions of Tina *had* appeared. At least, they were new to Marissa.

Local man recants admission of murder of Tina Lennox: former high school English teacher Marvin Miller claims police coerced a false confession.

That article was from four years ago.

In another one, dated nine months earlier, on the anniversary of Tina's death, Miller repeated his claims of innocence. *I've spent half my life sitting in a cell while the real killer walks free,* he was quoted as saying.

Marissa had stared at the screen, her hand over her mouth, feeling nausea rise in her throat.

If their English teacher hadn't killed Tina, then who had?

It had been a struggle to get through dinner and Bennett's bedtime routine, knowing this reckoning was finally coming. She'd tried to act normally, but more than once she'd caught Matthew studying her with a puzzled expression.

Now Marissa stands looking through the double glass doors leading from their family room to the backyard, to where Matthew stands by the fire in the stone hearth. It's a cool, starlit evening, and Matthew has brought out a blanket and bottle of good wine. Bennett is sound asleep in his race-car bed, his thumb covered with a fresh bandage and his dinosaur diorama nearly finished.

The scene is set for a quiet, romantic night. Until Marissa throws a grenade into it.

She slides open the door and steps onto the patio.

Her husband is tending the flames, using a poker to arrange the logs. The firelight playing across his face conjures an image of another, long-ago evening by a bonfire.

Not that she needs the reminder.

"There you are." Matthew puts aside the iron poker and sits down, patting the cushion next to him on the settee.

Marissa walks toward him as he reaches for the white Burgundy and twists the corkscrew before pulling it out with his strong fingers.

He pours them each a glass. "Cheers."

"Cheers." She takes a tiny sip. She notices that on the eve of their anniversary, he has selected their wedding crystal.

She's so cold again, despite her fleece leggings and top and the heat of the fire. She feels as if she hasn't been able to get warm since this all began.

Matthew reaches for the blanket, tucking it over her legs. "You okay?"

Marissa makes a noncommittal noise. "Can I ask you something?"

Matthew looks calm; he has no idea what's coming. "Of course."

She takes a deep breath and speaks the question that has the potential to unravel everything: "Why did you lie for Skip all those years ago?"

Matthew sets down his glass and turns to face her, as if he recognizes the importance of this moment.

"Because it looked bad for him, and I knew he didn't kill Tina," Matthew finally answers. "You and I know Skip sometimes went to work on his boat at night, when he was taking clients fishing early the next morning. But if the police knew he was out there alone, near the spot where Tina was killed? They might not have believed him. He was about to go to college on a scholarship. Even if he was cleared later, that cloud of suspicion could have cost him everything."

Marissa nods, remembering the scratch Tina had inflicted on Skip's arm. "You were such a good friend to him," she whispers.

The false alibi had seemed harmless when Marissa first heard about it from Matthew shortly after they started dating: *Skip was scared. The police were questioning everyone. He came to my house to ask my dad for advice, but my dad was in the city. I knew he hadn't done it, so I told him to just say he'd been with me at home watching a movie that night. My mom covered for him, too; she trusted me when I told her Skip wouldn't hurt anyone.*

The lie stopped seeming harmless when Marissa learned about that open window in Matthew's office, and about the English teacher recanting his confession.

The fire makes a loud popping sound and Marissa flinches, but Matthew doesn't even glance at it. He's staring intently at her.

"Why are you bringing this up now?"

Marissa's mouth is so dry she needs another sip of wine. "I googled the case this afternoon. Did you know our English teacher claimed the police leaned on him so hard he gave a false confession?"

Matthew reaches for her hand and begins to massage it. "Sweetheart, ask any man in prison if he's innocent. They're all going to say yes."

"How well do we really know Skip anymore? We've only seen him a few dozen times over the past twenty years. He lived across the country until last summer."

Matthew's fingers stop moving. "What are you saying?"

Marissa begins to shiver. This reminds her of her first confession in Avery's office, when she sat shaking from a combination of chill and fear.

Then, Matthew hadn't responded to her discomfort.

Now, he wraps an arm around her. She leans into his warm, hard body and inhales his woodsy scent, trying not to think about how it could be for the last time. Then she pulls back to face him.

I have to tell Matthew the truth, she reminds herself, and not only because we can't have a real marriage without honesty. Her simple lie has spread and morphed, like an invisible virus that sickens everyone it touches. And like a virus, the lie could turn lethal.

It would be one thing if Skip's behavior had affected only Marissa. She could have thrown away the roses and note and soup and lived with the pressure and guilt as a kind of penance.

But if Skip is the one behind the vicious attack on Matthew and the apparent break-in this morning—she hates to think like this, but who else could it be?—then his escalation is downright terrifying.

She recalls a line she once read: *You can never truly know what is inside another person's heart or head.* Perhaps Avery has been guiding me toward this moment all along, Marissa thinks. This could be the ultimate test. If Marissa tells Matthew the truth and he forgives her, they really could start to heal.

And if he doesn't . . . well, it is far more important to protect Matthew and Bennett than to protect her marriage.

"Skip has been acting so strangely lately," she begins.

"Yeah, it was kind of weird that he stopped by uninvited last night and then dropped off all that soup." Matthew shrugs.

"It's more than that. This is so hard for me to say. But I think Skip could be behind the other things that have been happening lately."

Can Matthew feel her leg trembling against his? She swears she can perceive the shift in his energy; he must sense the grenade is in her hand.

"Why would you think that, Marissa?" Matthew's tone is even and measured, the way it sounds when he's conducting a difficult talk with a concerned client.

"Those roses . . . I called the florist the next day. The Venmo account was @Pier1234. There's that long pier near where Skip and I grew up. He used to love fishing off it. And the note you and Polly found? Ray, the homeless man who hangs out by Coco, told me someone paid him to deliver it. The same man also gave Ray a pair of gloves. Gloves I know belonged to Skip."

Matthew stands up and reaches for the poker. He jabs at the fire. A thick wave of smoke drifts toward Marissa, making her feel briefly dizzy as she inhales it.

"Matthew." She takes another sip of wine for courage. "I lied to you. I didn't sleep with a guy from the gym. . . . It was Skip."

Matthew is perfectly still for an endless moment. Then he slowly turns to face her, the poker still gripped in his hand.

Half of his face is in the darkness, the other half illuminated by the flickering firelight, making him appear both familiar and like a stranger. Just like Skip looked on the night she first kissed him.

Matthew doesn't speak. He stares at her, as if he is peering deep into her soul.

The first time I kissed you, it was like glimpsing the ocean for the first time. All these years later I still feel the same way.

Her husband will never feel that way about her again.

Tears spill down her cheeks. "Matthew, please say something! I'm so sorry."

Matthew sets downs the poker.

He sinks back into his seat and stares straight ahead, as if he's in shock.

"You and Skip," he whispers. "Are you kidding me? How long has it been going on?"

"It only happened once; I swear."

"You've been lying to me this whole time." Matthew's voice is preternaturally calm and soft. To Marissa it has the feel of the trembles that precede an earthquake.

"I didn't know what to do. I thought if I told you, you'd leave me and I couldn't bear that. But I should have. You deserved to know."

"I just—I can't get my mind around this. Skip was in our *house* last night, Marissa. We all sat around talking about old times and all the while, you and he . . ."

Matthew reaches for his glass and drains the wine. "Does Avery know about all this?"

Marissa hesitates. Will it make it better or worse for Matthew when he hears the answer?

"She does, yes."

With a swift, powerful motion he hurls the empty crystal against the stone fireplace. She flinches as it shatters into a dozen pieces, shards cascading everywhere.

"Everybody was in on it but me! You all think I'm a fucking fool!"

Marissa shakes her head. "No! I'm the fool, Matthew. I ruined everything! You're the only one I want."

"Yet the evidence doesn't support that." Matthew is back in control, his sharp legal mind countering whatever she says.

"I told Skip it won't ever happen again. I begged him to leave us alone. But . . ."

"But Skip won't accept that?" Matthew is looking straight ahead, as if he can't bear the sight of her.

"It seems that way," Marissa whispers.

In a way, she's grateful she can't see the fury and disgust that must be filling Matthew's eyes. "I'll do anything to—"

He abruptly stands up. Without a word, he begins heading toward the house.

She knows exactly what will happen next: He'll pack a suitcase and stay at a hotel.

There will be no anniversary celebration tomorrow.

There will be no more anniversaries at all.

She watches as he reaches the glass doors.

But instead of pulling them open, he turns around and walks back to her. She is prepared for him to yell or tell her to move out.

But when he gets closer, she can see his eyes are wet. She has only seen her husband cry once, when his mother died.

Marissa feels as if something is breaking inside of her, too.

"Are there any more secrets?"

Of all the hundreds of questions Matthew has asked her throughout their lifetime together, this is the most important one, the one she must get right.

She shakes her head. "That was the last one."

Matthew nods, and in that moment Marissa feels time shudder to a stop.

Matthew looks at the house again, as if weighing his options. Then he looks back at her.

She waits, afraid to even breathe.

"I thought it was over," Matthew finally says. "But I can't let go of you."

CHAPTER FORTY

AVERY

I SETTLE INTO A COMFORTABLE rhythm as I jog along Rock Creek Drive. Beside me, Romeo easily keeps pace. It's our first real run since his stitches dissolved, and he seems to crave the exercise as much as I do.

It's not merely a physical release I'm seeking. Something about the steady, repetitive motion of my feet along a familiar path tends to free up my mind. And right now, I desperately need clarity.

Marissa phoned me earlier this morning, while I was drinking coffee and reading the Sunday papers, letting me know she'd finally told Matthew the truth about Skip.

He still wants to try. Her voice was filled with wonder. *He says he can't let me go.*

It's not that simple, I'd told her. *We've got a lot of work to do.*

Of course. We'll be there tomorrow night.

Session eight, I'd thought to myself. The Test. I have one in mind, but I may change it up based on what I learn today.

I'd asked to speak to Matthew, but she'd told me he was in the shower and would phone later.

It has been two hours, and I'm still waiting for that call.

Just as I think this, I'm nearly jerked off my feet.

"Romeo, no!" I pull on his leash to draw him back. The squirrel that caught his attention scampers across our path and climbs a tree. I wince and rub my shoulder with my free hand, then resume running, passing a pair of women who are walking together along the path.

Usually by this point in my process I've identified my clients' issues and have a treatment plan well underway.

I think back to the notes I jotted on my yellow pad, beneath Matthew's and Marissa's names, during our first session.

Marissa's confession: Infidelity.

Probable root cause: Emotional distance.

If my progress was being judged solely by the quality of the Bishops' relationship, I could view this case as an emerging success. Their marriage appears healthier now than it did when they first walked through my door.

Appearances.

I'd also written down that word during our initial visit and underlined it twice. Now I mentally add to it:

Appearances lie.

Nothing about the Bishops or the people around them is straightforward.

The dirt trail veers sharply uphill. My legs begin to burn and my lungs feel tight, but I force myself to maintain my pace, knowing I'll reach the crest and the downhill soon. Beside me, Romeo is still running easily, looking at me every now and then as if to make sure I'm keeping up.

I reach the halfway point of my run, which is marked by a fallen tree, its intricate root system exposed.

I've warmed up, so I stop to unzip my fleece jacket and adjust one of my earbuds, which keeps slipping out.

I've seen a half dozen people on this trail, but no one is around right now. A breeze rustles the trees, and I inhale crisp air. "Ready to head back?"

Romeo seems agreeable, so we turn and begin to retrace our route.

A minute later, my phone buzzes in the side pocket of my leggings. I slow down to see who it is, then hit the button to accept the call.

"Hey, Matthew." I stop again and try to catch my breath. "How are you?"

"How am I?" It sounds as if I'm on speakerphone. Perhaps he's phoning me from his car.

I wait for him to continue. I want to hear Matthew's version of the evening.

"Completely pissed off. Like I've been sucker punched."

"It's a terrible betrayal." Even if on some level Matthew suspected it was Skip, to have it confirmed must be devastating. "And I apologize for being complicit in it."

"You're the one I'm the least pissed off at." Matthew exhales loudly. "Marissa obviously fucked up royally. She shouldn't ever have let Skip in that night. It's gonna take me a while to get over that. But these past few weeks, I've done a lot of soul-searching, and one thing I know for sure is that I want to stay married to Marissa. I can't help it. I love my wife."

"How do you plan to deal with Skip?"

"I want to beat the crap out of him, but I'm just going to call him and tell him I know. And not to come near me or my wife again or I'll kill him."

"I get it." I lean forward to stretch one of my calves, which is tightening up.

"I told Marissa I didn't want to know a single detail about what happened that night. I don't want that picture in my head." Matthew hesitates. "Honestly, I think she's relieved Skip will be out of our lives. I think she's a little scared of him now. All the stuff he's done . . . he could be violent."

Behind me, I hear the crack of a stick breaking.

I spin around. The trail is empty.

"We can look into a restraining order if he does anything else," I tell Matthew. "But I hope it doesn't come to that."

"I'm still taking Marissa out on the boat later today. Skip's not going to ruin that for us. It's not going to be the anniversary celebration I wanted, but . . . I don't know, maybe it can be a new beginning."

"It can be anything you want it to be."

"Okay. I guess we'll see you tomorrow night. Maybe you should have that tequila ready."

I laugh and promise I will.

When we hang up, I adjust my earbuds again and resume running. I seem to be alone in the woods, but I'm prepared. I've got Mace on my key chain, and I can hear anyone coming.

Because appearances lie: I'm not a carefree jogger listening to a playlist; there's never been any music playing through my earphones.

Romeo begins to bark and tug on his leash again, pulling me forward.

We round a corner and I spot a woman power walking ahead of me. Romeo and I pass her, and then a few minutes later, two bicyclists whip by me.

The woods that briefly felt menacing seem safe again.

Romeo and I reach the end of the trail and exit. My car is parked where it always is when I do these Sunday runs—along a stretch of Western Avenue.

A man is leaning against it, clearly waiting for me. It's a terrible spot for an ambush. Not only is this a busy road, but plenty of people are around.

Still, I reach for my Mace, ready to fight to protect myself and my dog.

I'm sick of being threatened and followed. If it's one of Acelia's henchmen, I'm going to blast him with Mace, kick him between the legs, and call the cops.

But it isn't.

It's Skip.

I take a few more steps toward him, ready to tell him off. Then I look down at Skip's hands and gasp.

It's cold out, and he's wearing gloves.

Blue leather gloves.

CHAPTER FORTY-ONE

MARISSA

THE TRADITIONAL ANNIVERSARY GIFT for twelve years is silk or linen. Marissa hadn't been able to find anything inspiring along those lines, so her present to Matthew is a vintage Rolex. She'd ordered it weeks ago and had thought about having it engraved with the message EVERY MINUTE I LOVE YOU MORE. However, getting it inscribed proved more challenging than she'd expected, so she planned to give it to him unadorned.

She'd intended to wrap it earlier today, but hasn't had a moment alone. Even though Matthew slept in the elephant room again, he woke early and showered in their bathroom. By the time Bennett padded downstairs in his pj's, Marissa and Matthew were in the kitchen drinking coffee.

Things weren't right between them yet, but Matthew had agreed to try, and that felt like the best anniversary gift he could have given her.

He seemed to have something else up his sleeve, though.

After they'd eaten lunch, Matthew helped Bennett pack an overnight bag and was currently taking their son for an unprecedented school-night sleepover at Charlie's.

Marissa had felt a sharp pang when Bennett hugged her goodbye; she was gripped again by the yearning to be near her son, keeping her eyes on him at all times.

But she didn't let on. Bennett had only been on two sleepovers in his life, and even though both were at Charlie's house, Bennett was still a little nervous.

Don't forget to feed Sam, he'd said, chewing on a thumbnail.

I won't. She'd smiled brightly at Bennett. *I'll pick you up after school to-morrow.*

By then, she'd hopefully have hired a new assistant and given Polly notice. And Skip would be out of their lives.

Instead of being filled with a sense of peace, her unease intensifies when Matthew and Bennett leave.

She keeps busy, tidying the kitchen and loading the dishwasher with their plates from lunch, then removing the watch from her hiding place in the garage and bringing it into the kitchen to wrap. She's folding down the last corner of the package when the Scotch tape in the dispenser runs out.

There's more tape in her makeshift office upstairs, but a closer roll is likely in Matthew's study. She leaves her gift on the kitchen island and walks into the room, the hardwood floors cool against her bare feet.

Across the room, the window by Matthew's cherished Picasso sketch is firmly shut. She averts her gaze. She won't let thoughts of Skip intrude today.

There's a letter opener, Matthew's laptop, and a pencil holder on his desk, along with a silver-framed family photo, but no tape. Marissa walks around behind the desk and pulls open the top drawer. Like everything in Matthew's office, it's well organized, with scissors, envelopes, paper clips, and a stapler in neat sections. The tape is toward the back.

She pulls the drawer out a little farther and sees another object next to the tape: a woven white rope.

She stares at it in confusion, even though she knows exactly what it is: Bennett's missing Cub Scout rope.

What's it doing hidden away here?

She pulls it out and stares at it. It's tied in an intricate knot that resembles a figure eight.

It's called a sailor's knot. She knows because she grew up on the water, and even though she never learned to make them, she's seen them a hundred times.

Bennett wasn't practicing sailor's knots, though; he doesn't even know how to form them. He was working on square knots.

Her skin prickles.

She hears the sound of Matthew's car pulling into the driveway and quickly pulls off a piece of tape, putting back the roll along with the rope and shutting the drawer.

She hurries into the kitchen and finishes wrapping the gift, sliding it into her handbag by the time Matthew has unlocked the door.

He steps into the kitchen. He's wearing a black jacket and dark jeans and his expression is grim.

Then he sees her and smiles. "It's just the two of us now."

For some reason, her stomach clenches. It's because of everything that happened last night, she tells herself.

"I should get changed so we can go." She desperately needs a minute alone.

"There's no rush." Matthew walks around the island to stand next to her, taking off his jacket. He's wearing a light blue oxford, one that Marissa bought him because it complements the color of his eyes. "Come, sit down. There's something I need to tell you about."

She doesn't want to sit, but she acquiesces.

Matthew, however, remains standing, setting his jacket down on the stool next to Marissa's. He's close to her. She feels penned in.

"I just spoke to Skip. I told him I know what happened between the two of you and that he needs to stay away from us."

"How did he take it?" she manages to ask.

"He apologized. He seemed to understand. But he's been acting so unhinged lately, I don't think we can count on this being the end of it."

An image of Skip flashes into Marissa's mind: Skip at seventeen, gently cleaning away the blood on the back of Marissa's hand from the oyster shell cut. *I'm not hurting you, am I?* he'd asked.

She would never see Skip again. Never hear his voice.

A deep sense of loss sweeps through her.

Matthew is staring at her. "Everything okay?"

She nods because it should be, but it isn't. Matthew is so close she feels as if she is inhaling the breath he exhales; her lungs are growing tight.

An almost overpowering sense of claustrophobia grips her as Matthew reaches out and strokes her hair.

"Oh, I just remembered!" Marissa's voice sounds strangled; she clears her throat. "I need to call Charlie's mom to make sure Bennett turns in the permission slip tomorrow for his field trip."

Matthew's hand dips down lower and he begins to massage her back, his fingers digging into a painful knot in her right shoulder.

"I already told her." Matthew's fingers are too strong; it hurts.

She winces and pulls away. What Matthew said makes no sense; she's the one who filled out the permission slip and tucked it in the pocket of Bennett's backpack. She wasn't even aware that Matthew knew about the field trip.

"You did?"

Matthew responds with a question of his own: "Why are you so tense, sweetie?"

She can't stop seeing that white rope in his desk drawer. If Matthew would just back off, she could try to make sense of the puzzle. Then he finally does move away, and she gulps in air.

He walks around to the other side of the island and pulls out a bottle from their wine rack.

"I thought we could have a drink before we leave."

"Sounds nice. I'll get the glasses." Marissa starts to get up, but Matthew waves her away; he's already taking them out of a cabinet.

Before she can do anything, he's back beside her, pressing in even closer than before, his legs against hers. He pours them each a glass. She reaches for hers with a trembling hand. The last thing she wants right now is alcohol; she has to keep a clear head.

Matthew clinks his glass against hers. "To my beautiful wife."

His words sound false, as if he's reciting lines.

He stares at her, as if trying to gauge her reactions to his toast. She feels an overwhelming desire to push Matthew away so she can finally get off this barstool.

She takes a small sip. Matthew is still standing; she has to crane her neck to look up at him. He's smiling broadly.

Given the news she delivered last night, something seems off. He's too happy, too carefree.

Too perfect.

"I almost forgot." He moves away from her again, and she sucks in another gulp of fresh air. Why is it hard for her to breathe when her husband is near? She doesn't know how she's going to get through the rest of the afternoon and evening with him.

That white length of rope; she last saw it in Skip's hands on the night they slept together. He was absently toying with it while they spoke. Then, he set it down on the end table, right before he leaned in to kiss her.

After Skip left, Marissa had hand-washed and dried the wineglasses they'd used, returning them to the cabinet. She'd buried the empty bottle of Malbec Skip had brought deep in the recycling bin. She'd tossed out the uneaten nuts from the little serving bowl, rinsed the bowl, and put the tin of mixed nuts back in the pantry. She'd fluffed all the cushions on the couch.

She'd erased the evidence.

Had she left the little white rope on the side table?

Possibly. It had seemed so innocuous.

Her pulse is pounding in her ears, making it difficult to think.

She sets down her wineglass. Matthew has gotten something out of the pantry and is back by her side. He's holding a tin of mixed nuts. He pulls off the top and selects a Brazil nut, offering it to her. She shakes her head; she fears she'll choke on it.

He pops it in his own mouth. "Mmm." The kitchen is so quiet she can hear him crunching. He leans in and brushes a strand of hair off her face.

She instinctively flinches.

"How's your wine?"

"It's good." She forces herself to take another small sip. Then another idea seizes her and she blurts out, "If we start drinking this early, tomorrow might be a little rough. Let me quickly call Polly and let her know I might be late."

Inquisitive Polly will pick up on something in Marissa's voice. Marissa can stay on the phone with her for a few minutes, coming up with some fabricated tasks she needs Polly to take care of in the morning.

Marissa would just feel better if she could speak to someone right now and let the person know she's in the kitchen of her house with her husband, alone.

But Matthew's next words drain every ounce of hope from her body.

"I already told Polly you'd come in a little late. I called her right after I dropped off Bennett. You need to relax, Marissa. I've taken care of everything."

"You called Polly?" This makes no sense: Matthew has only met her new assistant twice, maybe three times, tops. She doesn't even think Matthew knows Polly's last name. So how does he have Polly's cell phone number?

Matthew smiles. "Polly knows how worried I've been about you. And she's been worried, too. All those hang-ups. That crazy note."

He reaches into the back pocket of his jeans and brings out a white piece of paper, folded into quarters. As he smooths it out, Marissa sees it's been taped back together, like a completed jigsaw puzzle.

She releases a small, high sound. The last time she saw that note, it was in pieces in the trash can at Coco. She'd assumed it was gone forever. Polly must have fished it out of the garbage and reassembled it, before giving it to Matthew.

Have her assistant and her husband been meeting in secret?

"I asked Polly to look after you," Matthew murmurs. "Kind of be my eyes and ears when I'm not around. To help me keep you protected. She took my request very seriously. You know Polly; she's nothing if not overly conscientious. I suggested she keep a log of all the hang-ups and other incidents, since someone is clearly obsessed with you. Just in case."

Marissa begins to tremble. The kitchen has two exits: the door to the garage, and the opening that leads to the hallway and front door. A knife is in the block by the sink. Her car keys are in her purse, which is sitting on the end of the island, a few feet away. Her cell phone is upstairs, in the charger on her nightstand.

She catalogs all of this information instinctually.

The wine bottle is within reach on the island. The glass looks thick and substantial, and the bottle is nearly full. Her hand creeps out toward it while her eyes remain fixed on Matthew.

"I'll get that." He scoops it up. "I made sure to buy a case of your new favorite."

Matthew picks up the bottle and begins to slowly turn it around to display the label. She doesn't need to see it; she already knows it is the same wine Skip brought over.

Her husband no longer looks merely joyful. He seems filled with a triumphant glee.

You can never truly know what is inside another person's heart or head, Marissa thinks wildly.

What was Matthew's first clue? Maybe the rope; Matthew is highly attuned to details. If Skip left it in this nautical knot and Matthew saw it when he got home from his trip, his mind would have begun to whirl.

She'd buried the empty bottle of Malbec in the recycling bin, but Matthew had been the one to take the bin out to the curb. He'd know she would never drink an entire bottle of wine alone.

And those mixed nuts that Matthew just offered her. Marissa never ate them because they were so salty, and Bennett didn't like nuts, but Matthew loved them. He often snacked on a handful or two at night. Would he have noticed the tin had been nearly emptied on an evening when he'd been out of town?

Yes, he would have.

Dread fills her. "How long have you known?" she whispers.

"Forever. Skip has always had a piece of your heart." Matthew's lip curls. "But in terms of you fucking him? I confirmed it the following night, when you went into the shower and left your cell phone in your purse. You were clever enough to delete any text exchanges between the two of you. But you didn't think to erase the record of Skip's incoming call. He phoned you at eight twenty P.M. on the night I was out of town, and you two talked for forty-seven seconds. Not long enough for a proper catch-up with an old friend, but more than enough time to invite one over."

Matthew suddenly lifts his head, as if a noise has caught his attention. Then he looks back at Marissa and says, in a tone so conversational it's chilling, "You didn't think I was really going to take you away for an anniversary celebration, did you? It was so much fun to tell Skip about all my romantic plans for an overnight boat trip, though."

Marissa begins to tremble. Matthew has been creating fictional scene after fictional scene. And she believed every one of them.

He was never the unaware, wronged husband. That was an illusion; a gifted con artist's sleight of hand.

Blackness crowds her field of vision and she grows light-headed; she is on the verge of passing out. She fights the sensation with everything she has, grabbing the counter to steady herself.

"If you knew all along, why did you pretend?" she manages to ask.

"I've always been good at the long game. Especially when it comes to Skip. He thinks you're pregnant, by the way. I told him so when I invited him over the other night for a drink. The look on your face when he dropped off all that chicken soup . . ."

Matthew laughs and takes a deep sip of his wine.

Bile rises in Marissa's throat. She knew she and her husband had drifted apart. But she never suspected he'd been a stranger to her all along.

Marissa's eyes dart to the note on the kitchen island. The threat has been staring her in the face, in black and white. But the words belong to Matthew, not Skip. "You wrote this."

Matthew smiles. "Clever, huh?"

She's reeling from the layers of deception. Why would Matthew want to make it appear as if Skip wrote that message?

Matthew picks up the note and folds it again before tucking it into his back pocket. "I even made sure to buy a pair of those blue gloves for Ray. I figured you'd see them sooner or later. I also picked up a new pair of gloves for myself."

He pulls a pair of thin black leather gloves from his jacket pocket and slips them on.

This action makes no sense, yet it fills her with a bone-chilling terror. The kitchen is warm. Why would Matthew need gloves?

Her head is swimming. She struggles to think, to make sense of things. She leans back in her chair, as far away from Matthew as possible. Matthew counters her move, leaning in closer. He seems to be relishing her fear and confusion.

"Can I give you a bit of constructive criticism, babe? You're a terrible actress. The look on your face when you thought Skip had broken in here and dropped those Life Savers . . ." Matthew runs a finger down the side of her cheek. The cool leather of his glove against her skin makes her shudder.

"Tell me the truth," he whispers. "Did you wonder if Skip hired someone to attack me? You did, didn't you? But anyone can inflict bruises. You can even do it to yourself. All you need is determination and a brick. You can even pretend to pass out to make it seem like your injuries are more serious."

She can't breathe.

How easily she'd been fooled by all the fake evidence Matthew had planted. She believed Skip was a threat, but the threat lives inside her home.

An explosive noise erupts from the front of the house; it's the sound of fists pounding against the front door.

"Marissa!" Skip's yell is muffled, but it's unmistakably him. The doorbell rings several times in furious succession, then the pounding resumes.

Skip has come to save her.

She twists her head to look in the direction of the door. Matthew is still penning her in, but if she kicks out, she might be able to get past him. She can run to the door and fling it open.

Matthew reaches for his jacket, fumbling with it for a moment, and when she glances at him again, her heart stutters.

He's holding a gun.

She tries to scream, but her vocal cords seize up.

There is utter silence for a moment.

Then on the side of the house where Matthew's office is located, Marissa hears a window shattering.

Matthew cocks his head toward the sound. He looks perplexed.

"Seems like your obsessive lover has resorted to breaking in. Skip must be really panicked to forget I gave him the code to the back door a while ago. Our little reunion was supposed to happen right here, but that's okay. We can move it to another room."

What is her husband saying? Before she can try to make sense of it, he makes a movement with his thumb, and she realizes he has taken off the safety. His index finger is curled around the trigger of the shiny black weapon.

They don't keep a gun in the house. Matthew must have been planning this for some time.

Matthew lifts the pistol a bit higher, so that Marissa is at eye level with the little round tunnel the bullet will fly through. All she can see is that tiny circle; it's as if the whole world has narrowed to its circumference.

"I could call the police . . . or I suppose I could try and stop him." But instead of heading toward the noise, Matthew continues pointing the gun at Marissa. "No one would blame me for shooting the man who killed my wife."

Marissa's eyes widen. It's far too late, but she sees everything clearly now. He's going to kill her, frame Skip, then murder Skip, claiming it was self-defense.

Her husband is a master illusionist.

Their happy life together has been a mirage.

She has no idea how he lured Skip here, but it doesn't matter.

Marissa cheated on her husband and thought he forgave her.

But he didn't.

She only knew half of their story. Matthew has been operating from a different script.

"I need you to stand up, Marissa." When she doesn't move, Matthew reaches for her arm and yanks it roughly, pulling her to her feet. She gasps in pain. Her legs are so rubbery she nearly falls to the floor.

"I've wanted to hurt you ever since I found out you fucked our friend in my house," Matthew hisses in her ear.

"Please," she begs. "Bennett . . ."

"Let's go greet Skip. You first."

He steps behind her and, when she doesn't move, digs the gun into her shoulder blade. She rises and walks out of the kitchen, down the hallway toward the study, then stumbles.

She is going to be sick. The thought of leaving her precious little boy is too much. Matthew will be viewed as the heroic, grieving widower. He'll have full custody of Bennett.

She retches, then starts to cry.

"Get a grip, Marissa," Matthew barks, jabbing her again with the cold metal until she resumes walking.

At the threshold of Matthew's office, she sees Skip pulling himself through the broken window. He's got his coat draped over the bottom to protect himself from the sharp shards, and his upper body is through the jagged hole while his lower body dangles outside the house. Blood drips down from a cut on his forehead. His eyes widen as Marissa and Matthew step into the room. Skip looks frantic.

He's too late.

Matthew will shoot them both. The final scene he is directing will be complete. He even has witnesses in place who will testify to Skip's obsession, and to Matthew's seeming devotion to Marissa: Polly and Avery.

Marissa hears the noise of a distant siren, but if the police are coming, they'll be too late as well.

"Walk toward the window," Matthew instructs her. "I'll shoot you now if you don't."

Skip shouts, "I'll kill you if you hurt her!"

"Actually, it's going to be the other way around," Matthew replies.

Marissa keeps her eyes locked on Skip. There's nowhere to run. She might be able to grab the letter opener from Matthew's desk, but he will surely fire his gun before she has a chance to wound him.

She takes a step toward Skip, then another, as if she were walking down a gangplank.

Skip stops moving. "Look, Matthew, it was my fault, okay?" Skip's voice is pleading. "Not hers. You don't have to do this."

"Keep walking," Matthew orders.

Marissa takes another step.

Skip's words tumble out: "Marissa picked you, not me."

"Sure she did," Matthew snaps. "Just like my dad prefers me to you. Just like Tina did, too."

Marissa freezes; she can't take another step.

"Things didn't end up so well for Tina, either," Matthew continues. "Do you know she thought it was *you* chasing after her when she was sitting on the pier alone that night? She looked so disappointed when she turned around and saw me. But not for long."

Three things happen as Matthew speaks those horrible words.

Skip abruptly drops backward through the open window, vanishing.

Matthew shoves Marissa roughly to the floor and runs toward the window.

And a gunshot explodes, the sound so loud and powerful it seems to reverberate through Marissa's soul.

CHAPTER FORTY-TWO

AVERY

THE BLUE LEATHER GLOVES aren't my only clue. But the second I see them on Skip's hands, everything else clicks into place.

There is no way Skip could have given his gloves to Ray and still be wearing them himself. But someone else could easily have purchased a near-identical pair and passed them to Ray along with the anonymous note. That same person could have ordered the yellow roses from Bloom, made the phone hang-ups, and even orchestrated the attack on Matthew.

I think I know who it is, but I need one question answered to be certain.

Never before has so much hinged on The Test.

"The night you and Marissa slept together—where did it happen?"

Skip looks bewildered.

"Her house, your place, your car—*where*?"

"Her living room. But listen, I came looking for you because there's something else I need to talk to you about. It isn't about Matthew or Marissa. It's about Matthew's father."

I don't hear anything he says after that. I'm recalling the words of a different man.

Marissa shouldn't have ever let Skip in that night.

Only a few minutes ago, Matthew told me he hadn't wanted to hear any details about the night Marissa and Skip slept together. So how did he know that one?

"Matthew has been setting you up," I tell Skip.

At that moment, Skip's phone rings with an incoming call. Skip turns around the screen to show me. "It's him."

"Answer it."

I can't hear what Matthew is saying, but as I watch Skip's expression transform from anger into a kind of primal terror, I act on instinct. I pull Romeo into the back seat of my car, jump into the driver's seat, and start my engine, while Skip leaps into the passenger's side.

"He's going to hurt her!" Skip shouts. "I'm calling 911!"

I'm already making a U-turn, my wheels squealing against the pavement, as I head towards the Bishops' house. There's no traffic on a Sunday afternoon, and I'll run any red lights we encounter. We're only a couple minutes away.

Matthew must know his threat will bring Skip to his door, but he won't expect me to be there, too.

Matthew had a long time to plan this. But I've got the element of surprise on my side.

I've got something else, too. As we race toward the Bishops' house, I steer with one hand and reach across Skip to unlock the glove compartment of my car with the other. I take out my fully loaded .38 pistol and set it on my lap.

"I know the code for the back door. Give me the gun." Skip is leaning forward, one hand on the door handle, ready to leap out the moment we get there.

"No!" I instinctively say. "He'll be expecting you to go in that way."

Then I tell Skip what we're going to do.

By the time we pull up by the curb down the street from the Bishops' house, Skip has his jacket off. He leaps out before my car comes to a stop and sprints diagonally to the front door, banging on it and yelling Marissa's name.

He's creating a diversion. If Matthew is watching out a window, his eyes will be on Skip.

I lock Romeo in my car, then quickly survey the terrain. The Bishops have neighbors on both sides. To their left is a house with a manicured lawn and two cars parked in the driveway. The one on the right is surrounded by trees and thick bushes. I opt for that one, hoping the cover of the foliage will camouflage my movements.

By the time Skip is breaking a window at the side of the house, as I told him to, I've arrived at the back door.

I punch in the code Skip gave me—S-A-M-B, for the name of Bennett's pet gecko—praying no one has changed it recently. The light on the lock switches from red to green.

I'm in.

The kitchen is empty, but I hear the sound of retching, then Matthew barking, "Get a grip, Marissa!"

They're in the hallway, heading toward the noise Skip is making.

I step into the hallway, a half dozen feet behind them. My gun is raised. It's difficult to shoot a moving target, so I aim for center mass, envisioning a bull's-eye on the back of Matthew's light blue shirt.

We move almost in unison toward Matthew's office, my footsteps light and nearly soundless in my running shoes. I'm like a ghost, creeping unseen behind the Bishops.

As I step into the office, I hear the distant siren of a police car, then see Skip struggling to pull himself through the window.

"Walk toward the window," Matthew instructs Marissa. "I'll shoot you now if you don't."

"I'll kill you if you hurt her!" Skip is shouting.

"Actually, it's going to be the other way around."

I scan the scene, knowing I've only got a few seconds to act. Matthew is going to shoot Marissa just as Skip clears the window and heaves himself into the room. Skip will lunge at Matthew, and Matthew will shoot him, too.

Then Skip stops moving. He has spotted me.

"Look, Matthew, it was my fault, okay? Not hers. You don't have to do this."

"Keep walking."

Marissa steps forward. Skip is trying to distract Matthew, while my gun remains fixed on the invisible bull's-eye.

I can't shoot Matthew, though. Marissa is directly in front of him. My bullet would probably tear through him and hit her.

"Marissa picked you, not me." Skip's desperate, playing to Matthew's ego. Skip must have done the mental math, and he knows there is no way he can get to Marissa in time.

"Sure she did," Matthew replies sarcastically. "Just like my dad prefers me to you. Just like Tina did, too."

Marissa stops moving.

"Things didn't end up so well for Tina, either." Matthew's tone is pure evil. "Do you know she thought it was you chasing after her when she was sitting on the pier alone that night? She looked so disappointed when she turned around and saw me. But not for long."

You sick bastard, I think.

Matthew raises his gun slightly, and I know this is it: the moment he's been planning ever since he discovered his wife and good friend betrayed him. Marissa is completely silent; she must be in shock. Skip is still too far away to help.

I've only got one possible move.

I flatten out my left hand and gesture in a swift, downward motion— the same one Skip taught me on the night he met Romeo. *Down.*

Skip's eyes widen briefly, then he gets it. He flings himself backward and disappears.

Matthew leaps forward, grabbing Marissa and shoving her to the ground. Then he runs toward the window, leading with his gun.

The instant Marissa is clear, I pull the trigger.

A tremendous boom echoes through the room. Matthew collapses to the ground, dropping his weapon. Before I even realize I'm doing it, I run over to him and kick the gun away.

A widening bloodstain blooms across Matthew's chest, and he makes a faint gurgling sound. His eyes flutter, then roll back in his head.

Marissa is still lying on the floor, her arms curled around her head and her eyes squeezed shut, as if she's waiting for the next gunshot.

My eyes flit from Matthew's body to Skip hurling himself through the window.

When Skip reaches Marissa an instant later, he wraps his arms tightly around her.

I step closer to Matthew and nudge him with the toe of my sneaker. He doesn't appear to be breathing anymore. I move over to Marissa and Skip, but keep my gun trained on Matthew.

He seems to be dead. But he has tricked me before.

He's not going to do it again.

Marissa finally opens her eyes and stares up at me. She whispers, "Tell me it isn't real."

"It is," I say gently. "And it's also going to be okay."

CHAPTER FORTY-THREE

MARISSA

TIME IS A CHAMELEON. It's ever changing, cannily adapting to circumstances.

It stretches out some tiny moments for an eternity. Then it shifts course and swallows up whole days, years even, as if they never existed. It's as slippery and elusive as water running through the cracks in a tightly cupped hand.

It has been eight days since Matthew's death—a stretch of time that felt endless yet far too short, because it brought Marissa here, to Monday, her scheduled reentry point into the world.

Marissa thought she could do this; she imagined Coco would be a refuge again.

But all the scented candles and gorgeous objects and shiny fixtures provide her no peace.

They're just beautiful things.

They have no importance at all.

Marissa has spent the morning desperately bargaining with time, wishing for the clock to spin forward so she can pick up Bennett. Other than when Marissa needed to give statements to the police, the two of them have not been apart since Matthew died. Marissa sleeps curled next to Bennett in a double bed; for the first days at her parents' home on the Eastern Shore, and since then in a guest room at Skip's town house. She takes Bennett to see a child psychologist and gives him ice cream every night, as if the sweet treat were a balm. When Avery asked to come over to meet with her, Marissa scheduled their talk for after Bennett's bed-time and kept his doorway within view the entire time.

Now her son's absence is like a missing limb.

The bell over Coco's door jingles as two customers enter. Marissa and Polly have been busier than ever this morning, but most of the people coming in aren't shoppers. They're gawkers, thrilled by their proximity to danger.

Marissa can already tell these women have come to her store to collect a story to serve up to their friends. They're not looking for new coasters or robes. They're looking for her.

"I've got this," Polly announces, and she marches up to the women while Marissa slips into the back room.

Marissa can hear Polly deflecting the women's nosy questions: "If you're not here to buy anything, we cordially ask that you leave."

Polly steps briskly into the back room a moment later: "Just some lookie-loos. I got rid of them."

"Thank you," Marissa replies quietly.

Polly reaches out to touch Marissa's shoulder, then withdraws her hand. Marissa can tell Polly has been gearing herself up for this conversation all morning. "If I had known, I never would have told Matthew anything."

Marissa nods. "How did it all start?"

Polly's chin trembles and her eyes grow wet. "Matthew came by the store one afternoon right after I began working here. You'd gone to pick up Bennett from school. He introduced himself and told me you were trying to get pregnant, and that you'd had some fertility issues. He asked me to look after you—to make sure you were eating enough, and that you didn't lift any heavy boxes."

All the offers of tea and muffins and salads. Polly's distress when Ma-rissa tried to pick up a box of pillows. It makes sense now.

"Matthew paid me, too," Polly blurts. "He insisted. He'd come by when you weren't here, usually at closing time. He'd give me some cash and ask how you were doing. I thought it was so sweet, that he loved you so much."

Marissa should be upset, but it's such a small betrayal, in the grand scheme of things.

"After we found that creepy note, we started talking more frequently. I'm such a dummy. He really made me believe he was trying to protect you, Marissa."

"I believed him, too. It's okay, Polly. Truly."

Polly twists her hands together. "Well, if there is anything I can do, anything at all . . ." Polly hangs her head and begins to walk away.

Marissa doesn't feel as if she has much to give—she needs to save it all for her son—but she can offer Polly this one small thing.

"Actually," she calls out, "I would really love it if you could make me a cup of tea."

Polly spins around and wipes away the last of her tears. "Coming right up."

After Polly serves her the hot chai and goes back to the front of the store, Marissa sips it and stares into space.

Learning more about the extent of Matthew's depravity only increases her desire to be with Bennett. Her son is the antidote to Matthew's poison.

Marissa keeps recalling how Bennett had looked walking up the front steps of Rolling Hills this morning, holding his dinosaur diorama in both hands, his big backpack resting on his small shoulders.

Would the other kids stare at him or ask him upsetting questions—or worse?

Marissa has spoken to the principal, and Joan in the front office, and Mrs. Tanaka. They all promised to look out for him.

But children can be vicious, and teachers couldn't be there all the time. Someone could taunt Bennett in the hallways or in the bathroom: *Your dad tried to kill your mom!* Or: *It's a good thing your dad is dead!*

It's too much for Bennett's little shoulders to bear.

She imagines him sitting alone in the lunchroom, or leaning against a tree at recess to hide his tears, and Marissa bends over, wrapping her arms around her waist. Aching for her son.

She'd been so foolish to imagine they could step back into their old lives as easily as slipping on a soft pair of shoes. A week, a month, a year . . . There would never be enough time to recover.

She's about to call the school to check in when she hears the jingle of the bell over the door again, then Polly saying Marissa is busy right now.

Leave us alone! Marissa wants to cry. She curls into a tighter curve, wishing she could disappear.

"I only need to talk to her for a minute!" The loud voice is close—and familiar.

When Marissa opens her eyes, she sees Natalie standing on the threshold to the back room in her sky-high heels and leather leggings, her shiny black hair flowing.

"This is a restricted area!" Polly practically shouts. She's tugging on Natalie's sleeve, trying to pull her away.

"Jesus, let go of my blouse! It's Stella McCartney!"

"It's fine, Polly." Marissa lifts her head wearily. Why fight it? Whatever Natalie has come to say, she's clearly determined to say it.

Polly shoots a final angry look at Natalie, then moves away.

"Nice guard dog you've got." Natalie rolls her eyes. "I guess I'm to blame for that. I heard you were looking for an assistant and I knew my boss wanted to help Polly because he's close to her dad. So, I told him she should apply here. Matthew thought it was best if you didn't know about my involvement, but I couldn't resist rubbing it in the other day. Sorry about that. But you have to admit you and I haven't always had the easiest relationship."

Marissa blinks. "Is that what you came to tell me?"

Natalie brushes at her sleeve, as if she's erasing Polly's touch. "No, this is: I remember how worried I was about Veronica when her father left me. I get that this is a million times worse."

Marissa looks at Natalie a little more closely and finally says, "Thank you."

"So don't worry about Bennett. I'm on it."

Marissa is bewildered. "You're on it?"

Natalie looks at her levelly. "All of us moms are. We've got him, Marissa."

Then Natalie turns on her heel and saunters back out.

Three o'clock takes forever to arrive.

Marissa is in the passenger seat of Skip's Tesla, waiting for the students to come streaming out of Rolling Hills.

Skip is behind the wheel. He went to work today, too. But he left early to pick up Marissa and Bennett. Together they will drive back to his town house. She doesn't know how long they will remain there, but Marissa can't ever imagine wanting to go back to the house she shared with Matthew.

For the moment at least, the town house is their home. Skip took care of everything to make them feel comfortable there.

He'd picked up Sam and his cage, along with clothing and personal items for Bennett and Marissa, so they'd be surrounded by familiar things. He cooks for them—salmon on the grill, or simple pasta dishes— and talks easily with Bennett about the habits of hummingbirds and the mysteries of the solar system. At night, after Bennett falls asleep, Skip's solid presence is a comfort to Marissa. Sometimes she talks to him about Tina, sharing some of the good memories she has of their friend-ship. They also discuss Matthew, reassembling the image of the man they both thought they knew.

Matthew knew how I felt about you, Skip told her. *But when he offered me an alibi the night Tina was killed, he convinced me I owed it to him to let him have a shot with you.* Skip had shaken his head. *Turns out I was the one giv-ing him an alibi. I always thought he was a jerk—but I had no idea he was evil.*

As the days go by, they talk less about Matthew. More often lately, they've simply been watching television together, or reading side-by-side in the living room.

Skip has been the best friend she could imagine.

Nothing more than a friend, though.

Mourn your marriage—or what you thought your marriage was, Avery had said when they'd met for their ninth session. *But don't ever forget the pos-sibilities life holds for you.*

Marissa can't think that far ahead.

But as she unfastens her seat belt and Skip comes around to open her car door, she does allow herself to recall this:

What did you say back when we were teenagers and you told Matthew how you felt about me? she'd asked Skip just last night.

He didn't blush or look down. He'd simply replied, *I told him the first time I kissed you, it was like the first time I saw the ocean.*

Skip hadn't asked why she'd burst into tears. He'd just hugged her.

At three o'clock sharp, the big double doors to the school open. Ma-rissa scans the faces of the students coming down the front steps. A pack of rowdy boys are in the lead, with a teacher loudly admonishing them to walk, not run.

Then she sees Bennett.

He's all alone.

Her heart leaps into her throat. She wants to race to him and throw her arms around him.

Then she hears a boy call out, "Bennett! Wait!"

It's his best friend, Charlie.

Then another boy joins them: Lance, the baseball player who wears his sister's hand-me-down pink cleats. They're flanking Bennett, one on either side.

Bennett comes closer, and Marissa studies his face. His eyes are clear; his skin tone is even. There are no signs at all he has been crying.

She feels the tightness around her heart ease.

"Bye, Bennett!" a boy calls from a dozen yards away.

Then a small girl wearing a chic little leopard-print jacket calls Bennett's name, waving. "See you tomorrow!" It's Veronica, Natalie's daughter.

As the crowd of kids disperses, Marissa sees Natalie a few yards away, leaning against her shiny Jaguar, surrounded by her usual hangers-on.

But Natalie isn't talking to them.

Natalie is watching Bennett carefully, too.

Natalie seems to feel Marissa's gaze. She turns and meets Marissa's eyes.

Someday soon, Marissa vows, she will call Natalie and suggest they get together for a cup of coffee, or a glass of wine. But for now, she settles for mouthing, *Thank you.*

When Bennett finally arrives at the car, he is smiling.

CHAPTER FORTY-FOUR

AVERY

You might think, watching them, that they're an ordinary mother, son, and grandfather enjoying a beautiful spring afternoon at the park. But the Bishops, like the rest of us, are far more complicated than they appear.

I slowly walk toward them, along the trail that winds through the Candy Cane City park, pausing every now and then to let Romeo sniff a dandelion or—and this bit of his progress delights me—wag his stubby tail at another dog.

Romeo is healing from his traumas, but he still bears scars.

We all do. Some of ours are just more visible than others.

Marissa puts an arm around her son's shoulders and bends down to kiss the top of his head. I wonder if Bennett is recounting the story of his rocket getting stuck in the tree, and his dad lifting him up to retrieve it.

Bennett chose this spot when Marissa asked where he wanted to go to remember his father. Matthew hadn't spent much time with his son, but at least Bennett has a few good memories.

Bennett doesn't seem to be grieving much, Marissa had said to me last night at Skip's town house, when I'd seen her for our ninth session: Reconciliation.

For Marissa, like most of my clients, this means reconciling her new reality with the loss of her former life. Because if I've done my job right, my clients are in a completely different place—emotionally, and often physically—by this point in the process.

I told her what I tell all of my clients who are struggling with loss: Grief is a shape-shifter. It defies logic, sneaking up on you when you least expect it and leaving you empty-handed and hollowed out when you go searching for it.

Bennett knows you're here for him, and that's the most important thing, I'd advised Marissa. *Answer any question he has, but don't feel the need to make sense of it all for him now.*

She'd nodded and reached for a tissue. *Do you know what some people used to call us? . . . The Golden Couple.*

I do know, I'd thought as I pictured Marissa and Matthew gliding into my office for their first session. They'd almost convinced me, too. Then I'd put a hand on her shoulder while she'd cried.

Her tears were mostly for her son, but they were also for herself, because even though Matthew wasn't ever the man Marissa tried to pretend he was, grief breaks all the rules.

Marissa and I still have one final session left: Promises. The tenth meeting is when my clients embrace their new futures. I suggested we schedule it whenever she is ready. I also told her there was no expiration date. But I have the feeling Marissa will reach out to me before the end of the year. I also have a pretty good idea of who will be in her future, but Marissa needs to find her own way to him.

"C'mon, Romeo," I say now, giving his leash a little tug.

Marissa hadn't wanted to hold a memorial service for Matthew. Given that detectives are now investigating whether Matthew was responsible for Tina's murder in addition to trying to kill Marissa and Skip, any public event would have turned into a media spectacle.

So she planned this little private one at the park.

Marissa knows I'm coming, but her father-in-law, Chris, does not.

I'm counting on the element of surprise to continue to serve me well.

On Bennett's other side, Chris leans over to say something to his grandson. Chris looks like a doting grandpa. He appears to be the kind of guy who would stop and help if you got a flat tire or would stuff a pillow under his shirt to play Santa for a holiday party.

Until you see his eyes.

Matthew inherited his icy-blue eyes from his father.

I've put together a timeline since Matthew died, casting back in m memory in between my questions to Skip, fitting in the pieces until the narrative finally flows.

It began with Finley, of course.

But the next person who entered my life was Chris. Not Skip, and not Marissa and Matthew.

I just hadn't seen him coming.

Like his son, Chris is an invisible architect of destruction. He has been behind the curtain all along, wreaking havoc.

I now know that Chris works in the shadows. Many of his clients seek him out for the kind of services they can't dirty their own hands with. Men like Chris have always been around: They protect the interests of the biggest players in the most powerful cities in the world. They're the jury fixers, the eyes in the sky at billion-dollar casinos, the dirty political operatives who take down national candidates.

Chris's name doesn't appear on Acelia's list of employees, but he's one of their most valued assets.

Shortly after I called in my tip to the FDA, I burst onto Chris's radar. Chris began looking into my life, searching out potential entry points.

He found out I was single, then he asked Skip to befriend me.

That meeting at the Matisse bar was no accident.

Skip didn't know many details then. He just thought he was doing a favor for the man he'd known since he was a teenager, the man who'd helped him get a scholarship to Dartmouth and had given him a start in business.

But after a few dates, Skip explained to me, he defied Chris. *I liked and respected you too much to try and trick you into giving me information about your clients.*

The rest of what Skip had already told me was true: He'd begun to suspect Matthew could be dangerous, so he sent Marissa the *Post* article about me. He hoped I could help her see who her husband really was and break free from her marriage. At least one part of Skip's desperate plan worked: Marissa did make an appointment to see me. He just hadn't counted on her bringing Matthew along.

Skip had no idea that Chris was increasing the pressure on me on behalf of Acelia, sending his henchmen to move my Synthroid medication onto my bureau, follow me to my doctor's office, and even pose as a new client.

I was looking at your appointment calendar that night when you caught me coming out of your office, Skip confessed. *But it was only to see if you were meeting with Marissa. I swear I had nothing else to do with what Chris did to you.*

When I got over being pissed off at Skip, I told him I was flattered by the faith he'd placed in me.

Now I walk a little farther down the path at Candy Cane City, enjoying the feel of the sun warming my face and the laughter of a group of kids tossing around a Frisbee.

Marissa catches sight of me and waves me over. "Avery, you made it."

Her father-in-law whips around at the sound of my name.

Chris's poker face is impressive. He must need one, in his line of work. His only other reaction to me is a tightening around his lips.

I've taken precautions to prepare for whatever he might do next—I did kill his son, after all, and now I know exactly who Chris is, whom he works for, and how he's connected to my life in ways that have nothing at all to do with his family.

But Chris merely nods at me. I exhale and slide my hand out of my coat pocket.

Marissa turns to Bennett. "Sweetie, this is my friend Ms. Chambers."

"Can I pet your dog?" Bennett asks.

"Sure. His name is Romeo."

Bennett holds out his small hand to let Romeo sniff him. "His tongue tickles."

"Do you want to take him for a walk?" I suggest. "Maybe your mom can help."

Marissa nods; she's in on my plan. I hand Romeo's leash to Bennett.

Romeo ambles off with the two of them, looking back a few times to make sure I'm not going anywhere.

When they are out of hearing distance, I say simply, "I'm sorry for your loss."

Chris shakes his head. "I lost my son when he was sixteen and came home with blood on his shirt the night that girl was murdered. My wife went to bed early that night, but Matthew told her to say he and Skip watched a movie with her, so she did. She always covered for him."

Chris knew all along what his son was capable of.

I take another good look at Chris, finally putting a face to the dar menace that has been looming over me ever since I blew the whistle on Acelia.

Chris knows where I live, and where I keep my prescription medication. He knows what kind of car I drive and where my doctor's office is located. But Chris still doesn't know the singular piece of information that led him to infiltrate my life in the first place: the name of the client who told me about the faulty Rivanux drug trials.

He's *never* going to know that.

I've spent the past few days collecting more information on Chris than he'll ever be able to amass on me. With Skip's help, it has been easy. I know who many of Chris's other secret clients are. I know where he lives. What keeps him up at night.

I stare at Chris for a long moment.

"Skip told you," Chris finally says. "I can tell."

I nod.

Chris spreads out his hands. "It was only business."

"I understand your clients are important to you," I tell Chris as he watches me with his flat eyes. "Mine are important to me, too. I know a lot about them and their families. For example, I know Bennett is allergic to shellfish. I know the parking lot at Bennett's school gets busy at pickup time and can be dangerous if the children aren't carefully monitored. I know random criminals break into private homes in expensive neighborhoods like the one Bennett lives in. And I know that in another year or two, Bennett will be old enough to take the bus to school all by himself."

The most important bit of information I've gathered about Chris is his weak spot: his grandson.

Bennett is the only person in the entire world that Chris loves.

I would never hurt a child. But I'm good at bluffing.

"So, nothing is going to happen to my clients or their families, right?" I lean closer to Chris. "*Any* of my clients."

He continues to stare at me.

In the distance, Bennett's sweet, high voice calls out, "Grandpa! The ice cream truck is here. Do you want a strawberry shortcake?"

"That would be great," Chris shouts back, still staring at me.

Then he breaks our gaze and replies, "Understood."

I'm not done with him yet. "Someone contacted an insurance company and leveled a charge against me." I shake my head, as if I'm bewildered by the very idea of it. "Apparently they got an anonymous tip that my husband's death wasn't due to natural causes."

Chris folds his arms. "What do you want me to do about it?"

It's not a challenge. It's a question.

I smile. "Do what you do best. Make the problem go away, Chris."

An hour later, I unlock my front door and tap in the code for my security system, then remove Romeo's leash and give him a pat on the back. I don't bother resetting my alarm. I'm sure I'll need it again someday, but for now, the threat against me is gone.

"Go get your bunny."

My fierce-looking dog's favorite new toy is a fluffy stuffed rabbit. Instead of chewing it, Romeo has taken to carrying it around tenderly and sleeping curled around it at night.

Love is an eternal mystery, I guess.

There's a lot I should do today. My voice mail is full; I've gotten media requests from as far away as Hong Kong, and offers from film producers, and messages from Oprah, Hoda Kotb, Jimmy Kimmel, and dozens of others who want an exclusive interview.

MAVERICK EX-THERAPIST KILLS CLIENT.

That headline does sound pretty irresistible.

I could keep turning down the interview requests, or put in the order for the dinner I'm having delivered to eat with Lana tonight, or answer emails from a surge of new prospective clients.

D.C. is a peculiar city. My notoriety has only made me more in demand.

Instead, I slip off my shoes and walk upstairs. I turn right at the top of the hallway, heading in the opposite direction from my bedroom.

I've been planning this short journey for a while now. It's surprising how long it has taken me to get here.

I open the door and walk into Lana's old bedroom, the one with bird feeders outside the windows and photographs of Paul, Lana, and me or the walls.

The old Crosley turntable is still in one corner of the room. I lift the lid and see the last record I ever played for Paul.

Miles Davis, *Out of Nowhere.*

Paul used to argue that the composition is Davis's true masterpiece. Most people prefer *Kind of Blue,* with the legendary John Coltrane on the sax, but the first time Paul ever invited me into his home, he played this record.

I blow the dust off the vinyl and set down the needle, listening to it bump and scratch before it settles in.

The title song is the one we danced to at our wedding.

There aren't any lyrics. The music is pure, magnificent emotion.

I look at the space that once held Paul's hospital bed, remembering my husband's final words to me. He'd mouthed them through dry, cracked lips, but they were unmistakable.

I'm ready.

I'd been amassing morphine in preparation for the moment.

I always do my research; I knew exactly how much it would take, and how to insert it into his IV. When the needle was empty, I'd climbed into bed with Paul and held him in my arms while the morphine seeped into his veins.

He was gone by the time the record finished playing.

Now I step into the center of the room and close my eyes and remember. I don't see Paul as he was during his final months—bone thin and weak, a shadow of his former self. A man I'd stopped loving long ago.

I see the husband who completely captivated me, spinning me across the dance floor in my long white dress while our guests applauded, his dark eyes promising me everything.

God, I love you, he'd whispered in my ear. Then he'd dipped me down low and scooped me back up into the air.

The space Paul inhabited is empty. It's still hard for me to wrap my mind around that.

Maybe it will always be.

I sink down onto the floor and wrap my arms around my knees.

Miles Davis's trumpet sings to me while I cry.

Grief isn't linear. It isn't logical. There's no structure or civility to it; it grabs you when you least expect it and digs in its nails until you succumb.

So I give in to it, until the final notes fade away.

Then I get to my feet again.

I look around the room, imagining it not as it was, but as it will be: with a guest bed in one corner, and a pretty rug on the floor, and a potted tree by the window. Or maybe I'll transform it into an exercise room, with a yoga mat and treadmill and wall-mounted TV.

The space has so many possibilities.

I walk back out again, this time leaving the door wide open.

ACKNOWLEDGMENTS

From Greer and Sarah:

Our thanks always goes first and foremost to our brilliant editor and publisher, Jennifer Enderlin, who helped to launch this book by conjuring the delicious title and to land it with her incisive, spot-on edits. Our publicist, Katie Bassel, whose enthusiasm for us and our books lifts us up.

The amazing team beside these two women nurtures our novels through the publication process with meticulous care, boundless energy, and limitless creativity. We are so lucky to have them working on behalf of our books. Thank you to Robert Allen, Jeff Dodes, Marta Fleming, Olga Grlic, Tracey Guest, Brant Janeway, Sara LaCotti, Sallie Lotz, Kim Ludlam, Erica Martirano, Kerry Nordling, Erik Platt, Gisela Ramos, Sally Richardson, Mary Beth Roche, Lisa Senz, Michael Storrings, Tom Thompson, and Dori Weintraub.

At William Morris Endeavor: we are incredibly grateful to our agent, Margaret Riley King, and her assistant, Sophie Cudd, who were our early readers. Their thoughtful contributions made this a better book. We are beyond appreciative for Sylvie Rabineau and Hillary Zaitz Michael, who champion us and our books in Hollywood, and to Jack Beloff and Victoria Nunez. We also send our deep thanks to Tracy Fisher at WME, and to Holly Bario at Amblin.

Our gratitude to all of our foreign publishers who have shared our work around the globe, especially Wayne Brookes at Pan Macmillan UK whose exuberant emails always make us laugh. And thanks to Julianna Haubner for helping us navigate social media (because of you, we now understand the difference between "stories" and "posts").

And last but never least, a bundle of gratitude to our readers. We love connecting with you, so please find us on Facebook, Twitter, and Instagram. Please visit our websites: greerhendricks.com and sarahpekkanen.com.

From Greer:

Sarah, what a journey this one has been. *The Golden Couple* was written entirely during a pandemic and despite not having our usual systems in place (Google Hangouts, hotel visits, solo writing spaces), we did it! Thank you for . . . well, everything.

I am incredibly grateful for my friends both inside and outside the publishing industry. Extra appreciation goes to Marla Goodman, Alison Strong, Megan De Valle, and Vicki Foley, who did double duty as early readers. Thank you also to Karen Gordon, Gillian Blake, and my Nantucket Book Group. Special thanks to my family of origin, Elaine, Mark, and Robert Kessel. A super shout-out to my mom, who read the first draft and offered keen psychological insights. Huge gratitude to my father for his wise counsel on the pharmaceutical sections. And to my brother, our 4:00 p.m. "walk and talks" always enlighten and lift my spirits.

Since I began writing, I have worked alongside two noisy dogs, but during the creation of this book I had additional company! Paige and Alex, my greatest creations, thanks for the love and the laughter. And finally to John, "my happily ever after"— your love, support, and encouragement make it all better.

From Sarah:

Greer, from cutting short our book tour and completely changing up our work process, this has been a year unlike any other! We not only got through it, but produced a novel to be proud of, and I'm so grateful for that—and for our many years of partnership.

One of my favorite perks of being a writer is the connection it creates with fellow book lovers. Two of the women I've met along the way turned first into friends, then early readers of *The Golden Couple*. Thank you, Napheesa Collier and Stacey Kruml, for your insights and assistance (especially Stacey's last-minute reconnaissance trip to the Wharf, bringing me along via FaceTime!). And to Jamie Desjardins, who always lets me know if the new manuscript is creepy enough to keep her up at night.

My gratitude to Rachel Baker, for the weekly porch sits and heart-to-hearts that helped keep me sane during lockdown. To Isobel Aarons, for weighing in on everything from the addition of Romeo the pit bull to the big twists in these pages. And to Kathy Nolan, for the tech support and website fixes. I would also like to acknowledge the enduring influence of one of my first and favorite editors, the late, great Al Eisele.

I'm lucky to have a therapist in the family for many reasons, and credit my sister-in-law Tammi Pekkanen for ensuring certain details about Avery's mindset and methodology didn't strain credulity. My love to my parents, John and Lynn; my brothers, Ben and Robert; and to Saadia, Sophia, and little Billy.

Roger Aarons, you are my rock. You read every single draft of this manuscript, in between giving me neck rubs, cooking delicious meals, and sharing nonstop laughter (and nonstop home renovations, but I'd rather think about the laughter).

To my sons, Jackson, Will, and Dylan: thank you for putting up with a mom who paces the house, conversing with imaginary people and dreaming up creative ways to commit murder. I could never write kinder, funnier, or smarter characters than you three.

OUT NOW

You Are Not Alone

By Greer Hendricks and Sarah Pekkanen

Shay Miller wants to find love, but it eludes her.
She wants to be fulfilled, but her job is a dead end.
She wants to belong, but her life is increasingly lonely.

Until Shay meets the Moore sisters. Cassandra and Jane live a life of
glamorous perfection, and always get what they desire. When they
invite Shay into their circle, everything seems to get better.

Shay would die for them to like her.

She may have to.

★

'This is the latest excellent offering from the classy double act
that gave us the *The Wife Between Us* . . . Intelligent and disturbing'
Daily Mail